"KISS ME!"

She looked into his blue eyes. *Kiss me,* she willed wordlessly. *Kiss me.*

He held her face gently. Then, with infinite tenderness, he brushed her lips. She tried to draw a breath; she felt weak, and for a few seconds darkness covered her eyes.

"Michelle!" Instantly he lifted her and carried her to the settee. "Do you always faint when you're kissed?"

"I've never been..." She stopped herself. "I've never fainted in my life!"

Other Regency Romances from Avon Books

WORLDLY INNOCENT

JOANNA HARRIS

AVON BOOKS ◆ NEW YORK

AVON BOOKS
A division of
The Hearst Corporation
105 Madison Avenue
New York, New York 10016

First Avon Books Printing: May 1989

For my three Georges
and Bea
beloved each, all, always

1

"RICHARD, Richard, you are here at last."

Before Richard de Varennes could brace himself against the door frame of the inn bedchamber, a flash of pink muslin and dark, fragrant curls had flung herself into his arms. The girl hugged him impetuously around the waist and drew back suddenly when she heard the sharp, ragged intake of his breath. Cautiously she opened the man's coat, her small hands exploring quickly, possessively, demandingly. When she saw the streak of dried brown blood that had soaked through his bandages onto his shirt, a small sob escaped her throat; cautiously she felt the shape of the padding over his heart and ribs. "It's a wound! You've been hurt, and we knew nothing! The blood has dried—the wound must be days old. Are you all right?"

Small lines of weariness, etched with road dust, marked the strong, sunburned features of de Varennes's face. His breeches and boots were spattered with mud. He had ridden for sixteen hours, right through the night to meet Michelle for the first time in over a year; now, looking down into the intense violet of her eyes, their shade deepening with a shadow of anxiety, he knew with certainty he had been right to come. He drew her to him, cradling her gently against his unbandaged side, and kissed her resolutely on the top of her head.

"Michelle, Michelle, hush; of course I'm fine—a light saber slash, nothing serious or I would have told you." Not serious—God forgive me yet another lie in this treacherous

1

business of loyalty to one's king, thought Richard as he eased his tall frame over to the window and drew the slender woman after him. "Now, just let me feast on looking at you for a moment," he said, pushing her back to arm's length. "Stand away, child, and let me see how you have grown."

"Only if you stop calling me 'child,'" Michelle said pertly, with a defiant lift of her chin, "because I'm not. I had my eighteenth birthday four weeks ago, and Jane said I was quite old enough to wear the most sophisticated styles Ninette could make."

"As I see," said de Varennes, appreciatively eyeing the slim figure turning with slow and natural elegance in front of him, "although it quite astounds me that your old nurse, Jane, would have allowed such décolletage at this hour of the morning."

Michelle's eyes twinkled; she pouted teasingly. "And I'll wager you've never made *that* remark before to any other woman, Richard de Varennes, and you only make it to me because I am your little sister, and you are a positive prude where I am concerned." She noted her half brother's slight blush and relented a little. "I must admit that Jane would not have allowed me this design had you not written and said I was to have a new wardrobe 'befitting the daughter of a *comte* about to enter society,' although I'll tell you right now, if you think for one minute I'd cross the threshold of Napoleon's court, I'd ride a wild stallion first. I'll never betray Papa's Royalist sentiments."

Richard's gaze became stern. "You know full well, Michelle, that is something I would never ask of you. I loved the count as much as you did."

It was Michelle's turn to be embarrassed. "I'm sorry, Richard, but when your letter came to us in Paris a month ago, with the money for my new wardrobe, what was I to think? What other society is there?" Suddenly her voice grew earnestly quiet. "And why did you write last week that we were to pack so quickly and meet you here in Ostend? We arrived on Monday and have waited three days for you—and here you appear, wounded. Richard, tell me, what is going on?"

De Varennes gazed down at Michelle. Her face was so young and trusting in its beauty, and he knew he was right to get her out of France, where she could so easily be held hostage if he should ever be arrested.

Yet, he thought as he drew back, Michelle had changed since he had last seen her. It wasn't only the becoming fashion of her dress and the sophistication of her dark, shining ringlets caught back with combs in the new Greek style that had changed his sister. She had gained a certain charming, ineffable quality—an ability to be still, to be gentle, with an earnest watchfulness. It was familiar. He remembered: Michelle's young mother, his stepmother, had exactly the same grace of bearing—yet that gentleness had not deterred her from running away from her home in England to marry her penniless French count. No doubt Michelle shared this same strength and determination. His task was not going to be easy. He eased himself into a chair by the window and spoke with deliberate casualness.

"I want you, Jane, and Ninette to leave for England, to go to your godfather in London for a short while."

Michelle's eyes grew wide. "Leave Paris? Why, Richard, you are home little enough with all your traveling to deal in art. But you are the only family I have, and if we leave France, we will never see you till this wretched war is over."

De Varennes smiled. "Exactly why I want you to leave now, my pet. Since his defeat in Russia, the tide against Boney has turned; the allies smell his blood and will pursue him like bloodhounds on the scent to the very gates of Paris. We may yet see battling in the streets—and I don't want you in danger."

"Oh, poof, Richard. Things truly aren't that desperate—and anyway, I'm not afraid."

He chuckled warmly. "My deceptively demure, but audacious Michelle! It is precisely because you are not afraid that I am asking you to go. What you really want to do is charge off through enemy lines, disguised as a maid, and stab Napoleon as he lies sleeping in his campaign tent." Michelle grinned at her brother's humor, but frowned when he added, "That is why I want you out of Paris—now."

"This is ridiculous," snapped Michelle. "Surely there are other places. Go to London—to a godfather I have never heard of? Why?"

"Partly because it is what the count stipulated in his will—that upon his death you were to go to your godfather's and were to remain as his ward until you were twenty-one, or married. And I know that both of us would want to honor his request."

The girl's eyes narrowed challengingly. "Papa died last year. Why didn't you tell me of this plan sooner?"

"Because I didn't receive the notary's letter detailing the count's will until two months ago. No fault of his, mind you," said Richard, his voice tinged with weariness. "The letter evidently followed me in my travels since last May and finally caught up with me in Warsaw in late November. I wrote you as soon as I knew. Michelle, you are precious to me. Have I ever been arbitrary with you? Go to England for our father's sake."

Michelle was quiet for a moment; Richard's argument had quelled her; he knew she would never disobey her father's last command. The girl nodded, thoughtfully. "Who is this godfather I have never heard of? How will he receive me?"

"An English duke father met while he was in England during the Revolution. I believe it was at a ball he gave that father met your mother." De Varennes looked steadily at Michelle: a petite vision in pink, her violet eyes wide with concern; he could easily surmise the reaction of a kindly, conservative old gentleman to her. "A moment the old duke will not regret when he sees you, my pet."

Michelle blushed. Compliments from her brother were rare, and this one sounded as if he truly approved of her changed appearance. "He might be glad to see me as a visitor—but as his ward, for the next three years?"

Richard drew a small, neat pile of letters from a leather satchel. "The notary forwarded to me the count's copies of his letters to the duke, and the duke's responses. Take them with you, and read them, Michelle. He and Father were obviously very close, even if he didn't visit us often."

"Does he sound like a pleasant person?"

"From the letters, he appears to have quite an interest in foreign affairs and the arts, as Papa did. The count obviously found him good company, so most likely you will too. My guess is you will be sharing books before the first week is out."

"Have you ever met him?"

Richard mused for several seconds. "Once only, when you were baptized. I remember Father and him poring over some da Vinci drawings on the library table. The duke was delighted when Father showed him how to tell Leonardo was left-handed by the direction of the stroking."

Michelle thought for several minutes. It would be wonderful to meet someone who had known her parents just as they had fallen in love and married! Perhaps her godfather could tell her more of what her mother was like at Michelle's own age. "Certainly a visit to the old gentleman can't do any harm," she said. "If he is kind, I will stay as you request; if not, I'll come right home to France. I'll show these letters between Papa and himself, and your letter of introduction, referring to the will—"

"No, not my letter of introduction."

"Without your letter of introduction? Why ever not?" Michelle was incredulous; though charming as always, her brother was asking the impossible. "I am supposed to land on his doorstep like some homeless waif, hoping, because of these few letters, he will believe I am the French god-daughter he has never seen since baptism?"

The most difficult moment Richard could anticipate had arrived. Would Michelle be content to stay in England without knowing the true nature of his work, and also agree to have no contact with him until the end of the war? Not without a fight, he knew, for her sharp response had revealed her rising anger. Yet she would have to accept the explanation he had prepared—or both their lives would be in danger. He rose stiffly from his chair and pulled his sister to him, cradling her in his arms as he spoke.

"Of course not. It is just that I have a little more experience in the way of the world than you do, my pet, and I know that a careful and precise English duke would be even less likely to accept you if you offered a letter from the bastard son of the count. Remember, it was most unusual of Father to acknowledge me, and raise me in his own household. I have no credentials in the English *ton*. Do you know how your godfather remembers me? As an inquisitive nuisance of eleven, who made his horse bolt by setting off my homemade gunpowder near the bridle path."

He had worked hard to make Michelle accept the impossibility of his writing a letter—and hoped his painting the ridiculousness of it would help to convince her. Noticing her faint smile, he hurried on. "Of course, I would not send you without some proof of your claim. I haven't had a chance to return to Paris to obtain a notarized copy of the original will, so I have drafted a copy exactly according to the terms in the notary's letter, signed it with Father's signature, and impressed it with his seal."

Suddenly Michelle withdrew from his arms. and stepped back, anger flushing her cheeks. "I have just realized what you are asking me to do! Without any clear reason at all, other than your saying Papa wanted it, you expect me to go to a country I have never visited and present an old gentleman, a friend of Papa's, with a *forged* will!"

With lightning quickness, she drew off her bracelet and

threw it at him; it struck the door of the adjoining chamber with a resounding crack.

"Forged!"

In the room next door the word rang out more effectively than an alarm bell; the following sharp crack jolted Black Jack Sharkley fully awake. His eyes snapped open, then shut again. The light streaming into his room was blindingly bright; it felt for a moment as though his entire head, rather than just his eyes, had opened, but the brandy had been worth it. Quickly, gently, Black Jack eased his complaining body out of bed, trying not to jar his thumping head, but the word "forged"—that was an opportunity not to be missed, even on a morning such as this.

Stealthily he crept over to the door leading to the adjoining bedchamber. While it was firmly bolted on either side, he could at least see through the keyhole. For several seconds he could see nothing through the narrow slit but the whitewashed wall, then a tall frame of a man—blue coat seamed with road dust, white vest—stooped to retrieve an object near the door.

"Well, I am relieved to see the sophistication of fashion and hairstyle does not mean you have been completely tamed, Michelle." The gentleman's voice was tinged with teasing laughter. "As cool and demure in public as ever one could wish, but still, in private, a sharp aim with the jewelry! I had not realized how I missed dodging your missiles all these months, my dear. Nonetheless, I vowed to the count on his deathbed that I would take care of you. And that I mean to do. So, my pet" (here the man's voice assumed a tone of unquestionable authority) "even a fourth dent in this bracelet will not change my direction that you leave for England, now."

Sharkley caught a glimpse of the man's hand catching up a small, graceful one emerging from a rose-colored sleeve, and slipping a heavy gold band back on the woman's wrist. With his touch, the woman's voice became gentler, but still pleading.

"Please, Richard, I don't feel comfortable carrying a forged will."

"It is *not* forged. As soon as the war is over, we will be able to verify it, every clause."

"Richard, this document you have written *is* forged. I am carrying a *forged* will to an English duke. He is, after all, my godfather. Perhaps, if I spoke to him, showed him the letters, a simple explanation would do."

Exasperation edged the man's firm voice. "Michelle, I have told you, I do know the ways of the world, and I do not consider mere charity and goodwill strong enough to safeguard a woman I love and am sworn to protect. 'Where compassion fails, legality oft succeeds'—the count's motto. You should understand it by now."

"Is my godfather compassionless, then?"

"I do not have any doubt, since the count selected him for your guardian, that he is a good man and would always give you shelter. But even a good man should always be astute, and therefore he himself will be much happier if he sees the will for himself. It is a temporary deception of mere paper, that can be proven later."

Reluctantly, the girl's hand accepted the proffered sealed envelope. "Only if you will promise me that after the war—"

"Of course! Now, think of the pleasure of being ensconced safely in the bosom of the English *ton*. You will be so much better off."

"Better off away from you? Oh, Richard."

Sharkley could see a man's tanned hands drawing a slim beauty to him, his voice reassuring her even as he cradled her gently. Black Jack could make out the girl's shapely shoulders and slim waist, and he knew by instinct that she was quite a filly. Now, if he, Sharkley, had held her in his arms at this moment, the embrace would have been very different.

"You know, my pet, in Paris you are only a daughter of yet another impoverished Royalist count. We would have to spend what would be your dowry simply to keep alive over the next three years."

"But how will things be different in England?" The woman's voice was flat and unhappy.

"Because there, my love, you will be under the guardianship of a duke of the realm. That you are the daughter of a Royalist French count will not be a liability; in fact, it will make you a little exotic. With your bewitching smile, reasonable income, and French taste in fashion, you should have little difficulty in English society—*au contraire*, you will be quite the attraction."

"Reasonable income! Why would my income be better in England than in France?"

"Because I will give you your dowry immediately, in full."

"The sketches?"

"Yes. You know that I would not allow you to arrive at the duke's penniless, so I brought a portfolio for you. I am sure your godfather would be more than pleased with the presentation of two or three da Vincis as memorials of your parents' esteem, and in gratitude that he has undertaken to become your guardian."

"Two or three?" The woman's voice filled with cautious wonder. "Exactly how many of the sketches did you put in that portfolio, Richard?"

"Quite a few."

"How many?"

"Twenty-four."

"Why, that is all we have, including the Rembrandts and Rubenses. You have included your share." Her voice was hushed, overwhelmed. "Of course I can't take them all."

"You can and you must. What other security do I have to give you, Jane, and Ninette? Give three drawings to your godfather, sell the others one at a time to pay expenses that come up until you are well and truly married; and if twelve or so are left, you will not be a great heiress on your marriage, but you will be well enough dowered."

"Oh, Richard! First you were talking only of leaving France until the end of the war. Now you sound as if I will be married off to some dull English lord within three months of landing in London. That is not at all my style. How dreadfully boring! Englishmen!"

"And what would have happened if your radiant English mama had felt the same way about Frenchmen?"

"Papa was her *grande passion*. Look at all she went through for him and France. And who ever heard of a *grande passion* among the English?" The girl sniffed at such an impossible notion, then her voice became quiet with concern once again. "And then what security remains for you?"

He laughed. "My wits, my knowledge of art—and the deed to the Paris town house. Quite enough, my pet, to not only survive but prosper."

Prosper! Heaven forgive me yet another lie, he thought, but if his impetuous little half sister ever discovered how dire the situation was, she'd never leave. Yet he claimed an indulgence he could afford, and treasured the warmth of Michelle in his arms for two or three more minutes. Finally, he gave her a last brotherly squeeze and released her. "Come; I must leave in half an hour, and before I say good-bye to Jane and Ninette, I want your promise you will leave on the next packet for London."

Rarely in his career had Black Jack heard as much damning information in one conversation, yet the man was leaving in half an hour, and Black Jack had not seen enough of the couple through the keyhole to identify them! He had found gold and intended to mine it thoroughly. He turned quickly from the keyhole and, with his foot, nudged his valet sleeping in a blanket roll at the foot of the bed.

"Roland, quickly. I've found two pigeons to blackmail. Something about presenting a forged will to an English duke —now, that ought to be worth a pretty penny. The woman is petite, in pink muslin. The man's in blue and leaves in half an hour, for where I don't know, and we must learn their identity before he departs. The innkeeper or the stable boys may know. Never mind me—I'll dress myself. Hurry." Sharkley gave a last quick glance through the keyhole, then turned to shave and dress.

Roland didn't need a second command; as often as not, he didn't need a first one.

They had come to make a good pair, Black Jack and he, thought Roland, as he slipped speedily into the modish, cheaply made clothes that marked him among other servants as a Covent Garden dandy. "Aye," he said to himself, "fortune surely found us when you overhead this plum. We do need a little blackmail, what with the earl being so miserly with our payments. The gods favor the wicked, I always say."

If the gods seem at times to favor the wicked, they also protect the innocent, for Black Jack had turned from the keyhole before he had heard the most damning facts—facts that would have brought a far higher price in blackmail than any number of forged wills; facts that Michelle herself was having a difficult time in drawing from her brother.

"Come, pet, we must go to Jane and Ninette." Richard de Varennes tried to guide his sister toward the door, but she stubbornly refused, and looked at her brother with quiet determination.

"Richard, I will go with Jane and Ninette to England, but only after you tell me the real reason for our being sent. It is only partly our father's will, isn't it?"

The weary man sucked in a long breath; the wound in his side began to hurt intensely. So the moment had come.

"I know that you were not at the auction of the archduke's collection last month," she went on," because the Princess Marina stopped her carriage in the Rue de Faubourg to call me over and say how much they had missed your presence. They had hoped to see you purchase the small Rembrandt self-portrait you have always so much admired."

Richard sat wearily in the straight-backed chair and remained quiet. To tell his sister too much would endanger her very life.

The girl walked to the window, and began quietly to reminisce. "And I've been remembering. When we traveled with Papa to sell or transfer painting collections, you both took a far greater interest in the goings-on at the court than you truly needed to know; and neither of you were simply gossips." Humor tinged her voice at the very idea; Richard flushed and said nothing.

Suddenly she turned and, walking to where he was seated, placed her hands on her brother's shoulders and looked at him with a compelling, level gaze. "Why did it matter to you and Papa that I report, after my week with Countess Leiden, which minister appeared in or out of favor? Why did you and Papa always pull out the maps in the library when you returned from trips?"

For seconds, he returned her gaze with one as level and direct as her own. Bright child! She had surmised too much, too accurately, already. His mouth tensed in a grim, firm line, and, grasping her wrists, he drew her hands from his shoulders and stood up. "What a child you are, Michelle, what an intelligent child. You do not realize that if I answer that question, I place you in danger."

"Must I tell you again, I am eighteen, and no child," she exploded. "Richard, you are being truly unfair. On one hand, you send me away to exile in a foreign country, perhaps to become a wife. You trust me to use wisely all the meager wealth the family possesses. Neither of which you would trust a child to do; yet when I ask you why, you insult me by calling me one."

The man sucked in his breath as the wound in his side stabbed. "I apologize, for I truly didn't mean to insult you. It wasn't that we didn't trust you or respect your intelligence. You *were* a child when we started."

The girl drew back and looked intently at him, as if searching his face to read the validity of the apology. She nodded her acceptance—and then demanded more. "Started exactly what?"

Richard paused thoughtfully. "I guess you have concluded enough for me to tell you—the count and I have always worked to restore the monarchy to France."

"A monarch for France?

"When the count lived in London during and after the Revolution, he began to realize that there was some measure of justice in the complaints against the king and aristocracy. He did not support the Revolution—to the very last drop of his blood, he was a Royalist. When Napoleon had the audacity to crown himself emperor, the count worked to see Louis restored to France, but only as a constitutional monarch, based on the English model, where the king is head of state, but the prime minister is head of government."

"Did Papa believe Louis would bring this type of government back to France?"

"We certainly hoped so. The count sent many papers outlining various forms of constitutional government to King Louis while he has been in exile in England. Louis's sympathy for such a constitutional monarchy is one of the reasons that the regent has granted him refuge in England."

Michelle's voice became fervent. "So you and Papa worked as spies for King Louis. And that is why you have missed so many auctions. Oh! Richard, I'm so proud of you, carrying on Papa's tradition!" Michelle hurtled herself into Richard's arms and kissed him on the cheek. "How I hope Louis's return comes soon! Do let me help!"

Richard held her for a long instant, as if allowing himself the luxury of her embrace, then pushed her away, gripping her shoulders firmly. "You can help, if only you will do as I say. When you are in France, I constantly worry that some of Napoleon's men may seize you as a hostage, to countermand my activities, or force you, under the threat of saving my life if I am captured, to spy for them. When you, Ninette, and Jane are in England, there is no such worry. None of Napoleon's scoundrels will touch you while you are under the guardianship of an English duke."

"Oh, Richard! Now I understand, and of course I'll go. If only you had explained sooner."

Richard was grim. "Even knowing that the count and I have spied puts you at considerable risk. There is one more thing you must do. From now to the end of the war, we will have no direct contact with each other. I will not write to you; you must promise never to try to contact me in any way. It would endanger the security of us both."

Michelle's eyes were shiny with tears. "Surely you cannot be serious. *No* contact? Perhaps through our priest, Père Vanasse?"

"*No* contact, through Père Vanasse or any other. This war is not for children. One letter between us could cost us both our lives; neither of us would want the guilt of the other's death on our souls. Do you understand?"

Michelle felt the harsh earnestness of her brother's grip on her wrists, looked up into his eyes, and read the same trustworthy compassion in them that she had always known. She nodded sadly.

"But now I have thoroughly terrified you, there is one small ray of hope," he said with a smile. "Occasionally, at the English court, you will come across the Duc d'Anton. He is the aide-de-camp to King Louis, and he is acquainted with my work. He knows also that you are my sister, and that you will be staying with your guardian, the Duke of Calvern."

Michelle was indignant. "It seems the Duc d'Anton knew my plans before I did!"

"Only for your security, my pet. Now, if you meet him in one of the public crushes—the best place not to be overheard is always a large crowd—I'm sure he will inform you about how I am."

"The Duc d'Anton—another of King Louis's spies?"

"Such words are not appropriate, my pet. The duc is simply a kind friend, who knows what goes on. Trust him—and *never* try to contact me directly."

"Never, Richard," his sister murmured, and tears overwhelmed her.

"Now, dry those eyes before we meet nurse Jane and Ninette, or Jane will lock me up in the room as punishment for brotherly abuse."

"That would be one way to delay your departure," said Michelle, trying to smile through her tears as they walked rapidly to meet the servants in the inn's dining hall below.

2

As HE SCURRIED in search of the innkeeper to find out more about their quarry, Roland gave a small, self-satisfied grin. His protégé, Sharkley, was, indeed, learning the ways of the underworld from his "servant," spotting pigeons to blackmail like that! A few more months in each other's company, the dandy thought, and they both would be as rich as Midas.

It was hard to believe it was on a night only a year ago that Roland had put his clever idea into effect. He prided himself that he was as clever as a fox and had no trouble surviving on the tricks and petty crimes of a street thief. But the street was not where bags of gold were to be had—those were in the pockets of the *ton*. He was smart enough to know that there were many things he could do, but Covent Garden dandy that he was, in his stylish, cheaply made clothes, he would never be mistaken for a member of the upper classes. He had only to open his mouth to confirm it. What he needed was a front man who was himself a member of the *ton*, yet in desperate enough straits to appreciate the lucrative advantages of Roland's wily arts.

Right then he had noticed a tall, distinguished, and thoroughly foxed gent leaning on the lamppost outside White's Club. Distinguished, maybe, but the cuffs of his neatly tailored jacket were frayed, and his boots, though well polished, were more worn than a solvent gent would tolerate. Aye, he had class—and equally clearly, pockets to let.

Was this fellow one Roland could use?

In the early hours of that fateful, foggy morning, the gentleman in question, John Sharkley, was attempting, somewhat unsteadily, to negotiate his way home.

It had been a particularly dispiriting day.

As the second son of a minor baronet, Sharkley had long accepted the fact he would receive nothing from the small estate his family had—there was barely enough income for his father to hold on to the mortgaged land. And all the whiskey Sharkley had drunk couldn't block from his mind that this was his fourth season as a bachelor in London, and he had as yet failed to entice an heiress into marriage. Why, this morning as he had taken Lady Jane Willington's small, plump hand and looked into her blue eyes, he could have sworn he caught a glimpse of tears as she said, with gently condescending firmness, that she was so sorry, but she was certain her father would not entertain his suit. What was unspoken between them was understood by both: Lord Willington knew the generous dowry he was offering could purchase a husband of much higher rank for his daughter than a mere second son of a baronet, and however much she might have been enticed by Sharkley's striking looks and ribald humor, Lady Jane had most certainly concurred.

After four seasons of futile effort, Sharkley had finally been forced to accept the truth: an heiress will flirt with a handsome, untitled, and impoverished man—but never marry him. What was that saying the chaperones oft recited to their charges to warn them away from penniless but engaging suitors—dance with the daring devil, but marry a prudent prince?

Aye, well, he suspected the plump and petulant Lady Jane would wait long for her prudent prince.

Sharkely gave a small, drunken grin at his own wit, then subsided again into despondency, for tonight insult had been added to injury when he had attempted to make enough money at the gaming tables to pay this month's rent on his suite of dingy rooms and had lost even his last, small stake.

For some time, Roland had hung back in the shadows, noting the man's every move. Having himself experienced more twists of bad fortune than he cared to remember, he recognized despair when he saw it—and the tall, well-dressed figure leaning on the lamppost was it.

Under his breath, Roland asked Dame Fortune for a lucky wink and sidled up beside the tall figure. Before the two had walked as far as Picadilly, he'd discovered enough of the fellow's plight to know he had found his man. Quickly, the dandy threw the net of as fine a story around Sharkley as his imagination could invent and began to pull the drawstring.

He was a a valet, he said, and a fine one. But his young master had been killed in France. He was rather vague about which battle, but he roundly cursed Boney in language that made his knowledge of military life most convincing. He'd been back only a few weeks, he said, and as dead masters don't give references, he was having a time of it finding employment. Now, he knew a particularly fine member of the *ton* when he saw one, for all the world could clearly see that was exactly what Sharkley was, Roland reassured him. Now, if he, Sharkley, would consider employing him as a valet, he would be more than grateful; indeed, it would help the servant of a dead hero find his feet after the wars. No salary necessary—just a fair share of the profits.

Profits?

Little of the loquacious dandy's story had struck through the haze of Sharkley's inebriation, but the word "profits" certainly did. He turned unsteadily to confront Roland full in the face.

"Eh?"

Roland's eyes glittered with anticipation; he drew the drawstring of the net a little tighter. No, the wily servant said, he wouldn't dream of taking a salary, just a small share in some discreet undertakings that he might, from time to time, suggest to Sharkley—ventures, he assured him, that had already approved financially successful for this dead master.

Even in his present state, Sharkley was not to be gulled. Why, he demanded, if Roland knew of these various profitable *ventures,* did he not practice them for himself? Why did he need Sharkley?

The answer, Roland claimed with obsequious charm, was obvious. He prided himself that he was an intelligent man—intelligent enough to realize he would always be identified as a working stiff, and never as a member of the *ton.* One had to be *born* to that, as his companion obviously was, said Roland, casting a slight bow in his direction. (Even though he recognized it as flattery, Sharkley warmed to the suggestion; indeed, it was the only pleasant thought he had had all this chill evening.) But, Roland continued, the true rewards, the real piles of gold, were to be found among the *ton.* Now, if he could suggest a few devices, and Sharkley, with his *entrée* into high society, could practice them, poverty would be a thing of the past for them both.

Poverty a thing of the past!

Even this canny street rogue could not realize how close to the bone Sharkley was living at this moment.

Until last spring, Sharkley had been surviving, for he had acted as a private secretary to his uncle, for which he had received a small stipend, but the uncle had since died. The money he invested with friends in a stable of racing horses had evaporated faster than a summer mist. Why, in the last few weeks, he had become so desperate as to think of borrowing from his brother to purchase a commission in the army, but the thought of facing the Napoleonic bloodbath had made him postpone such a presposterous move, and opt for the slightly more pleasant and definitely more secure option of marriage to Lady Jane—the proposal of which had led to this morning's embarrassing debacle.

It was no surprise then that by the time the two men had walked to Sharkley's rooms, they had agreed to become a team, living, and in time hopefully prospering, by their wits. True to his class and intelligence, Sharkley had made only one stipulation: although they were accomplices, Roland was never to forget he was, in fact, a servant, and that he, Sharkley, as master, would control the purse strings. Roland relaxed: he knew that success would come to anyone cautious enough, even when drunk, to make such conditions.

The very next week, they had started working for one of the major importers of contraband goods into England—an earl, as Sharkley had been shocked to discover when Roland had arranged a meeting. Over the year, they discovered the earl's pay wasn't particularly good, and the risks were high, so a few discreet ventures in blackmail offered a welcome chance to line their pockets.

To a degree that surprised even Roland, Sharkley had proved a most adept student. The demimonde, quick to appreciate his genuine flair for both the black market and blackmail, bestowed on this elegant figure with the striking dark hair the sobriquet of Black Jack—a title, Sharkley joked, he was pleased to have earned, for it certainly had paid more than any bestowed by the king. And when talking to his cronies, Roland always boasted of one thing: his master was as true a gentleman in honor as he was in manner, for whatever the take, meager or rich, Black Jack shared it quickly and fairly with his brother in crime.

This morning, Roland returned from his successful mission in a scant fifteen minutes, and his report to Sharkley was precise. The man's name was Richard de Varennes. He had arrived late last night, "on as fine a piece of 'orseflesh as the grooms 'ave ever seen, sir," said Roland. Mademoiselle Michelle Langois de Bellevue, and her two maids, had waited for the gentleman for three days here at the inn. Upon his arrival the ladies had ordered wine and a joint of beef to be sent to the small private parlor the women shared; the maid called Jane had herself gone to the kitchen to select the meat. De Varennes had left soon after the encounter Sharkley had witnessed. Right this moment, Mademoiselle Michelle was breakfasting at the corner table.

"And," said Roland, tossing a heavy leather coin purse into the air, "look at what I cadged."

"I'll take that, thank you," exclaimed Sharkley, snatching it midair. "Aye, it's quite a catch you have here, my man, if weight is any indication. How did you lift it?"

Roland grinned. His master always acknowledged true skill. "That Frenchie Varennes left his saddlebags for a minute while he sought the stable boy. *Et voilà!*" he exclaimed, offering the French phrase with a flourish.

"It's a credit to our trade you are, Roland. Well, let's see what we have here." Sharkley emptied the contents of the purse onto the bed. He whistled softly as a multitude of gold coins ran through his fingers. "Quite a traveler our man Varennes, I see. French, Belgian, Austrian, Italian coins. And this"—Sharkley held up a watch fob engraved deeply with a family crest—"may be worth a hundred times the money if we play our game right."

"Aye, sir, that is what I thought when I saw it. Now, if we can seal the letters we sent to Mademoiselle de Bellevue with this crest, we won't even 'af to blackmail her—just write on behalf of her so-called 'brother' pleading that 'e's in desperate straits and to send money to 'im with you, on your 'trips' back to France. And we pocket the money and destroy the letters."

"That would only work if we had an example of his handwriting."

"I'll take care of that, sir. The innkeeper 'as 'elped once already."

"Roland, at times you are worth your weight in gold." Sharkley flipped several gold coins over to his valet, for he had long since learned that a well-paid accomplice stays loyal.

"I'd take my weight in copper pence, if you 'ad it, sir, for even though I am as thin as a beggar, it would still be worth more than this," he said. "But thank 'e, sir." He buttoned the coins carefully into his pocket, then continued. "And a bit of a dazzler for a 'sister,' sir. Why, the bloke didn't even take the pains to match 'is name to 'ers. She's de Bellevue, and 'im signing de Varennes. Now, a true gentleman such as yourself, sir, would never make that slip like that."

Black Jack smiled at his servant's appreciation. "Now, Roland, come help me finish dressing before Mademoiselle de Bellevue leaves the dining hall."

In exactly ten minutes, Sharkley, attired in his best cravat, descended the stairs to the dining hall of the small inn and tipped the innkeeper handsomely to be placed at the table nearest to Mademoiselle and her companions, where he could observe them more closely. He thought he knew exactly what to expect, for Roland had given him a detailed description, yet he was not prepared for what he saw.

"Bit of a dazzler," his valet had said. He got it only half right, Sharkley thought.

Black Jack was used to beautiful women—yet Michelle de Bellevue startled him. The high cluster of dark curls was caught up pertly with intertwined ribbons of lavender and rose. Two long ringlets touched her shoulders, their darkness emphasizing her unusually fair skin. The rose of her dress highlighted the delicate flush of her cheeks. But it was her eyes, above all else, that captivated him. They were not blue —no blue could be that deep. They seemed almost as lavender as the ribbons in her hair.

The girl's honestly breathtaking, Sharkley thought, and began to warm to this adventure.

In minutes the jolly little French maid whom Michelle called Ninette caught Sharkley looking at them and winked. He returned the compliment. But despite Ninette's willingness, approaching Michelle, he knew, would not be easy, for the other servant, a straight-backed, sharp-eyed older woman, Jane, was undoubtedly an English governess—the breed was unmistakable—and Black Jack knew from previous experiences that such a woman would be a growling Cerberus in defense of her charge. Overhearing their conversation, however, would not hurt, so he ordered a rasher of bacon and a mug of ale from the innkeeper and, seemingly preoccupied with his breakfast, settled in to listen.

"Well," said silver-haired Jane, her severe and proper tones overlaid with affection for Michelle. "Richard has certainly changed your attitude about going to England. Ever since you received his letter, you've been bemoaning the idea—and now, after an hour's conversation with him, you are sparkling at the thought!"

Michelle shrugged prettily. "He has simply convinced me that it is another adventure that we might enjoy."

"I do hope that my beloved England is *not* an adventure. I have quite enough adventures, what with revolutions, wars, blockades, and popinjay emperors these past years," Jane said tartly.

Michelle studied her nurse, who had never once complained before. Now, as they were about to leave for the security of England, her old home, Jane had ventured for the first time to express her true feelings. Michelle suddenly understood what a trial this past year had been for her, and reached to touch her hand reassuringly: "And haven't we survived the experiences of these past months since Papa's death quite well?" she asked, seeking to give the conversation a more positive turn.

"If poverty is an experience, with more experience than any sane body needs in a lifetime," snapped Jane.

"Jane, we never would have discovered your superb skill at bartering and Ninette's magic needle. Why, I am costumed more beautifully than any woman wardrobed by Sophie of Paris."

Ninette nodded, pleased. "But I would still give my best ear bobs for three lengths of good silk."

Sharkley was fascinated. So all was not as it appeared to be! He had expected a young woman traveling with two companions to be substantially supported—and there certainly had been the mention of some sort of dowry Michelle was bringing to her godfather. Yet when he looked closely at Michelle's clothes, he noticed that while the finishing stitches were very fine, and the colors enhanced their charming wearer to perfection, the dress was plain muslin, not fine, and the lavender cloak beside her was of a serviceable wool.

"I promise you, Ninette, with the first sale of one of the drawings Richard gave me, we shall try to find some fine silk remnants to give your art its glorious due. Yet," added Michelle, turning to Jane and looking at her directly, "I worry about Richard's involvements. Do you think he will be safe?"

Involvements? Jane's eyebrows rose in surprise at Michelle's choice of words: obviously Richard had told Michelle a great deal this morning, for previously his sister had not known of his spying. The girl was obviously probing to see if Jane, too, knew the secret.

The old nurse looked thoughtfully at her charge. Now that Michelle was eighteen, perhaps she should know—especially as Richard had already revealed part of the truth. "Don't worry, pet. As well as being quick-witted, Richard is brave but not foolhardy. There is much I can tell you later to reassure you."

Michelle nodded. It was clear her dear companion would talk no further now, for Jane regarded Ninette, however skilled a designer and seamstress she was, as a feather-topped parrot, likely to repeat everything she heard.

Ninette was not at all sure she understood the drift of the conversation, for she knew nothing of Richard's "involvements," but always the romantic, despite her thirty years, she knew one thing: Richard was handsome. "No one would hurt an Adonis such as he, Michelle. Handsome men always find assistance."

"Aye," said Jane sharply. "I only wish we had some handsome Adonis to find assistance for us in this next dilemma. While you were with your brother, I checked at the dock. In waiting for Richard these three days, we have missed our passage on the *Overton,* and the other British packet, the *Lark,* leaving today, is already booked."

A tiny wrinkle creased Michelle's brow; she was aware of how meager the sum in their little communal treasury was, and one week more in expensive Ostend would deplete it entirely. She would have to sell one of the last three of her father's cherished antique books.

As he observed the intensity of Michelle's beautiful face, for the first time in his criminal career, Sharkley began to hope that, for him, there might be a far fairer prize in this escapade than simple gold. This turn of events might mean he would surrender his own passage on the *Lark,* but he realized that, whether for blackmail or other ends, this opportunity to place Mademoiselle in his debt should not be missed. Experienced with women as he was, Black Jack knew how to approach Michelle. A beauty as rare as she probably would be used to seeing abject devotion, and it would not impress her; he would be polite, but not obsequious.

His moment to address Michelle had come.

He rose in his place several feet away and bowed, but not too deeply. "Mademoiselle," he said, offering slight nods of acknowledgment to Jane and Ninette as well, for he never forgot Roland's comment that servants are a blackmailer's best friends, "John Sharkley at your service. I could not help overhearing the matter of your distress. My man and I are booked on the *Lark* for departure this afternoon at high tide. It would give me the greatest pleasure if you would allow me to offer you the accommodation reserved in my name. A few days delay in Ostend would be a small price for me to pay for your comfort and security." He finished with another discreet bow.

A small flush of anger had crossed Jane's face, as she realized from Sharkley's remarks they had been overheard; Ninette beamed, pleased by his gallantry. Black Jack was most surprised by Michelle's reaction: her look was almost like—the thought was preposterous—the cool self-possession of an experienced gambler at cards. How could a young woman like this have learned such an expression of guarded impassivity?

Little did he realize that Jane had trained Michelle in restrained self-possession in tense, difficult moments such as this, not merely as a social grace, but although Michelle did not realize it, also in order to safeguard her identity, and perhaps her very life. The daughter of a Royalist count, Jane knew too well, was never safe.

Her pupil was most adept, but beneath her seeming calm, Michelle was, indeed, perturbed. She was embarrassed to realize they had been overheard, but she quickly decided that poverty had not yet forced the daughter of the Comte de Bellevue to depend upon strangers to solve their problems.

"Why, thank you, sir. We see that the age of courtesy is not dead in England." Michelle rose from her seat and, offering Black Jack her hand, gave him a small curtsey that precisely matched the degree of his bow. "However, we cannot allow strangers, however thoughtful, to be inconvenienced on our behalf, Mr. Sharkley." With a shy smile, she quickly slipped on her pelisse, and murmuring, "Thank you again," departed, with Jane and Ninette quickly following.

Black Jack was completely charmed. He sat down to order another serving of bread and bacon, and not until his man Roland joined him did he realize that Michelle had not offered her own name. Roland thought that it was merely a slip in manners of an inexperienced girl; Sharkley knew better, for while that delicate cameo of a face had been innocent, its guarded caution had been deliberate.

What a dilemma! He had found out the de Bellevue name and circumstances by spying, but he had no way of knowing her destination and final address. Without that, how was he to make further contact with Michelle? It was clear: he would have to ensure that the three women sailed with Roland and himself on the *Lark*.

How expensive would it be to bribe the captain? He hoped not too much, for the master smuggler for whom Sharkley imported the contraband had always been miserly, and even with the added boost of using de Varennes's gold, after paying the most urgent of his gambling debts, Black Jack calculated that he had but a month's living expenses, then his pockets would be to let.

Then he remembered Michelle's shy smile, and a warmth came over him. The richness of the prize added to the excitement of the chase, and John Sharkley was not one to take his hunting lightly. Yes, regardless of the cost, he would do it! He would bribe the captain to make room, then announce to the ladies that through his good offices the sea master had found a vacancy, and let them pay for their own passage. They would most certainly put his success with the captain down to influence rather than bribery, and that would only increase his image of respectability, which was exactly what he needed. The only remaining question was whether or not obtaining passage for the ladies would make them grateful enough to allow him to converse with Michelle sometime during the voyage between Ostend and London, but his way with women was well-known, and he had few doubts on that score.

"Roland," he announced, "we're going to use some of this morning's treasure to bribe the captain of the *Lark* to find space for the Bellevue party. It's the only way we can discover their destination."

Roland grunted. Giving up gold, he always found hard.

Sharkley pushed his argument. "We're priming the pump, my man. We're buying something worth much more than the few coins in this pouch—the lady's trust. After we've bribed the captain, we'll return the purse, and a third of what is in it, to the mademoiselle. That will convince her of our integrity."

Roland physically winced at the thought of "returning" any gold at all, and for one mad moment, Black Jack thought of telling his servant that he wanted Michelle to trust him in order to win, rather than blackmail, the lady, but he knew his hardheaded servant would regard that as "silly, slobbering sentiment." Black Jack threw in a morsel to appease his valet. "Of course, we'll keep the watch fob with the crested seal."

Roland's face eased, and he chuckled. "I can see the letters between these lovers taking some mighty strange turns, sir—and pretty rich ones at that. I don't think our Season at 'ome will be 'alf bad, sir. We won't be poor."

Sharkley rose. "Then I'll be off, to see if a substantial gift to the captain will help him discover room for our lady and her maids."

While Sharkley departed in search of the captain, the Bellevue party, needing to consider their dilemma in private, walked to the lookout. Quite a picture they made as they strolled along the promenade: the glorious Michelle, with her pretty lace parasol, seemingly oblivious to the looks and nodding bows of unknown gallants; quick-eyed Jane marching alertly two steps behind, watching for any untoward move of an ill-mannered male toward her beautiful chick; and Ninette, yet farther back, enjoying the sun, the people, not averse to giving a quick, friendly smile to the nicest of the seamen or tradesmen who smiled at her.

On their arrival at the lookout, Michelle and Ninette selected a bench with a clear prospect of the sea; Jane insisted on standing to discourage intruders and listeners. To any innocent viewer, they looked like happy chatterers, but the conversation was most serious.

"Precisely how much money do we have left?" asked Michelle, mastermind and strategic planner of the trio, for there was a slim possibility she might avoid selling the beloved book.

"Fare for our voyage and three English pounds," stated Jane, the treasurer of the little group.

"Dear me," said Ninette, her jolly face creased into one of its rare frowns. "Does that mean that we shall have trouble affording the inn for the week until another British vessel arrives?"

"Precisely so, *ma chérie*," said Michelle. "But do not fear. We will inquire and find a local *pension*—a less expensive rooming house that will be happy for boarders during the winter. And I noticed on our promenade that there was an excellent antiquarian book shop. Surely they will be delighted to purchase one of Papa's books, for here they probably rarely see works of such quality. That sale will cover our expenses until we get to London. Once there, Richard's plan will work beautifully—even if I *do not* marry an English lord" (Michelle's delicate nose wrinkled slightly at the mere suggestion) "and I return to France when the war is over, which will not be very long at all."

The two older women said nothing, for they both had seen enough of life to know that wars do not end easily. And poor child, thought Jane, although she calls Paris home, they had barely lived there since Michelle was ten. Who could tell what would happen? Richard's suggestion that his sister might marry in England seemed quite possible.

"Jane, please," Michelle said earnestly, "tell me all you know about my English family, of my godfather. I'm no longer a child, and can't be shocked. In fact, the success of Richard's plan depends on *all* of us" (there she cast a significant glance in Ninette's direction), "especially me, not being caught off guard. If I do not know the details of my past, he might suspect we are imposters, which we are certainly not. Papa would never talk about it; he said it hurt too much, although"—here Michelle's chin went up and tears shone in her eyes—"although you have told me so often the part about how Mama and Papa were each other's *grande passion.*"

Ninette leaned forward, eager to hear at last the story she had speculated about for the last five years. The part about the *grande passion* even she knew, for who in the household had not been aware of the distinguished, prematurely aged count, striking with his fine features and silver hair, standing quietly for a few moments each morning before the small formal portrait of his lovely, young English bride? No matter in what city they were living, that small portrait always was on the mantel of the salon, almost a holy shrine. The count had had a small traveling case made for it that only he himself was allowed to carry.

Michelle sat on the bench nervously twirling her parasol, awaiting her companion's decision.

Jane recognized the validity of Michelle's request; reluctantly, she agreed even loquacious Ninette should share some of the information, for doubtless the duke's servants would question the little seamstress relentlessly. The old nurse steeled her thin shoulders. Even these eighteen years later, it was painful to recount, loving her Anna and wanting to do justice to truths hidden too deep in the heart for words.

Yes, she decided, the time to tell the whole story had come.

"The Duke of Calvern, your godfather, was a most generous man, as I remember, old enough to be your grandfather. Your father was an established scholar, having gone to the

Sorbonne and the university of Padua to learn about manuscripts and art. He had come to London for further study. He met the duke at an art dealer's in Old Jermyn Street—Derby's, I believe. The two men had so many mutual interests in the arts, they became close friends.

"It was the terrible winter of ninety-three, when the French Revolution turned mad and beheaded the king and many of your father's noble compatriots. The duke realized your father, as a French count, could not go home, so each holiday and summer for his three years in London, the duke invited your father to his estate in Surrey. Count Pierre and the old duke got along like a well-matched coach and four, for both were ardent scholars. Then, in that spring of ninety-five, the year of your dear mother Anna's come-out, she met your father at one of the duke's balls."

Even now, Jane found it painful to recall; she paced uneasily back and forth in front of them, halting her tale whenever passersby might overhear.

"My Anna was love-foolish, the child. What did she know of the way of the world? She was seventeen, and the count twenty-eight.

"Her father, Robert Warner, was so haughty when he inherited the title of Earl of Silkington from his great-uncle. He raged that he had paid for Anna's come-out and had 'bought' her the offers of one English duke and two earls, and she *would* choose a penniless French count of uncertain future. In fact" (here Jane's face flushed with a decades-old anger) "the truth of the matter is her father had been rather miserly in my Anna's clothes and *début* entertainment; it was her own sweet beauty and winning ways that brought those beaux to her feet. The more her father raved and threatened, the more my Anna stood silent and firm. Count Pierre she would have, and Count Pierre would have her.

"They were married in the Duke of Calvern's private chapel. Her father disowned her within a day of hearing of her marriage, vengeful miser that he was. He willed his entire estate to a witless nephew in Shropshire; what has become of him, we never heard, and I do not want to find out.

"It was ninety-six. The count, wanting to shelter Anna from her father's scorn and treachery, brought her home to his only remaining property, the town house in Paris. She begged me to come with her—as if I would desert my motherless Anna, whom I had served since she was born!

"It was a content and innocent time. There was laughter and happiness. Although Anna was rather surprised to discover your half brother, Richard, the ten-year-old illegitimate son of the count and Madame de Varennes, his long-vanished mistress, in the household, she cherished the boy as an elder sister would have, and loved the count even more for not casting off his responsibilities as so many men do; and her generosity toward the boy made the count cherish your mother even more."

Ninette's head nodded in romantic sympathy: "Some say love is blind. I say it just reaches a little deeper than most ways of looking."

Jane cast Ninette a rare look of appreciation.

"Ah, Michelle," Jane continued. "The joy when you were born. The count was ecstatic. My Anna herself gave me charge over you—no other but herself and the count would she allow to touch you. The count wrote to Anna's father; of course, there was no response. What a treasure he has missed!" Jane stopped her pacing; her hand rested affectionately on Michelle's shoulder for a moment.

"The Duke of Calvern was in Paris, and came over to the house within hours of your birth. The duke was most flattered to be your godfather, I remember. He bought a bottle of cognac, and he toasted you, wishing you to live to the age of the cognac, which was very, very old. How your parents laughed! How could we know that our Anna would die of childbed fever within ten days?"

For several minutes, the stern lapping of the ocean waves was the only sound on the pier. Each of the three women looked fixedly out to sea; Michelle's cheeks glistened with tears. She felt a wave far warmer than that of the ocean at her feet wash over her: the bravery of her young mother in following her love, her father's joyous pride in her, the understanding generosity of the Duke of Calvern.

There were other chapters to come, although Ninette, of the three, did not realize it. Jane looked at her with concern. Ninette had come to the count's household only five years earlier as seamstress and lady's maid to Michelle, but she had never been privy to family secrets, for both Jane and the count had thought of her as a feather-top.

Michelle read Jane's worry instantly and, looking around, caught sight of an attractive young pie-man selling his wares some distance down the breakwater. Removing the last small coins from her reticule, she exclaimed, "Oh, Ninette, we will soon be hungry, and those pies smelled so delicious as we passed. Would you get us some before that fine young man moves on?"

Ninette, who could see even from this distance what a fetching figure the man cut, was off immediately.

"Now," said Michelle earnestly, "although I will mention them to no one, I should know some details about Papa and Richard. When did Papa take up his profession?"

Jane became thoughtful. "I would hazard a guess at about ten years ago. You were eight and Richard eighteen. Until then, your father had been quite withdrawn, for in his mind, no other woman, no other interest, could take my Anna's place. When Napoleon crowned himself emperor and started out to conquer Europe—that was the turning point. He felt that Napoleon was a false monarch, who, although he said he supported the reform, was an absolute dictator in the worst sense. And the new nobles he appointed! Loyal to neither the country nor the people's government. When your father was in London, he was most impressed with the constitutional monarchy of England. He wrote to your godfather, who encouraged him to explain his views to Louis, Comte de Provence, who will become King Louis after Napoleon is routed. Louis was most sympathetic, so your father found a new focus, a goal beyond his grief: bringing a constitutional monarchy back to France."

"Richard told me exactly this in our talk this morning, Jane. But what precisely did Papa do?" Michelle could feel herself growing tense with interest.

The old nurse's answer was cautious, the words she sought precise. "I'm not sure. A scholar in manuscripts and drawings can travel freely in Europe even in wartime. All one can say is that France's rightful king, Louis, in exile first in Poland and now in England, knows many details of Napoleon's military and court."

Michelle's eyes widened questioningly. "How did Richard become involved?"

"With great persistence," answered Jane. "The count was most unwilling that his only son should undertake such a risky endeavor. He would have preferred your brother to become a quiet scholar and then serve the government of free France, once it was well established, in a public capacity. Richard would have none of it. He adored your father and wanted to be his compatriot, his colleague, right then. Don't you remember four winters ago, the nights the two of them sat in the library, arguing till dawn?"

Michelle nodded.

"Finally, your father consented, on condition that Richard safeguard himself by assuming the name of his mother, de

Varennes, and by never referring to the count as his father. Have you not noticed that Richard never calls you sister, and always refers to your papa as the count, even when speaking of him in private?"

"You're right! Richard started that habit years ago, and I thought it was a strange affectation. Why did he do it?"

"That way, if anyone overheard them speak, they could never identify them as father and son, and so one was never held hostage for the other. Perhaps it was not such a bad thing, after all. Richard has told me that this saved his life on one or two occasions."

"I am so proud of them both," exclaimed Michelle, her eyes shining. "Richard told me this morning that when we are in England, safe under the duke's protection, he will rest easy and work much better. Now can you see why I'm so ready to leave our beloved France? Even though I will feel as if I'm in exile, it will be for King Louis, but most especially, for Richard."

Jane cast her charge a look of pride. Her young mistress was beginning to show the grace and courage of a great lady.

Just as Ninette returned with the steaming meat pies, Black Jack approached the de Bellevue party on the pier and told them that through his good offices, the captain had found accommodation for them on this day's voyage. Further, it was his pleasure to return to them a coin purse dropped by a gentleman the innkeeper had identified as a member of their party.

Ninette wept, Jane thanked him, and Michelle gave him such a radiant smile that Sharkley banished the remotest thought of blackmail and believed, for the moment, in his own goodness.

It was as an honest suitor that he asked Michelle if, once on board, she would grant him the pleasure of her company on a stroll around the deck; on that walk, as a would-be lover, and an honorable one at that, he asked her destination in London and if he might call on her. She responded very prettily that if the Duke of Calvern, her guardian, agreed to receive him, she would be delighted.

Roland grunted when he heard the news. He had never seen his master in such a softened state. Right unnatural, he thought, but held his tongue.

3

"**I BEG YOUR PARDON?**" Edward Radcliffe, Duke of Calvern, rose to his feet and rested his hands on the library writing table in front of him. "I don't believe I understood you correctly. Would you please repeat what you just said?"

Mr. Justin Straighton, solicitor, was distinctly uncomfortable. He had been the family lawyer since Edward, the present duke, acceded to the title at twenty-one, and for thirty years before that, he had served Edward's father and grandfather. Nothing Mr. Straighton had said before in those thirty-nine years had caused a Radcliffe to rise to his feet.

"I said, Your Grace, I have in my possession a signed copy of the will of Pierre Langois, Comte de Bellevue, deceased in November 1811, requesting that your father—dead these nine years, rest his soul—as Michelle de Bellevue's godfather, assume guardianship of the child until she reaches the age of twenty-one or is married, whichever shall come first."

"Thanks to your guidance over the years, sir, my father was unusually fastidious in his legal affairs, yet in the index of legal commitments he left with his will, there was no mention of such a guardianship agreement. Are you sure it is authentic?"

"Your father once purchased a small property in Paris from the comte. The seal on that deed of sale and on this will is identical."

"Is the child in London now?"

"Yes, sir. She arrived with her nurse and maid two days

ago from Ostend. The nurse came to my office to deliver the will and to request an interview between Mademoiselle de Bellevue and yourself. I, of course, said I would consult you immediately.

"Yes, of course. Quite proper of you, Straighton."

The duke walked toward the nearest of the four glass doors leading from the spacious library to the garden and looked out.

Straighton settled back into the comfort of his wing chair and prepared to wait. He hadn't known the duke since the week he was born without discovering precisely how he would react to such a surprising situation: Calvern would withdraw into himself for some minutes, think things through most rationally, then announce his conclusion.

Straighton adjusted his spectacles so he could see the duke more clearly. His granddaughter Phoebe spoke of the duke as "that unattainable Norse god." Seeing his tall, athletic build framed in the sunlight, Straighton understood the girl's phrase. The sun caught the sheen of Calvern's silver-blond hair; his lightly tanned skin was flushed from the exertion of his morning gallop. The flawless fit of his blue coat, beige breeches, and highly polished riding boots emphasized the lithe, muscular lines of his body. He was, without doubt, a remarkably handsome man.

Phoebe, after listening to Calvern discourse at dinner on issues currently in the House of Lords, also commented on "the cool command of authority" that matched his Norse looks. And almost all the *ton*, thought Straighton, would have agreed with her; they were blind to the more profound nature of the man.

Straighton had to admit, the duke himself was as much responsible for that reputation as anyone. His witty, aloof manner was not merely social sophistication: it was founded on a commanding presence, a quiet sense of authority that made him the center of attention whenever he strode into a room, even if he chose not to say a word. That demeanor imparted strength to friends, intimidated foes, and, the older solicitor conceded, attracted the sparkling ladies of the *ton* as a flame does moths.

Yet, the astute old lawyer wondered, who other than the duke, the Cresswells, and he himself recognized the loneliness, the passionate concerns, that underlay Calvern's worldly suavity?

In all his fifty years of practice, Straighton had never met a man—not even Edward Radcliffe's father—more intensely committed to things he valued: his family (his younger brother Tom, his maternal uncle, General Cresswell, and Cresswell's wife and daughter were all that remained), the honor of the family name, the well-being of the estates, and perhaps most of all, the Radcliffe tradition of service to king and country. Straighton knew whereof he spoke, for he had encountered the young man's passion for his family and his estates at their first meeting after the old duke's death.

The new duke had been barely twenty-one; his face was still drawn from his grief at losing the father and companion he had so loved and respected. He was truly alone as the head of his family, for his mother, Lady Mary Cresswell, had died when his younger brother Tom had been born, and his father had never remarried.

The news Straighton had brought to young Edward Radcliffe that day was not good. The old lawyer knew that since an early age, his father had inculcated in both his sons pride in the integrity of the family name and the responsibility of keeping up the estates and supporting the family retainers, loyal for generations. The butlers of the three estates had come to offer their reports to the new duke, and Straighton suspected the young man would not like what he heard.

Although Radcliffe's father had been a frugal and compassionate man, he had not maintained the three estates consistently, or improved the land. The income had fallen, and within two or three years, the stewards and old solicitor estimated, one of the estates would have to be sold for debt. Why not sell one of the estates now, release some of the retainers, and start with a clean slate?

The look of fire and courage that had crossed the young duke's face was one that Straighton would never forget.

"Sir, I am Edward Radcliffe, Duke of Calvern; and the only fitting memorial I can give my father is to enhance the family name, not diminish it. By not one acre, or one loyal retainer, shall this estate be lessened while I am duke."

He strode from the room.

Over time, as it became apparent that the lad was profoundly committed to what he said, he won both Straighton's heart and unqualified support. The skillful management of three estates and the guardianship of a rambunctious younger brother were not easy tasks at the best of times, but the young duke put aside his long-held ambition to serve his country in international affairs, and shouldered the responsibilities fully.

Soon after the young duke inherited the title, the British blockade of France started to wreak havoc on the English domestic economy. Many older aristocrats and landowners known for their business acumen fell heavily into debt, but young Calvern was determined to succeed. He weathered the initial financial crisis by following Straighton's suggestion, painful though it was, of going through his father's extensive art holdings, keeping the most select pieces for the estate, and selling the rest. He invested the proceeds in developing new farming methods for the estates, but even this was not easy. His own estate managers jeered at such radical notions as rotating crops rather than allowing the land to lie fallow; at times they flatly contradicted the young duke.

It was then Calvern developed his defense. Gone were the heated tirades and endless explanations and compromises. Under Straighton's guidance, the young duke learned how to give the managers once, and once only, detailed explanations for his decisions, and then to expect that his instructions be followed to the letter. Under no condition would he countenance defiance. At first, his air of authority was assumed, but it rapidly came to be part of his being. It seemed that the coolly aloof manner, once learned, was too valuable a tool to forget.

Straighton sighed.

What his granddaughter Phoebe and the rest of the *ton* would never recognize was the ardent passion of struggle and concern that lay behind Calvern's light, witty demeanor. Yet in just the past four years, the farms began to pay substantial incomes. Further astute investments in West Indian spices and in the timberlands of British North America (all the more vital now because of the need for ships to maintain the blockade of Napoleon) meant that the family fortunes were truly flourishing. Straighton estimated conservatively that Calvern was now one of the ten wealthiest men in England.

Nor in all the stress and strain of financial rebuilding had the duke forgotten his brother, Lord Thomas. He put the young rascal through the Regal Military Academy at Woolwich, and purchased for him a prestigious commission. Tom acquitted himself brilliantly with Wellington in Spain. Even General Cresswell was heard to confess the lad had shown exceptional mettle that did the family proud. Indeed, the younger Radcliffe was fast on his way to becoming an established military force.

At last, in the past two years, Edward had been able to turn attention to his own long-desired career. He had a genuine flair for politics and foreign affairs. Cool reason and authority of manner, so effective with rebellious young brothers and recalcitrant farm managers, worked equally well in the House of Lords, and brought his opponents to a standstill more effectively than any tirade. Lord Castlereagh, as foreign secretary, was coming to rely more and more on this insightful peer's suggestions and policies. In the rebuilding of Europe after Napoleon, Castlereagh made very clear to the duke that there would be an opportunity for his name to be imprinted on history. In fact, the foreign secretary confided to Straighton one night at their club, with Edward as a diplomat and Tom as a military commander, the name Radcliffe could become, in their generation, one of the glories of the British Empire.

Straighton adjusted his spectacles again and looked at Calvern as he leaned his arm on the door frame and thoughtfully overlooked his garden. The seemingly relaxed elegance of the duke's stance did not fool the old solicitor: he knew it was as deceptive as the easy strolling of a lion circling his pride. Threaten Calvern's family duty and honor, he knew, and one would be faced with the full, leonine strength of the duke's rage. The young man's upper lip was taut—a subtle but sure sign Edward was annoyed, and Straighton sympathized. The last thing the man needed now, at this crucial stage of his long-awaited and well-earned career, was to be saddled with his father's godchild!

The solicitor had been mulling the matter over ever since the child's old nurse had approached him, and he thought he had a suggestion that would both satisfy the duke's sense of duty and leave him free to follow his career. Judging that he had left Calvern enough time to contemplate, he broached the topic directly.

"It might be inconvenient for you, sir, to assume full responsibility for your father's godchild. There is, in fact, no legal necessity for you to do so. Any moral duty could be taken care of by making sure the child is not in need, and arranging her placement with a family of suitable class."

Calvern looked at the wary old solicitor and burst into a full, throaty laugh. "You cut right to the bone, Straighton. Here am I, trying to master the diplomatic art of appearing inscrutable, and you can read me like a book. I can only be thankful that you are not an opponent of mine in the House of Lords or at the negotiating table."

Edward walked back across the library and seated himself in the wing chair facing Straighton's. "You well know my most cherished value is the Radcliffe name; it must never be said I failed to honor a Radcliffe obligation, no matter how inconvenient. But once again, my old friend, your solution is precisely the one I have just been contemplating.

"It certainly would be inappropriate for me to have the child here at such a bachelor establishment." (The solicitor smiled to hear this magnificent Adam mansion on Portman Square described like rented chambers in a lodging house.) "I shall ask my mother's sister-in-law, Lady Deirdre, to take responsibility for chaperoning the girl, though heaven knows her hands are full with her own daughter Emma, who has been out for two years and has not yet received an offer. If she cannot do it, perhaps she knows of some suitable family among our cousins which would take the girl in return for a generous support allowance. By the way, what age is the child?"

"I don't know, sir. I must confess that I was so startled by the event that I forgot to ask the woman. One may assume, Your Grace, that as your father died nine years ago, she must be at least ten or eleven."

"Bring the schoolroom miss and her nurse here tomorrow at four, Straighton. I will have Lady Deirdre in attendance, and we'll straighten matters out then."

"I beg your pardon, Edward?" said Lady Deirdre, wife of General Cresswell. The red-haired Irish beauty was tastefully *déshabillé* in a white satin peignoir overthrown with a light morning robe of yellow India silk. Only intimates were allowed to approach her at the ungoldly hour of ten in the morning in her private boudoir, but it was no secret that her handsome nephew Edward Radcliffe, Duke of Calvern, only seven years her junior, was one of those so privileged.

"A godchild, you say? How utterly absurd!" Unlike Edward, Lady Deirdre had no pretensions to diplomatic service, and so allowed herself a full display of amazement and a rich, warm chuckle. Catching a glimpse of Edward's stern countenance in her vanity mirror, she stifled the laugh, motioned for her hairdresser to leave, and assumed a deep, sympathetic frown.

"Of course you are serious. Straighton has never joked in his life. A godchild; how surprising! Well, we must do something, but in a crisis, tea first, I say. It is the only safeguard of sanity, especially at this hour of the morning."

Deirdre motioned to a delicate Chippendale table placed by a window, already set with a tea service, chocolate pot, large breakfast cups, fruit, and scones. Edward realized he hadn't eaten since his vigorous morning ride and the interview with Straighton. Seated, with a cup of steaming tea and a scone or two, he was able to be quite objective about the problem. His aunt Deirdre he understood thoroughly. Although on the surface she accepted, indeed cleverly used, the *ton*'s foibles, in family affairs she always gave precedence to her kind and intelligent heart.

"My obligations at the Foreign Office and the House of Lords are at a crucial stage," said the duke, "and I must admit I don't want my personal responsibility for the child to become an unfortunate interruption. There is, however, one acceptable alternative: who can we find in the family to foster her? Of course, the child's governess and maid would accompany her, and I would certainly provide a substantial income for the service. Any impoverished vicars on your side?" Edward joked lightly. "I can't imagine the daughter of an *ancien régime* count is an heiress, so of course, at a later date, I'd pay for her come-out and dower her well."

Tea and a dish of fruit had also made Lady Deirdre quite clear-sighted about the matter, and she understood the indirect question Edward had asked. The major realities of life could not be avoided, as her daughter Emma was proving. Despite a lavish *début* two years earlier, fashions from the best London modistes, and a good training in social graces, things were not going well. Emma was too retiring. If the old duke's godchild was difficult, as a young, uprooted French *emigrée* would probably be, she would have two social problems on her hands.

"I truly regret that I can't assume responsibility for the girl at present, at least until Emma is married, I hope next season if not this. Our house is a little crowded." She noticed Edward's twitching lips, for even he would laugh outright at the thought of the Cresswell mansion, which was the second largest on Grosvenor Square, being cramped, so she added quickly, "At least in the servants' quarters. You mentioned she had both a governess and a maid. Why does a child need a lady's maid?"

Lady Deirdre paused significantly to let the strenuousness of her list of objections settle in. If Calvern did not believe them all, he did not make the mistake of countering them.

Deirdre continued, "If not an impoverished vicar, would an impoverished earl do? With this blockade of Napoleon, it seems impoverished earls are more common. Would you consider my brother and his wife? They are older now, and being childless, they might actually enjoy becoming family to a lonely young girl."

"Quite suitable, quite suitable, thank you," murmured Calvern, gratefully.

"Now to basics, Edward. Is the child pretty? Well-mannered? Speak English or only French?"

The duke raised a quizzical eyebrow. "My dearest Deirdre, I never considered. Of course, even if I had, and Straighton had met the child as well as the nurse, I can imagine the nature of Straighton's report: 'Legally correct, and financially not yet responsible, Your Grace.' I guess we do have to wait until tomorrow teatime to find out. You will join us?"

"I've never been one to forgo family duty, Edward, as this morning proves."

"You wouldn't miss a good occasion for family gossip, my dear, even at your own funeral." They both grinned, and he kissed his aunt lightly on the cheek. *"À bientôt!"*

"I beg your pardon, ma'am. Are you Jane Malton, in service to the Comte de Bellevue?"

Ninette, standing immediately behind Jane in the reception room of the Duke of Calvern's elegant Adam mansion, watched in amazement as Charles, the duke's tall, distinguished butler, bowed deeply to Jane, and nodded to herself. Jane beamed.

"Charles Wilson, after all these years! We used to see you so often in Paris with His Grace. It has been so long! Eighteen years exactly, for the last time was the baptism of my lady, whom you just announced to His Grace in the library."

"That was the infant we saw baptized? A beauty!" he beamed. "And, as I can tell from her entrance, as well-mannered as she is lovely. The eighteen years have been most gracious to you both," Wilson concluded with the slightest of bows.

Jane blushed.

Ninette's eyes widened. She tried to say to herself once again that love was not blind, that it reaches a little deeper than most ways of looking, but the saying couldn't quite stretch to cover the present situation. Why, in the five years she had been Michelle's maid, had not Jane's hair become grayer, her figure thinner, the features of her face more stark? Perhaps the good butler's eyesight was failing.

"Has Mr. Straighton spoken to the duke?" said Jane. "Do you think His Grace recalls her situation?"

"Oh, Miss Malton, didn't you know? The old duke has been dead these nine years. Young Lord Edward is now duke—and a fine one, at that. He kept his own valet and appointed me senior butler of this household."

"Congratulations, Mr. Wilson," said Jane warmly, then a sudden frown creased her brow. "Good heavens! That means my poor little Michelle has entered the lion's den, with no one there who knows her."

"His Grace the duke may be a social lion, Miss Malton, but he is not carnivorous. May I remind you that the British lion roars only to guard and protect? And from what I saw when I announced her, no one was going to roar."

Just the reverse, Charles thought. He knew the duke and Lady Deirdre had been expecting to encounter a child. Wilson had lingered just long enough, before he closed the library doors, to note that her ladyship's breast had heaved by several inches as she drew her breath in surprise; and for one of the rare times in his life, the duke, for a few seconds, came close, very close, to gaping.

"Come. Let me escort you both to the servants' parlor, and I will join you there after I have served tea for the duke." Wilson offered Jane his arm, and Jane took it.

Ninette followed behind, eyes wider than ever, mumbling in French, "I don't like lions."

Had she heard Ninette's opinion, Michelle, standing at this moment just inside the door of the duke's sunlit white and gold library, would have shared it. She felt as if she were, indeed, in a den of lions. The butler had announced her name but, quite correctly, left it for the occupants of the room to introduce themselves. She looked quickly around for someone elderly enough to be the duke; he obviously was not there. She had evidently intruded on this lean, elegant man and magnificent red-haired woman in a moment of intimacy, for they both were clearly startled.

Had Michelle been able to see herself as the duke and Lady Deirdre saw her at that moment, she would have understood their reaction.

The chit is a raving beauty! thought Lady Deirdre. "The child" was obviously seventeen or eighteen, and clothed in the very latest fashion. Standing as she was at the threshold, her petite form was highlighted by the large white and gold doors, which were literally twice her height. And her clothes. She was wearing a lavender traveling gown, banded with dark blue and lavender ruffs at the hem, and carrying a

matching blue shawl and reticule—any modiste on Bond
Street would have exclaimed approval. But it was the girl's
dark hair, threaded through with lavender and blue ribbons,
and those wide, compelling eyes that quite overwhelmed
Lady Deirdre. Every thought she had on how to handle Michelle instantly went out the window. Obviously, she could
not send a fully grown young beauty to the home of the earl,
her brother, and his slightly obese, jealous wife. What to do
now?

If Lady Deirdre had been caught off guard by Michelle's
beauty, Calvern had been instantly, utterly captured. He
hadn't missed the girl's graceful fragility, the dark hair offset
by the unusually white skin, the eyes as violet as a king's
amethysts. Michelle de Bellevue was beautiful—but such
beauty, though rare, had intrigued but never yet captured the
worldly-wise Calvern

Those eyes! That was it, he thought later.

For a few fleeting instants, they had been veiled by a
shadow of confused embarrassment, yet she had collected
herself without the least fluster, with only a slight heighten-
ing of her delicate color to reveal her discomfiture.

"I beg your pardon. Indeed, the butler must have mistaken the room. I am supposed to meet with the Duke of
Calvern. Would you be so kind as to direct me—"

If her ladyship did not know what to do, Calvern certainly
did. Before Michelle could finish, in five long strides he was
in front of her and bowing deeply.

"Excuse me, Mademoiselle Langois. I should have introduced myself more readily. I am Edward Radcliffe, Duke of
Calvern; may I present my aunt, Lady Deirdre Cresswell."

He came so quickly in front of her, she found herself
looking first directly at the top button of his waistcoat, and
then up into blue eyes so clear and discerning that she felt,
for a moment, as though he were reading her very thoughts.
A blush rose to her cheeks—would he see how astounded
she was by his youth, how the lithe elegance of his figure, his
quick, perceptive smile, disconcerted her? Quickly, she collected herself, turning first to curtsey to Lady Deirdre, and
then the duke. "I had expected you to be somewhat older,
Your Grace," she said softly.

"And I expected you to be somewhat younger, mademoiselle," said Calvern, with another slight bow.

"I daresay we are all somewhat surprised," ventured Lady
Deirdre, her breath having returned, and rapidly fanning
herself to cool a sudden flush.

"I gather you were expecting to meet with my late father, your godfather," continued the duke. "He died nine years ago, but I know he would have been delighted to be of service to you, as am I. Please, be assured that you are no less welcome because it is I who receive you."

As delighted as any man in his right mind would be, thought Lady Deirdre, catching Calvern's intent gaze on Michelle. Her ladyship certainly wanted a chance to assess the girl, and to think, before any decisions were made. In a crisis, she thought—and instantly rang for Wilson to bring the tea.

As Lady Deirdre poured, Calvern noticed that his aunt was most watchful and keen-eyed—sure signs that she was in an interrogating mood, and her questions, he knew, could be closely probing and intimidating. The duke leaped into the breach. "Mademoiselle Langois de Bellevue—"

"Michelle! If you stand in my godfather's stead, please call me Michelle. It would mean so much to me."

"It would make you like one of the family," said Lady Deirdre.

Michelle smiled her thanks. "Precisely. One feels so alone. How quickly you understand."

Lady Deirdre turned away. The remark had been intended to point out how familiar such a request was, and so discourage it. The girl had chosen to give it the kindest possible meaning. Was she, for all the fashion of her dress and composure of manner, that naive about society?

If Michelle appeared not to catch the intent of the remark, Edward did, and he covertly shot Deirdre a look of severe warning.

"Of course I will. And will you please call me Edward?"

Michelle looked down. "Your Grace, would it not seem too familiar to call my guardian by his first name?"

Her ladyship hid a quick smile. The girl had done it. Edward had been feeling like a knight rescuing some damsel in distress, and Michelle had just reminded him of his proper role, and how ancient the age of thirty appeared to her.

Calvern flushed. "Call me by whatever name makes you comfortable."

Deirdre, feeling a little sorry for the tone in which she had approached the girl, ventured a compliment. "I see by your lavender costume that you are still in the last stages of mourning for your father. Yet how charming it is, Michelle, the style becomes you so. Sophie of Paris is without equal, is she not?"

Michelle chuckled with delight. "How flattered my maid will be when I tell her, madame. I am afraid the daughter of a Royalist count could not afford to walk through the door of Sophie's. My maid Ninette's eye is infallible. She can see a gown once, only for a minute, and copy it exactly. How fortunate I am to have her."

An uneasy silence fell, and the duke racked his memory to find a topic to make his guest comfortable. "Tell me—I remember my father mentioning yours was a superb art collector. Is that so?"

Michelle looked from the guarded face of Lady Deirdre back into the face of the duke. His eyes were compassionate, reminding her of Richard's. She was drawn toward him, knowing instinctively that this man she could trust. As for the question—he was her godfather's son, after all; indeed, he should know some of her background.

Edward smiled encouragingly at her, and she opened to him, like a flower in spring sun. Although she was shy, and answered only with two or three sentences at a time, she obviously enjoyed talking about her father and art, and spoke with disarming innocence. With Calvern's gentle leading, a remarkable story emerged.

Of course, Michelle said, her papa and his papa before him had enjoyed paintings, particularly the Dutch and Flemish masters. Lush Rubens and haunting Rembrandts had decorated the public rooms of her grandfather's chateau; bright Vermeers and witty Brueghels had enlivened the family quarters. (She spoke of the works as if she remembered them, but the chateau had probably been confiscated before she was born, Edward thought.) What few works the revolutionary and Napoleonic governments had not taken from the count's estates had been sold to maintain the family in Paris. What remained to the family was easily portable—a few pen and chalk sketches by Rembrandt and Rubens, some particularly valuable because they were the working drawings for larger masterpieces; others were simply charming, intimate portraits. Her father, the count, had given her a small sketching sheet of da Vinci's scientific drawings of human musculature, but Leonardo was not so popular now, was he? Would His Grace like to see one or two drawings she had brought with her from Paris?

"Is Rembrandt not the same artist that Prinny thinks so highly of?" asked Lady Deirdre, a little overawed by the recital of names she had just heard.

Michelle nodded. "The Prince Regent bought Rembrandt's *The Shipbuilder and His Wife* for Carlton House just two years ago. I believe he was most pleased that Papa wrote to inform him it was for sale."

Calvern's face expressed genuine surprise, so Michelle hurried to explain that in his last years her father had become an art dealer, buying and selling major works for friends who had great respect for this gentle scholar's knowledge and fine taste. In these last five years, her father had taken her on his extended trips through Europe, with Jane, her nurse, and Ninette, her maid. Often they would live in one European capital or another for months on end while her father negotiated the purchase and transfer of important collections. In Amsterdam, she had close friends. She had enjoyed Florence, where they had passed a winter, but Venice was hot and smelled in summer. She had not traveled in Germany as much as she would have liked, because of "Napoleon's escapades." Nonetheless, her German as well as Italian was fluent. Her Russian was "schoolroom," for she had never visited the country, although her father contended that she should learn the language, for the czar was making Saint Petersburg one of the great capitals of Europe, and the art collections of Catherine the Great, although composed largely of pillaged works, were among the best in the world. Like the czar, the Prince Regent, her father said, was one of this generation's few rulers to assemble such a world-class collection.

Calvern cast his aunt a sidelong glance, his lips twitching. Only last week at dinner, he had listened to his uncle, General Cresswell, railing against the regent's exorbitant expenses, the folly of his interests in art and architecture. Lady Deirdre uttered a small choking sound.

"But I do not imagine," Michelle hurried on, eager to tell her hosts how pleased with England she was, "that the czar is nearly as interesting as the regent. The regent is said to be imaginative and playful. The Pavilion at Brighton is so unusual. I have never seen it. It looks Moorish, does it not? Some of the emperor of Austria's favorite works share the same playfulness."

Lady Deirdre uttered another small, choking sound and quickly poured herself a third cup of tea.

"Have you met the emperor?" Calvern asked.

Catching the glint of sympathetic humor in His Grace's eyes, Michelle laughed merrily at the suggestion. "Never, but"—her eyes sparkled with laughter—"I have met the crown prince. He wanted Papa to come with him to see a certain picture at an auction. It was four years ago, in our hotel suite in Vienna. My dancing master had come to give me my first waltzing lesson. The prince whirled me around the room at the end of my class, before Papa had arrived. He was most kind, actually. He was charming to pay attention to me, for I was only fourteen."

This time Lady Deirdre did not cough. She placed the cup and saucer gently on the table and took another long, searching look at her nephew's new ward.

The girl was self-possessed, a little shy, and obviously not saying these things to be deliberately shocking. Evidently the regent's preferences in art, and waltzes with crown princes, had been a normal part of her life, and she was honestly unaware of how inappropriate the ruthless matrons of the *ton* would find such statements. Unless this Michelle was taken in hand, her reputation would be destroyed within the week. And, Deirdre thought, suppose her own daughter, Emma, had been orphaned, and were sent to a strange country? Her throat constricted at the thought. Yes, the girl deserved every consideration. In fact, she mused, Michelle's dark-haired beauty would form a pleasing contrast to Emma's silver-blond locks. If the two girls could get along, in fact, become friends—Lady Deirdre's course was clear.

"Well, my dear, you have certainly experienced some adventures. It must have been quite lonely for you without a mama. But you and your papa were very fortunate to have each other, as you lived in all those foreign places."

During the course of the interview with Lady Deirdre, Michelle had come to expect the penetrating questions. This last remark, so sympathetic in its insight, almost unnerved her, and she fought to keep the sudden, hot tears in her eyes from betraying her. "You are right, madame. We were both very lonely and very fortunate, at one and the same time."

Her ladyship rose to her feet, giving a small nod and a genuinely warm smile to Michelle. "It has, indeed, my dear, been most interesting to meet you, and I hope my family and I may have the pleasure of your company soon. Would you pardon me if I detain my nephew for a few minutes? We have several matters to discuss."

Calvern rang the bell for Wilson, instructed him to bring Michelle more hot tea, and excusing himself, accompanied his aunt from the room.

As she awaited the duke's return, Michelle looked with awe and pleasure at the library. The room itself was glorious: sunlight poured through the four French doors; white and gold columns separated the bookshelves and flared to the sixteen-foot ceiling. Could this room have been designed by Adams? It certainly looked like illustrations of the master architect's work. And the books! Three entire sections of French and German histories and literature. This young duke looked so—so English, yet had such sophisticated European taste! And his eyes were kind; they had almost twinkled with enjoyment at some of her remarks.

Michelle's thoughts turned to Lady Deirdre, and a small frown creased her brow. It was obvious that, unlike her nephew, who had enjoyed the recounting of the young girl's adventures, she had been slightly shocked. Why? wondered Michelle, for she had carefully edited anything in the telling that had touched on the uncertainty and poverty that had marked life with the count. She had not revealed that the reason they had traveled with her father was that he had rented out the town house in Paris to provide capital for his business, and they had no home but the flats and hotel rooms in strange cities. Nor did she say that one day, when she was twelve, Jane had pointed out to the count, that a young lady needed dresses and bonnets, and her father could only afford Ninette as a maid and seamstress after he had dismissed his own valet.

Michelle had been so careful to tell only the positive things, yet for one moment in the interview, she had almost faltered. When the duke asked if it had been difficult since her father's death, she felt as if his eyes, so kind, could see every image of pain she was hiding; yet she had said nothing.

How could anyone—even this strangely perceptive Calvern—understand the loneliness, the struggle, the sad disillusionment of the thirteen months since her father's death? She had been shocked by how many wealthy nobles and patrons of the arts who had, at the best of times, been slow in paying her father his commissions on their purchases, after his death, had defaulted entirely. They had survived only because Jane, Ninette, and she had practiced a thousand small economies. For all the brave front she had put on, there had been times when fear of the future, loneliness for her brother and a real home, had overwhelmed her—and if the duke had looked at her thirty seconds longer with those kind eyes, she would have told everything—all in a flood of tears. Would Calvern have then judged her to be a foolish, sentimental child?

Surprisingly, she cared what this Englishman thought of her.

Her brother—dear Richard. How she longed to be able to write to him, to tell him how right he was to send her to England. She knew he had expected their family drawings to be her chief financial security; she was glad she had them, and would use them wisely. Yet something told her that this Edward Radcliffe, Duke of Calvern, would be her guardian in more than name, that she might even have a real home with him.

For the first time since her father's death, a little of the loneliness and fear lifted; she felt almost safe. Michelle gave a small twirl of happiness before settling down to read and wait.

Calvern and Deirdre withdrew to the salon near the front door to await her ladyship's carriage. For several minutes neither of them spoke.

Calvern, while anxious not to interrupt his diplomatic career with any more involvement than was necessary, was surprised at the degree of his own concern for the young woman he had just met. Yes, he admitted to himself, Mademoiselle de Bellevue had caught his interest with her unusual dark-haired, fair-skinned beauty; her intelligent, perceptive mind intrigued him.

Yet there was something that now, as he mulled over their encounter, he realized had touched him even more. Was it the candor and modesty with which she had told her story? He'd enjoyed the way in which she'd shared her humor and knowledge of the world. While she did not have the sophistication of judgment that comes with experience, she already knew and accepted the differences of language, custom, and people. He suspected that this was one woman to whom one might be able to talk about such unfeminine, interesting things as politics. Yet although her wit and worldly innocence were undoubtedly part of her attraction, that was not all.

Was it the intensity of her emotion? Although the expression on Michelle's delicate features had been carefully controlled, at moments as she spoke of her childhood, like the shadow of a large bird cutting across the sun, pain would flicker across her eyes, and he knew with certainty that interwoven with the happy memories, there had been some painful ones of which she made no mention.

The eyes—that was it!

The hurt she had attempted so gallantly to hide had been fully revealed in her eyes, and now aroused in Calvern a protective tenderness he had almost forgotten how to feel.

And then there was that first awkward moment at the door of the library: she had appeared, like a small Dresden figurine, so dainty was she in her perfection. Yet there had been a particular quality to her gaze at that moment—yearning, haunted, perhaps a little hopeful. He knew the look, oh, how well he knew that look, for it echoed something he had felt so often himself. Particularly in the two or three years after his father's death, for a short instant when he first met people, he had allowed the vulnerability of his loneliness to surface as he searched for a particular understanding, a friend. He had been fortunate and found several. But Michelle was alone in a strange land, without even her own godfather.

Quietly, sitting in the receiving salon, a realization came upon Calvern. Until this afternoon's meeting, his concern for Michelle had only been a legal responsibility, to be fulfilled carefully, conscientiously—but only to the limit of the law. Now, he admitted to himself, he felt very differently indeed. He no longer wanted to offer Michelle a shelter, a modicum of financial support. He wanted to give her a home; he wanted to see laughter, instead of loneliness, in her eyes. For some reason, that had become important to him.

The duke glanced up from his contemplation and noted that Deirdre's jaw was set, determined—a sure sign she had come to a decision, probably a negative one—and despaired. "I take it, Deirdre, I now have a serious responsibility on my hands, for you don't think that Michelle, with her liberal education, is suitable to be placed with either your brother, the earl, or yourself?"

To Calvern's surprise, Deirdre responded with her most winning smile. "*Au contraire,* my darling nephew. I would be most happy if you, as her guardian, should arrange for her, *and* the maid and nurse, to stay with us at Grosvenor Square." She glanced at her nephew's surprised face and chuckled. "Although I cannot think of it as flattering for a member of the family to register shock because I choose to make a generous gesture."

"You would understand my astonishment, Deirdre, if you had seen your face during the interview. You, the most sophisticated of women, were utterly nonplussed when Michelle said she had seen drawings of human musculature, which, I admit, knowing Leonardo, were probably amazingly, gloriously male."

"It is precisely because she makes such remarks that I wish to take the chit under my wing. Suppose she had said such a thing at a court occasion? Her reputation would be destroyed by the next morning. Michelle has traveled in Europe more extensively than most men on a grand tour, but for all her travels, she is most innocent in the ways of good society, or else she would not have revealed to us all she has this afternoon. In fact, I would venture Mademoiselle Michelle will benefit as much from my guidance in society as yours, Edward. Agreed?" Deirdre asked with a lift of her lovely face.

Relieved, indeed delighted by his aunt's response, Edward bowed over her hand in thanks. "Undoubtedly she will benefit more from yours than she ever would from mine, for you run the *ton* like a puppet show for your own amusement. But," he pressed, "why the sudden change of heart?"

"Michelle's vivacity and sense of style will enliven my Emma and set her off nicely by simple contrast. Perhaps some gentleman, in calling on our little *émigrée,* will discover and appreciate my daughter's quiet grace. But first, of course, Michelle must make her *début.*"

"Ah, I see I am to become a victim of one of Lady Deirdre's magnificent, mad campaigns." Calvern grinned. "Well, if you choose to make her so, Michelle will become the nonpareil of the season, and I shall enjoy paying for the privilege of watching you do so."

"But understand, Edward, I assume responsibility for Michelle only if she and Emma enjoy each other's company. If they do, why, their friendship may be the making of them both."

"I've underestimated you, Deirdre. But," he said, humor warming his voice, "shouldn't the *ton* be forewarned? When did you last encounter a girl who has not yet made her comeout, yet who dresses in such height of fashion that she would drive the modistes of Bond Street to sketching her? Who speaks four languages, and apologizes because her fifth is 'schoolroom'? And who knows who Rembrandt and Rubens are, let alone when Prinny last purchased one of their paintings?"

"What would Sally Jersey and Lady Castlereagh say if they knew a girl who had not yet had her *début* had been allowed to waltz?"

"Not only allowed to waltz, madame, but *taught* to waltz —with the crown prince of Austria as partner?" He chuckled again, and even Deirdre was amused.

"Have Michelle, her nurse, and maid come to Grosvenor

Square this evening." And Deirdre allowed her nephew to show his gratitude with a kiss on her cheek.

As she rode in the carriage, her ladyship thought of the amiability, indeed interest, her nephew was showing in this ward that he had termed, before meeting, an "unfortunate interruption."

That Michelle would be an interruption in his life, Lady Deirdre had no doubt, but "unfortunate"?

Time would tell.

4

IT WAS NOT without significance that Lady Deirdre was the wife of one of England's cleverest military strategists; for the maneuvers and battles for which the general was famous were matched, or indeed, as certain dowagers of the *ton* averred, occasionally surpassed, by the "magnificent, mad campaigns" of come-outs and matchmakings for which his wife was justly famous.

The marriage of the ravishing Lady Deirdre O'Hearn, daughter of an impoverished Irish earl, to the older, well-placed Lord Christopher Cresswell, brother of the Duchess of Calvern, had been interpreted by the *ton* as an alliance of political convenience and financial necessity on the part of her family, and on his part yet another example of the Cresswell family penchant for marrying outstanding beauties.

Perhaps it had been precisely that in the beginning—that is, until Major Cresswell, as he was at that point, had had a chance to fully appreciate the range and sparkle of his young bride's intelligence and quick wit, and she began to understand his genuine love of his country, and passion for military tactics. She quickly learned the goals of his career, and set about to aid him in every way possible. Her dinners were as excellent in company as in food; the spring picnics she gave on the grounds of Hampton Court palace were always one of the most festive highlights of the season. As a result, her invitations were always valued, and the Cresswells' company was much sought after. The army, never oblivious to the social graces, did not fail to notice Lady Deirdre's flair, which, along with her husband's genuine military talents, ensured Lord Christopher's promotions were rapid.

During her husband's absences in the early stages of the Peninsular War against Napoleon, Deirdre Cresswell neither pined nor was unfaithful. In fact, it was then when she, only seven years older than her husband's young nephew, the lonely new Duke of Calvern, had discovered they had much to give each other in understanding and support, and developed the honest and frank relationship that carried through to the present moment.

When Lord Christopher returned from Spain, he had become one of the key generals in strategic planning, and husband and wife both rejoiced. Whatever hour he came home from the War Office, his wife would be waiting with a well-stoked fire against the foggy chill, a hot toddy, and a listening ear. It was no small wonder she learned the principles of strategy well, and she rapidly realized they applied just as well to society as they did to the military. In fact, the private talk of the Cresswells might have easily been mistaken for strategy sessions in the general's tent.

"Well, m'dear, preliminary preparations underway for the launch of m'nephew's ward?" The straight-shouldered, silver-haired gentleman removed his dress uniform jacket and bent from his great height to kiss Deirdre's lovely neck as she sat at her dressing table, brushing her hair. She patted her beloved's cheek.

"Preliminary preparations initiated, my love. You have taught me the first thing I must do is know the nature of my troops, then arm them. It will take me a while—two or three weeks at least—to know how Emma and Michelle will get along, but at this point, they seem to like each other. They are different enough in both looks and temperament to complement one another, and that bodes well. As for arming them" (Deirdre grinned at her own metaphor), "this morning I consulted with Michelle's seamstress about wardrobes for both Michelle and Emma. That Ninette has quite the flair, and I expect we shall have some pleasant surprises for you in a month's time. I believe you will be quite pleased with us, milord."

"As always, particularly with you, m'dear," he said as he raised her from her chair in front of the vanity and drew her to him.

Lady Deirdre was as pleased with herself as her husband was, for she recognized that her real stroke of genius had been in her use of Ninette. When Michelle had been with the family for three days, she had summoned the two girls, along with Jane and Ninette, to her boudoir. She had placed the girls side by side, Michelle petite and dark, Emma slim, silver-blond, and gray-eyed, and sought Ninette's advice. Ninette took one look at Emma, and frowned.

"Oh, *non*, madame, *never* pastels *alone* on such a silver beauty, *jamais, jamais*. Perhaps pastels, but always with a rich color about the face and neck."

Ninette slipped a cranberry silk scarf around the neck of Emma's pale pink dress and drew a crimson rosebud from a flower vase on the tea table. Her hands quickly brushed out Emma's tight curls into a sleek chignon with tendrils escaping only around her dainty ears; the rosebud in the chignon was the perfect touch.

Emma turned to look at herself in the pier glass mirror, and both her mother and she gasped. Instead of a pale and insignificant figure, a striking, light-haired beauty had emerged. The sleek chignon emphasized both the sheen of her fair hair and the delicacy of her features. The drama of the reds had formed a frame for the softness of her own coloring.

Lady Deirdre stamped her foot. "For years I have been patronizing the best modistes here in London, and here, in an instant, Ninette has shown us such art. What am I to say? Emma, my dear, I have never seen you look lovelier. And, Michelle, you must need so many costumes. Ninette, what will you do for her?"

Ninette beamed. "Of course, madame, for Michelle it is entirely different. She has enough"—Ninette paused, searching for the English word—"drama with the hair and eyes. For her, clear colors—dark, pastel, *ça ne fait rien*. But Michelle and Emma, when they go out together, they must be two flowers in the same bouquet, *non?* If Emma wears a darker rose, then Michelle wears pink or blue. Michelle is smaller. No ruffles around the neck—very plain, simple."

Emma turned, a flush of genuine excitement in her cheeks. "Please, Mama, may Ninette make all the clothes for Michelle and me? She is right here in the house for fitting, and understands exactly what we want. Please do let her!"

Lady Deirdre paced for a moment. "How long does it take you to make a dress, Ninette?"

"About three days for a plain dress, madame, maybe ten for a ball gown."

"If I hired about three or four seamstresses to work under

you, would you be able to do ten or twelve costumes for each girl in a month?"

"Oh, madame!" Ninette's eyes shone.

"Then that settles it. Of course, you must select the materials, the laces."

Michelle laughed. "Then, my lady, you must speak to Jane as well as Ninette, for Jane is the one who finds the superb materials at the best price. Why, she waves a magic wand and finds three lengths for the price of one."

"It seems we have found an answer to many things. Michelle, you have brought us not only the treasure of yourself, but Jane and Ninette, as well. It is an opportunity we must not waste." Lady Deirdre was pacing thoughtfully. "I believe I know just what to do."

By the end of the next week, Ninette had her own workshop in a large sunlit room over the stables with seamstresses she herself had selected, cutting and sewing to her designs.

Lady Deirdre was amazed when she accompanied Jane and Ninette to look for yard goods. Of the materials found in Bond and Oxford streets' best shops, little satisfied the two women. If a piece was fine enough to satisfy Ninette, which was rare enough, the color was not right, or Jane found it too expensive and would march resolutely away. It was Jane who thought of the solution.

"Lady Deirdre, I have noted that the silks Ninette finds light enough are mostly from China, imported by the East India Company. Perhaps if we saw the warehouse before the best lengths were sold."

"The very thing," she cried. "Why, the general himself is a director of the company. Of course—that's ideal!"

Two days later, the three women were standing at a large oak table in the warehouse office, selecting from bolt after bolt a veritable rainbow of diaphanous silks and rich Turkish embroideries. There were carved ivory fans and parasols frames from India, chests of sweet-smelling sandalwood in which to store handkerchiefs and delicate lace underclothing, and—the warehouse master was accompanied by a guard when he showed this—a small leather chest with brass bindings, which was opened to reveal a king's ransom in cut, unset jewels.

"Is this not Ali Baba's cave?" exclaimed Ninette, her eyes wide.

When the bill was tallied, frugal Jane did not utter one complaint. And when Lord Christopher discovered that, while attiring his ladies in the height of fashion, having the family's own private modiste would save him substantial sums, he was pleased with what they had accomplished.

Perhaps the most satisfied was Lady Deirdre herself. Not only did she see her Emma blooming into a beauty, but every one of the dresses of the three women would be an original, kept secret till the day of wearing. Never again would her ladyship pay handsomely for a gown, only to see the same model on another lady of the *ton,* or have her especially chosen fabric or color revealed by an indiscreet seamstress, and copied before an event. In fact, she knew that now every outing of the girls and herself would be more carefully watched than ever, as eager eyes noted the costumes. Why, they might even become fashion leaders!

Certainly, the first stage of her campaign was proceeding better than she had dared to hope.

The second question that concerned Lady Deirdre, and, much to his own surprise, the Duke of Calvern himself, was how Michelle and Emma would get on together. The duke had expected, once his aunt and uncle had agreed to take the girl, that his concern for Michelle would rest, except for the odd formal occasion where it was expected that her guardian appear; but it was not working out that way. For some reason that he couldn't explain to himself, how Michelle was faring still mattered very much to him, and he began inventing occasions to see her. Within five days of her arrival at the Cresswells', he offered to take his aunt and the two girls in his carriage to Hyde Park at the fashionable hour between four and six, but Deirdre said that if he suggested the girls appear in such a public place before they each had enough costumes to see them through at least the first four weeks of the Season, and she had prepared the *ton* for their launching, she would run him through with the general's own battle sword.

If Calvern was not yet allowed to take the girls into the public world, he would visit them privately. Two or three times in the previous fortnight, he found himself leaving the Foreign Office earlier so that he could join the Cresswells for dinner. He took to arriving in time to join the girls in the library, and would sit quietly in a chair, presumably reading, but in fact enjoyably watching his cousin and his ward together.

This particular evening, as it was only three weeks since her arrival, Calvern thought that Michelle would probably still be feeling a little strange. He had noticed on his previous visits that the general's library had few volumes in French, so he had brought Madame de La Fayette's *La Princesse de Clèves* over for Michelle. Her delight at his thoughtfulness shone in her face, and made it quite worth his coming over in the chill drizzle, he thought, as he settled in a wing chair before the bright fire.

Emma was intent upon her embroidery, her canvas held firmly by a large tambour screen tilted at a comfortable angle in front of her. She bent over the frame, working with two or three colors of silks at once in complicated patterns of different stitches in overlay. The design looked, Calvern thought, like a bouquet of wildflowers.

Michelle had been leafing through her favorite passages of *La Princesse,* but after several minutes of watching Emma work, she walked over behind her. "Your embroidery is quite, quite exquisite, you know—just as fine as any art done by the French or Spanish nuns, for which they are so renowned. Many people must have commented on it."

Emma flushed deeply. "Why, thank you. Not many people notice embroidery, you know—I just do it for my own pleasure. I've never seen any Spanish or French stitching."

"Your Grace, you have seen the finest European stitchery. Isn't Emma's just as well done?" Michelle turned to Calvern for confirmation—and, to her pleasure, discovered he had already come over behind them to give the picture in silk a more detailed look. She gave him a trusting smile.

The duke was as moved by Michelle's genuine interest in Emma, and her confidence that he would support that interest, as he was surprised by the competence and strong design of his cousin's work. "Yes, Emma, what Michelle says is true. In the finest Spanish homes, such a piece would be framed and much sought after as a wall decoration. I should say the family, myself included, have been remiss in not noticing the quality of your work. You are a fine artist. Are the flowers in your bouquet botanically accurate? They seem so."

Emma beamed. "Why, yes. I designed this after I had seen Edward Kean's performance of *Hamlet.* I call it *Ophelia's Bouquet,* for it contains all the flowers she mentions, and I copied them from Osgood's *English Flowers,* which is superbly illustrated." She opened a volume on a nearby table to show them the exceptional hand-colored prints.

"Sir William Osgood, the botanist? Why, I went to Oxford with the chap. He is never in London for the Season, you know—he says spring is one of his best collecting times, and goes off to all sorts of places. Saw him at my club several nights ago. This year he is planning to collect in Scotland. He has an extensive greenhouse and a laboratory in his home on Berkeley Square, I understand. I believe he would be quite flattered to know how his science has inspired you artistically."

"Your Grace, do you think if you approached Sir William, he would show Emma his greenhouse?" Michelle turned the full intensity of her pleading gaze upon him.

Calvern hesitated a moment. "I'm sure it is not a common request. Many of us at the club take his work for granted, Michelle, as we in the family have taken Emma's. Both undeservedly neglected, I say. Certainly, I'll ask him."

Michelle fairly bubbled. "For Papa, I used to write to an art and book dealer on Jermyn Street, who had a fine collection of tapestries and fabric art. May we take Emma there also? I know Lady Deirdre doesn't want us to be seen by the *ton*, but surely if we made an appointment with Mr. Derby, and went early in the morning, there would be no harm."

The duke agreed, and before three days passed, he found that he had organized a morning outing to Derby's Book Shop on Jermyn Street, to be followed by luncheon for Lady Deirdre, the girls, and himself at Sir William's residence.

Why, Calvern wondered as he knotted his second cravat —an unheard-of lapse in the duke's renowned concentration —was he so unsettled at the thought of going to a bookstore with Michelle? Then it came to him—he had always been somewhat alone in his family in his appreciation of art and books, but since his father had died, no one had accompanied him as he went quietly about his collecting. A month ago, the idea of taking any lady of fashion to one of the finest book and art dealers in London would have appalled him, for fluttering feminine presences were not acceptable in such scholarly haunts. But he already knew that Michelle was no dilettante in her appreciation of art, and he had been pleased to approach the renowned Mr. Derby to arrange the appointment.

If Calvern had been aware of his own nervousness, he was more than surprised when, as he handed Michelle into the carriage, he felt her small hand tremble. "Do you think," she said, her voice quiet with hesitation, "Mr. Derby truly remembers my papa, and will be glad to meet me?"

"I'm sure he does," the duke answered. He did not add that Derby, when he heard the name de Bellevue, had practically danced. "A collector, a truly outstanding collector, sir, and an even greater gentleman. His daughter! Imagine! Such an honor!" No, Calvern thought, he would let Michelle discover for herself the esteem in which her father was held.

The portly merchant, resplendent in a red satin waistcoat and blue jacket, was awaiting them at the door of his shop. Derby greeted Michelle with particular enthusiasm, kissing her on both cheeks in the French manner, and speaking with warm respect of her father's knowledge and taste; Michelle fairly glowed. Then, with a great flourish, he insisted the ladies take tea and almond cakes at a small table in the back garden, while assistants hurried back and forth with small pieces of tapestry and especially intriguing books. Only after half an hour of such flustering attention did Derby consent finally to allow Michelle and Emma to browse at leisure through the shop, on the condition that the instant he could be of service, they would call.

Calvern, ostensibly browsing through maps of British North America, watched as Michelle guided Emma through the embroidery collection with gentle tact, allowing her to discover her own interests, yet by means of an occasional comment on background color, the use of gilt thread, or the effect of various borders on overall designs, giving his cousin a new appreciation of her art.

Finally Michelle, content that her newfound friend was well on her way to discovery and enjoyment among the tapestries, asked Derby if she could see any drawings he had recently purchased. He disappeared into a back room and returned instantly with a small, worn portfolio. Calvern and Michelle were hushed and intent as Derby flipped page after page, each one a Rembrandt portrait sketch. At one, Michelle's spoke softly, her voice trembling on the edge of tears.

"Look, the head of a sleeping child—about three or four years old, would you say? It is probably his son who died so tragically later. Did you ever see an artist capture a moment of such tender peace?" She stared at it for several minutes, and passed on. "Of course, Mr. Derby, I cannot afford to buy such a magnificent drawing, but thank you for sharing such treasures with us."

The old man nodded at her fondly.

While Michelle returned to Emma and the silks, encouraging her to buy several fine pieces as examples for herself, Calvern quietly purchased the drawing of the sleeping child. The duke did not know quite why he did so, or on what occasion it would be appropriate to give it to his ward; he only knew that Michelle should own that drawing, and it was important to him that he be the one to give it to her.

The rest of the day went just as pleasantly. When they picked up Lady Deirdre to go to luncheon at Sir William's, her ladyship commented that she had never seen Emma so enthused and happy. Naturally not, thought Calvern, for none of us has ever given Emma the totally appropriate and caring attention she has received from Michelle in these past few days, but he said nothing.

Most fortunately, Emma's buoyant mood carried over at Sir William's luncheon—she was more open and charming than Calvern ever remembered seeing her. And Osgood, who had always struck the duke as rather a dry sort of chap, responded to her with genuine warmth and wit.

When Sir William offered the tour of the greenhouse, Lady Deirdre, never one to miss an occasion to gossip, stayed in the salon to have another cup of tea with her host's quick-witted and acerbic mother. Calvern and Michelle followed Emma and Osgood; and when they were shielded by some heavy foliage in the greenhouse, Michelle gave him a wicked wink.

"I take it," Calvern whispered, "the study of botany does not entrance you."

"Quite right, sir," Michelle responded. "I prefer watching people bloom, and I believe these two are. Look!" From the hothouse Osgood had collected a bouquet of exactly the flowers that Emma had shown him in her embroidery of *Ophelia's Bouquet*. "Quite romantic, *non?*" Michelle's gleam of delight was unmistakable.

As the two couples returned to the salon, Michelle's small hand slipped easily through Calvern's arm. "Thank you for arranging today's outing, Your Grace. Papa and—" (she had almost forgotten and mentioned her brother Richard's name) "others rarely used to take my madcap suggestions seriously."

"I don't think it's a madcap suggestion at all to bring these two together. Creative people are often little appreciated, and it appears these two have each found pleasure in the talents of the other."

Michelle felt her cheeks become pink under his gaze. "You have understood why I did this for Emma."

"And I am delighted by what I understand of your consideration for others," said Calvern quietly, almost as surprised as she by his confession.

The duke had given in to his aunt's pressing invitation to stay for dinner at Grosvenor Square, and he suspected the first reason for the invitation was her desire to talk privately while the girls and Lord Christopher changed for dinner.

"Please do not misunderstand what I am about to say, Edward. I'm more than pleased that Emma and Sir William Osgood have met. It is an introduction I never would have thought of making. Thank you for contacting him, although I suspect I should most properly thank Michelle. Quite the little matchmaker, your ward," said Lady Deirdre.

Calvern listened to her, then thought back to the afternoon. He remembered the charming tilt of Michelle's head and her slight, attentive smile when she listened, fascinated, to people. Whatever other attributes Michelle possessed, her gift for drawing others out was most remarkable; her very presence seemed a catalyst for pleasant happenings.

"On the contrary, Deirdre. I do not think Michelle suggested this meeting out of any sense of deliberate manipulation. The considerations that normally cross matchmaking minds—age, fortunes, appropriate social standing—have never entered her innocent head. She genuinely enjoys people and listens very carefully to what interests them, then simply brings together people who share the same interests —quite successfully, apparently."

"You are precisely right, Edward, to have noted the girl's innocence. In fact, that is the problem I wished to draw to your attention. I gather from talking with the old nurse, Jane, that while Michelle's father was fastidious about the child's education, she never sustained contact with one society for any length of time—a result of all that moving about, I suspect. She may be educated—charmingly educated—in languages and manners, and may handle people well when they are as straightforward as Osgood and Emma, but she is totally unaware of how society reads and reacts to dubious characters. Michelle does not yet know the existence of evil, Edward. It is her very innocence and enthusiasm that may cause her to make a serious error of judgment."

Calvern rose and stood beside the fireplace, slowly twirling the glass of sherry. While Deirdre deliberately acted the part of a light-headed gossip, Edward, as well as her husband, knew how deucedly insightful and correct in the reading of situations the woman could be.

"Madame, I read a warning in your words," said Calvern.

"It cannot be too strong, I fear." Deirdre pursed her lips thoughtfully. "In a few weeks, we will be launching on the scene the girl who is certain to become the nonpareil of the Season. She is as quick-witted as she is beautiful, and after the defeat of Napoleon and the return of Louis to the throne, to be French, I assure you, will be all the rage. While she does not have a fortune in her own right, she is to be dowered by you, one of England's wealthiest men. These things alone would make her a target for every impoverished, debt-ridden, scheming rakehell in England. Add to that her lack of discernment of English society, and she will be ready prey."

"Aside from donning my armor and lance, mounting my steed, and charging the nearest dragon, which I am prepared to do in defense of my ward—"

"As is most apparent by your recent numerous visits and intense interest, Edward," said Deirdre, smiling kindly. "That even my beloved Christopher, who doesn't usually observe things that can't charge or fire in battle, has noticed. No, it will be quite unnecessary for you to ransack the halls of the family estates for armor, but playing Saint George in modern dress will be quite appropriate when the girls take their outings in Hyde Park, let me assure you."

"Yours to command, madame," Calvern smiled, clicking his heels and bowing.

Lady Deirdre nodded. She knew that under the exterior of urbane good humor, her message had struck home, for the duke was nothing if not responsible.

"As for Michelle's coming-out entertainments," she continued, "it is most useful that until June, she will still be technically in half mourning for her father. We will use that excuse to limit the number of the guests to exactly those of whom we approve."

"But I should like these occasions to be especially fine."

Deirdre laughed. "Truly determined to spoil the chit, aren't you? Of course, I will make them as lavish as you and your banker advise, Your Grace. The restricted guest lists will give the events a certain cachet. People will be clamoring for invitations, I assure you. I will make Michelle's come-out the Season's event, and you will see her married well."

At this point the girls and Lord Christopher entered the library, and the tête à tête ended.

* * *

Later, as his coach turned home toward Portman Square under the clear, bright moon, Calvern relaxed his elegant frame. He had not enjoyed a day so thoroughly in a long time. He had also paid careful heed to his aunt's warning, but one remark bothered him like sand in an oyster. He had not realized until tonight that Deirdre fully intended to have Michelle married off in a matter of a few months, and, he admitted to himself, despite the time away from work consumed by his guardianship, he was almost reluctant to let Michelle, with her amusing ways and mischievous smile, leave his charge in so short a time.

5

LADY DEIRDRE was a master of social manipulation. Nobody, not even Lady Sally Jersey herself, could titillate the *ton* as effectively. Deirdre decreed that the first appearance of Calvern's ward in public would be an outing in Hyde Park, and she planned that appearance of the "matchless Michelle" with a degree of study, ingenuity, precision, and timing that delighted her husband, the general.

On the Monday five weeks after Michelle's arrival, ladies bending over the tea tables of Grosvenor Square twittered with the news that the Duke of Calvern's charming ward—so French—had brought her very own *modiste* from Paris with her, a modiste who positively insisted, rumor had it, on ruffled hems. On Wednesday, the frequenters of the bridle paths of Hyde Park heard that Calvern's charge, Michelle, daughter of the Comte de Bellevue—quite, quite lovely said three people who had spoken to Sir William Osgood, who had actually seen her—would be driving out at the fashionable hour one day next week. On Friday evening, the gaming rooms of the venerable St. James Street clubs buzzed, as the Tories of White's Club, the Whigs of Brooks's, and the nondeclareds of Boodle's speculated about the violet-eyed dazzler of a French count's daughter whom Calvern had placed for safekeeping with the family of General Cresswell, a man known to brook no nonsense.

"Well, m'dear, congratulations," said the general, patting his wife's hand, which she had slipped through his arm on their way home from Lord Castlereagh's Saturday dinner.

"The chat over port was of nothing but Michelle. Young bucks kept asking me when she would appear next week. Said I didn't know—that it was as big a secret in my house as Wellington's next move. They kept on pressing, you know. When *is* she appearing?"

Deirdre shrugged, with a slow smile. "Next week when the weather is fine—but certainly not before Wednesday. Building tension, you know."

The general roared with laughter. "You've certainly done that—and you left stern old Emily Castlereagh smiling like a cat in a cream bucket. What did you tell her?"

"I just mentioned that when King Louis comes out of his exile in Buckinghamsire and visits the English court before leaving for France, he will undoubtedly recognize the de Bellevue family name, so of course, Michelle will probably be presented to both the regent and the French king. *That* whetted Lady Castlereagh's interest. She asked me if she could be the first to give a private entertainment for Michelle. What could I say but yes to such a dear friend? Emily is, of course, declaring her reason for entertaining Michelle is her husband's wish to thank Calvern for his fine assistance at the Foreign Office. The *ton* will soon note that not only has Michelle been admitted to Almack's, but she has also been received by Lady Castlereagh privately first! It will be the making of the girl."

Lord Christopher looked admiringly at his wife. "Well, m'dear, when you have finished with Michelle's launch, we could use you at the War Office."

Monday offered a foggy drizzle, and Tuesday a chill and blustery wind. Wednesday dawned cool, crystal-bright, and still—a perfect day for a drive in the park, declared Lady Deirdre.

From the boudoirs and dressing rooms of the second floor to the attic servants' quarters and out to the coach house stables, the excitement passed in waves. Ninette, as judge-in-chief, with Lady Deirdre and Jane, comprised the Council of Final Decision, as Michelle laughingly called them, for the choice of gowns for the ride. The two girls tried one new costume after the other, which had to be modeled in tandem, for the two chosen costumes would have to complement each other.

Michelle looked striking in blue, as did Emma in deep rose, but the combination was too usual, was it not, asked Ninette? Lady Deirdre and Jane agreed. Perhaps Emma in cranberry, which suited her well, and Michelle in a richly embroidered variegated silk. But Michelle looked a little too exotic for her first fashion showing—better to keep it classic, *non?* Jane and her ladyship concurred. Then again sun yellow for Michelle—it brought out the raven black highlights in her hair, and contrasted beautifully with her eyes—and Emma in forest green, with a magnificent green plume on her bonnet? She looked so well in darker colors. No, the green was too heavy for the bright day.

Why not, suggested Emma, violet with yellow, the way the flowers themselves are found in the woods? Exactly! Assent came from every one in one breath. Soon Emma, in a soft violet gown, with a single small purple plume wrapped around her silver chignon, and Michelle in a narrow yellow silk with a ruffled hem, and rich yellow ribbons on her small bonnet, were ordered to stand and walk together. Perfect! Lady Deirdre, not wanting to detract from the spring dazzle of the girls, chose an understated India cream silk, with very deep ruffles and a matching small daytime ostrich plume in her titian hair. For the girls' outfits, there were already matching parasols; for milady one would be sewn on an ivory frame within two hours.

"Will it be that sunny?" asked Jane.

"My dear little one!" chided Ninette. "Please do not be so English. Parasols have *nothing* to do with the weather, and *everything* to do with completing one's costume."

The room echoed with happy laughter.

In the stables, all three stable boys had been set to blacking and shining the four-in-hand reins and polishing the brass bells. The Duke of Calvern had lent his open landau with the family crest emblazoned on each side for the occasion, for both he and Lady Deirdre wanted to make very clear to the world that Michelle was his ward. His footmen were well attired, but Deirdre had twitted Edward into buying his coachman a handsome new uniform, not with buckled breeches, but slim trousers, thought by some to be so radical, but quite appropriate for daytime, she assured him, especially with a hip jacket and beaver felt top hat. She knew that by this final touch she could guarantee both the male and female fashion worlds would be buzzing.

The duke and the general had been summoned home to luncheon at the Cresswells' to ensure their punctuality for the ride, but at sitting in the carriage, both men rebelled. For his part, Calvern said, he refused to play Saint George with-

out a charger, a remark that amused the general and her
ladyship, but confused the two girls utterly. The general said
he had not escaped death in battle to be suffocated by ruffles
or beheaded by a parasol, for which Deirdre slapped his
hand with her fan. It was obvious, she said, that the general's
place beside her in the carriage would be well taken by her
lapdog, for at least the pug looked at her with properly adoring eyes, and did as he was bid. There was a burst of laughter, and it was cordially agreed the two men would ride
alongside on their finest mounts.

In fact, both Michelle and Emma were very nervous, they
confessed to each other as they reclined on chaise longues in
Emma's boudoir (for even Lady Deirdre realized that to demand proper naps was testing even her formidable powers to
the limits).

"I can't remember being this excited on the very afternoon of my presentation at court," said Emma.

"Well, if I didn't have you to sit beside, or Edward
nearby, I would be in quite a state."

Emma sat up, then reclined again. "That is the first time I
have ever heard you refer to my cousin as 'Edward,' for you
always 'Your Grace' him to distraction. Why do you find him
so comforting? He has always seemed so aloof."

Michelle flushed. "'Edward'—that's the way I refer to
him in my head sometimes; I would never hazard such an
informality in public. I really do like him nearby. Haven't
you noticed he is always there exactly when we make a comment, or have a question? When I don't know quite which
way to take these strange English witticisms, he will wink, or
smile, or even frown. Just watch his face."

Emma wondered why she had never noticed her cousin's
responsiveness in such detail; Michelle must be especially
observant—or was it a new characteristic of Calvern's?

At exactly four o'clock, as the three ladies swept out the
front entrance of the house on Grosvenor Square, the entire
Cresswell household down to the scullery maid and smallest
stable boy came for a peek, as did half the staffs of four
houses immediately neighboring, and behind drawing curtains open to the afternoon sun, so did the mistresses and
masters. Lady Deirdre, with the slightest turn of her head,
noted it all and felt that her campaign had gone well.

As Michelle was handed into the landau by the footman,
her eyes searched among the outriders for Calvern. He saw
her instantly, and almost before she had time to beckon to

him, he drew up quickly to her side of the coach. Michelle caught her breath: with his blond hair and ruddy cheeks, he looked so outrageously *anglais,* so dashingly handsome. Yet it was not only the light tan emphasizing the clean, strong lines of his face, or the muscular leanness of his body, that made her throat grow tight, her heart jump a little, when he rode toward her. It was something less definable, more compelling—a sense of authority, of presence. It was so clear even in the way he rode: his gray horse looked so tall and fierce, yet the duke controlled it with unconscious but undeniable self-assurance. For a fleeting instant, she wondered what kind of woman would ever capture and hold a man of such disciplined power, then flushed a little at her own thought.

"Your Grace, would it be imposing upon you to ask you to ride on my side of the carriage? I am not sure of my English manners, and her ladyship and Emma may be occupied by others while I am addressed on this side."

Calvern looked down to Michelle. She had never looked lovelier, he thought, with her two heavy, dark ringlets falling from her small bonnet to her shoulders, a light blush rising to her cheeks. Yellow truly became her. Her face was calm, but very serious; for this moment at least, the mischievous sparkle had evaporated. His heart went out to her. Deirdre's events could be most intimidating, especially for someone as socially sheltered as Michelle had been. At that moment his stallion, Smoke, snorted and pranced a little, and she visibly started.

"It is not your manners, Michelle, for they would be perfect in any country; it is English gentlemen that might be a little unsettling at first, for they sometimes are more roughly mannered than European men. I will never be farther from you than one glance, I assure you. I won't even let Smoke take one nibble of you either, until the end of the ride," he said, stroking the horse's neck.

Michelle laughed, a little of her sparkle came back, and they started off along Upper Grosvenor Street.

If only Michelle had had time to notice it during the ride, which she certainly did not, she would have found the duke's face a classic study. Deirdre had warned him that every breathing eligible male of the *ton* in London would be waiting to greet the "matchless Michelle" (her sobriquet for his charge had taken well), and on this occasion, Calvern conceded, Deirdre could not be accused of exaggeration. Before they had reached Park Lane, they had greeted two of the general's brightest young officers and one of Calvern's long-forgotten Oxford friends. When Emma recognized the regiments of the soldiers, and commented on their recent service history, her father beamed almost more than the dashing young men themselves.

On Park Lane they met several of the duke's friends from White's Club, each looking more immaculate and dapper than Calvern remembered seeing them in a long time. Robert Pinkerton, who cared little for horses and never worried about the nags he rode, had been anxiously haunting Tattersal's horse auctions for the previous week, and when Edward saw Robert's showy new black mount curried to a mirror polish, he began to understand the remarkable scope of the occasion that Deirdre had generated, to inspire such undertakings.

To each new introduction, both Emma and Michelle responded with grace. Sometimes, when Emma knew the gentleman, she would remind him of a funny event that they had shared, and retold it in such a way as to bring Michelle into their world. Emma was exhibiting some of her mother's flair for putting people at ease in a most charming manner, Calvern thought; he had never noticed that talent before.

As they turned from Hyde Park Corner into The Carriage Road, Michelle gave a cry of glee, looked immediately to the duke, then beckoned warmly to a gentleman unknown to Calvern: a distinguished-looking man whose riding clothes were tailored in the very crack of fashion.

"Your Grace, I am delighted to have you meet Mr. John Sharkley, the gentleman whom we met in Ostend. He not only returned a lost coin purse to me, but also his intercession with the captain of the crowded packet to England spared us a week's layover in the port. He was so helpful. Jane, Ninette, and I are surely obliged to him."

Sharkley was more than a little surprised to realize this handsome, forthright figure was the duke; he had gathered from the conversation he had overheard in Ostend that he was much older. However, he recovered quickly, and when the duke reached out to shake Sharkley's hand, Black Jack gave him a slightly obsequious bow.

"Sir, had I known of my ward's coming, I would have had her escorted from Paris; as I did not, I was not able to make arrangements on her behalf, and so am indebted to you for your kind service."

Aye, sir, how could you have made arrangements for circumstances that had just been invented, such as a forged will? Sharkley thought, but he said: "The occasion of being of service to Mademoiselle was a highlight of my travels, Your Grace, and no inconvenience at all."

"You travel much in Europe, sir, in these unsettled times?"

"To serve one's country in whatever capacity, sir, is not only a duty but a privilege."

"But you are not in the military, sir." The duke offered it as a statement rather than a question, for he knew enough of the general and his own brother to recognize military bearing when he saw it, even out of uniform.

"No, sir," Sharkley said, and with a small, enigmatic smile, said nothing and implied everything.

"Perhaps Mr. Sharkley may join us at one of my coming-out entertainments, to express our thanks more fully, Your Grace?" asked Michelle.

Both men turned to look at her guileless, lovely face. By asking Calvern's permission in front of the man, he could not be refused, although the duke should have liked to know more about him. Calvern saw too clearly what Deirdre had called dangerous innocence, but nonetheless, he supported his ward.

"Michelle is quite right, sir. We should like to have you join us—please leave your card with my man, and we shall be in touch."

Sharkley nodded, bowing to the duke, and more deeply to Michelle, presented his card to the footman, and rode back to the livery stables where he had rented his horse, feeling the entire effort was well worth it.

Had either Calvern or Michelle known the extent of that effort, they would have been incredulous.

Michelle had mentioned on the cross-channel voyage that she was the ward of the Duke of Calvern, but Sharkley's man, Roland, had ascertained by watching the duke's house for several days that Michelle was certainly not staying there. Showing his usual invaluable initiative, Roland had befriended the duke's rather fetching second cook as she went to market, and learned that Michelle was residing with General Cresswell, whose discernment and severity were legendary. That blocked off all possibilities of calling, Black Jack realized; however, he was too obsessed to be deterred. Sharkley knew that as surely as the sun rose and set, every family of the *ton,* even General Cresswell's, would appear in Hyde Park eventually, and he set Roland to find out when.

Exercising his usual quick-wittedness, Roland began investigating General Cresswell's household, and fast discovered Ninette's role. He had developed the habit over the last two or three weeks of being exactly at those places on Oxford Street where she would be most likely to come for dressmaking supplies. The talkative French woman, susceptible always to flirtation salted with usefulness, had almost come to expect Roland to appear as she came out of the door of a shop, take her packages, and help her to the Cresswell carriage, and she repaid the convenience by bubbling out with more information to Roland than even Sharkley needed. When Roland thus discovered that Lady Deirdre and the two girls would ride out the following week, Sharkley had invested the last of the de Varennes gold in renting rooms at a respectable address, having a fine new riding habit tailored, and hiring a decent horse.

Despairingly, Roland recognized his master's new image for what it was: He had seen the disease of lovesickness before, with its symptom of incipient respectability. It was not a luxury any self-respecting crook could afford for long. He knew now that Sharkley had no intention of blackmailing Michelle, but actually loved the woman. Blimey, he thought, the master will be thumping the Bible on the street corners of Soho like a Methodist preacher if he ain't careful. A servant with Roland's special talents worked on a commission basis, and he mentally gave the master two months to fall off the straight and narrow, or he'd move on.

But to Sharkley, the honest warmth of Michelle's smile, and the open delight with which she had introduced him to the duke, had made his hopes bloom even brighter.

If Sharkley's hopes could be said to be blooming, so, said General Cresswell later, was Lady Castlereagh's flower-bedecked hat. Shortly after the Cresswell procession turned into Carriage Row, her open landau pulled aside the duke's.

"My dear child," she said, looking astutely at Michelle, "I cannot express enough how welcome you are to London. Safe at last, with our poor France so—so violated."

The duke, whose horse was between the two carriages, pulled ahead and circled, as much to hide his grin as anything. The dear lady, whom he much respected, made Michelle's voyage sound like an escape from a fate worse than death. But then, that was what being French was, in some English eyes.

"I have come to discover, your ladyship, that one is saved from the chill of the English winter fogs by the warmth and kindness of the British people, especially one's own," Michelle said, lightly touching Emma's hand and smiling at the duke.

Lady Castlereagh opened her lorgnette and took a long look. This was a young woman to be reckoned with.

"Your frock is most becoming. I understand you brought your own modiste from Paris."

Trap number two, thought Calvern.

"Ninette is most gifted, Lady Castlereagh, but I assure you her talents have blossomed a tenfold with the superb English goods. In France, the blockade so sadly limited us, you know."

Advantage to Michelle, and a gracious stroke at that, said the duke to himself.

Lady Castlereagh resettled herself in her carriage, took a commanding survey of her domain, and fired her last volley. "The viscount and I are most pleased that your first entertainment outside will be the small supper dance at our home next Saturday evening. However, I understand from Lady Deirdre that in Vienna you learned to waltz. I do not approve of *débutantes* indulging in such intimate behavior. Furthermore, it is not an English dance."

Michelle's eyes sparkled with mischief, and Lady Deirdre and Calvern exchanged tense glances.

"Of course, your ladyship, I shall respect your wishes. It makes eminent sense to me that the English, known for their straightforward political thinking, should resist going around in circles, especially in a foreign dance," she said.

Game! exclaimed Calvern to himself. Michelle had acquitted herself in the high-stakes gamble marvelously, closing it with an indirect compliment to the negotiating skills of Lady Castlereagh's husband as Britain's foreign secretary, and at the same time parrying the challenge with humor. Even the general was grinning.

Lady Castlereagh chuckled appreciatively and beckoned Calvern to her. "Enjoy her company now, sir, for she will not be your ward for long. Our English gentlemen are no fools, and with such beauty and wit, she will be wed before you turn around. In another country, she would probably become a princess." She turned to Deirdre. "Superb touch, those parasols. *À bientôt!*"

Calvern rode up beside Michelle, and he reached for her proffered hand. "I'm proud of you. Emily Castlereagh has unseated more than one *débutante* in her day."

"I do not believe that she is intentionally stern, Your

Grace. It is her knowledge of passion that makes her so heavily stress decorum, I think."

Calvern looked down into Michelle's shining eyes. In all his years he had not heard Lady Castlereagh so insightfully or charitably judged, and felt a surge of protective tenderness. Please God, nothing would make Michelle's beautiful nature cynical. He could think of nothing to say that could bear overhearing by others, and so only squeezed her hand.

"Oh, look! Sir William!" cried Emma delightedly, for Osgood was waiting by the Serpentine Bridge. The instant he spotted the Cresswell carriage, he cantered smartly forward and presented the ladies with three bouquets: a large one of purple violets encircled with contrasting yellow for Emma, a smaller one of yellow surrounded by purple for Michelle, and orange-gold roses for Lady Deirdre.

"Imagine such flowers in March! They must be from your greenhouse, Sir William. They are truly magnificent, and smell so sweetly." Emma's smile was beatific.

The general drew Calvern aside. "I say, how did Osgood do that? Did you tip him off, or did Deirdre write him a note? The colors are right on, you know."

"Neither, Uncle. I noticed Osgood's groom, mounted, when we entered Park Lane. I suspect he rode back to Berkeley Square, described the dresses, Osgood had the bouquets made up by his gardener, and here he is."

"Osgood is some sort of flower gatherer, isn't he?"

"A botanist."

"Shame, you know. We could use men who think like that in reconnaissance," the general said, and rode up to greet Osgood warmly.

As they crossed the Serpentine on the Ring Road, the Calvern carriage literally formed the center of a procession, with the duke and general now joined by Osgood as immediate outriders, some friends from the House of Lords, large clusters of fellows from White's Club, as well as smaller ones from Brooks's and Boodle's riding fore and aft. Calvern saw chaps he had not seen literally since Oxford days (one of whom still owed him fifty pounds). Deirdre was glowing, and rightfully so: the girls had had a string of continuous greetings and introductions since the moment they had entered the park, with the laughing, flaxen-haired Emma attracting almost as much attention as Michelle. One beau, after having been introduced to Michelle, asked Lady Deirdre to introduce him to the other beauty.

"Why, George," she exclaimed, "that is Emma, with whom you danced twice at her come-out."

"Emma, I am sorry, but you are truly in full, radiant bloom; at your *début* I must have been blind."

"You owe me at least two dances at our next ball together for that, George," she said laughingly, then whispered to Michelle, "Heaven bless Ninette."

All of a sudden, there was a rustle among the crowd. A tall broad-shouldered figure in a hunt master's coat trotted down the Ring from Bayswater Road. Men clustered forward to meet him, hailing him on all sides; he was obviously outstandingly popular, and it took several minutes for him to work his way through to the landau. Even the general and Osgood rode forward to meet him; only Calvern hung back, moving a little nearer Michelle, a slight frown on his face, though the girls did not notice.

"Who is he?" Michelle whispered to Emma, all the while smiling prettily.

"David Richmond, Earl of Malfet. Well liked. Good speeches in the House of Lords, and almost as wealthy as Edward. He went to school at Eton and Oxford with Edward. He was married six years ago, and has a four-year-old son, but Edward has refused to speak to him since his wife, Katherine, was killed in a hunting accident three years ago. It is quite embarrassing at times."

"How unlike His Grace," said Michelle, frowning a little herself.

When Malfet finally drew close, Michelle was a little startled. The glowing virility of the man, with his dark hair and eyes and charming smile, was almost overpowering. There was no edge, only easy authority and charm in his voice, when he addressed the general and asked permission to speak to Emma, then turned immediately to Calvern and asked the same for Michelle. The general assented willingly, but Calvern gave his with an unsmiling, guarded face.

"I had thought your ward, sir, would be missing Paris. How can one not miss a city of such beauty? We English have pined for Paris these last seven unhappy years, mademoiselle," he said, turning to Michelle, "so I see Paris has sent one of her glories to us." He held her hand several seconds longer than was necessary, and gazed right into her eyes.

At all times Michelle was beautiful, and until now she had been completely unconscious of the effect her violet, mischievous eyes or dark hair falling against her luminously white skin created in men. The Earl of Malfet was different. His gaze gave to Michelle that moment that must come to every lovely woman: the instant when she discovers she is intensely desirable. That knowledge caused Michelle's cheeks to flush and her breathing to heighten; in front of their eyes, she became even more radiant.

Calvern's reins drew tight, and his horse pranced uneasily.

"I found something that might bring Paris a little closer to you." Malfet smiled down at Michelle, as if he and she, and only they, shared a secret. Michelle felt herself growing almost dizzy. He drew a small package wrapped in fine silk from his breast pocket. Her fingers trembled as she opened it.

"Oh!" she exclaimed, finding it difficult to catch her breath. "It is a porcelain miniature of Notre Dame, in precisely the way I saw it from the end of our street. My lord, however can I thank you." Michelle's eyes were glistening.

"I only hope that it gives you as much pleasure, mademoiselle, as meeting you has given me." He turned away, well aware that if he pressed his advantage a moment longer, she would be in tears.

"I say!" said the general.

Calvern pulled so sharply on his horse's bit that the animal reared slightly, and Deirdre glowered at the ungracious duke.

The procession continued.

Later that night, Michelle, her soft angora wool robe wrapped around her, tapped on Emma's door.

"Come in." Emma was arranging Sir William's violets in a shallow bowl. Michelle sat down on Emma's bed and wrapped her arms around her knees.

"How do you feel when Sir William is near?" Michelle asked.

Emma glanced up from the flowers and saw the earnest look on her new friend's face. "Safe. Happy. I can say all sorts of things that I feel, that I never could say before, and he understands. He really cares about what I am doing; but today is only the fifth time I have seen him since the luncheon."

"Do you love him?"

"With six meetings it is much too early to tell, but"—Emma put down the flower clippers—"yes."

The answer was so direct and self-assured, Michelle envied her.

"What you are describing for Sir William is what I feel about Edward sometimes, such as today. Did you notice how he never let me flounder with anyone?"

Emma grinned. "The look on his face when you spoke to Lady Castlereagh—he practically whooped with delight when you answered her so well."

"Yet *safety* is not at all what I felt with Lord Malfet looking at me. He made me feel—adventurous, almost as if I could become something I never knew I could be. I don't believe I could talk to him very much, either—certainly not the way I do to you or Edward. I don't think he would be in the least interested. He seems only to want to—possess."

There was a short pause; the girls, confidantes that they were, did not yet have the words that encompass the intensity they had recognized in the earl's face, but Michelle persisted, urgent in her need to understand. "My mama died when I was born, but Jane tells me she had *une grande passion* for my father. Is that what the earl makes me feel?"

Emma thought a minute. "Are you asking me if love feels comfortable, and passion feels dangerous? I don't know, but I'll tell you one thing: the gaze that Malfet gave you made *me* tingle."

"I wonder if he will be at Lady Castlereagh's supper dance," mused Michelle.

6

LADY CASTLEREAGH scorned giving "crushes" where the entire *ton* was invited to appear in the same room—even a ballroom—at the same time. Relying on her husband's diplomatic sense and her own keen awareness that exclusivity lends cachet, Lady Castlereagh invited only those who were "appropriate" for Michelle's first social gathering. It was a very European group, capped by the Duc d'Anton, aide-de-camp to Louis, the French king presently waiting out his exile in Buckinghamshire, followed by several senior officers of the Austrian, Prussian, and Russian legations, looking remarkably dashing in their dress uniforms.

Lady Castlereagh had asked for Lady Deirdre's "preferred list," so there were several of Calvern's close friends and, of course, Sir William Osgood. Lady Castlereagh had heard from several sources about Malfet's glance at Michelle in the park, and because both she and Lady Deirdre knew the value of a little spice in one's gatherings, and since the Cresswells were not about to indulge Calvern's apparently petty bad form, the earl was most certainly invited.

For this special evening, Ninette exhibited her masterstroke: she allowed both girls to wear the same color—claret—but in styles that complemented their unique beauty so effectively, the women of the *ton* fluttered at the audacity of it for days afterward.

Emma's dress was classically simple, an unadorned bodice with a fine overskirt of sheerest silver voile emphasizing her tall, slim figure, with wine-colored rosebuds and silver ribbons in her fair hair. By contrast, Ninette had emphasized the intense drama of Michelle's dark hair and white skin: her dress had a bodice of gold and silver Turkish embroidery interspersed with colored brilliants on a claret background, with a skirt of the matching plain silk. Her black hair was swept back by a semicircular comb of three inches height, fanning out in a peacock's tail of the finest gold and colored stones; from behind it tumbled a cascade of raven ringlets. One was caught, said the Austrian chargé d'affaires later at his club, between a luminous orchid and an intense, exotic rose.

The Duc d'Anton was the first to reach Michelle, no mean feat in the face of the crowd surrounding the girls. He strode toward her purposefully, as if to meet her were, in fact, not only a pleasure, but the chief aim of his evening. "Ah, so here at last we see the daughter of the Comte de Bellevue. Your father, my dear, had the best eye in Europe for significant treasures; now we see that his finest was you, mademoiselle. It is only a pity he did not live to see your *début.*" His deep bow over her hand seemed not the least condescending, but inspired by genuine sympathy and appreciation.

"You knew Papa?" Michelle asked, searching his face earnestly.

The duc correctly read the beautiful intensity of her expression. He swept up her hand and held it high as he led her to the head of the second column of dancers for the opening quadrille, beside Lord and Lady Castlereagh leading the first. The music covering his words, he whispered, "His Royal Majesty, King Louis, appreciated your father's artistic sense, his ability to bring to the king's attention treasures of national significance—a tradition being followed by your equally talented brother, who even now is enjoying excellent health, I understand. The king hopes to be able to thank both you and your brother in person one day soon, we pray."

Michelle's violet eyes glistened luminously. "You could have said nothing, Your Grace, that could mean more to me."

The duc smiled knowingly, squeezed her hand, and they passed to their next partners in the column.

If the Earl of Malfet had not been the first to Michelle, it was not only because he was well enough mannered to defer to the duc as guest of honor and senior ranking diplomat. He had some considerable business interests in common with the duc, and hesitated to anger a valued client. Immediately after the first dance, Malfet was beside Michelle, instantly reserving the dance leading into supper, and the closing one. In every other way, he attended on her. It was he who removed the lemonade from the footman's tray and handed it to her; it was he who, seeing her fan ribbon break and the fan flung to the floor while she danced with the Austrian, Count von Reichertz, retrieved it.

The gallery of matrons in the corners whispered wickedly and could hardly wait to see Michelle's dance with Malfet before supper.

Meanwhile, Calvern, his tall, well-tailored form relaxed and elegant, had reserved two dances with Michelle for himself, which he performed in his own friendly manner, whispering his pleasure that the Duc d'Anton had spoken to her, and telling her that she was the most beautiful woman present. After dancing with Michelle, Calvern seemed, with deliberate discipline, to turn to several new *débutantes,* who were reduced to fluttering charm by his elaborate attentions. Ah! thought Deirdre, he is trying to avoid hovering over Michelle. Yet when it came Malfet's turn to escort his ward, Deirdre noted Calvern excused himself from the company and watched the dance from the vantage point of the stair to the musician's gallery.

There is little, one would have thought, that can be done to make the long lines and great distance between partners of the formal quadrille an intimate and stirring moment, but whatever could be done, the Earl of Malfet did. Each time the partners came together to hold hands, he held Michelle's high, near his lips, his fingers caressing the inside of her wrist. Each time the partners gracefully circled each other from a distance of three feet, his eyes caught hers and never wavered, a slight, intent smile on his lips. The heat of his gaze brought a delicate flush to Michelle's cheeks, and the sparkle in her eyes heightened; between the two, one could almost sense a physical force.

Halfway through the dance, Calvern, white-faced and severe, left the room. He did return in time to escort Lady Jane Willington to supper, as he was pledged, but she found him to be a very quiet partner.

If the Earl of Malfet succeeded in serving Michelle at all during supper, said Lady Deirdre later, it was by dint of a supreme effort, for at every turn he had to compete with von Reichertz and the head of the Russian legation. Even the Duc d'Anton joined them for several minutes. Michelle sat happily on her small gilt chair, smilingly accepting or refusing offers of more lemonade, cold meats, relishes, sweet tarts, chocolates, or fruits.

Asking Malfet's permission to do so first, in the prettiest way (for he spoke English and French fluently, but no German), she sat, a small sovereign in the middle of her court, rapidly switching between German, French, and English, and even laughingly attempted a few words in Russian. The *ton* knew of Michelle's many languages: they had suspected it might be a prima donna performance on the part of a gifted, spoiled darling. Lady Castlereagh, her lorgnette in place, and the watching matrons could observe that speaking different languages was as natural as air for the interested and lively young woman; to have read it otherwise would have been a travesty.

The evening ended as it began: an outstanding success for the two young beauties. Lady Deirdre was particularly pleased to note that, although Emma had been surrounded at every turn, Osgood had stayed firmly nearby, and escorted her to the Cresswell carriage.

However, it was Michelle, without question, who was the belle of the ball. The Earl of Malfet had to fend off what he described later as "clamoring hordes" to escort Michelle's departure. As he handed her into the Cresswell carriage, he asked Calvern directly if he might have permission to call on Michelle.

The duke bowed, but was less than gracious in his dismissal; he would write the earl, he said, of his decision.

Deirdre gasped; Malfet's face flamed. His lips became an angry, thin line, and he left with a wordless bow.

In the carriage on the way home, not a word was spoken. Emma and the general were silent, Deirdre tapped her fan on the windowpane in a steady rhythm of annoyance, and Michelle sat opposite the duke and stared out the window into the darkness, her eyes large with injury.

Although it was very late, before Deirdre went to bed that night she wrote a note to Calvern, demanding his attendance in her boudoir at ten the following morning, and gave it to her footman, asking him to deliver it to the duke before breakfast.

When Calvern entered her boudoir, Lady Deirdre was formally dressed and sitting rigidly by her tea table. She did not ask him if he preferred tea, coffee, or chocolate, but poured tea directly.

"Your Grace," she said, the formality of the address reflecting the severity of her mood; "I do not know you to be either irrational or a boor. Your behavior to the Earl of Malfet bordered on both. I am trusting in my long time of respect for you when I say I *presume* you had a reason." She handed him his tea without his usual sugar, and began to pour her own.

"Of course I have, Deirdre. You have known me long enough and well enough to recognize that." His tone was equally annoyed.

"Then please declare it." Her voice had an edge he had heard only once before, when some matron had questioned the general's integrity. She obviously would brook no nonsense, and he would give her none.

"Quite simple, Deirdre. I am convinced without a doubt, although I do not have proof, that the Earl of Malfet murdered his wife."

Her tea missed the cup, and splashed into the saucer.

"One does not lightly go around, Edward, charging anyone, let alone an established and respected member of the *ton,* with murder."

"I am not charging him with anything, Deirdre, for I have no evidence, and no firsthand knowledge. I simply have my own conviction, which I believe is well enough founded to be just, and because of it, I don't want him near anyone of mine, especially Michelle."

"May I hear the basis of your conviction?"

"Malfet and I, as you know, were at Eton together; he was two years ahead of me. In his final year, his cricket team played mine for a championship; we defeated them rather soundly, if I remember correctly. As we left the field, he came after me with a cricket bat."

"You are not going to tell me that a simple boyish quarrel is the basis for your reaction."

"Deirdre, it was no simple case of fisticuffs. He came at me from behind, at top speed, and swung his bat at my skull with full force. The blow knocked me unconscious, but even when I was limp on the ground, he jumped on top and started to pummel me. It took three of my team and the sports master to pull him off. There was talk of sending him down from the school, but as he was an outstanding student in his final year, and would be leaving within weeks, he was only given a stiff caning. Why he attacked, I do not know. Perhaps he could not stand to be bested by a captain two years his junior. It seems so irrational, even now."

So there was a reason! Deirdre served him a peace offering of a scone and jam, which he took, and they both settled back in their chairs. "Do you have any other grounds for suspicion?" Her tone was conciliatory, her look intent.

"At the Royal Opera seven years ago. I was there with Ghiselle, who was so perceptive."

"Your first mistress—the dark one?"

Calvern, surprised that Deirdre could identify both the name and the woman, blushed slightly and nodded—but then, this was a converstion of unusual frankness. "Malfet had the box next to mine, and he was there with his mistress of some long standing, Charlotte. Ghiselle knew her quite well, I think. I remember clearly—Ghiselle was sitting beside me, and she gasped. 'Look,' she said, 'someone has tried to strangle Charlotte.'

"I looked, and sure enough, she was right. Even the choker Charlotte was wearing could not hide two deep bruises the size of thumbprints at the base of her throat. And when she turned around, one could see an elongated bruise around the back of her neck, rising slightly in the center, as would be made by eight fingers pressing. In the world of lightskirts a woman does not leave a lover of the stature, wealth, and looks of Malfet without thought, yet only two weeks later Charlotte had transferred to the protection of a minor cit, not at all wealthy."

"The circumstances are suspicious, Edward, but not conclusive," said Deirdre, serving him more tea, this time with sugar.

"The final straw for me was the death of Katherine. When we were children, Katherine lived on the estate next to ours in Surrey—she was about my brother Tom's age. When she was twelve, on her first hunt, her horse refused a fence. She fell, cracked her head, and broke an arm. She never again—not once—rode on horseback. Her father, a passionate horseman, tried to convince her to try again and again. He bought our gentlest mare from us, expressly for her. She wouldn't look at it.

"Several months after she and Malfet had their son, rumor had it that their marriage was stormy. They said Katherine knew that Malfet had kept two lightskirts during her confinement, and she was upset because he was in London far more often than with her. Because of that, she had refused to assign the money from her estate over to him, but kept it for herself.

"Deirdre—Katherine was killed supposedly jumping a fence on an early morning ride with Malfet!"

Calvern was silent for a few minutes to let the full significance of his remarks settle in, and then continued: "He put about the explanation that, to please him, she had tried to take up riding again, and the horse bolted. Oddly, though, he had purchased no gentle animal especially for her, and they had left in the morning before the grooms were up. Now do you see why I cannot let the Earl of Malfet address Michelle?"

Deirdre looked drawn. "As I said, Edward, I have never known you to be irrational or a boor, and I presumed you had a reason." They smiled wryly at each other, each clearly remembering the tone in which she had first made the remark. "Such things as these are often deemed unspeakable in polite society, yet warning others discreetly, fully, at the proper times prevents tragedy. You have been wise." She reached over and touched his hand; he nodded his acceptance of her apology.

Calvern's face tensed. "Yet we are faced with the problem of the earl. Michelle's come-out is in two weeks. Of course, because the invitations went out before this talk, you invited him?"

Deirdre sighed. "Of course."

"Then how do we stop his attentions to Michelle?"

Deirdre pursed her lips in thought. "With the exception of the attack on his mistress, the circumstances of which you don't know, the times Malfet has seemed most violent are when he is thwarted in his immediate desires—the winning of the cricket match, the obtaining of Katherine's estate."

"Yes."

"His immediate desire is to court Michelle. If we stop that directly, we will be fostering his wrath—particularly if we are blatant enough to rescind the invitation."

"Agreed." Calvern's face was uneasy.

"Well then, we do nothing socially to exacerbate the earl's temper, but inform Michelle of the situation, and help her at every point to keep a safe distance from him. By our not offending him directly, but forewarning and guarding Michelle, he will eventually have to accept her lack of interest, but no direct affront to arouse his passion will have been offered."

"Deirdre, your plan has only one flaw—we have to tell an innocent young beauty about a most violent and despicable situation."

Lady Deirdre rose swiftly, walked to the window, then turned to face the duke directly, anger staining her cheeks.

"Oh, Edward, do not be one of those men who believe women are too delicate to be told difficult truths. That is ridiculous! More women have been condemned to lives of living hell because people believed they were too delicate to be told that their suitors were drunkards, excessive gamblers, or obdurate rakehells—but not too delicate, evidently, to be condemned to living with such men. In other words, the only safeguard of Michelle's innocence is not ignorance, but truth."

"It will not be an easy conversation."

Deirdre shrugged. "No. But how often in this very room have you been praising Michelle's insight to me? And I have found her to be gifted not only with intelligence but also common sense. Pay her the compliment of trusting her to exercise those qualities. If she is as fine as we both believe, she will respond well. Just choose an appropriate time to tell her."

When he took his leave, Calvern bowed low and kissed Deirdre's hand. "My dearest aunt, you are one of the constant treasures in this treacherous world."

"Edward, consider yourself blessed, for I believe you have another such treasure in Michelle."

The opportunity for Calvern to talk to Michelle came soon enough. Sir William Osgood had proposed an outing for a small group to see the Royal Botanical Gardens at Kew, and Deirdre had managed to limit it to Emma and Osgood, Michelle and Calvern, and herself.

It was a clear, sunny April day, not a cloud to be seen. Sir William chose his best-sprung open landau and had its trunk packed with a small table, linens, cold champagne, and every conceivable picnic delicacy. Two strong young footmen who would set up the picnic hung firmly on behind. While the three ladies had brought pelisses in case it turned chilly, they were dressed gaily in flowered spring muslins and matching parasols, with bonnets that were, indeed, large enough to fend off the sun.

As Calvern and Osgood escorted the girls to the carriage, they chimed in unison the naughty political line:

> I am my master's dog at Kew
> Pray tell me, sir, whose dog are you?

With a burst of hearty laughter, the entourage set off.

Once at the gardens, Sir William had arranged that they

were to be greeted formally by Sir Joseph Banks, the director and the distinguished voyager and botanist who had, from his own travels, brought back so many rare plants to Kew. Emma shone with pride when Sir Joseph, singing her William's praises, took them on a short tour to see the most outstanding of Osgood's own contributions. After this, when Sir Joseph invited the group to the far end of the lake to see some new, rare water iris, Deirdre demurred. Emma and Sir William were quite safe, she was sure, chaperoned by Sir Joseph; Michelle was with her guardian. For her part, she could think of nothing lovelier than strolling up the long vista, coming to rest at the renowned ten-story pagoda, where she was quite content, she said, to supervise the setting up of their picnic. She set off, her parasol twirling, with the two brawny footmen looking aghast at the distance to the pagoda, and heaving the picnic trunk behind them.

Very soon after the four had reached the water iris, Calvern and Michelle strolled the see the lilac bushes farther down the walk. Michelle's small hand slipped easily through his arm; she was so relaxed, chattering happily.

"How is it you know precisely what I want, almost before I do? I dearly love Emma and Sir William, and now I do believe I can distinguish between four kinds of blue iris. Emma has her watercolor box, and will escape into doing the most charming washes of the flowers, to embroider designs from them later. But if I had to listen to an endless string of Latin names for another half hour, I believe I would be reduced to tears or giggles. You have just rescued me so gallantly."

They smiled at each other, relishing their complicity.

"How did you enjoy Lady Castlereagh's supper dance?"

"Immensely! I cannot remember an evening that has delighted me more. It felt so familiar to be surrounded by people from so many countries. Less constricted, *non?* And the best of all—the Duc d'Anton knew Papa and—" She stopped.

She turned to face Calvern on the walk. Never had she been more tempted to tell the duke of Richard. Earlier on, she had hesitated to do so, for she had felt she did not know him well enough to trust him with the life of her brother. Now she did—a more honorable or trustworthy man than the duke, she could not imagine. A new thought was stopping her—shame.

Shame in the forged will.

From what she understood today of Calvern's integrity

and compassion, she knew she could have come to London,
stated that she was his father's goddaughter, and shown him
the correspondence between the two men as proof—there
was no need for Richard's elaborate deception. But now the
will had been presented. Even if she had explained Richard's
concern for her safety, Michelle felt sure that disclosure of
the forgery would make her a deceiving, scheming opportunist in his eyes. Now he cherished her—a feeling that she
would not have recognized before her encounter with the
Earl of Malfet in Hyde Park taught her the meaning of looks.
Michelle, glancing shyly into Calvern's strong, open face,
knew the truth about her own feelings for him: more than
anything, she wanted his cherishing, his good opinion of her,
to endure. His implicit trust in her had already given her
such strength and grace in many moments in this strange new
world. She had not felt as secure since her Papa died.

Whatever else, even if it meant keeping silent about the
will, she would not risk losing this.

Edward held both her hands close to his chest during her
minutes of silence. He watched her intently as she almost
told him something, and then withdrew; a dark shadow of
pain crossed her eyes, and she decided not to speak. His
heart went out to her. If only she could trust him! He had
known for a long time that the life of an impoverished Royalist count in Napoleon's Paris could not have been easy.
Deirdre had deduced from many remarks made by Jane and
Ninette that their poverty had been very real, that all the
travel had been from necessity. It was obvious also that at the
ball the Duc d'Anton had shared something with her that she
did not yet feel free to tell him. For now, he thought, so be
it, restraining the urge to kiss her hands lest the intimacy
startle her.

". . . and of course, I may tell you the rest, for you know
Lord Castlereagh, and have assisted him in the Foreign Office: the Duc d'Anton says King Louis is soon going to issue
a manifesto declaring himself in favor of a constitutional
monarchy modeled on England's. This statement will make
him so much more acceptable to the people of France after
Napoleon falls. If only Papa had lived to see it, for that was
his greatest dream!"

Calvern knew, intuitively yet with certitude, that this tidbit of information was not that which she had intended to
share with him initially, yet he *was* surprised. D'Anton was a
discreet and canny politician, who did not go around telling
his king's plans to every featherheaded *débutante*. Even in

the British Foreign Office, the pending announcement of such a manifesto was still highly confidential. Certainly, d'Anton must have been very sure of Michelle's family background, and trusted Michelle herself, to share such a confidence. What exactly was her involvement with the duc?

"And then there was that marvelous Count von Reichertz. Do you know that he whispered in my ear that had we not been at Lady Castlereagh's, he would have led me in a waltz that would have stopped all the other dancers on the floor in amazement. Those dashing Austrians! Do you think it was too naughty of me to pledge him the first waltz at my come-out?" Her eyes twinkled with mischief. "I do hope Lady Castlereagh is there to see it, even though I may be banned for life from Almack's."

They both chuckled at the image of the grande dame of Almack's confronted with this glorious scene of "seduction in public," as she had labled the waltz—all too obviously exactly that, smiled Calvern to himself, since it would be performed by an Austrian and a Frenchwoman.

"Did you notice any others?" Calvern asked.

Michelle eyed him steadily. "Here I am babbling about trivia, and my guardian is anxious to know if I am aware that I am being courted by one of the most eligible peers of the realm, the Earl of Malfet."

Calvern blushed. "I did not mean to be that unsubtle. But how *do* you feel about Malfet?"

Michelle looked straight down the arch of lilac bushes ahead, a small frown creasing her brow. Her answer was slow in coming, but it was not because she was guarded about it; she wasn't. He could see she was trying honestly to assess some difficult feelings.

"When I am with him, Your Grace, it is as if the part of me that exists when I am with you—that cares about King Louis, about Emma meeting Sir William, about being fascinated by drawings, or how the war in Russia is going—doesn't exist; it is irrelevant. He looks at me very intensely and draws me into his private world. He makes me feel as if I am being burned alive by the heat of his emotion, but I have no desire to pull away, no will of my own. In fact, I never feel more beautiful than when he looks at me so."

Calvern was astounded. He had never heard a more disarmingly innocent yet articulate description of aroused passion, but Michelle, he knew, had only been in Malfet's close company at Castlereagh's. Fully as much had been communicated in that quadrille as he had feared.

"Do you love him?" he asked gently.

"Love him?" Michelle turned away, blushing a little, and began to poke a flower bed with the tip of her closed parasol. "I am not sure. He is certainly more intriguing than any man I have ever met. Perhaps I will be his *grande passion,* and he mine. I do not really know what *une grande passion* is; Jane tells me only that it is what my parents felt for each other, but she never describes it." Suddenly she turned back to Calvern, her voice a shaken whisper. "My heart is so confused. You know, after the ball, I would have given everything I have to speak to my mother, eighteen years dead."

Michelle's cheeks were shining with tears. This time Calvern did not restrain himself from taking and kissing her hands.

She drew a deep, ragged breath and forced herself to continue. "I feel the earl wants only to hold, to possess me; somehow I am afraid to share all I am with him. Yet Jane says Mama and Papa talked and read and laughed and rode and looked at pictures for hours together, as well as knowing this passion. Perhaps I have not a heart as rich as my mama's, that I cannot feel both the fire and the sharing together."

At that statement, Michelle's misery surfaced fully; she broke into choking sobs.

"Michelle, look at me."

She did glance up at Calvern, her bonnet disheveled, daubing her eyes with her glove. He reached for his large handkerchief and wiped her tears away, feeling all the while the wildest gamut of emotions: bitter anger at Malfet, who had awakened such a raw, surging passion in an innocent girl; sharp disappointment in his own failure in tact, yet not knowing, even now, how he could have been more sensitive.

Damn the circumstances that made him her guardian, and did not allow him to court her!

He had a compelling urge to let his finger trace the path of the tears down her finely hollowed cheeks, and kiss her lips, which were redder now than he had ever seen them. Yet such a move would not only appear to be a belittling of her pain, it would violate his position of trust as her guardian, and he would not, could not, do that.

"Michelle, look directly into my eyes while I tell you this; I want you to feel the truth of what I am saying as well as understand it."

She looked.

"The reason that you feel only the intensity of Malfet's

passion, and cannot give anything else, is because that is all he wants, all he allows you to give. The irrelevance of interest in other things is on his side, not yours."

"Is that true? With another man will I feel both the passion and the sharing?" Her eyes were pleading with him, wanting to believe.

"I vow, yes, you will."

She ventured a shy half smile. "Then perhaps I am my mother's daughter."

"Undoubtedly."

Dear God, if Michelle was just beginning to comprehend the tempestuous, compelling passions her young mother had known, and her mother, in turn, had been this desirable— Calvern suddenly had a surge of sympathy for the Comte de Bellevue, and for the exquisite, teasing torture the innocent, virgin trust of Michelle's mother must have put him through.

Calvern drew a deep breath, reclaimed his handkerchief, and withdrew a step. "There is something else. I do not want you to allow Malfet to pay his attentions, or to be alone with him ever. Lady Deirdre and I will not prevent him joining us socially, but if he ever approaches you closely, come to one of us immediately."

"Why? Now that I understand him a little better, and realize he may not offer my true *grande passion,* the thought of his company does not nearly distress me so."

"Because I am convinced he can be dangerously, irrationally violent—particularly toward women. Certainly the circumstances of his wife's life—and death—were not happy."

"Should I know those circumstances?"

"Only if you want to."

Michelle drew back, her eyes narrowed thoughtfully. She was exercising the discretion that had already saved her often in her young life. She knew she could trust Calvern: he had not insulted her by demanding mindless obedience; he had given her his reasons.

"I think, Your Grace, I would trust my very life to your judgment, and I cannot bear more gloom than I have already inflicted on us both—especially on such a sunny day. I will do as you say."

Calvern was hit by such an overwhelming sense of relief he almost felt weak-kneed.

Michelle only mentioned Malfet once more, as they walked the long distance back to the pagoda to join the others for the picnic tea, and then not by name.

"I think," she said, "I understand his violence. It is that

same intense passion that makes me feel so alive, turned inside out. Good or bad, there is no reality for him but that intensity."

Calvern stopped walking, and looked at her. In all his years of pondering since he left Eton, he had never seen that connection between Malfet's passion and his violence. Deirdre was so right about knowledge being the defense of innocence, yet he would never have believed that one so innocent could understand so profoundly.

7

EVEN THE DISGRUNTLED Roland was impressed.
Late one May morning, the brass bell of John Sharkley's bright new lodgings was pulled resoundingly. Grumbling, still adjusting his jacket, Roland sleepily opened the door, and his eyes widened. Before him stood a small page —no more than six or seven, he told Sharkley later—clad in white satin knee breeches with gold buckles, a blue satin coat, and a small blue turban upon his head, fastened with a large red brilliant. Behind the lad stood a brawny footman, clad in the same uniform without the turban.

"Invitation for John Sharkley, Esquire, of forty-four Albemarle Street (here Roland, much to his own amazement, found himself coming to attention in the best form of the good servant, and giving a nodding bow), to the come-out of Mademoiselle Michelle Langois, daughter of the late Comte de Bellevue, and ward of the Duke of Calvern, on Friday, the seventh of May, the year of Our Lord 1813."

A small arm jutted forward and handed Roland a neat square wrapped in blue silk, with a red seal. Then the little page executed a well-rehearsed bow, turned smartly on his heel, and, followed closely by the footman, hopped into a crested carriage and departed.

Indeed, the whole town was buzzing about the little turbaned page.

Lady Deirdre had struck again.

"By Gad, so I've got one!" exclaimed John Sharkley when he came in. "In every club and gambling hell chaps are asking if the page has come. Some posh event it will be, let me tell you, and the cards are limited—number only two hundred, I understand."

With Roland peering over his shoulder, he broke the seal and unwrapped the silk. Both men whistled.

On the front of the white card, engraved in blue, were the Calvern and de Bellevue crests, side by side. Inside, *face à face,* French on the left, English on the right, the formal invitation. At the bottom, clearly written, John Sharkley, Esquire, Number 168.

Roland whistled again. "Bet that card would fetch a pretty price in the clubs on St. James Street," he said, then catching Sharkley's look of stern outrage, which he had seen so often of late, added, "which, of course, we would never do, seeing it's got your name and all. We'd better find some pigeons to play for the new evening clothes you'll need. Fine satin breeches and gold buckles and a jeweled cravat pin, for a start."

Sharkley nodded. Ironically, while he had taken the new *ton* address, and outfitted himself on Saville Row, only for Michelle, news of his apparent prosperity had spread fast, and now he was received into the more elite clubs and gambling dens, where, for the past month, he had subtly plied his trade of fleecing the ignorant and holding debt notes as blackmail more lucratively and, surprisingly, more easily. The higher a man's position in the *ton,* Sharkley discovered, the less likely he was to tolerate scandal, and he, more than members of the merchant classes who were often wealthier, would more readily pay well to avoid it.

Furthermore, Sharkley strictly limited himself in the damage he would do to any one person. "No gentleman," he said consistently of late, within the hearing of influential people, "would drive another to debtors' prison," and his adherence to the statement won him not only grudging respect, but also continued entrance to the better establishments. Even Roland was reluctantly coming to admit that respectability, at least within limits, makes a handsome profit. But neither the enamored Sharkley nor the cynical Roland ventured so far into the seducing depths of respectability that they destroyed the de Varennes's seal hidden in Sharkley's desk.

Lady Deirdre was in the throes of preparing for Michelle's come-out. As their gowns were already complete, the girls were at loose ends, not participating in the whirlwind of tightly scheduled preparation that preceded a major Cresswell event.

A heavy fog had settled on London. Calvern had dined early, and was at work in his library preparing a brief for the Foreign Office on the possible structures of European countries after Napoleon's defeat (news from the Russian front made clear that if not imminent, the defeat was at least certain) when Charles announced crisply, "Mademoiselle Michelle and Miss Jane Malton."

The duke rose, startled, but on this occasion he was not immobilized, and strode across the room, both hands outstretched to welcome her.

Michelle stood shyly at the threshold, remembering she had not crossed it since that first fateful interview. How could she explain her reasons for coming to the duke, she asked herself, when she could barely explain them to herself? Since seven days ago in Kew Gardens, two thoughts had been pounding constantly in her head. The first was that she could barely tolerate another instant of the dishonesty of the forged will; for one wild moment as she stood on the threshold, she thought of telling him the truth about everything— the will and Richard.

Yet as she saw him striding towards her, lean and strong, his welcoming smile so warm, she knew that her second thought had more weight. Ever since he had so perfectly understood her feelings in the gardens, and kissed her hands, she knew only one thing: she wanted him, needed him, even more than her own brother. How could she risk losing Calvern, having him cast her aside as a scheming opportunist? Furthermore, even Richard's existence was a secret she had sworn not to reveal. There was but one way: she would share everything that she knew of her past that she could, without that final revelation to discredit herself or break her vow to Richard. How glad she was she had brought the letters!

"Lady Deirdre said it would not be inappropriate to visit my guardian, if Jane accompanied me, for there is so little chance to talk privately at Grosvenor Square."

Michelle looked questioningly at Calvern, awaiting his response even before entering. He took her hand firmly and brought her into the room.

Jane stayed outside the threshold. "I'll come to the library to accompany Mademoiselle home in one hour, with your permission, Your Grace." The duke nodded curtly, and Charles left the door open a discreet crack, as propriety demanded. At last, Michelle and Calvern stood alone.

He beckoned to the two deep wing chairs before the fire, and put on another log. "What brings you all the way from Grosvenor Square in this drizzle? I know Deirdre's events can be staggering, and this time she is constructing some sort of domed tent, isn't she? Has she turfed you all out for the evening while she rebuilds the house?"

Michelle laughed. "The general swears he is going to set up his old campaign tent in the back garden and move into it if there is any more disruption, but that is not it, sir. I have wanted to share something with you for several weeks, but there seemed so little private time. With my *début* so soon upon us, and a positive whirlwind after that, I thought to-night . . ." She shrugged gracefully, embarrassed by her awkward explanation, and handed a small black portfolio to the duke.

He seized a five-branched candelabra for better light, cleared the papers from the desk, and opened the case. On top there were six letters—three of his own father's in their original envelopes, and three copies of the count's. Underneath, a small pile of drawings, the first of which he recognized as a Leonardo da Vinci. He turned to Michelle, standing next to him.

"Why, Michelle . . ."

She held her fingers to her lips, smiling softly. "Sh-sh, read the letters first, and then talk."

He did, and he was moved.

It is rare enough for men to have a profoundly close friendship, and rarer still to see that relationship articulated. That it was his own father's and Michelle's made the moment incredibly intimate—the children of the two friends sharing their deceased parents' thoughts.

In the first letter, the duke told the count of his utter fascination with one of Leonardo's drawings of the fantastical flying machines. The count was still urging him to accept it as a gift; the paternal duke would not, reminding de Bellevue that life in Paris with a young English bride would be most expensive, and the count should guard his assets. In the next letters, the count wrote happily of his wife's coming confinement, welcoming the duke's visit to Paris at any time, and expressing the wish that the duke be godfather to the coming child. Edward's father accepted eagerly, rejoicing in his friend's news, because of the joy the birth of his own sons had brought him.

In the final exchange, the letters were strained. Dated six years after Michelle's birth, the duke almost chided the younger man at not living fully after his wife's death, suggesting that if he could not love another woman, he did at least love his country, and in its service he might be revitalized. In his closing letter, the count mentioned cryptically that he was in continuing contact with King Louis, and enclosed a list of his art holdings and their value, asking the duke's aid in finding London buyers.

Then Calvern picked up the first drawing: it was of Leonardo's flying machine.

Michelle talked nervously, afraid to look up from the drawings. "I would be delighted to have you select two or three of these drawings that you like for yourself. I know my father would be so pleased for you to have them. I'm sure that when he named your father as my guardian, he thought only that I would be brought under his protection; he would have been overwhelmed by the great generosity and warmth with which you have welcomed me. We are so beholden to you for your kindness, Jane, Ninette, and I. I only wish I could offer you more, but you see, I intend to sell the rest for my wedding dowry."

She finally risked a glance up at the duke.

He looked down into her small, perfect face. He had marveled so many times at the color of her eyes. Tonight they were more richly violet than the flowers themselves. Her hair, not formally bound up, but caught back in loose curls, shone in the firelight. From the low bodice of her gown, modest enough by current fashion, he knew, he could see the shadowed cleavage of her breasts and white skin. Whether the slight scent of rosewater came from her hair or warm body, he did not know or care; he only knew that she was nervous, and a little frightened that he might not understand her offer of something of tremendous value to her. He reached for her and drew her to him; she came readily.

"Silly, silly child. These drawings are the only treasures a father who loved his daughter above all else had to give her. If you think for a minute I would countenance their sale to pay for your dowry, you do not know me. They are your father's tangible love for you. They will never leave your hands."

As he had longed to do so many times, he traced the hollow of her cheek with his fingers, brushing back the tendrils of her hair. She reached up for him, her arms around his neck; he felt their smooth undersides like the finest silk, warm on his skin. Her eyes were shuttered, a faint half smile on her lips.

When will he kiss me? she thought. Will he never kiss me? His touch on her cheeks, in her hair, was thrilling her; her body was almost shaking. When she put her arms up to draw him down to her, even the silky sheen of his blond hair in the fire light mesmerized her. Will he know that I've never been kissed? she wondered. She looked into his blue eyes. Kiss me, she willed wordlessly. Kiss me.

He held her head gently, exploring her face with his mouth almost as if it were a sculpture. First his lips brushed her cheeks, her ears, her temples, incessantly, rythmically. Unaware of it, she gave a soft little moan of desire; her fingers curled into his hair.

"Slowly, my love," he murmured.

Then, with infinite tenderness, he brushed her lips. Hers trembled slightly under his, wet, half-open. His tongue entered, and she drew a small, sharp breath of surprise. He slipped his fingers through her hair, supporting her head. His tongue was insistent; she felt possessed, urgent. She gave another moan, and responded with the passion that was sweeping her. There was no reality, nothing except his mouth's magnificent taking of her. She tried to draw a breath, felt weak, and for a few seconds, darkness covered her eyes.

Calvern felt her body crumple against him, a dropped weight against his supporting arm. He drew back; her face was white.

"Michelle!" Instantly he lifted her and carried her to the settee facing the fire. No sooner had he placed her there than she struggled to sit, drawing deep breaths.

"I'm so sorry, Your Grace. For a moment I felt I couldn't breathe, I couldn't get air."

"Michelle, lie back." His voice was commanding, gentle, as if he were addressing a distressed child.

She shook her head furiously. "Nothing is wrong!" But he was already at her side with a glass of water and his handkerchief moistened from a jug beside the whiskey decanter. He bathed her face as if she were seven, and she shut her eyes tightly.

"Do you always faint when you're kissed?" His voice was lazy, cool, but his eyes were smiling.

"I've never been—" she stopped herself. "I've never fainted in my life!" Bright pink stains of embarrassment and fury flooded her cheeks.

"It is just that I was a little overwhelming, is it?" he said with a chuckle. She could have hit him with her fan.

They sat quietly together on the settee for several minutes, his hand holding hers.

"Do you think that now we know each other just a little better, you could stop calling me Your Grace and call me Edward—not in public, if it makes you uncomfortable, but at least when I'm kissing you?"

She did hit him with her fan.

For the next twenty minutes, until Jane came, Calvern and Michelle, as self-possessed as churchgoers, careful even not to brush against each other, sat at the library table and, with reverence and care, leafed through the drawings. She was engrossed by Rembrandt's studies for *The Descent from the Cross,* wondering how he could capture such agony in the few rough lines of a figure. Then there were the Michelangelo male nudes. Almost any other girl of Michelle's age in the *ton* would have been reduced to giggles or fainting, but she was fascinated by their beauty, he noted with a smile.

"Please"—Michelle was close to tears—"do select some of these drawings for yourself. It would give me such great joy for you to have them. It would almost be like sealing our fathers' friendship."

He could read in her glance how much it meant to her.

"Our fathers' friendship was sealed when you felt free to come to me, but for my father's sake, I would enjoy the Leonardo sketch of the flying machines that so fascinated him."

Michelle's face shone with pleasure.

When Jane came, the duke took Michelle's pelisse from the footman and placed it around her shoulders himself. As he did so, he whispered in her ear, "Remember, next time it's Edward."

Jane did not miss her mistress's flush and half smile.

Michelle was grateful for the darkness and silence in the swaying carriage on the way home. She wanted to turn the evening over in her mind the way a jeweler turns a fine stone in the light. The duke had savored their fathers' letters just as she did; he had, without her expressing it, understood the immense importance of her father's drawings to her, and accepted one (only one, not three or four, as she had hoped), but that one did, in fact, form a bond. And he had called her "my love." *My love*—she turned the phrase over and over in her mind.

Yet he had teased her about fainting, kindly, when in fact

she must have appeared the greenest schoolroom miss. Even now, in the dark, she could feel herself flush.

What did he really think of her?

If Michelle could only have overheard Calvern's thoughts at that selfsame moment, she would have discovered they were centered on precisely that question.

He carefully measured a small amount of brandy into his glass; there were only two bottles of the thirty-year-old vintage left, and he refused, as a matter of principle, to buy any on the black market, although many of his friends did. He stood, an elbow on the marble mantel, swirling and warming his brandy in its snifter. From time to time, he kicked a piece of glowing ash back into the fireplace with his boot.

He was distinctly annoyed with himself. Perhaps this had been the one moment in his life when only the art of his loving could have expressed his feelings, which were so profound, no words could encompass them. But with such a result! He hadn't rushed his fences with a woman in years! How the bucks at the club would smile if they knew—and he certainly couldn't excuse himself on the grounds of inexperience.

In the nine years since his father's death, he had had only two mistresses. For the first six years, until the courts of Napoleon looked richer, his paramour had been the legendary Ghiselle, dusky, warm, temperamental. Although only three years his senior, what a teacher she had been, and he, a willing and skilled pupil. It was she who taught him that it is not the number of women a man takes, but how satisfied his lovers are, that determines a man's reputation. With her, he had made his reputation. Then, until last spring, his lover had been the exquisite and perceptive Lilianne, known for her superb arts, strangely insatiable until Calvern became her protector, and under whom she became as monogamous as a purring, satisfied kitten.

Yet tonight, when it truly mattered, be damned, it had not gone well. Calvern rehearsed carefully in his mind what had happened.

He had known Michelle was innocent—that was obvious —but he had not guessed she was totally inexperienced! In that case, he would have expected the demure manner, the coy shyness—sometimes, he thought, a sad affectation, but often enough the sign of a genuine novice. Not that Michelle had come with anything like the warm response, practiced, deliberately teasing and seductive, of more experienced women. She had come simply as herself, open, ready, without affectation or calculation, responding to his every move, implicitly trusting him not to injure her in any way.

Had he (the renowned lover!) not been so swept away by the intensity of his own pleasure in her response, he would have realized when she started as he entered her mouth what an innocent she was. And the fainting: when he thought back, he realized she had had no control—her breathing had been startlingly erratic for several minutes. He roundly cursed his own lack of perception and caution. The more he considered it, the more he realized she had no understanding whatever of the end from the beginning; the urgent, seductive power she had exercised so artfully was also completely unconscious.

As he sipped the brandy, a sick thought struck: suppose, instead of himself, the first man to kiss her had been Malfet! What a frightful outcome there might have been. Yet there wasn't a man alive, even the despised earl, whom he could have justly blamed for seducing Michelle on the spot, for her totally unguarded response could have so easily been misread as willing experience.

He would have to speak to Deirdre about Michelle tomorrow. Surely there had to be something his aunt could say to the girl that would teach her to protect herself, for such rare innocence stood in ready danger of being viciously mauled.

And that, to the limits of his power and being, he would not allow.

He sank into his favorite wing chair, stretched his feet to the brass fender of the hearth, and studied the firelight through his raised glass.

The strength of his own feeling about the matter startled him. Why all the consternation? It had only been one mistimed kiss—surely no catastrophe. He had regained his wits and light touch soon enough afterward, so Michelle, thank God, seemed neither frightened nor appalled by the experience.

Why then was he so concerned?

He thought back to the first instant that he had seen Michelle—so self-possessed as she stood at the library threshold. And that evening at Castlereagh's, Michelle sitting on her gilt chair like a princess on a throne, so easily switching languages—he had never seen anyone, let alone such a beauty, perform the feat with such easy grace and wit. A perfect diplomat's wife. In the garden at Kew, his most vivid memories were of the moods of her incredible eyes. The sparkle of appreciative enjoyment and mischief as she glanced at Emma and Osgood had changed suddenly to concealed hurt, almost fear, as they had strolled together on the lilac path. The memory of her pained vulnerability caused such a surge of protective passion in his being that Calvern was astounded.

Suddenly it came to him: it was not only Malfet he did not want touching her, it was any man at all. He was no less angry at the thought of her intimacy with any other than he was at his own indelicate handling of her.

What was he so zealously safeguarding? Through the amber liquid in the snifter, he watched the flames in the hearth dance.

The open radiance on Michelle's delicate face as she came to him was vivid in his memory. Her trust in him was absolute. She had swept into his arms so trusting of his protection that she felt free to respond to any passion he aroused. She had presented to him the opportunity that comes so rarely to a man—to form from innocence the nature of a fully awakened and loving woman.

Sometime in the moments of the kiss, he had accepted the gift of her vulnerability; he wanted her now, and all that she was to become, for his very own. The intense jealousy of his passion, he realized, was not a wish to dominate Michelle. He was safeguarding the joyous, uninhibited, sensual nature of the woman he wanted for his own bride!

Marriage to Michelle.

A soft smile played over his lips for several minutes as he swirled the brandy slowly. "Damn the chit!" he suddenly exploded aloud, and with a deep oath, buried his head in his hands.

He was her guardian!

Whatever else Calvern was, he was her guardian, by honor bound to act in the place of her father. Tonight, when he had accepted the Leonardo drawing, it seemed as if a sacred seal had been put on that responsibility. An honorable fulfillment of that responsibility clearly forbade any use of his privileged position as Michelle's guardian to win her for his own.

He thought about her emotions. She had certainly been flattered by Malfet's first attentions. The earl was a past master at the art of seduction, and Michelle was the easiest of prey. Her saving grace was that she learned quickly; how readily she seemed to grasp the significance of what Calvern had said to her in Kew Gardens.

But did she really understand, in the depths of her being, that her much-cherished ideal of *une grande passion* had to be based on her lover's enjoyment in, and fostering of, her total being? It was a concept even mature lovers sometimes failed to comprehend. Was there a chance that Michelle, with her intelligent heart, had understood that he, Calvern, offered precisely that kind of love, and had chosen to respond—splendidly? The desire and tenderness that the very thought aroused overwhelmed him.

Yet, as compelling as the thought was, Calvern's honest, insightful knowledge of human behavior refused to let him believe it. It was much more likely, her reaction had been a naive appreciation of his "rescue" of her and his concern for her as her guardian.

How temptingly easy it would be to prey upon her inexperience with tempestuous lovemaking, lock up her heart, and marry her within weeks! Yet as surely as night proceeds from day, he knew the results of such a course, for he had seen many innocent country debutantes marry worldly-wise older men within weeks of the start of their first Season.

With Michelle, the results would be the same: she did not know the world; his was the only love she had yet had a chance to encounter. What would happen in several years, or even just months from now, when she realized others—probably many others—could have held similar passions for her, and he had abused his power and position as her guardian by failing to give her the right to choose? Her love for him could so easily turn to hate, and his possession of her, a bitter jailing. He knew well enough where that would lead: she would withdraw into a mood of enraged betrayal, and her possible infidelity would crucify him.

Cursed dilemma!

If he were not her guardian, he would be free to pursue and win her now, with the best of them—and he would have, no holds barred. Even now, Count von Reichertz, scion of an old and honorable diplomatic and military family, was after him constantly at the club to be allowed to call. Rumor had it that the Russian legation officer who had been incessant in his interest in Michelle was to be made his country's ambassador to Paris after the fall of Napoleon. Even Sanderson, the best of his friends in the House of Lords, whose name and nature were above reproach, had been pressing.

There was only one course that he, Calvern, as her guardian, could follow, for it alone was both honorable and offered the possibility that one day Michelle, a little wiser in the ways of society, a little more aware of her choices, might choose him. It was his clear duty to safeguard her from disaster, to welcome all those whom he knew and trusted to call on her, yet discreetly to keep his own oar in, at least until she had some time to experience and understand the world; then he would press his own suit relentlessly.

What would happen if she should immediately, and honestly, find her *grande passion* with someone else?

The thought did not bear thinking; he fired his brandy glass into the flames.

When, the next afternoon, Calvern had unexpectedly dropped by for tea and, in private, requested Deirdre to talk with Michelle about discretion in response to gentlemen, and then asked her to add the name of several "eligible good fellows" he knew to the guest list, she had raised a questioning brow. No instance she knew of should have prompted concern, nor did she understand his sudden urgency to introduce Michelle to such a plethora of eligibles. Why, she said, the child would be like a hummingbird with too many flowers to choose from, and so would not select any.

Precisely, Calvern thought, and said not a word.

Deirdre ordered another serving of his favorite watercress sandwiches, gave him a thick slice of dark fruitcake, and poured him a third cup of tea, then ventured to probe a little more. She received only his charming, diplomatic mask, which revealed nothing. Her ammunition was depleted.

Never before in their relationship had there been such a silence.

Well, she decided, she could think of no one whose judgment she trusted more, so she held her peace and did as she was bid.

8

"**D**AMN BRUMMELL!" exclaimed Sharkley as he attempted the complex folds of yet another white linen cravat around his neck; four crumpled failures lay on the floor. In a few minutes of intense and intricate manipulation, both Black Jack and Roland were satisfied with the knot, and the new ruby and diamond stickpin confirmed its success.

Sharkley stood up and walked to the pier glass.

Roland whistled softly under his breath. "Well, sir, after all these months together, we've done it. You look as you deserve—as rich as any man and more 'andsome than most. With thighs like that, the lightskirts will be begging you to wear satin breeches all the time."

Sharkley looked at himself in the mirror, and smoothed the perfect fit of his jacket. He agreed with Roland, for he could clearly see that he had never looked better: his distinguishing height, the slight gray at the temples, his muscular frame (for he had lost a little weight at his new fencing lessons), certainly meant he presented an attractive figure. He was pleased, for tonight was important.

It had been six weeks since Michelle's first outing in Hyde Park, when she had introduced him so willingly to her guardian. He had not risked calling on her at the Cresswells', for to do so, he knew, would bring an immediate investigation of his credentials. He had seen her twice more in the park; the second time she had deliberately stopped the carriage to ask if two days earlier he had received the invitation to her come-out, for she hadn't yet opened that day's responses. When he confirmed his acceptance, her smile was one of genuine pleasure; it had inspired Sharkley's efforts for days.

Now, indeed, he felt ready to withstand the probing of Calvern and Cresswell. He intended to remind them that he was, indeed, the son of a baronet, even if untitled himself. He had memberships in two of the "right" clubs; he would not mention they were obtained within the past two months. There were no outstanding gambling debts against his name —he'd had to threaten a discreet few of the *ton* to shake out the money for that one—and he could offer a small but growing income from "foreign investments," to which his somewhat affluent appearance and address would attest.

Surely this would be enough to allow him the prerogative of calling on her, and it was this right he could claim tonight.

Eventually, his winning card, he believed, would be that he would genuinely inspire her love, and he could offer, if not wealth, at least happiness. Calvern would endow his ward handsomely, and Sharkley would be genuinely confirmed in respectability—except for the occasional, irresistibly lucrative adventure, which he was sure the *ton* would tolerate, as he could name more than a few of them who indulged in questionable dealings themselves. After all, any of his activities would be for the sake of "the matchless Michelle."

"Wish me luck tonight, my man."

He turned and looked at Roland. He would actually have liked to confide his plans in his servant, for they had been through much together. He didn't, though, not because Roland wasn't completely loyal—he was—but because the delicate fabric of his desires could not withstand the cynicism of Roland's look. He'd share when the bird was in the hand.

He would have been astounded to know how much Roland had already guessed, and how accurately. The servant-accomplice had been surprised at the success of the change to date in his enamored master's life-style, and pleased by it, for as always, Sharkley had evenhandedly shared the benefits. But if Roland had one iron-clad belief, it was this: the *ton* only admits its own, and the two-month make-over his master had undergone certainly wouldn't qualify him as a full-fledged member. He wondered when the rebuff would come.

"I always 'ave wished you luck, sir, and with the swells, you'll be needing it."

Sharkley was too rapt in his own plans to hear.

* * *

"Lord and Lady Dundurnham!"

Two pages in blue and white satin blew a short fanfare, and yet another privileged couple entered the fantastical world of Michelle de Bellevue's come-out ball.

Lady Deirdre had excelled herself, which was no mean feat, and she had done it by following her own golden maxim: find the essential characteristics of the guest of honor that society most enjoys, and build. For Michelle, it had been easy. All the *ton* had talked about the *exotic* beauty of this daughter of *l'ancien régime*, so Deirdre focused on exactly those two phrases.

L'ancien régime: the colors of blue and white, so these became the choice for the ball, although Lady Deirdre deliberately interpreted blue to mean a shade very close to the violet of Michelle's eyes. *Exotic:* now, there was the challenge, and it was that which inspired what the general, with his usual military accuracy, referred to as "Deirdre's raid on the East India Company warehouse."

The ballroom remained much as it was normally, although the musicians' gallery had been draped in blue and white, and around the pillars of the ballroom, tied with broad blue bands, were circled the largest white ostrich plumes yet seen in London.

Three sets of French doors in the ballroom swung wide onto the balustraded terrace and the steps into the garden. Over each alcove, brightly lit with swinging lanterns, a blue and white awning had been suspended. The ground was covered with Turkish carpets, satin pillows of blue and gold were heaped into settees, and small sandalwood tables carved in the shape of elephants held large brass platters on their backs heaped with fruit and nut cakes. Standing in the shadows of each setting were footmen, attentive to every need. Michelle never suspected that the brightness of the lights in the alcoves, or the bevy of footmen in the garden (extra staff lent to the Cresswells by Calvern), were part of the duke's consideration of her safety.

It was the long, high-ceilinged dining room of the Cresswell mansion that truly fulfilled Deirdre's imaginative vision. From the gigantic, sparkling chandelier in the center of the ceiling, she suspended literally hundreds of yards of broad blue and white silk, arching low, and caught at the walls at a ten-foot height, where they descended to the floor. From fifty standards around the room swung brass lanterns, each shedding a circle of soft light on small tables for four covered in blue and gold silk. Male servants, dressed in blue and white satin with ornamented turbans on their heads, as the little page had been, served rich curries, tropical fruits, strange honied sweets. They offered six kinds of steaming teas and thick Turkish coffee. Dining in the summer tent of some gracious sultan could not have been more exotic.

Calvern, the general, Lady Deirdre in cream satin with a magnificent aigrette of matching ostrich plumes in her titian hair, and Emma, glowing in rose, received the guests. Following the French custom, Michelle was to make a grand entrance: she would sweep down the mahogany staircase at the end of the ballroom, on the Duke of Calvern's arm, at precisely nine. When she descended, she would accept signatures on her dance card. At a quarter before the hour, both the Earl of Malfet and Sharkley were among the small cluster of men at the bottom, positioned to be in the front line; at five to the hour, the group had swollen to a crush.

Behind the curtain at the top of the stairs, which had not yet been drawn open, Michelle turned to Calvern and asked, with an earnest half smile on her lips, the immortal question: "How do I look?"

He took two steps back and circling his hand, beckoned to her to turn around. For a minute, he was so caught by her beauty, he couldn't speak.

While Deirdre had planned the evening to be one of glittering, ornate exotica, it had all been designed to offset its richest jewel, one of utter simplicity. Michelle's dress was of sapphire-blue silk so light and fine, its lines were liquid against her slim form. The high waist was banded with a thin ribbon of brilliants that emphasized the high firmness of her young breasts. From the back, a small train, separate from the narrow skirt, on which Emma had embroidered a simple de Bellevue crest, fell from the high waist. Ninette had looped the end as she had learned to do in Vienna, so when Michelle waltzed, the train would waft lightly from her wrist. Her long gloves were white; in her hair she wore two small egret plumes. blue and white, and carried a matching fan. Drops of single sapphires, borrowed from Lady Deirdre, hung in her ears.

There was no clutter, no artificial dazzle. The immediate effect was to bring forth the quiet radiance of Michelle's own beauty.

Once again the very whiteness of her skin against the raven hair caught Calvern by surprise; the blue of her gown made her eyes sparkle even more. Calvern looked straight into her eyes and spoke softly: "Because it is what you might expect to hear, it is no less true: you have never been more beautiful than you are right now." His hand slipped into his vest pocket; he removed a small leather case, opened it, and handed it to Michelle.

Her eyes widened, and then shone. Three oblong pearls of richest luster formed the shape of the fleur-de-lys of the *ancien régime,* set in a medallion of exquisite sapphires. It hung from a simple broad velvet chocker, exactly the shade of her dress.

She glanced up at Calvern. "It is incredibly beautiful; the fleur-de-lys represents my heart's dearest desire." She hesitated, trying to articulate a subtle awareness; for a rare moment, her English felt awkward. "Every time you speak, or give support to me, as at Kew, or share, as you did with the letters and drawings, or now, with this treasure, you always know what I feel but cannot say. You understand my heart."

A smile of rapt pleasure on her lips, she traced the flower with her slender fingers, and circled the medallion. Handing him the ribbon, she beckoned for him to put it around her neck.

For the last two weeks he had been ranting at himself about self-discipline where she was concerned, but the small, jumping pulse at the base of her throat and the familiar scent of rosewater made his vow of restraint almost impossible to keep. His hands were shaking slightly and, he hoped, imperceptibly; he succeeded in fastening the clasp.

"C'est belle?" she asked shyly.

"Seulement moins belle que la dame qui la porte."

She smiled one of her dazzling, intimate smiles, and waited. He felt an incredible surge of desire toward her, but he had anticipated it. His self-control was impeccable, and he smiled back.

"Merci, Edouard," she said, whispering his name in French. Coming forward and standing on tiptoe, she kissed him on the cheek, then slipped her hand through his arm.

Before they signaled the curtain to be drawn, he noticed she took several deep breaths and straightened her shoulders. The aura of unruffled composure that had so intrigued him on their first interview in his library settled on her features; her smile became public.

Her *début* had begun.

To say that both Malfet and Sharkley were furious when they saw Michelle's dance card would not be an understatement, although both men were masters enough of self-re-

straint to have their feelings show only in a quick flush, easily
explained by the crush and the heat. The Duke of Calvern,
of course, would lead his ward in the opening quadrille. The
first waltz had already been signed for by Count von Reichertz; the Duc d'Anton was to lead her to supper, and General Cresswell had the closing dance. Calvern, damn him,
they both thought, had left no holes in Michelle's defenses,
and they both scribbled their names where they could:
Sharkley immediately after the first waltz, and again near the
end, Malfet right after supper.

The general and Lady Deirdre, Emma and Sir William
Osgood, led the flanking columns of the quadrille, while
Calvern and Michelle crowned the center. The appropriate
waves of whispers surged through the sidelines on her
beauty, her graceful bearing, the artistry of her dress. Calvern seemed to hear every one, but Michelle was oblivious.
She gazed evenly in his eyes, disarming him to the very core;
only the formality of the dance enforced discipline on his
rising passion.

Sharkley, watching like an acute, still cat from the sidelines, did not miss his beloved's glances at the duke, or the
duke's subtle, but undeniable, response. His lips set in a
firm, angry line.

At the finish, as Calvern led Michelle directly to von Reichertz, he whispered, "Now, my dear, enjoy yourself. I want
to see Lady Castlereagh blush."

"She shall, Your Grace, or I am not my father's daughter." Michelle winked wickedly and, looping her train over
her wrist, turned to curtsy deeply to the waiting Reichertz's
courtly bow.

By the gods, thought Malfet, dancing with Lady Jane
Willington, Reichertz must have bribed the maestro.

Indeed he had.

It was obvious that between last week, when the same
orchestra had played at Almack's, and now, it had learned
something new about waltzes. No longer the staid, mathe-
matical tempo; the strings indulged in lyric, singing sweeps,
faster runs, swirling, building momentum. In ever widening,
twirling circles, at almost incredible speed, Reichertz led Michelle, her light train swirling high behind her, through intricacies of dazzling waltz steps London had never before seen.
Even Calvern was amazed. Not another couple could keep
pace: the floor was conceded to the count and Michelle
alone, and they held it in a spectacular display for fully five
minutes.

After their bows, the outburst of applause was sharp and immediate. Michelle and the count disappeared in search of cold champagne; the orchestra took a well-deserved break, and Lady Castlereagh demanded that a footman bring an entire pitcher of lemonade right to her table, for it was so stifling hot, she was flushing.

Nearby, Calvern laughed with genuine pleasure.

If the Duke of Calvern was enjoying himself, John Sharkley, Esquire, distinctly was not.

He had noticed the intensity of Michelle's glances at the duke; he had seen how completely, freely she had yielded to the German count's dominance of her during the waltz. He felt the first woman he had ever truly cherished slipping away, and he would not allow it. The next dance was his; he would not yield a moment of it. Like a relentless hound, he went out on the terrace to search her out. Away from the light of the open ballroom doors, and the candles of the alcoves, in the shadow of the house itself, stood the figures he sought.

Beside a covering bush, he froze.

Reichertz had seized Michelle's hand and, in an exaggerated, melodramatic gesture, pressed it over his heart. She laughed, tossing back her head, displaying the lovely long line of her throat. The pace changed. Slowly, with complete deliberation and tenderness, the count raised her gloved hand to his lips and held it there. Sharkley was so close, he could hear her quickened breathing.

The count was not finished.

After a moment, he gently turned Michelle's hand over and undid the two buttons of the slit on the inside of the glove's wrist. He raised the inside of Michelle's wrist to his lips. Sharkley heard the sharp intake of her breath.

He felt sick; he could take no more; he went inside to wait.

When Reichertz brought Michelle to Sharkley in time for the next dance, Sharkley was completely composed; he knew exactly what he wanted to do. He smiled apologetically at Michelle.

"The dance I have spoken for is a schottische, which, I am afraid, is not one of my best. Would you care, instead, to sit in an alcove?" Michelle nodded happily. She needed a little time to be easy, to talk, to collect herself.

In oriental fashion, the low settees in the alcoves were

heaped with cushions, and in sitting down in her narrow
skirt, Michelle lost her balance, and the full length of her
warm, scented body tumbled against Sharkley. He hurriedly
picked her up; they both flushed and laughed. He compli-
mented her on her dress; she delightedly showed him the
crest Emma had embroidered on the train. He remarked on
the fleur-de-lys; she fingered it, smiled softly, and said her
guardian had just presented it to her.

Damn it, thought Sharkley, I will not tolerate this one
moment longer.

"When may I call on you, Michelle?" His tone was the
imperious one of a schoolmaster demanding work, but
Sharkley's intense anxiety made him unaware of it.

Nothing, not one thing, that Michelle could have said or
done could have injured Sharkley more. She looked surprised—surprised for at least a full minute.

In actual fact, Michelle was rehearsing in her mind her
past relationship with Sharkley, to see whatever she had
done to entitle him to ask that question in such a tone. She
was at a loss, but her kind heart took over. It could well be
the heat of the evening. She looked up at him, uncertainty
making her smile a little coy—a rare instance. She remembered Calvern's instructions, and his reasons. "My guardian
has asked that all requests to call on me be referred to him.
I'm sure he is not the least insensible of the debt of gratitude
we owe to you, and he will be most kind."

Sharkley appeared to be as nonplussed by her formal
speech as she was in giving it, though she looked into his eyes
and lightly squeezed his hand as she did so. He was thoroughly miserable, and it was with a downcast face—if that
was possible for one who had just been with Michelle,
thought her next partner—that Sharkley handed her on
early. Michelle escaped into the intricacies of a Scottish court
reel with relief.

The Countess of Willington allowed it was definitely The
Waltz, but the Marchioness of Bridgeport contended that it
was, without refute, Michelle At Supper that was the best
Entertainment, for it involved a Contest.

A contest it truly was.

For the opening minutes, it looked as if it was to be a
replay of Lady Castlereagh's supper, for Michelle was holding court at her small table, chattering happily in different
languages, only this time with the Duc d'Anton, as had been
carefully prearranged, dancing attendance at her side.

If Michelle's magnificent triumph of the evening had dispirited Sharkley, it had only served to stoke the fires of David Richmond, Earl of Malfet. If Sharkley had been shocked by the prearranged card, Richmond was not: he knew the ways of the *ton* much better, because he was one of them. He knew too well Calvern's dislike of him, and understood clearly the duke's defensive intentions. Where Sharkley had misread Michelle's warmth to her various partners such as the Count von Reichertz as proof of the woman's flirtatious inconstancy, Malfet was much wiser. He recognized all her escorts were as air to her. There was only one man whose glance she had sought after the first waltz, during the reels, when she came in from refreshments. It was Calvern's.

Suddenly the attainment of Michelle meant more, much more to Malfet than the possession of those eyes in which a man might drown his passion, and of a body that promised more delight than he could stand: it also promised the satisfaction of revenge. Through Michelle, Malfet's injury to Calvern, and his damned honor, might well be mortal.

Malfet went in to battle.

He was a wily, patient foe.

He knew, without a doubt, that all private access to Michelle would be stopped; he was only grateful that he had been afforded the opportunity of this evening, and he knew that, for his purposes, this evening was only supper, and his following dance. Michelle had to be caught and won in less than forty minutes. There were few men who would ever have attempted to win a woman in such a short space, and fewer still who had ever done so and succeeded: David Richmond, Earl of Malfet, was one.

For the first part of supper, he reviewed the characteristics of his prey. He knew that she was totally innocent, and so would frighten easily; but he also knew that on the two previous occasions she had opened completely to gentleness with an underlying intensity of passion. He would have to hold precisely that mood in the most delicate balance, but if he did, she would, he was sure, agree to meet him secretly, and so be ripe for abduction.

When the sweets were served, he started his campaign.

The Duc d'Anton and his equerry had been waiting on Michelle most attentively, but as the duc shared her knowledge of languages, they both were occupied in speaking animatedly to several people at once. The earl moved in most subtly. Was the light from the standard a little too near her eyes? He changed its position an inch. Were the honeyed fruits, which the duc had just offered, a little sweet? He had discovered a small dish of fresh orange. Was her lemonade a little warm? He had just obtained this well-chilled glass from the footman.

Within only a few minutes, the duc was clearly aware of the intruder; he glared at Malfet, who appeared not to notice, so intent was he on Michelle. Finally, the duc signaled his burly equerry to position himself between Michelle and Malfet; Malfet simply murmured, "I await your pleasure in the next dance, Michelle," and, bowing gracefully, departed.

Sharkley, indulging in his despair as deeply as others indulge in food, watched in uninhibited misery as the "two titans of the *ton*," as he called them later to Roland, vied over possession of his own beloved. "An even match," he said later; "a perfect draw," the Marchioness of Bridgewater roundly declared.

Both experts, for this round, were right.

It was in the next round, the dance itself, that Malfet knew the battle had to be won. To disarm the enemy, he carefully escorted Michelle to the floor under Calvern's very gaze, and moved off in a most sedate and distant waltz; it even passed the scrutiny of Lady Castlereagh herself, to whom he ostentatiously nodded. That accomplished, he quietly broached Michelle herself; the very courtliness of his speech made it less threatening.

"My lovely Michelle, you have not graced me with even one of the lovely glances or dazzling smiles you gave me on the two previous occasions. If something troubles you in my attentions, I will desist immediately, but I want to hear it from you, and you alone. Surely I am owed that. Should we step out onto the terrace, right by the door?"

No other request but an appeal to justice, with a guarantee of safe closeness to the house, could have removed Michelle from the dance.

Sharkley followed discreetly, careful not to be seen either by Michelle or Malfet. The earl had definitely recognized Black Jack; he had looked straight at him several times, but offered no sign of recognition. Sharkley feared Malfet's anger, and could ill afford it, but despite the dangers, he was determined to drain the glass of his sorrows to its bitter dregs.

In the very shadows where Reichertz had plied his dastardly arts (later Roland marveled at the rolling riches of

Sharkley's newfound vocabulary of misery), Malfet bent to Michelle. Sharkley could not hear their words, but the earl's voice was soft, rhythmic, persuasive, and Michelle's, for the first time in Sharkley's hearing, had a tense edge. Their talk was long, so long—perhaps seven minutes, he told Roland. Suddenly, Malfet moved. His back was to Sharkley, Michelle was completely obscured from view. There were the sounds of a scuffle, and a sharp, tense, muffled moan. A small, gloved hand splayed across Malfet's back.

Fear and terror were Sharkley's stock-in-trade, and he needed to see no more. His beloved was in trouble; he went straight for Calvern as fast as he could.

Calvern had been vigilant all night. He had not joined the dance until he had seen Malfet and Michelle on the floor. He had since lost sight of the earl's tall frame, and his partner was troubled by the duke's seemingly erratic pattern of movement; actually, he was on a waltzing search for the missing couple. He had spotted Sharkley's distressed look as soon as he came to the ballroom door. The duke knew that the man had been following Michelle like an ignored lapdog all night, and that his coming meant Michelle was in trouble. With a quick word of excuse he abandoned his partner and, almost running, beckoned to the two footmen he had stationed by the doors for just such an eventuality. He was at Sharkley's side in seconds. The duke didn't ask him to explain; he simply said, "Where?" and the four men ran.

For the first time in her life, Lady Jane Willington found herself deserted in the middle of a dance. She ran off the floor. Her mama may have thought the duke was the most eligible man in the realm, she said, but he was a boor, a rapscallion, and perhaps not even a gentleman. He had been impossibly quiet at the supper dance at Lady Castlereagh's, and now he deserted her with a simple "Pardon." Were he not a duke, muchless a duke of the blood royal, he would have to walk over a bed of hot coals, cover himself with the ashes, and bow to the ground three times before she ever spoke to him again.

A trifle excessive, didn't she think? said her mama, the Countess of Willington.

But so entertaining to see, said the Marchioness of Bridgewater.

"Sir!" Calvern's voice cut the shadows like a blade. Malfet whirled, still holding Michelle's wrist tightly. She was dazed, ashen; a bright spot of pink was at one corner of her lips.

"Unhand my ward immediately, or I will order my men to run you through on the spot."

The earl looked carefully. He was confronted by the duke, no mean opponent at the best of times, and now in a mood to brook no quarter. Behind him stood two massive footmen, armed, to Malfet's shock, with swords. He did not see Sharkley hovering in the shadows, but from the ballroom, Malfet recognized the tall form of General Cresswell moving swiftly toward them. He let go of Michelle's wrist, and she flew behind Calvern.

"If I find that any one of my family or General Cresswell's have so much as been spoken to by you, or anyone in your pay or service, I will take it as a deliberate, mortal threat to their safety, and conduct myself accordingly."

Calvern's words were very quiet, but not a man within hearing doubted their veracity.

The breath hissed between Malfet's teeth. "I have come as a guest to your house, and find myself confronted with the most abominable threats. I will take my leave now, and my justice later."

He strode from the terrace, surrounded by the general and the footmen.

Calvern turned instantly to Michelle. "Quickly! The servants' stair to your boudoir." She responded as if in a trance.

As soon as they reached the narrow wooden stair, he swept Michelle into his arms and bounded up the stairs. At the turn he banged into a hapless scullery maid with a tray of cutlery; it clattered down the stairs with an incredible racket.

"Don't stop to pick them up," Calvern commanded her. "Have Jane Malton and Lady Deirdre come to Mademoiselle's boudoir instantly!" He ran on.

Calvern and Michelle had been in her room no more than two minutes when Jane rushed in. Michelle was sitting rigidly in a chair, her hands limp in front of her, she seemed to be dazed. Calvern gently grasped her shoulders, saying over and over, "I'm with you. Jane is with you. You are safe; Malfet has gone. It's all over."

Over and over. Again and again.

The corner of Michelle's mouth was bleeding. A small trickle of blood ran down her chin.

"Oh, my God," Jane cried, and returned in seconds with a damp, clean linen. She wiped, Calvern still grasping Michelle's shoulders. The cut was very small.

Slowly, Michelle began to focus. She looked first at Calvern, then at Jane, then back to Calvern. Her voice was quiet, disbelieving still.

"When I refused his attentions, he forced them on me and wouldn't let me go. When I said I wouldn't meet with him secretly, he slapped me." She put her hand to her mouth, and all of a sudden saw specks of blood. She went to the mirror and touched her face gingerly.

"Oh, Edward, it wasn't a nightmare. He really did slap me."

Suddenly the reality of her experience broke through, and she ran to Jane's arms, and sobbed and sobbed. Jane stood, cradling the petite Michelle in her arms, crooning and caressing her back.

Calvern had never felt more useless, upset, disconsolate, and unhappy in his life. He had failed Michelle, now he could only leave.

"Oh, Edward, stay! I'll be so frightened if you go." She ran into his arms.

For an instant the scented closeness of Michelle's fragile vulnerability disarmed him completely, but trying to quench his sudden, aching surge of desire for her, he cradled her, crooned to her, just as Jane had done, while she sobbed all the more.

Even as the heavy waves of a swelling tide crest, then perceptibly begin to ebb, the shivers of Michelle's sobs became fewer and fewer. The silk facing of Calvern's jacket rubbed her cheek; the light spice of his cologne mingling with her own perfume caught her senses. In Jane's hug she felt only comfort; enfolded by Calvern's strong arms, it was as if she was not only being comforted, but being held close in the magic, protective circle of his presence.

She was truly safe.

Yet there was more than safety here. It was as if his very power, while encircling and protecting her, was also drawing something from the well of her own being: sensations she had never known before. She clung to him, not knowing how to deal with this new dizzy spinning of her bruised heart.

Hearing Michelle's sobs quiet, Calvern eased her innocently tempestuous, teasing body away from his own and, delicately brushing a wayward strand of hair back behind her ear, kissed her chastely on the forehead.

There was a quiet knock at the door.

Deirdre entered, carrying a tea tray in her hands, and cold compresses in a bag. "Here then. Some tea and sweet chocolate. After your hair is redone and you have had cold compresses on your face for five minutes, you will feel just the thing and be ready to go downstairs, the 'matchless Michelle' once again."

Edward turned on Deirdre and exploded. "Good God, Deirdre. Don't be senseless and cruel. The girl can't go down and face those people tonight. She should be put to bed, and comforted, and probably given a good dose of laudanum so she can go to sleep."

Deirdre's cheeks flamed, and she shot Calvern a withering glance. She strode over to Michelle and, in a commanding tone, spoke to her directly.

"Look, Michelle, you have just suffered a very big emotional shock, but thank God, a small physical one. The man who assaulted you is a sick man, and a very evil one. The guests saw him thrown out of the house bodily by my husband and two footmen. His reputation is in ruins. There is no way he can regain it. To get back at us, and probably Edward in particular, Malfet will deliberately attempt to destroy your reputation in the most vicious way possible.

"If you do not reappear, the gossips will have it out in every house by breakfast that you have been beaten or violated, preferably both. You will stop these nonsensical rumors immediately by appearing downstairs intact, smiling, able to carry on dancing. And then you and Edward will stand with the general and me, and we will bid every guest good night. You are strong enough to do it, and we all, especially Edward"—she cast him a commanding look—"will help you."

Jane, who had never stopped rubbing Michelle's back, whispered, "She's right, my love."

"Certainly I am," said Deirdre, popping a chocolate directly into Michelle's mouth. "Jane, bring me Michelle's hairbrush, and go to my room and bring me my pot of rouge. Don't gape. Of course I use rouge, and tonight so will Michelle. Edward—don't stand there like a mantel ornament. Serve each of us tea with lots of sugar, then go downstairs and tell the maestro to play a waltz when you enter with Michelle, and not to stop until you signal. But no Count von Reichertz arrangements."

Even Michelle smiled.

For hours, it seemed, Sharkley had waited at the entrance to the ballroom. He wanted the second dance he had signed for on Michelle's card. He wanted to know she was all right.

He wanted to be her hero.

Calvern reappeared, and gave him a small bow. "Once again, thanks to your gallant vigilance, Mr. Sharkley, Michelle is safe. Our gratitude will be expressed appropriately." The duke bowed once more and passed on to speak to the maestro.

When minutes later the duke, this time with a pale, unseeing Michelle on his arm, walked by with no acknowledgment at all, but swung immediately onto the ballroom with his ward, Sharkley's disappointment crested at full flood, and he went home.

As Michelle danced with the duke, she discovered why Lady Deirdre had specified a waltz: it allowed her to escape, just as she had upstairs, into the tenderly protective security of Edward's presence. She had to face no other person, acknowledge no one else. She was safe within his arms; that was all that mattered.

For the first few minutes of the waltz, Calvern found Michelle absolutely rigid in his arms, like a wooden doll. He didn't glance down at her, or she up at him, yet he was aware of every breath she drew. Moments later, he felt her notice the music. The rhythm began to enter her body, she began to sway a little more.

Three circles of the room later, she looked up at him and smiled. "I'm fine, Edward. Why don't we form the closing reception line now?"

He pressed her lightly to him, and nodded to the maestro.

Later, as the door closed on the last guest, Deirdre placed her arm around Michelle's waist, and with Emma on Michelle's other side, the three women ascended the stairs. As Deirdre swept past Calvern, she muttered, "Bed and laudanum, indeed. I will recommend that treatment for you the next time you have a crisis at the Foreign Office."

Sharkley arrived home an hour earlier than Roland had expected, but one look at his master's face told him he had been right to set out a bottle of French brandy beside his favorite chair. Tonight, he knew, Sharkley would not talk; it would be several days before he told Roland the tale. For his part, Black Jack worked at getting soddenly, roaringly drunk. In his outbursts of anger as he stared at the fire, he would repeat one or two sentences.

"He is not the least insensible of the debt of gratitude we owe to you, and he will be most kind," Sharkley slurred, raising his glass to toast himself. "Our gratitude will be expressed appropriately."

"Very appropriately," he muttered to himself. He went to his desk and drew out the little chamois bag containing the de Varennes seal, then returned to drinking. His head fell back, and he snored loudly, his hand still fondling the chamois bag.

Roland lifted the bag to place it on the table and, heaving the heavy body of his master to bed, smiled with relief. "'E may be steps up the ladder now, but at least 'e's off the straight and narrow."

The Earl of Malfet, cursing viciously, directed his coachman to an establishment near Covent Garden where some of his more unusual needs had been met in the past. The madam, called to the door by her massive footman, took one look at the mood of the earl's face and informed him that her entire company of women had been spoken for. The door slammed shut.

Calvern paced his library until dawn.

And Michelle slept, exhausted, safely in her own bed.

9

The new growth of the willow trees barely touched the surface of the languid, green-brown stream. The water lilies had opened to scented luster in the warm midafternoon sun. Here and there in the shade of the willows, a daddy-longlegs walked on the water, creating tiny circles on the surface with each step. The world was perfect in its lazy June newness.

Michelle lay back on the large cushion in the bow of the punt, and closed her eyes. She had already committed the gravest of sins against beauty—that of removing her broad-brimmed sun hat. She relished the gentle warmth of the sun on her face and loosened hair, and deliberately put out of her mind the chiding Jane would give her on the pinkening of her white skin, and the lemon paste that she would have to use tonight to bleach out any freckles. The day was too perfect to ruin with such thoughts.

Clear, sweet, on the still air, came the gentle whistle of the man poling at the stern of the boat. A Scottish air, low and melancholic. She understood its mood, and savored it in her soul.

In her mind's eye she could see the duke there, pushing the long pole easily into the bed of the stream. Edward's shoulders were always so powerful. But his hands were long-fingered and fine, she had noticed as he turned over drawings, and she liked that too. His hair was becoming almost silver in the summer sun. The muscles of his legs and thighs as he gripped his stallion, as he rode into the early morning

117

mist—there was nothing about the man that did not delight her. She sighed.

"Weary?"

"No. The sweetness of your whistle was making me a little melancholic." She opened her eyes and gave a wistful half smile, not to the Edward of her daydream, but to Robert, Lord Sanderson, a friend of Calvern's from Oxford, punting at the stern of the skiff.

"Not too melancholic, I hope."

"Not at all. Just the touch of sadness that makes the happiness real."

He smiled, and said nothing.

His smile is kind, she thought, and he knows when to be quiet—a true virtue.

Unaware, she sighed again. There was a real sadness growing in her heart; she knew its cause, and could do nothing.

Shortly after the triumph and almost-disaster of her come-out, Edward had proposed a fortnight's country holiday for some thirty people at his Holton House estate in Surrey. He had planned everything with such thorough foresight—picnic excursions, lawn luncheons, musicales in the evening, punting on the stream. In her bedroom every day there were fresh bouquets of violets. He had brought some of the French books down from his library in London so she would not be bored. His interest in her, his attention to every detail of her comfort, could not be faulted, except for one thing.

He avoided her.

A wry smile twisted her lips. Odd how that last incident with Malfet should lead to such different reactions in Calvern and herself.

Before the fateful come-out, Edward had enjoyed much of what she loved, shared much of her international world, and made her knowledge of languages and cultures relevant by his diplomatic insights. In fact, she had thought from his comments that he understood her inmost being. Even the one instance of his lovemaking had thrilled her so, that she often lay awake, recalling the sensations of every minute of it, although she had been foolish enough to faint. She flushed now, thinking of it. (Robert Sanderson, seeing Michelle blush lightly in her daydream and become, if possible, more beautiful, was intrigued.)

Then all had changed.

It was as if the confrontation with Malfet at her come-out

had hurt Calvern almost more than it had hurt her. Afterward, he seemed to withdraw from her company—why, though she had pondered it for days, she could not fathom. He had ceased being her possible lover, and became once again her aloof guardian.

Even as her guardian, his care and concern for her were evident. It seemed that he had vowed that no man who could remotely conceive of injuring her would ever come near her again. In fact, she thought, it seemed as if he had planned this carefully select house party solely for one purpose: to introduce her to eligible men—each, for different reasons, an appropriate suitor for her hand. The would-be suitors were not only titled, handsome, and well established; they were also, without exception, fine and honorable gentlemen, men one could trust instinctively. She liked every one of them, and enjoyed their company.

Yet she loved only Calvern.

A small frown creased her brow. Ungrateful wretch that I am, she thought. There is no law that says a guardian must fall in love with his foolishly romantic ward. He has been so generous. If I had honest respect for the duke's wishes, I would seriously consider every suitor here.

With one last, unconscious sigh she pulled herself from her melancholic thoughts and smiled up at Lord Sanderson.

Both in his nature and his handsome, rugged virility, Robert Sanderson resembled the dramatic granite outcroppings of his beloved Scottish highlands. He was fully three inches taller than Edward—well over six feet. His black hair shone in the sunlight; his eyes were blue-gray. His smile was easy, open. But it was his jawline that attracted her most—square and strong.

"You're a lady who has traveled much, and seen all the capitals, but you have not seen wild and sublime beauty until you've seen my highlands. The thunderheads roll down the loch, gusting rain before them, and the heather scents so rich you can feel it in your throat."

Michelle smiled. "It sounds compelling—a peculiar beauty that gets in the blood, and one would hate to leave."

"Aye, but it's the crofters too. They are as rough and strong as the hills they live on, but are hospitable to the very dregs of their pots. Never a one has left the hills hungry who needed food."

She smiled. "In contrast with such beauty and generosity, the London Season must seem very shallow to you."

He looked at her, surprised by her perspicacity. At the

club, Calvern had once spoken of her "seeing heart"; he now knew what the duke meant. His eyes became earnest. "I'm one of the few Scots nobles appointed to sit in the English House of Lords, Michelle, and our people need a voice."

"His Grace says you are very good in the Lords."

"Not surpassing the likes of the duke himself, who understands the world beyond our shores, but strong for my own people. Would you like to see the highlands sometime?"

Michelle's smile strained a little. She knew exactly what that invitation implied; the Count von Reichertz had issued a similar one last night to Vienna—at least after the wars were over, which, he said, would be only two or three months. She, chaperoned by Lady Deirdre and probably escorted by the Duke of Calvern himself, would visit the estates of the chosen suitor. If she enjoyed the country, and her host, an offer would likely be made for her hand, and she would be wed within weeks.

"This day has been enchanting, my lord, and perfect in every way. I have enjoyed your company deeply; but I am afraid I left my mind in the rose garden where we had our picnic, and I have vowed to do not a thing but *feel* this glorious June world, and not to *think* until Sunday next. At that time I will speak to my guardian, and we will see."

Sanderson, a deeply caring man, had been studying her attentively all day and knew full well that, except for the brief rest in the bow of the punt, she had been doing nothing *but* thinking all day. Although she was young, he realized that she was preparing for her most profound decision, that of her marriage, and he respected her for the care she was giving it.

But at this moment, he deemed, she needed some fun.

Sanderson had just tied the punt to the small dock at the foot of Holton House's long, sloping garden. As she took his hand to disembark, he caught her waist in his broad, strong hands and tossed her, like a child with skirts flaring, high in an arc from the boat to the shore.

"How does that feel, my wee lassie?" He laughed and, swooping down, seized her sunbonnet right from out of her hands and ran, at half his normal speed but twice hers, waving the hat and calling "What fine kindling for tonight's fire."

Michelle took off up the gentle slope after him, her dark hair streaming and glinting in the sun. Her narrow skirts made running so difficult that, without thinking, she hied them up to six inches above her trim ankles, and ran. He led her a merry chase, crisscrossing the lawn, often allowing her to come within three feet of him, then dashing away.

"You quicksilver fox," she cried breathlessly. "I'll need a pack of hounds and a horse to catch you!"

He slipped into the hedgerow maze. She caught a glimpse of his coattail around the corner and went pelting after—straight into his arms.

"Well, my dear, the fox has got the hunter, but you have caught me."

He kissed her full on the lips, laughingly placed her hat askew on her head, and took off again, with Michelle in pursuit. As Sanderson pulled open the garden door to the library, Lady Deirdre's lapdog dashed out, and Michelle tripped over him. She fell headlong, but Sanderson caught her before she hit the flagstones. As he raised her, he said in the primmest of tones: "My dear lady! Such a display! I believe that the virtue of every man in the house is at risk with your presence here!"

She chased him all the way to the lemonade jug on the sideboard in the dining room.

Two pairs of eyes had watched Michelle and Sanderson's game of fox and hunter.

Calvern had been sitting at a window desk in his private study next to his bedchamber, pondering the confidential list of twenty names that General Cresswell had just sent him by plainclothes military courier, who would take back the duke's answer the next morning.

Deuced bother, this spy business!

He intensely disliked his professional life to intrude here at Holton House, but during hostilities, what could one expect? If his younger brother could offer the country his life, Calvern would grant his country its intrusions. At least here, Michelle was safe from that madman Malfet. Deirdre believed there was no further danger from that source, but Calvern knew the earl's remarkable capacity for warped revenge too well to believe that.

Back to the unpleasant implications of the spy question.

Both the War and the Foreign Offices, Cresswell said, had known for some time that Bonaparte was receiving information leaked from the court in exile of French King Louis. Every time the king gave an important announcement in England, such as his upcoming Manifesto of a Constitutional Monarchy, Napoleon knew about it weeks in advance, and so was able to prepare speeches and influence the press against the king's statements. While such information was not as

damaging as the discovery of military secrets, it was seriously
hampering popular support for the return of the French king.

The culprit, the War Office suggested, probably had three
characteristics: it had to be someone who would be well received in court circles; who spoke fluent French; and who
had regular, easy communication with the Continent for
other purposes in order to shield the messages to Napoleon.
Cresswell had asked Calvern for all his personal knowledge
of each name on the list, any irregular transactions or unusual debts or liabilities incurred by them, and his assess-
ment of their characters.

Calvern scanned the list of names. The first ones were
painful, for it involved the questioning, in some instances, of
the circumstances and character of lifelong friends. The head
boy of his house during his first year of Eton, whom he had
idolized, was one. At the end of the list, he drew his breath
in sharp shock. The name was one of his current house-
guests—that of John Sharkley.

John Sharkley.

The duke would not normally have included him among
his intimates: he had invited him to the houseparty as a
thanks for his fine service to Michelle, at Ostend and especially at her come-out ball.

Calvern had had Sharkley, along with a considerable list
of others, investigated before the come-out, and he was
happy to tell the general what he knew. He was the second
son of a minor baronet, had recently had some commercial
success in trade with Europe, and had therefore joined two
of the better clubs and acquired new lodging. While he had
previously had excessive gaming debts, he was clear of them
now. It was rumored that formerly he had been a little
rougher in collecting debts owed to him than propriety would
allow, but that too seemed to be a thing of the past. While he
spoke French fluently, probably learned in the course of
trade, he had no access whatever to either the French or
English courts, and therefore was, in Calvern's estimation,
an unlikely candidate. However, the duke told the general,
he would certainly keep a watch on him.

Calvern had glanced up from his desk, his face drawn with
the thoughtfulness and worry of his task, and suddenly
smiled. He had spied Michelle, skirts lifted, her thick hair
tumbling in the sunlight, running as fast as any schoolgirl.
She was so free and happy, far beyond the unfortunate circumstances of four weeks ago.

Then the duke spotted Michelle's quarry. He recognized

clearly how handsome Sanderson looked in his summer trousers and boating jacket. From the height of his second-story study, he could see clearly into the maze; and when he saw Sanderson kiss Michelle, he stabbed the quill into the paper and broke the point. Involuntarily, despite his suffering, his eyes followed the couple as they entered the library door on the projecting wing of the house. Michelle had pitched forward, over what he could not see, but the look of besotted longing on Sanderson's face as he caught her reminded Calvern of nothing so much as his own feeling.

Damn the price of honor! thought Calvern.

For the honor of his country, he was examining and, however justly, perhaps condemning, old friends. For his honor as a guardian, he was losing the first woman whom he had ever profoundly loved.

He got up, concealed the papers, and roared to a footman to have the grooms bring around his most spirited steed.

Perhaps he could outride the torment.

An hour and a half later, a lathered horse and dusty rider returned to the stables. The duke had made his decision; how to put it into effect, he would think of tonight.

Down at a window in the far end of the library, one of the subjects of the duke's contemplation also contemplated Michelle and Sanderson. John Sharkley stood, shaking his head and muttering to himself, "Roland was right. She *is* just a toy of the *ton.*"

For almost a week after his attendance at the *début,* Sharkley, taciturn and sullen, had said nothing about the evening, but Roland was patient; he knew when his master had healed enough, he would talk.

Furthermore, he had heard by the networks of gentlemen's gentlemen that Malfet had been bodily heaved out of the Cresswell house for some approach to Michelle, but that she had reappeared and had gaily danced the evening out. Awkward, thought Roland, for his master to witness the prime client for whom they took black market goods into France, and to whom they sold most of the contraband goods returning, heaved out of both the Cresswells' house and respectability.

Five days later, Sharkley talked.

It was sparked by a personally written note from the Duke of Calvern, his crest in heavy black heading the page, thanking him for his most considerate service and prompt action on behalf of Michelle. Would he, therefore, do the duke the honor of joining a small house party on his estate two weeks hence?

Sharkley exploded. What did the high and mighty Duke of Calvern think he was, a servant? First, after the considerable expense and effort, he had not had a chance—not even a hope—of leading Michelle in the first waltz, or into supper, or in the closing dance. No, that had been given to family intimates well before. And she had flirted outrageously with at least three men before he danced with her—and by flirt, he meant beyond all bounds, for the like of the waltz she did with Count von Reichertz had never been seen. No, the count didn't hold her too closely—he just *dominated* her, Sharkley said in answer to Roland's request for details. She, who had flirted so, had the *temerity* to look *surprised* when he, the son of a baronet and as well established as any of them (here Roland controlled his smile), had asked if he might call on her.

And it had been Sharkley's alertness that had single-handedly saved Michelle from both a violation and beating at the hand of that monster Malfet. No, of course he had not let Malfet see him—Sharkley was no fool, to bite the hand that fed him. And what thanks did he get for this alertness? When Michelle came downstairs again, did she come for the final waltz to the arms of the hero who had saved her? No, indeed, her guardian, her guardian of all people, who could share her company every day at will, had usurped his, Sharkley's dance, without even a by-your-leave, and held her all to himself.

"An 'ero you are, sir, a real 'ero; an honorable gentleman of the old school, sir, if I do say so myself, and it is a privilege to serve you," said the masterful Roland as he placed a steaming bowl of beef stew in front of Sharkley, who harrumphed and demurred, but inside himself couldn't help agreeing fully with his astute servant.

As he watched his master ease into the warm glow of flattery and a good meal, Roland began to arm Black Jack for the attack. He had recognized that even now, his master would never hurt Michelle directly, so Roland simply removed her from the target.

"I wouldn't be too 'ard on the chit, sir. She didn't mean to 'urt your feelings by being surprised, sir, at you as a person; in fact, she probably finds you 'andsome and likes you as well as any."

Sharkley silently concurred.

"It's just that she has been brought up to be a toy of the

ton, sir, a simple toy of the *ton*, to be sold in 'er Season to the 'ighest bidder, and she knows you ain't got the stakes to be in 'er auction, sir, and all of 'er callers 'ave to 'ave the stakes. That's why the chit was surprised, sir, no dislike of you at all."

"Roland, that is a very crude way of putting it," said Sharkley, genuine shock in his voice.

"No cruder than the facts themselves, sir. Why, you yourself said a count, an earl, and the duke 'imself, sir, were *bidding* for her 'and. And you ain't playin' at that table yet, sir, not yet," he added gently, then was quiet for a few moments.

Roland's harsh vocabulary had, indeed, helped Black Jack to see the truth.

"The question is, sir, the toffs themselves. As I sees it, the duke and 'is company owe a good bit more than a week in the country to a gentleman wot is a genuine hero and 'as offered them invaluable service on several occasions."

Sharkley couldn't agree more.

"I was thinkin' there might be a way we can get the money wot the toffs *owe* you as a debt of gratitude, and get Michelle to be fonder still of you. We know the lady in question 'as little money of 'er own, so any money we gets from 'er has to come from her guardian or 'er 'usband, as the case may be."

"I don't want any money from Michelle," said his master sharply.

"Of course not, sir," said Roland, smiling. "That's the 'ole point. She hasn't got any of 'er own for us to take, so it 'as to come from 'er keepers."

"Please don't use the word 'keepers' where Michelle is concerned. It makes her sound like a courtesan."

Roland was smart enough not to score his point with the ready answer to that one.

"As I was sayin', sir, why don't we offer Michelle your services? We'll say we've 'found' Varennes, 'er young man in France, 'ho's not in the bidding either, it appears, and bring back letters from him—real artful forgeries. Nice, nuzzling ones." Roland grinned. "Only, in every letter, 'e'll be just a bit short of money, too short for 'is own safety, and she'll send it back to 'im via you, and we'll keep both the letters and the lolly."

Sharkley sniffed, but let Roland continue.

"And Michelle will think you are the king's crown, because you are keepin' 'er in touch with 'er lover."

Sharkley could follow that, but there was one difficulty. "How can we have letters from de Varennes forged? We have his seal, but not one manuscript to have the forger copy from."

"Now, sir, 'ave you ever known Roland to make a suggestion 'e can't follow through on? I paid the bloke as was the innkeeper at Ostend for the page from the ledger where de Varennes 'ad signed. A while ago I nipped over to our favorite friend in Carnaby Street, and 'e wrote a letter right then. He said 'e could write any number of letters from this page, because it gave samples of the man's 'ole alphabet but six letters, and 'e said 'e could deduce those."

Sharkley beamed with satisfaction. "Why didn't you tell me what you had done?"

"Because, sir, you was *in love.*" Roland couldn't erase all the scorn from his voice.

Sharkley blushed, thought a little, and then said, "I guess blackmailing Michelle for the forged will making the duke her guardian is a little too rough." He was a little perturbed at his own disloyalty to her in even mentioning it.

"And not all that quick-witted, sir. Not only would she 'ate you, sir, but if the duke disowns her, she 'as no way to the duke's pocket, no dowry, no rich 'usband, and no money for letters."

Sharkley no longer saw the duke's holiday as an insult, but as an opportunity to gain his rightful benefits and acknowledgment of service from the *ton.* He would write to the duke, accepting with pleasure the honor of the invitation bestowed upon him. Then he would speak with Michelle, who very soon would be in frequent contact with this de Varennes.

"As I've said before, my good man, you are worth your weight in gold."

"As I've said before, sir, I'd take it in pence."

They both grinned, glad to be back in the trade.

Sharkley stood now, at the far end of the library, with a twist of a wry, dispassionate smile on his face, shaking his head and saying, "A toy of the *ton.*"

Later that afternoon, he asked Michelle to join him in a walk by the river. She was pleased to go, for she somewhat enjoyed the company of her faithful friend.

Neither of them noticed that behind them, a trusted footman of Calvern's was walking Lady Deirdre's pug. His instructions had been to follow the couple discreetly, and match their pace. "Even" (to quote the duke) "if it meant carrying the animal on its walk."

"Michelle, I have a message for you," said Sharkley. "When my man was in France a fortnight ago, he encountered Monsieur de Varennes—"

The girl whirled from Sharkley's side to face him. "Oh, sir, how is he?" Michelle's face was shining with joy.

"Very well, by his looks, said my man, who also told him that we had returned his purse to you. He was most pleased, for he had thought he lost it outright. When he heard that I see you with some frequency, my lady, he was delighted, and asked if we might deliver letters from him outright."

Suddenly Michelle felt weak with shock; her throat became tight and dry. Richard had told her he would never contact her directly. Some extreme danger or need must have forced him to break this safeguard, and she must both protect him and respond. The girl looked uneasily around her and said in a suddenly quieter voice, "I must implore you, sir, never to speak of him to me in public, or give me communications from him where we might be seen."

She was tense with anxiety for Richard's safety, but Sharkley, as cynical now as he had been idealistic earlier, recognized a woman scheming to protect her would-be lover.

"My English friends have been most kind to me during this wretched war," she continued, "but if it were known I communicated regularly with a Frenchman, the action might be seriously misinterpreted."

Novel excuse, thought Sharkley. "The safety of my lady and her friend are paramount; this secret will not be drawn from me, though I be racked."

Michelle's eyes glinted with humor at Sharkley's medieval term. "Once again, you have been my most true and perfect knight, Mr. Sharkley." On the impulse of her happiness, Michelle rose on tiptoe and kissed him on the cheek, and for a minute, Sharkley felt intensely ashamed.

The footman, not close enough to hear, saw nothing untoward, and although he smirked at the light kiss, he reported only the uneventful nature of the walk.

10

MICHELLE WAS NOT the only queen playing on the romantic chessboard of Holton House's rolling green lawns that week.

Hidden from the house by a bend in the riverbank, on a high, grassy knoll beside a still pool, sat Emma, easel in front of her, sketching three water lilies arranged neatly, roots, leaves, and flowers, beside her. Sir William, easy in his new boots made of rubber that fitted well up to his strong thighs, looked particularly handsome, she mused, glancing up from copying the plants.

Dear William had gone to such trouble to have those boots made, she thought. When he had learned that Wellington had had rubber boots made for going into battle, he had written the War Office and asked which boot maker the general had used. Some headquarters officers had raved that nothing surpassed the well-greased and polished leathers, but good field officers and men had spent too many cold nights with socks literally frozen to their feet not to like Old Hawk-Nose's innovation. Yet those rubber boots were hard to obtain. The boot maker, when he had heard Osgood's request for over-the-knee ones so he could gather plants from pools and streams, thought he really had a strange one here, but that was what he had thought of Wellington at first, and look what that had done for his trade! He therefore obliged Osgood, and the "waders" fit beautifully.

Emma glanced up at William and saw him striding toward her with a fourth species of lily for her to copy, but some expression on his face made her lift her easel to one side, remove her wide-brimmed sunbonnet, and rise.

"Emma," he said.

"Yes, William." Her voice was soft with a smile.

"You know I love you very, very much, don't you?" he said earnestly from a ten-foot distance, a dripping water lily in his hand.

"Of course." Her pleasure at his words showed in her radiant face.

He came closer and dropped the lily. "You do love me, don't you?" he said, his voice husky, almost daring to make it a statement instead of a question.

She heard his tone, and her eyes shone. He had already come to have confidence in her love! "As much as you do me, William."

He reached for her, and she ran to his arms. He crushed her to him, and she could feel his strong, lean thighs, the dampness from his waders marking her muslin dress and petticoats where they pressed.

He cupped his hand under her chin and raised her shining face. "May I speak to your father?"

"Of course, William, and if you do not kiss me this minute, I will have him cite you as a national traitor."

And William kissed her, as a woman ought to be kissed when she has just been betrothed. She felt for the first time the opening floodgates of the passion of a sensitive, intelligent, and lonely man experiencing the reality of a woman who knows him for his very self, and takes delight in him.

He drew his mouth from hers, looked long into her eyes, and smiled. "Emma, I love you so much I believe I would buy a commission in the army if the general made it a condition of our marriage."

She laid a slender finger across his lips. "Sh-sh, my love. Do not even whisper such a thing. Father just might think it a capital idea."

The following day after dinner, when the ladies left the gentlemen to their port and adjourned to the withdrawing room, Lady Deirdre announced that the previous afternoon, Sir William had ridden to London to ask her father for Emma's hand, and the general had been delighted to approve their betrothal.

The room burst into a flurry of best wishes, whens and hows, offers of betrothal parties, wedding stories about torn trains and nervous flower girls.

"When is the wedding?"

Emma laughed. "In late November or Christmas, when the flower-gathering season is over."

"Will you take a wedding trip?"

"William did want to follow the Danube through Austria and Hungary, but seeing as the war is still on, we will probably go down to Devon."

In a rare minute when there was a small lull in the festivities, Michelle came over to Emma and took both her hands. Michelle's eyes were glistening with tears.

"It is so perfect, Emma. You two are parts of a greater whole."

Emma looked intently at Michelle. "It was your insight into my art and your love of people that brought us both together." The two young women stood silently for a moment, honoring their friendship as well as the engagement.

The party increased in swirling delight and chatter. When the men finally did join the ladies, the musical entertainment and games of cards were enlivened with the news, and the evening continued to be a festive celebration of laughter and new love.

That night, as Jane brushed Michelle's hair, she noticed her mistress's sad eyes.

"What troubles my girl?" the old nurse asked in her direct manner.

"For Emma and William, it has all been so straightforward and easy."

"Sometimes, my pet," said Jane, weaving Michelle's hair into its long night braid, "things may not be exactly as they seem. Why don't you ask Emma about the path of their courtship? She understands your situation, and may enjoy sharing her story with someone she loves and trusts."

"Come in!"

Michelle entered Emma's room, suddenly shy. "I . . . I just came to wish you happiness again."

Emma, who was rapidly developing the same insightful nature as her mother, quickly divined Michelle's true purpose.

"So you came to hear the parts that could not be said even in the drawing room, my dear minx. Of course, you and Mama are the only ones to whom I would ever tell all—well, almost all. We shall have the most delicious coze." She climbed up on the high, canopied bed, wrapped her arms around her knees, and patted for her friend to sit on the spot beside her. "So ask away."

"You have loved Sir William from the beginning."

Emma smiled. "You knew that already."

"And Sir William loved you from the first."

"I'm beginning to believe that is very probably so."

"So you both just very easily came together."

Emma chuckled. "Does it appear that way? How appearances can deceive."

Michelle's eyebrows rose.

Emma answered Michelle's astonishment. "You ninny-hammer! It is when two people love each other so much that it becomes more difficult to come together. Each is so convinced that they are not worth the beloved's love.

"First, William seriously believed that no woman could love a scholar who was consumingly interested in his subject. I really did like him and wanted to share his world, so I asked to borrow some books. How I would surprise my old governess, who thought I was a feather-top! Believe me, I have learned more Latin nomenclature for plants in the last eight weeks than I ever dreamed existed. I have studied the differences between species, and followed William's maps of where they were found. Do you know what William thought? That I loved botany, but couldn't possibly love him!"

The two girls giggled.

"Then what did you do?"

Emma became thoughtful. "At first I worked even harder, hoping against hope he would understand. He didn't. Then I tried showing him I wanted him for himself, for his presence alone, by arranging to have him asked to accompany me to any number of places, most with no botanical interest. Do you know what happened? At first, simply because he loved me and wanted to be with me, he came to events that held no attraction for him, but after several weeks he became moody, because he really wanted to be out collecting, at least part of the time."

"I never thought that shared love could be such a wit-puzzle," said Michelle, intrigued by the revelation.

"It was one I could not solve, so I went to Mama. Do you know what she advised? That I tell Sir William the truth—directly, in very particular terms, with only as much delicacy as did not prevent his understanding."

Michelle was shocked. "Wasn't that immodest?"

"That was my complaint to Mama. She said that the real

vanity was in hiding my true feelings in empty phrases, and that the true heart has its own modesty. It would not be at all immodest for me to tell my beloved of my own feelings if I did not presume to suggest his response."

"What did you say to him?"

"That I had only recently come to see my embroidery as an art—that you taught me," said Emma, squeezing Michelle's hand, "and that I could just as easily have chosen to design rich patterns modeled on the Persian or Chinese art you had shown me. Instead, I told him, I made designs of flowers because it brought me into his company, and that is where I wanted to be."

Even now, Emma flushed a little at her own boldness, and Michelle marveled at her friend's courage.

"What did he say?"

"He looked at me silently, quite strangely at first, as if he did not believe what he had heard. He said nothing at all that night. I came home and cried. Mama said that if he never proposed, even if I married another, I would never regret that, by having told him truly of my feelings, I had given him the occasion to speak for me."

Emma stopped and looked directly at Michelle. "I spoke with him three days ago. He proposed yesterday."

The candles in Michelle's bedchamber did not go out until well past midnight. She sat curled upon a cushion on her windowsill, thoughtfully contemplating as wisps of clouds concealed and then revealed the moon, like some teasing courtesan. Was it necessary for a woman, like the playful moon, to practice the seductive arts and then wait to be "chosen" in the marriage mart? Or was Lady Deirdre right in saying the true heart had its own modesty, and could reveal its feelings without shame?

The essence of the matter, Michelle thought, was to know those feelings.

For her, only three suitors were even to be considered—Lord Sanderson, Count von Reichertz, and her guardian, the duke. The lord and the count, she was just coming to know. To be just, they both were fine gentlemen, and she already had a fair inkling of what life with either of them would be like.

Robert Sanderson was a man who loved his soil and his people beyond measure; it was in his very bones. Her home, for a good part of the year, would be in the rainy, misty highlands, with short stays at his abode in Edinburgh, and at his house in London while the House of Lords sat. She knew without question that his wife and the "bairns," as he called them (Jane had translated that one for her), would be at the center of his private life, as his people were at the center of his public one. But he was not wealthy—those wild and craggy hills were not paved with gold; and so they would not be able to travel much. He would also want his bairns to stay in the highlands, and come to love them as he did.

She would be deeply cherished, she knew, but her European side, her flourishing languages and art, would die. She smiled to herself: what Ninette thought of Scottish fashion would not bear repeating in gentle company.

Ah! With the dashing von Reichertz her life would be another matter. Calvern had said he might well be one of the ten or twenty great diplomats of his age. Without a doubt, the count would become Austria's ambassador to major capitals—perhaps even her beloved Paris. She would be invaluable to him, she knew, for he relished her grace, elegance, stylish dress. He was very wealthy.

But she had been disturbed by a small incident between them.

Only a few days after the strain of her *début*, he had escorted her to a card party in the elegant lodgings of the Duchess of Oldenburg, a sister of the czar's, who was visiting London. After two hours in the heat, and the frantically earnest games of piquet, Michelle had felt drained, almost weak, and asked to be taken home. Count von Reichertz had stared at her for a few seconds and said gruffly that he had already arranged a game for her with her friend, the head of the Russian legation, and could she possibly find out for him how the Russian personally felt about the Prussian possession of Saxony? Such information was not confidential, and easily available from other sources. Nonetheless, for von Reichertz, Michelle was another piece, however "personally dear," in the chess game of his court intrigues; her fragile well-being had been of lesser importance.

As for a family, "his" children, he said, would remain with his excellent staff at the *schloss* while he and his wife fulfilled their state missions in other lands, a pattern his parents had followed, although during confinements and for the first six months after birth, he said, his very devoted mother had insisted on staying with the babes at home.

In those words, Michelle heard the agony of a tender woman who did not have the opportunity to give her mothering heart full play. It was sad. Michelle, so close to her father and brother, and so hungry for a secure and happy family of her own, gave a small, involuntary shudder.

Ah! Then she came to ponder her dear Edward.

On one hand, Michelle felt so complete with the duke, as if all her abilities—the languages, the cultures, the traveling, her flair for the arts and fashion—fitted into his diplomatic world. For him, she knew she could be that highly irregular, many-sided piece of a puzzle that, when it is finally recognized and played, brings the picture into its whole meaning. Together, they could bring so much to England's diplomacy.

Yet his interest in foreign affairs was balanced by his love of family. Look at the care and expense he undertook to provide outstanding cavalry steeds for his brother, Tom, so he would be safer in battle. Even now, when Michelle seemed to not be "his love," but only his ward, he had cherished and safeguarded her.

True, when Michelle had first met him, Calvern seemed a little too serious, almost lonely in his concern for his family, his estate, his country. Emma had said that the seriousness had come from assuming the dukedom at such a young age, which was probably so.

Yet the picture had changed as Michelle had come closer to him. Edward clearly had a wicked sense of humor—she remembered the mischievous gleam in his eye with which he had encouraged her waltz with von Reichertz at her come-out, and his enjoyment of the ensuing titillation of the *ton*. His gentle wit when she fainted during his kiss was a special memory. At that moment she could have died a thousand deaths, but with one humorous twist he took the responsibility on himself—'A little overwhelming, was I?'—and deflected the embarrassment. He then went on to accept the gift of the Leonardo drawing—a bond of their relationship.

The kiss itself? Surely it had not lied?

She could never believe it had!

Michelle's mullioned window was open. The frogs were booming heavily in the still, sweet air, and she thought deeply for yet another hour into the night.

Then it all became clear.

With the count, her superficial self, the spectacular, public beauty, would be satisfied—at the price of killing her deepest desires. Despite the more limited means, and life in the misty highlands of Scotland instead of Europe, she would prefer to be cherished by compassionate, insightful Lord Sanderson. Indeed, she knew now that she could come to love him, as many women in arranged marriages come to be devoted to caring husbands who have won their wives' respect.

But Edward—Edward, she knew in the depths of her being, could be her *grande passion*. Would she accept the duke's withdrawal without even trying to rekindle their first attraction?

What Emma said was true. The heart's desire had to be actively sought, not merely waited for. Had not her own mama chosen to leave her family and England, and follow her indigent, passionate count to a strange country? Jane said that even in the hours before her death, her mother had had no regrets, and murmured yet again that her short life had been one of joy and fulfillment.

As at Kew, at the thought of her mama, Michelle's cheeks were wet. This time, though, it was different; she did not think of her with the unsatisfied longing of a confused daughter. In this moment, when she understood that she had to risk much to gain her beloved, she recognized in her own soul that she shared the remarkable strength of her mother's love and passion and courage.

She was her mother's daughter and would do what she must.

Edward Calvern's world was international diplomacy. She would enter it, she would share it, and she would make known to him her desires.

Michelle turned, and the moon shone a bright, clear path to her bed.

As the duke strode into the sunlit breakfast room after his early morning ride, he was surprised, and more than a little delighted, to see Michelle there. She looked as fresh as the morning itself in her flowered pink muslin with a deeper rose jacket, one small pink rose in her dark hair.

"I am rarely joined by anyone but Sir William at this early hour, for you gentlewomen usually take breakfast in your rooms," he said teasingly. "To what do I owe this honor?"

Michelle shrugged lightly. "The sunlight pouring through my window was go glorious, how could I lie abed? The rose garden beyond the maze was still covered with dew and so heavy with scent. The housekeeper has allowed me to arrange some of today's bouquets."

She beckoned toward several large silver vases on a sideboard, filled with roses and daisies. The stiff formality of five or six select blooms had vanished; the arrangements were profuse and rich. He nodded appreciatively at them.

Turning to look at her open, welcoming gaze, he knew how right was the decision he had made on yesterday's ride. When he had arranged to give Michelle the opportunity to be courted by others, he had expected them to give her time to come to know society, and them, quite well. Instead, the suitors were snapping at his heels, eager to capture Michelle immediately. Von Reichertz had already asked twice for permission to ask for her hand; and although Sanderson did not pressure directly, from what Calvern saw yesterday, he knew the lord was not far behind. The duke had surrendered much to others in the name of fairness. Now it was his turn.

Looking at her fresh loveliness, his desire for her became so intense, he felt it must inevitably show. The invitation he had planned seemed mundane, yet it was important to him that she understand what the estate of Holton House meant to him.

"After breakfast, would you like to ride with me to check the farms on the south side of the estate? On the way, there are some lovely meadows by the river where we could picnic, if you too have got the Osgood passion for flower hunting."

"I should love to, but I do not ride well enough, I'm afraid. There was little opportunity in all my travels with Father."

True enough, Calvern thought, and seized the second opportunity presented—it would give him daily contact with her. "I have several very gentle mares in my stables here. I'd be delighted if you would allow me the pleasure of teaching you."

"You like to ride so vigorously, for I saw you both yesterday and this morning. I would simply be a hindrance, for I would be terrified at anything more brisk than a walk." She blushed at her admission.

The duke saw her embarrassment and was moved. It was not easy for anyone to confess a deficiency; yet she did so, in order that his enjoyment not be stifled.

"To tell you the truth, I am relieved. Then my fastest horses are safe from your poaching, at least for now. Do say you will allow me to teach you."

His smile was warm and encouraging. Once again he had done it—made her feel comfortable with her inexperience. Her heart jumped a little: he was inviting her into his world first, but she, too, had something to offer.

"Only if you will allow the opportunity of doing something in exchange. Do you remember telling me that you rarely have the time to read the international newspapers as you should? I used to read them for my father, and summarize articles that would interest him. May I do the same for you?"

It was a most unusual offer. The task was performed by secretaries at the Foreign Office, and none too well at that, and it would allow her a sense of contributing.

"I am surprised by your interest in such a dull task, but I would be pleased to have it done, I can tell you."

In order to allow Calvern his "most vigorous rides" before breakfast, they settled on time together in the library before luncheon, in which the duke and Michelle would read the international newspapers together, followed by short riding lessons through the estate later in the afternoon. Calvern surprised himself in accepting the agreement; he had never before consented to share his diplomatic work with anyone.

Michelle was well aware of the significance of his assent, yet she had one other demand concerning the riding. "Please, Edward, do make sure that my horse is not merely pretty, but is also so very old and fat, she could not possibly gallop."

The duke laughed and, that afternoon in the stables, showed her a dappled mare that satisfied only her first criterion, yet was so docile and well-mannered, it won her confidence.

"Then, Edward, I accept your offer of the riding lessons with pleasure." She smiled shyly, aware that, in accordance with her decision made in the moonlight of the previous night, she had addressed him by his first name, as he had invited her to do the night of the kiss. She risked glancing into his eyes, searching for any sign of displeasure. He had read her glance precisely, and his responding smile was one of amused delight.

Their rides promised to be interesting.

11

SOMETIMES THE GODS in their charity will grant specially chosen lovers a moment in which they stand revealed to each other in peace and intense joy before the coming storm; it is the lovers' belief in the reality and significance of that shining moment that holds them through the sweeps of trial and disaster.

Edward and Michelle were granted one such week.

Calvern had not realized how much he was looking forward to meeting Michelle in the breakfast room until he had to reckon with his intense disappointment when she was not there. However, he recognized the originality of the artful bouquets, and slipped into his crested silver napkin ring at his customary table place was a small note: "I am already in the library," signed with a humorous sketch of a very small lady behind a very large newspaper.

Off the library was Calvern's private reading room. He normally kept it locked, for it contained current issues of newspapers from across Europe, and he did not want guests wandering off with important copies before he himself had read them. Yesterday he had volunteered to share this inner sanctum with Michelle, and had given her the only other key. This morning, according to both Calvern's and Jane's explicit instruction, she had meticulously observed the rules of propriety and left the reading room door slightly ajar. The duke paused at the threshold to enjoy the sight of the slight figure at the kidney-shaped desk.

Michelle's hair was arranged in a classic raven-black chignon at the base of her neck. Her simple lavender dress, high-collared and lace-trimmed, might almost have been referred to as maidenly. She turned to look at Calvern: the flawless match of the dress's color with her eyes made them appear even larger. The soft pink rosebuds in her hair and at her throat were only slightly darker than the flush of her cheeks and her smile-curved lips. Seductive innocence, he thought; Gainsborough, were he still alive, would have sold his soul to have her sit for a painting, exactly as she appeared now. He watched for several minutes, until she became aware of his presence and turned to him with a smile of genuine pleasure.

"Edward! I did not realize when I volunteered how *many* newspapers you have sent. They are fascinating. I have not seen *le Moniteur Universel* from Paris, or the *Journal de Genève* in months! The *Gibraltar Chronicle* reports all the ships passing through the straits, which is most interesting for the Peninsular War. And three London dailies—the *Morning Chronicle,* the *Morning Post;* and the *Times*—I must admit I have been enjoying the latest *on-dits* quite as much as noting the war news. There is so much to condense. Your quills are very hard and straight, but I am already on my third sharpening of this one." She pulled out a small silver penknife.

"Here, let me. You are almost down to the feathers."

As Calvern bent forward to sharpen the quill, he saw what she was writing, and was surprised. He had assumed Michelle's father allowed her to make some sort of light reference notes on current events while he was away, more to keep his daughter amused than anything. Instead, in a clear, precise hand, without the flourishes of her social handwriting, a page entitled: *Peninsular War: Vitoria: French Reports.* She covered the page shyly.

"Please don't judge my work yet—it isn't ready for formal inspection. My reports for you should be ready by Friday."

"Of course." He smiled, but it did not quell his wondering how Michelle should know to title pages exactly in the formal diplomatic manner.

Calvern had always had an aversion to chattering nuisances, and so had always worked alone. Michelle was the first person he had ever invited to share his private reading room. While he worked on estate accounts, she was intent reading and writing, the only noise the slight rustle of papers. She was so intent on her work, he had to touch her on the shoulder before she noted it was time for luncheon.

This shared arrangement might work after all, he thought, as they wended their way to the dining room.

That afternoon, the weather was still bright and cool—perfect for riding, Calvern thought as he went to the stables to saddle Michelle's horse himself. For most women, seeing the farms on the estate would have been regarded as too mundane an outing. Michelle, by contrast, appeared to be genuinely looking forward to it. She had delighted him by asking about the tenants' villages on the estate, the people's work, and the schooling of the children; she had chosen to see first the small cluster of cottages where the housewives wove their wool by hand in the old way.

By the time the duke and groom brought their steeds to the broad front steps of Holton House, Michelle had already changed and was waiting. Overnight, from the magic of Ninette's needle and a costume already made, had materialized a striking summer riding habit of royal blue, trimmed in lime green, with epaulets *à la militaire* and a matching cockade hat with a jaunty lime-green feather—an outfit Calvern found most beguiling.

While Michelle looked beguiling, her mood was not. This morning in his study she had been as bright and dazzling as the day itself; now she had grown quiet, almost anxious. As he cupped his hands for her to step up to her mount, he noticed her lips tighten, and she grew a shade paler. Even her nurse, Jane, who rarely was seen in public, was on the steps, watching. Calvern was astute at any time, but it did not take much insight to see Michelle had been badly frightened in a riding incident, and this was probably her first time on a horse since.

The duke checked Michelle's position in the sidesaddle, which until today he had always taken for granted as usual and safe seating. Now, inwardly, he cursed. How was she supposed to maintain any security of grip or control with only one leg touching the horse's flank? Correct posture in the sidesaddle forced her into a tenuous, slightly lopsided balance—dangerous practice. Calvern could only be thankful that the mare was so well trained. Even so, he would take no chances, and would ride within arm's reach of its bridle.

As they set out at a walk, Michelle's body was rigid with tension. Slowly, as the steadiness of the mare's temperament became apparent, she relaxed, and at the end of three miles she was trotting gracefully in easy rhythm with her mount.

"They say good dancers make good riders, Michelle, and

you are proving it true, although I wouldn't suggest you teach your horse to waltz just yet."

As always, Calvern knew what to say to make her feel easy, and she smiled appreciatively.

Unexpectedly, a fox cub darted across the path, and the mare shied a little. Even before Calvern could reach for the bridle, Michelle had pulled her under control and began stroking her neck. The duke looked at Michelle anxiously.

"Edward, if Lady Castlereagh could not unseat me, I assure you this mare won't, for Lady Castlereagh was a lot harder to handle."

They both laughed, and Michelle relaxed her grip. Just then, the mother fox and three other cubs flashed across the trail, directly underfoot. Calvern's stallion shied and the mare bolted, flinging Michelle backward off the saddle, but not to the ground. By sheer strength of will, she hung on to the reins and pulled herself back into the saddle just as Calvern got the mare's bridle and brought her to a halt—the whole episode had taken place within barely twenty paces.

The duke looked earnestly at Michelle, without a word. She was pale, and her breathing was ragged, but she made no move to dismount. They sat quietly on the horses for several minutes.

Suddenly Michelle felt she was ten years old again and just outside Ulm, Austria. In the distance, the cannon were firing, the now familiar throaty roar followed by a sharp crack. With each burst Prince seemed to be wilder, to go faster. Her fingers, roped through the stallion's mane, pulled forward so sharply with each jerk of his head, she thought they would break. The pain of stretching her small legs across the horse's broad back to grip his flanks made her almost cry out. She was far too small to reach the long stirrups set for her brother, but she couldn't stop pressing, despite the pain.

Dear heaven, stop the pain.

Suddenly there was silence, darkness.

When she looked up, rain dripped in her face; when she moved, brambles scratched. Dark. The sound of men's voices, speaking German, very close. Prince! Where was the stallion? Gone! The terror of being alone in this bramble thicket on a dark night was greater even than the terror of riding Prince. Her body was a living scream; no sound came from her throat.

Restlessly, Michelle's mare moved under her, and she looked up—right into Edward Calvern's intently concerned eyes. She was not ten in a forest outside Ulm; she was eighteen, here in England on Calvern's estate. She had intended to show him how adequately she could share his world, to convince him she could be his beloved as well as his ward, and she had just made the veriest fool of herself slipping off the saddle. She could feel the dull red of intense embarrassment flame through her face.

If only she could explain! But she had never dared to tell that story to anyone.

Calvern continued to watch her intently.

Immediately after she had brought the mare under control, Michelle had withdrawn from him into some private hell. She became almost unseeing, and a veil of pain shadowed her eyes almost exactly as it had at Kew, only with far greater intensity. Wave after wave of unbridled terror crossed her face. He could see her wrestling with intense panic; she was attempting to control it by sheer exertion of will and raw courage, and was succeeding.

Calvern suffered with her, but he knew too well that each heart must conquer its own fear; he could only watch.

Slowly, Michelle mastered the panic; yet she knew that if Edward looked at her with his penetrating, understanding gaze, he would demolish any self-control she had left, and she would burst into uncontrollable tears. Without risking a glance in his direction, she set off at a gentle trot.

When, without even looking at him, Michelle heeled her horse and proceeded down the trail, Calvern was caught momentarily off guard, but he cantered briskly up and rode right beside her mare's head. Half a mile down the road, well before the village, a stream sparkled through the forest glade.

"The horses are thirsty. We'll rest them for a few minutes, then allow them to drink," Calvern announced, and without so much as a by-your-leave, halted, seized the reins from Michelle, and tied both the mare and his mount to a tree at the edge of the water. As he lifted her down, he felt the trembling right through her slender body, and drew her to him.

Michelle did not even need to look up at him. The feel of the heavy lapels of his jacket, the faint odor of horse, and the forest-fresh scent of his presence were enough. His shoulders were so broad, her whole body seemed engulfed in his encircling arms, his hand caressing her back. It was like the last dance at her come-out; she was safe!

Suddenly the terror she felt, and had been reining in more

tightly than the mare itself, resurfaced, and her voice shook. "Edward, I'm so afraid."

"I know, my love."

He held her gently, closely, his hand still soothing her back. Minutes passed. Slowly, slowly, the warm reality of his presence overwhelmed her fears, and the panic slipped from her. He cupped his hand under her chin and raised her face to him.

"You have won ten medals for courage today, my pet, if you have won one. Where was the accident—in Paris?"

"In Austria, near Ulm, when I was ten." Suddenly she realized the implication of this question. "How did you know there was an accident?"

For a minute his lips twitched. Did she really imagine such anguish was invisible? Then he realized that, in fact, she had not allowed the fear to force her to dismount, and others observing less closely than he probably would not have noticed.

"Only because I am coming to know you, my love. Have I earned your trust enough for you to tell me?"

Looking up into his face, she recognized in his eyes the same compassionate look he had given her that first day, the one he always gave her. To be fair, he had more than earned her confidence, she thought, for so much had happened since then, and at every point he had safeguarded and cherished her.

And he had called her "my love" twice today!

She remembered her decision in the moonlight of two nights previous—that she should risk sharing all except facts that would endanger Richard's life. She had to venture that risk now. "In a thousand kind ways you have earned my trust, Edward."

His gaze was so insightful, she felt almost naked before it; she would have to glance away to talk. Could she tell what happened matter-of-factly enough so her terror didn't show? "It is a hard story to tell. Perhaps if we walked a little?" She slipped her small hand through his arm, and they turned to the well-worn path by the stream.

"We were going from Vienna back to Paris. Papa, Jane, and I were in the carriage; my brother was an outrider on the new stallion Papa had just bought him—part Lipizzan, 'Favory's Prince.' He was a beautiful horse."

"Your brother?"

A slight flush rose to Michelle's face; she had expected this question and even now ached to tell her trustworthy Calvern Richard's name, to talk of his bravery, his present danger. She could not; the secret was not hers to reveal. She would not call him by name and would mention him as if he were only in the past, a figure of her childhood. "My half brother, Papa's natural son by his mistress many years before he met Mama. I was ten that summer, so he must have been twenty."

Calvern cast Michelle a sidelong glance as they walked. He saw her embarrassment, and was well aware how close to the bone this story was cutting; he pressed her hand as it lay on his arm.

"We did not know it, but Austria had just engaged Napoleon's forces. We were just approaching Ulm when an Austrian cavalry regiment came charging down the way. Our coach lurched, veered off the road, and landed axle-deep in the mud.

"It was fast becoming twilight, and we could hear cannon still booming. Papa and my brother were truly worried—here we were, a party of French nationals caught behind Austrian lines. The coachman and groom we had hired in Vienna had deserted. What were we to do?

"Papa and my brother quickly unharnessed the coach horses—they were powerful, but lumbering and slow. Papa said Jane and he would use those; but he insisted that I ride with my brother on Prince, for Prince was a far faster horse and would be much harder for attackers to overtake. Jane wrapped me in one of her large cloaks against the night chill, and we set off. We were all to meet some eight miles back at a small inn we had passed just two hours earlier. Papa and Jane would stick to the main road, for the carriage horses were too large and clumsy to do else; my brother and I were to travel a small path that went in the same direction, but would probably not have as many troops on it.

"Prince was marvelous, stepping through the woods lightly and quickly. But not lightly enough, for before we had gone more than two miles down the road, three brigands or drunken soldiers—to this day I am not sure which—came from the bushes. They were waving burning bulrushes for light, and threatening my brother's life if he did not surrender Prince and 'the bit of a girl in the cloak.' I did not fully realize until we discussed it later that they had been referring to me!"

Michelle fought to keep a tremor out of her voice.

"As they pulled him off the horse, my brother deliberately spurred Prince heavily, and he bolted, with me on his back. The stirrups were much too long for me. My fingers were threaded through Prince's mane; as he charged, the branches he brushed aside with his powerful frame snapped back against me. It was dark, and he stumbled badly once; I do not know how I hung on. After minutes of clutching Prince's mane, with my knees gripping his flanks, I thought I would slide off, because I didn't have the strength to hold one second longer. The reins had fallen forward, but I dared to let one hand go to reach for them. It took three or four tries, and during that time I slipped sideways badly; then a branch rebounded."

Michelle stopped and looked straight into Calvern's eyes for a few seconds, the horror in her eyes intensifying with the memory.

"I did catch the reins, and pulled with every ounce of strength I had. I know I was ten, and not that heavy, but Prince paid not the slightest heed. For all he responded, I might have been a fly on his back, at that moment not even worth a flick of his tail."

She turned her head away from the duke and continued walking. "Just then, a musket went off nearby. It terrified me out of my wits, if I had any left. Prince reared and then bucked. What followed, I don't remember. All I know is that I woke up in a bramble bush, with water from the leaves dripping into my face, and within feet of me I heard gruff male voices—soldiers, I presume. I guess they couldn't see me in the night, wrapped in Jane's dark cloak—which had also saved me from being badly scratched by the brambles. I remember crying without making a sound, for the only thing worse than being on Prince's back was being without him altogether. Where had he—and my brother—gone?

"I was so afraid in this dark night forest, until I realized that in daylight I would be very easily seen; then I became even more terrified of the approaching dawn. I made my way down the trail, and whenever I heard voices or saw campfires, I hid in the most thorny thickets I could find. It took me that night and all the next day to make it to the inn."

Had Michelle looked up at that moment, she would have seen an expression of grave astonishment on the duke's face. The self-possession and bravery of this ten-year-old child was almost beyond belief!

"Jane was waiting at the inn for me—they had arrived at midnight the night before, having encountered not one difficulty on the main road. Papa had ridden out to find my brother and me. He was heartsick when an Austrian cavalry officer rode by, leading Prince on a tether. Not only couldn't my father claim him—a French count was not about to challenge an Austrian cavalryman behind Austrian lines—he knew from the fact that Prince was scratched and limping that both my brother and I had been thrown and most probably injured.

"When Papa returned to the inn that night, he wept when he saw that I was safe.

"Although Papa rode out for eighteen hours a day for the next two days, he couldn't find my brother. Thank God, he turned up by himself late the third night, badly beaten, with a raging fever. It was two weeks before we could risk moving him back to Paris, where he convalesced for over three months."

Michelle stopped pacing and looked directly at Calvern.

"You see, Edward, it would be grossly unfair to a beautiful stallion to characterize what happened to me as an accident, for the horse was truly well mannered. I just didn't know how to control him when he was terrified. Papa tried to get me to ride again, but I absolutely refused. Today was my first attempt."

At these last words, Calvern excused himself and strode some distance ahead of her and, leaning his forearm against a tree, looked intently upstream, away from her, and fought to regain control of himself in the most powerful turmoil of emotion he had ever felt.

This delicate, refined beauty had just described herself in the most dangerous circumstances he had ever heard of any woman being in—and she, in strict fairness, wanted to make certain he would not blame the horse for her fear! Initially, he might have been tempted to chuckle at such "justice," for what ten-year-old could control a stallion in *any* situation, but then the full horror of her predicament at Ulm overwhelmed him. She did not seem to realize, even now, what had obviously been clear to her quick-witted brother: the bloody, terrifying, bestial fate of "the bit of a girl in a cloak" had any of the brigands or soldiers captured her. The mere thought of it made his blood run cold.

But the bravery!

Certainly the duke had known that Michelle was uniquely courageous and self-possessed in social situations. How many other girls of eighteen could have handled either the intimidating first interview with Deirdre and himself, or Lady Castlereagh's interrogation, or the strain of her elaborate come-out without once resorting to nervously fluttering, fidgeting, or hysterical behavior? Her aura of distilled calm and grace aroused his desire almost more than her radiant beauty.

But far beyond social courage, thought Calvern, this seemingly fragile creature had just revealed she had, as a child, made her way through miles of enemy battle lines to a safe refuge. He knew regimental commanders who would have paled at the mere thought of having to accomplish such a thing.

The duke was deeply angry with himself: had he only known of the profundity of Michelle's bravery before they set out, he would have read her pale, drawn face as much more than simple nervousness, and she would never have had to confront the terror of this afternoon's ride. He would have moved heaven and earth for her not to relive that horror.

Then his agitation turned to Michelle herself. He had done everything, said everything, to encourage her to confide in him. Why had she not told him the story before they mounted? Surely she had discovered by now he would never hurt her, always cherish her? Had he somehow failed in communicating his concern and trustworthiness?

Michelle stared at Calvern in surprise as he strode away from her. He was pacing back and forth now, at some distance from her, obviously deep in disturbing thought.

What had she done to upset him?

He had begged her to tell him about the "accident"—and she had told him the complete and total truth. Even though life with Lady Deirdre and Emma had made her realize that she was somewhat socially naive, she had been well aware, long before she arrived in London, that people often viewed with outrage and alarm even the smallest "adventures" she had had with her father. They obviously found her upbringing unorthodox. She had never before trusted anyone with the story of Ulm; could the Duke be among those who were embarrassed and shocked by her experiences? Yet the once or twice when she had glanced sidelong at him during the telling, he did not seem to be particularly annoyed; in fact, the familiar, compassionate lines were around his eyes and mouth.

The riding! That was it! That was why he was pacing.

How infuriated such a skilled horseman as he must be when she could not even control so gentle a mare as her present mount. What a dolt Calvern must think her! Here she was going to impress the duke with her competence to share his world, and look how incapable she must look! Tears filled her eyes at the humiliation.

But she loved him.

She was not sure if he returned the sentiment—but he *had* called her "my love" several times just today. Yet again, she harkened back to the decision she had made in the moonlight. She would ask his help with her riding. If he loved her, he would oblige; if not—well, she would cross that bridge when she came to it.

Had Calvern been not so engrossed in his own thoughts, he would have seen Michelle coming to him with straightened shoulders and deliberate calm.

Suddenly a small, clear voice spoke at his side. "I apologize if my timidity upset you. It is just that when the mare reared, it began to feel like that night and Prince all over again, and I lost my head."

She risked a glance to his face, and was astonished.

Fear for her safety, his agony at the terror he had unknowingly forced her to relive today—alone, unnecessarily —had wiped his face clear of every trace of aloofness, of polished self-control. His eyes blazed with outrage commingled with raw desire for her. His hands were heavy on her shoulders; he almost shook her.

"Timidity! Michelle, you little fool, you are bravery incarnate! You are absolutely terrified of horses, yet you came! But for God's sake, girl, if you had frozen with fear this afternoon, which would have been more than understandable, if you had been one iota less coolheaded, or the horse a fraction stronger, it would have thrown you, and you might be dead by now! You scared the very life out of me!

"What bullheaded pride prevented you from telling me, of all people, that you were afraid and why? Am I that fearsome? Was telling me more terrifying than going through that hell of today's ride alone?"

Suddenly she understood. He was angry because she had failed to share her fear.

"I had never spoken about Ulm to anyone. With you it didn't seem necessary. You were with me, and that was quite enough to give me the courage to try."

He grasped the significance of her comment, yet he could not help wondering if she understood it as fully. Was his mere presence, indeed, enough to give her such courage?

Suddenly, buoyant with hope, his intense longing for her surged, overwhelming his outrage. He tilted Michelle's head back and kissed her full on the lips with all the fire and passion he had held in restraint for weeks. No teasing, controlling, artful lover, this. He swept her along in untempered passion, not caring when her hat fell off and her heavy locks tumbled down her back. Her eyes, her cheeks, her ears, were covered with fast, tempestuous kisses. He sought her mouth and dominated it in seconds. She could not have stopped him had she wished, but she did not want to. She yielded, impelled unthinkingly by the flood of desire he aroused in her. She was pressed against the hard line of his body and felt his impassioned breathing, the strength of his thighs against her.

At first she was surprised by the intensity of his passion, then her own desire rose and crested. His touch, his scent, the wild urgency in his kisses, broke through any shard of self-control she had left. She wanted him, she wanted his kisses now, as she had wanted nothing else in her life, only this. Where seconds before he had been seeking her, now she sought him, her hands in his hair drawing him down to her even more closely. His warm, demanding mouth drew a fiery line from her lips to the base of her throat, covering the wild flutter of her pulse there, and she heard a strange, soft, wild moan, not recognizing it as her own, then again.

The second time, the sound penetrated.

Calvern drew up and, gently grasping the hair at the nape of her neck, eased her back to look into her face. Her dark hair tumbled about it in a rich baroque frame, emphasizing even more the delicacy of her small, straight nose and high cheekbones. Her lips were red from the pressure of his kisses, and slightly parted; her cheeks were flushed. But it was her eyes: half-open, shaded by the heavy lashes—they were so dark, they seemed almost black. The length of her slender body was languid, warm against him. Another move on her part, and he knew he would tumble with her into an abyss of delight that would create a hell for them both.

"Michelle." He said her name, and it hung sharply on the air. Slowly, she focused.

With a swish, he picked her up so lightly, she might have been a child; and placed her on sun-warm rocks forming a natural seat on the bank of the stream. He retrieved her cockaded bonnet, handed it to her, then began to pace again.

She watched him, still, wide-eyed. The heat of his kisses lingered on her skin.

He loved her!

Or did he? Did the pacing indicate he regretted his passion?

"Michelle, you *know* I am fond of you."

After such a whirlwind, he said he was *fond* of her? These English! Where was the declaration of passion?

She must have been holding her breath, for she suddenly sighed, "I had hoped so!" but her voice was taut and subdued.

He was surprised by the flatness of her response, and hurried to explain. "Don't you see, my love? I am your guardian, and must not allow the prerogatives of my position to usurp your choice for greater happiness with another, should you choose."

What was this—these formal, hard words? He loved her, but was prepared to give her to another?

Michelle's cheeks flamed in anger. By contrast, she thought, Sanderson certainly would brook no others approaching her—he simply crowded them out; and if looks and words could kill, von Reichertz could regularly be charged with murder of any other man even contemplating courting Michelle.

Suddenly she realized that neither Sanderson nor von Reichertz seemed to regard Calvern as competition. Had Edward said he was "fond" of her merely to make his lovemaking acceptable? She closed her eyes against the horror of the thought.

Calvern stopped in front of her; he saw her closed eyes and the tight, worried anger of her mouth. "Michelle, look at me."

She opened her eyes. He had stooped almost to her height; his eyes were filled with gentle humor.

"My precious ninnyhammer! Your face reminded me of a child braced to surrender a favorite toy. Do not misunderstand me, my love. I said simply that I would not abuse my prerogatives as guardian. I mean that I will not, because of our almost daily contact, use every minute available to us to pressure you to be mine. You have every right to reject me as your lover, and still come to me, freely, respected, cherished for as long as you will, as my ward. Nor will I ever actively impede the approaches of any honorable, suitable gentleman you should wish to see.

"I had hoped you would have more time just to grow a little into the ways of the world, but I am well aware that others are pressing. Sanderson, as you know full well, is besotted with you, and von Reichertz has offered that, where you are concerned, French blood would enrich, rather than sully, his family line—no mean admission from that one."

Michelle blushed heavily, but did not say a word.

Edward stepped back a little and, seeing her embarrassment, continued more moderately. "As for you and me, I have a campaign planned that would do the general or Lady Deirdre proud. The first phase of attack is to have you come to love Holton House itself, and one of the people to help you do that is Emily Sopwith. Her handwoven yard cloth is famous all over the shire. I'm sure Ninette will be inspired to even greater designs when she sees Mrs. Sopwith's work. When I was a child, I used to spend hours watching her husband, the blacksmith. Knowing Emily, I expect she's prepared a magnificent tea for us, and we don't want to be late."

Without another word, he cupped his hands for Michelle to step up to her mount, and at a gentle trot they rode the short distance to the ten-house village of Holton. Michelle controlled her bruised, confused temper by deliberately concentrating on the events at hand, but surely, she thought, those kisses must be true!

Although he was expected, the duke's entry into the village did cause a commotion; Michelle was unaware the interest was heightened because this was the first time His Grace had ever brought a lady guest. Women waved from the town well, men emptied from the blacksmith shop, children crowded around.

"Michael, I do believe it is your turn," Calvern said, and in one swoop he swung one of the smallest lads up into the saddle in front of him.

Before one of the largest cottages stood an upright, rosy-cheeked woman, her dress and pinafore so starched, Michelle truly wondered if they would bend when they sat down. Calvern drew to a halt here, bowing. "Mrs. Sopwith," he murmured to Michelle. In minutes they were ensconced inside the big, sunlit cottage with Emily Sopwith, four sturdy children reduced to momentary silence by shyness, and her brawny blacksmith husband.

Michelle had learned much about village fare in her travels, and she knew she and Edward were being honored with the best. There was trifle with morning-fresh cream, fruit compote, "and raisin cake His Grace has enjoyed since he were a lad." Michelle tasted it and could only concur with Calvern that it was, without a doubt, "the best in all England."

Then came, in Michelle's eyes, the pièce de résistance. Over a large table was unrolled yard after yard of the most beautifully woven wool Michelle had ever seen. The patterns were variegated and subtle—but the most exquisite feature of all was the colors. Azure blues, mint greens, orange-rose so delicate it might have been stolen from a sunset. Michelle was astounded.

"How do you produce such work?"

From the kitchen paraded three more women. "Mrs. Smith dyes—she knows more about the colorings from roots, berries, and barks than anyone in ten villages. Mrs. Lambeth spins. I weave. Mrs. Hodge sews."

"This material is splendid. I have never seen its like anywhere in England or Europe. Where do you sell it?"

"In town, on the big market days."

Michelle looked at Calvern. "I believe there are several ladies now at Holton House who would be most delighted to see your work, and pay handsomely for it. Might it be possible to bring these bolts up to the house tomorrow?"

The women flushed with pride, and nodded.

"His Grace asked us to make something for you, mademoiselle," Mrs. Sopwith said, curtseying, and handed Michelle a package.

She opened it rapidly. "Oh, it is exquisite!" she cried, and indeed the word was no exaggeration. It was a full-length cape and hood, in subtle stripes of lavender (how had Mrs. Smith matched her eyes so exactly?), pink, and blue, lined with the finest pink silk. Michelle instantly slipped it around her shoulders; its length was perfect. "It feels so warm, yet is lighter than other wools. However can I thank you for such a treasure? I will so enjoy wearing it."

The four women fairly glowed.

After their profuse thanks and good-byes, Michelle, robed in her new cloak, and Calvern, carefully watchful, rode back to the house, silent for the first miles. The duke was savoring Michelle's response to the village people: she seemed to understand and know them instinctively. Her manner of addressing the four women had not been in the least condescending, which might have been expected in a woman of her class; it had been generous, genuinely appreciative of the talent she had discovered.

For her part, Michelle was puzzling through the day. It had been such a mixture.

She was well aware that a magnificent work such as this cloak did not appear overnight. Calvern must have ordered it weeks before—perhaps well before her come-out; further, he must have gone to great pains to get the lavender exactly the shade of her eyes. Certainly, like the pendant on the night of her come-out, it was a gift that showed great thought and attention. He seemed to express his fondness in other ways, too. Here Calvern had allowed her into his private reading room, asked for and shared her inmost secret of Ulm, and had twice kissed her in a way that made her entire being burn toward him, for him; he had even called her, however lightly, "my love."

On the other hand, he had actually said only that he was *fond* of her; he spoke of allowing others to become acquainted with her; he had clearly organized this country house party to allow her to come to know Sanderson, von Reichertz, and the others. As for their relationship, all he planned was "a campaign." Guardian or lover? She truly could not make it out. The man drove her to distraction, but she did, indeed, owe him thanks for the cloak.

Near the forest glade where they had kissed, Michelle spoke. "I think, Edward, you weave a magic charm with your gifts."

He arched a quizzical eyebrow.

"On the very day I come to confess my terrors of a black night, on a stallion, wearing a dark cloak, you not only bring me for a daylight ride on a gentle mare, but give me this glorious cloak as well, although you must have ordered it weeks ago. It is as if you had turned the fears inside out and wrapped me in a glowing rainbow."

He was pleased with her comment.

"Does this mare have a name?" Michelle asked as they neared the house.

"Only a stable name. Why? What would you like to call her?"

"Edward—do not laugh, but she is like a new hope for me. May I call her Rainbow?"

"Rainbow she is, my love."

As the duke went to his room to change for dinner, he was whistling, for he had begun to believe he would, indeed, capture the treasure at the end of his own arc in the sky.

Calvern had, in fact, succeeded in reserving most of Michelle's daylight hours of that week for himself. Only the following day, when Mrs. Sopwith arrived at Holton House with her cloth, and every lady guest in the country house party was to be found in Lady Deirdre's suite, exclaiming, holding bolts of various colors against their complexions, and ordering myriads of garments from Mrs. Sopwith's seamstress, did he lose time with Michelle.

In the afternoons, they explored the estate together. The

day he had shown her the layout of the crops had bored her a little, he knew, but even then they had taken pleasure in each other's company and shared the triumph of her leap on Rainbow over a two-foot jump in a meadow.

Her greatest enthusiasm was for the two villages of the estate. It was she who suggested having a small school for all the Holton children in a small, bright, abandoned cottage. Michelle realized how unusual it would be for all one's cottagers to be literate—but perhaps it would be useful in this modern steam age? She had put the question so beguilingly that he had, in fact, begun to give the matter earnest consideration.

Ironically, he who had been so careful of his privacy relished her company. Her morning freshness, the faint scent of rosewater, the soft rustle of papers, in no way disturbed him. She never intruded on his thoughts; in fact, at many times she seemed more absorbed than he; one day, to catch her attention for luncheon, he had kissed her on the nape of the neck.

But the work she had accomplished—there was the surprise!

On Friday morning, neatly clustered into groups, he found a pile of reports, each labeled neatly: *Peninsular War: Vitoria: English Reports, French Reports, Estimated Summary of Active Troops*—each so concise, complete, and accurate in detail, it could have been equaled only by senior men in the Foreign Office.

For fully a quarter of an hour, before Michelle came in from breakfast, Calvern sat in intense thought. It was clear that the girl had been well and painstakingly trained by a professional rapporteur—most likely her father. What was a respected art dealer, concerned that his daughter should learn art, languages, and the waltz, teaching her such a skill as this for? It was equally obvious that the father's own interest in current events went far beyond the usual if he asked for and used these reports.

On a separate page, Michelle had clipped a cartoon from a newspaper of Louis-Joseph's troops confronting Wellington's. Each leader was overlooking the devastated battlefield littered with the dead of both sides. Under the picture, Michelle had written despairingly: "Perhaps a *chess match* would have been a better idea." Calvern once again was surprised and moved by her. Most women, kept deliberately unaware for as long as possible of the actual horrors of war, were given to frenzied huzzahs and fanatic national loyalty.

This comment, by contrast, sprang from the heart of someone who had both suffered and understood the horror of real battle. Was it possible for anyone—even Michelle—to be at once so naive and so wise?

At that moment, Michelle, flustered and pleased, came through the door to show him a white angora kitten the housekeeper had just given her. "Do you like my 'diplomatic reports'?" she asked, delight on her face as the little white ball, with a purr twice the size of itself, nuzzled under her chin.

Calvern looked at her closely; it was obvious she thought the reports were normal. To ask further questions of such forthright innocence was ridiculous. For her, such skills had no possible relation to their professional use.

"They will save me hours of work, my pet, and I will try to spend that extra time with you."

She regarded him with clear, wondering eyes. His expression was tender, but where was the overt passion? There again was the dilemma: guardian or lover?

This week with Edward had been intensely pleasurable, but as his hand stroked both her cheek and the kitten, she was no nearer the answer.

As Calvern had commandeered her days, the conventions of society demanded he accord the privilege of Michelle's evenings to her suitors. John Sharkley had taken a few bets among the less intimate of Calvern's friends and senior serving staff as to who would lead the little dazzler in to dinner each night. As Roland had introduced Sharkley to Ninette some weeks ago, Black Jack had inside information, weighted the odds in his own favor, and won handsomely. Tonight it was running Sanderson, three; von Reichertz, two.

If others did not have the answers this special week, at least John Sharkley did.

12

"**I**NCREDIBLE! The arrogant rakehell!"

General Cresswell slammed his coffee cup so hard on its saucer, it splashed up onto the *Morning Post* he held.

"James! James!" he roared. "Come here; I want you to read something."

James, the Cresswells' masterful butler, was rarely roared at by anyone for anything. And never, he thought as he scurried full pelt into the breakfast room at the Cresswells' Grosvenor Square house, to *read* the general anything—and most certainly not when the general was so angry that the saber wound on his neck was scarlet.

"You called, sir?"

"You damn well know I did. Here. Read this. Tell me if I have gone mad or not."

James read. His eyes grew round. "Most unusual, sir. In fact, I might venture to call it startling."

"Then I'm not mad, eh, James?"

"No, sir. In fact, if I might venture again, sir, it would be to say the one who perpetrated this insult might well be."

"James. Right on the mark, as always. Where's my demn sleep-noddy equerry? Rouse the fool and tell him to ride to the War Office pronto and tell them I'm unavailable until further notice. Family matter. No, cancel that explanation. They'll know soon enough when they read the *Post*. Tell the chief groom to bring Warrior around for me; he can mount Old Imperial." (James's eyes grew even rounder at this, for no one but the general rode even this second-best steed.)

157

"He'll ride with me in ten minutes to Holton House. The arrogant rakehell! Hurry!"

James hurried.

Sir William Osgood was breakfasting quietly at Holton House before setting out on his early morning gatherings. He turned a page of the *Morning Post*.

"Mary, Mary!" he shouted.

The breakfast maid was so startled, she tipped the tray of breakfast china she was carrying, and a cup rolled, fell, smashed. The man had only spoken to her once before, last week, to request extra butter, and now he was yelling. "Yes, Sir William," she quavered.

"Has His Grace left on his morning ride?"

"I don't know, sir."

"Well, has he taken his morning coffee?" he demanded.

"I don't know, sir." Osgood took a step toward her, and she felt tears spring to her eyes.

"Well, count the cups on the sideboard. Is one dirty?"

Mary thought she would faint. "One, sir. Fresh dirty. It don't have sugar in it, and His Grace doesn't take sugar, at least I've never seen him do so, but once last year when Hester burned it in the kitchen and it tasted foul, but he didn't say a word, just put sugar in it, sir, but other guests com—"

"Mary, be quiet."

He took another step closer, and Mary *knew* she would faint.

"Now run and tell the butler to send a footman to tell the grooms and stable boys that His Grace is to come to me immediately in my suite the *instant* he returns from his ride. Is that clear?"

Mary nodded.

Sir Osgood studied her face for a moment. "Could you please repeat the message for me?" His tone was gentler.

"I'm to tell the groom to tell the butler to tell the footman to meet you in His Grace's suite..." But Sir William had already left to tell the butler and grooms himself, the *Post* firmly under his arm.

Calvern stood beside the sun-filled window of Osgood's room, holding the *Post*, neatly folded, in his white-knuckled hands. He stood still. He had been standing there, his hands on the same page, for the last five minutes, his eyes fixed on the same place.

Osgood wanted him to move, to flinch, to shout out.

Calvern continued to stand statuelike.

Osgood could have sworn that the sun had changed position in the sky before the duke spoke; when he did so, his face was expressionless, but the botanist suspected His Grace's cheeks were damp.

"Well, he has done it and done it in five lines, the evil-minded madman."

Sir William nodded dumbly, sharing his friend's misery.

"The bloody bastard, Osgood."

"Quite so."

"He has had his revenge on me by trapping Michelle so securely that she has no way out but to become affianced immediately."

"Quite so, Your Grace."

"But not, under any condition, to Malfet himself."

Calvern sat down at a small desk in the room and buried his face in his hands, but he did not let go. He could not, until all was solved. But the solution—the fact that Michelle, just as she was beginning to understand the *ton* and enjoy the gift of her own remarkable social grace, should be coerced by Malfet's brutal action to choose her husband within the next several days—overwhelmed him. It was forcing a bud to bloom too early.

Osgood ached in sympathy with the tall figure at the desk. Suppose it had been Emma! But in the duke he could observe no movement, no sound. Osgood marveled at the apparent calm reasoning of the suffering man in front of him. They said Calvern's brother, Tom Radcliffe, was equally cool in battle, even when injured. It must run in the family.

When the duke arose some five minutes later, he was as expressionless as before. He spoke formally, as Sir William realized he did when under greatest stress.

"Osgood, I'm calling a family council. I'll tell Lady Deirdre personally, and summon the general from London immediately. Thank you beyond measure for the discretion you have shown in bringing this matter to my attention so quickly, and in getting the newspapers out of immediate circulation in the house."

Sir William nodded.

"You, of course, as my cousin's fiancé, are soon to be a member of the immediate family, and as the handling of this matter affects the family's reputation, it affects you. Your prompt and supportive action shows that you already consider yourself one of us. Would it be presumptuous of me to ask you to assist in today's council?"

"Honored."

"The girls, of course, are not to be told until the course of action has been decided upon, and I fully believe it will affect Emma almost more quickly than it will Michelle, for Emma will understand more quickly the implications of this announcement within the *ton.*"

Osgood agreed.

"As for Michelle..." Calvern's voice stopped, and his stony face broke into an expression of such intense anger, and agony so powerful, that it made Osgood feel that maybe, after all, Malfet *would* be forced to pay his price for this.

As befitted two gentlemen who had just confirmed a remarkable degree of trust in each other, the duke bowed deeply, and the scientist returned the compliment; Calvern departed.

Lady Deirdre's maid never forgot the event, for it was the only day in her long and faithful service that her ladyship had ever requested smelling salts.

Neither Emma, Michelle, Jane, nor Ninette was given to such affectations, and the remedy had to be borrowed from a twittering laundry maid who asked, for weeks afterward, if Lady Deirdre were not "increasing."

The family council was held in the study of Calvern's suite, because of its privacy. Deirdre, of course, had never seen the room before, and as she entered on the general's arm, one glance told her why she liked her nephew by marriage so well.

Most men's private chambers, she had found (her survey had been neither large nor unchaperoned) to be cluttered with favorite old, unrepaired furniture, stuffed animal heads, two-year-old hunt schedules, and unread books on antiquities.

By contrast, here in the duke's room the paneled walls had been cleaned and polished; there were adequate bookcases placed beside the two desks, one for writing, the other, much larger, for the spreading of maps. The chairs were newly upholstered in the same mellow gold as the drapes; the lovely old Turkey carpet was in good repair. Beside the fireplace stood a small sideboard, which normally held only brandies. In preparation for today's unhappy gathering it also held a silver tea service. On the walls was not one stuffed animal head, but a small cluster of paintings of Calvern's favorite stallions by George Stubbs, a small portrait of his deceased parents, and an interesting da Vinci drawing of some sort of winged machine. As a room, thought Deirdre, it bespoke care, comfort, taste, and active interests, not unlike the man himself.

However, the duke, it was apparent, at this moment knew no comfort. Having seen Deirdre, the general, and Osgood properly seated, he relentlessly paced the hearth before them like some just-captured lion, then finally spoke.

"You know, Uncle," he said, nodding in the direction of the general, "there have been times when, because Holton House here in Surrey is so near London, we have been excessively interrupted by visitors. I was never happier, however, to be near London than to see you ride up just after luncheon. You must have departed well before my message requesting your presence reached Grosvenor Square. Thank you."

"The least I could do, lad."

"To review the facts as we know them. Malfet has inserted in three London dailies, under my name, the announcement of Michelle's engagement to himself."

"*Three* dailies!" exclaimed Deirdre.

Calvern nodded sadly.

"Do we know," said Osgood, bringing his scientific thoroughness to bear, "that it is, *indeed,* Malfet who placed the announcements?"

The general had anticipated that question. "Before I left, I instructed my private secretary to visit each newspaper office to ascertain who had placed the announcement. A rider with his report reached us moments ago. In two cases, Malfet's man was recognized as delivering it on forged Calvern stationery. The third office didn't recognize the messenger, but the stationery was the same."

"*Forged* stationery!" exclaimed Osgood. "Then, indeed, it was not just a spontaneously wrathful act, but something premeditated, and truly sinister."

"Oh, dear," said Deirdre, looking pale. "That his action was one of deliberate premeditation is precisely what Jane and I concluded this morning after you informed us, Edward."

Sir William raised a quizzical brow.

Deirdre blushed. "If you will excuse me for indelicacy, Sir William, but I believe that false modesty here sacrifices truth." She turned to Edward. "Jane pointed out that had Michelle been compromised at her ball, we would have learned, just about now, whether she was with child. That would explain to the *ton* why we supposedly have 'accepted' a suitor who was literally evicted from the house before hundreds."

"I say!" said the general.

Osgood was astounded by the viciousness of Malfet's hatred, but Calvern said he was not surprised, for he had discovered the nature of the man long ago. "It is a simple plot, expertly timed, and because it plays so well to the *ton's* delight in believing the worst, it will succeed," the duke said.

"How can it?" exclaimed Sir William. "A lovely innocent like Michelle—especially if the family issues a correction to the announcement."

The general was a little surprised at his future son-in-law's lack of understanding of the *ton*, then he charitably recalled Osgood's scholarly reclusiveness until he met Emma, and how unwitting he himself had been until he had seen society through Deirdre's insightful eyes.

Deirdre answered Osgood. "It is quite simple, really. As you know, William, in public it is *always* the girl and her family who cry off, regardless of what has happened. Quite simply, if we correct the announcement, people will assume that Michelle's family issued it to force Malfet to the mark, and he did not oblige. *That* will imply that he, an 'honorable member' of the *ton*, did not accept responsibility for her condition, and she will be doubly damned."

"But surely when no child appears . . ." protested Osgood.

"The evil minds of people will simply assume that certain steps were taken. As a result, no respectable and worthy offer of marriage will be made to her again."

Osgood looked almost sick. "When I hear this, I am ashamed of my own class."

Calvern concurred. "It is an emotion each honorable one of us has felt, my friend. In fact, it is precisely such feeling that has caused many particularly fine people to withdraw from the *ton*. We can only hope such circumstances become more rare; right now, we must save Michelle."

"Aye, there's the rub," sighed the general.

Calvern looked around the room at the pale, weary faces of his friends. "Forgive me if my preoccupation with this matter overran my duties as host. Lady Deirdre, would you care for tea?"

The proud woman roused herself from her own sad thoughts. "Edward, I believe I would prefer a small glass of sherry, if I may."

Calvern and the general looked at each other. If tea would not suffice for Deirdre, it confirmed the extent of the disaster.

As Calvern served her ladyship, he proceeded. "However, a thought occurred to me which might offer a solution. If we do not contradict the news immediately, but in five or six days time simply run the announcement with the correct name of Michelle's betrothed, headed by the newspaper's own apology for its error (they will do this, for they were wrong in accepting entries not signed by me, no matter how the paper was engraved), it seems to me the matter would be solved."

Deirdre grasped the point immediately. "Of course! And while the engagement must be announced within a week, the wedding plans could proceed at a normal pace, with no special licenses but the reading of banns in the church, which takes three weeks, and so forth. The lack of rush would quell any speculation concerning Michelle's being in a delicate condition."

"I say!" said the general, relief flooding his open countenance. "Are any of her present suitors up to the mark of betrothal?"

"Three," said Calvern.

Deirdre and Osgood looked surprised.

"I don't know that fellow von Reichertz's personal nature, but he has a fine grasp of military history," said the general.

Deirdre sniffed. "If Michelle wants that, she would be better off to retire to bed with a good book, for I believe he is a stuffed popinjay."

"A superb diplomat," cut in Calvern.

"Which, believe me, has little enough to do with the realities of marriage," said Deirdre. Even Sir William could not repress a smile. "And who else?" she demanded.

"Lord Robert Sanderson. A man I much admire personally. Holds tight to his own ethics in the face of opposition in the Lords. Abolishing slavery in the colonies is one of his interests."

There was a murmur of approval around the room.

"I've heard Michelle speak of him often. She likes and trusts the man, I think. The third suitor?" This one really piqued Deirdre's interest, for she had heard nothing from Michelle or Emma about him.

"Me," said Calvern simply, with a slight blush.

Deirdre chuckled with delight. "I must admit, Edward, you totally disarmed me. Why, I even believed you were truly interested in simply showing her Holton House all this week."

·"I was!" protested Edward, but Deirdre continued to chuckle.

With the proffering of such an acceptable solution, and the obvious suitability of all three beaux, the mood of the room so lightened that Lady Deirdre immediately went to the sideboard and served the hot tea and cakes.

Calvern alone seemed unrelieved. "There is one slight disadvantage," he said. "Michelle is eighteen, and very inexperienced. That is very young to be asked to make a decision which will mold her life. I had looked forward to her having a two- or three-year period in which to grow to maturity."

Lady Deirdre looked surprised. "Some women Michelle's age are already practiced at dealing with sluggardly husbands and two babies, Edward, although it is not a situation I would advocate. I would concur with you, as much against the custom as it is, that women should marry in their early twenties, for their choice is usually much wiser. In balance, however, I have found Michelle to have unusual insight and common sense, and her heart will guide her aright. As for maturity—I guarantee you, anything a woman learns before marriage is child's play to what she learns after, and if the girls are as lucky as I"—she touched the general's knee with her fan—"most of that will be wonderful."

After Calvern had discussed how he would approach Sanderson and von Reichertz about their intentions, and then speak to Michelle about her upcoming week of decision, the gathering came to an easy close.

"Well," said the general in departing, "it's an ill wind that doesn't blow someone good. One of your guests, John Sharkley, is growing rich. I wonder what odds he'll be giving the servants on the engagement."

The family council departed from the duke's chambers in such good humor, the serving staff wondered what all the fuss and tension in the morning had been about. Even Mary had become so relaxed that she served Sir William his soup at dinner without spilling a drop.

As he expected, Calvern found his interview with Robert Sanderson totally satisfying. The man's outrage was a mirror of his own, his desire to protect Michelle just as intense. The implications of the announcement and its insidious timing for the vicious tongues of the *ton* did not have to be explained, nor did the social logic of the solution. Calvern confided to the handsome lord that he himself was a suitor, and although Sanderson was surprised, the respect that each man had for the other was neither diminished nor strained.

In one thing, both men pledged themselves to both present and long-term action: to take on the Earl of Malfet appropriate social and personal sanction at every possible turn. They started by agreeing, after the announcement of Michelle's true betrothal, to place Richmond's name before the board of every one of his clubs for dismissal on grounds of behavior unbefitting his station.

The interview with von Reichertz, Calvern found less satisfactory. The man seemed to enjoy, rather than to love, Michelle. That was probably because, as Calvern suspected and Deirdre had underlined, he loved only himself. Von Reichertz studied the brandy in his glass and suggested delicately that even speculation about the original announcement might tarnish the betrothal somewhat, a blemish that could, in fact, be hidden with an increase in her dowry.

Calvern was enraged at this suggestion, for to him Michelle would be a pearl beyond price with no dowry at all. But the duke concealed his anger in case, heaven forfend, von Reichertz might be Michelle's choice, and he mentioned a figure von Reichertz accepted as "suitable, generous."

Damn good negotiator, thought Calvern, but damn bad lover.

Von Reichertz left the room smiling, but the duke threw both glasses from the brandy the men had shared into the fireplace.

And finally came the interview with Michelle.

It was already ten in the evening, for Calvern had spoken with von Reichertz and Sanderson after dinner. It was decided that he should speak to Michelle in the sitting room of Lady Deirdre's suite. Deirdre would chaperone, but Calvern knew she would be two rooms away in her dressing chamber, with the adjoining doors open only a symbolic crack. Lady Deirdre had also undertaken to explain to Michelle beforehand the implications of the announcement in the *ton*, and why she had to be betrothed right away, but could be married when she wished. Calvern knew the explanations had not gone well, for as he passed Emma in the hall on the way to Deirdre's, she looked at him with the eyes of a slapped, rebellious puppy, and the duke knew Michelle's mood would be no better.

It was, in fact, worse.

For Michelle, it had been a difficult day. She had concluded that morning that something dire must have happened in the servants' quarters, for after Jane had spoken to Lady Deirdre, she had been sensitive and sullen; Ninette had drowned in tears sandwiched between romantic sighs—moods both women indulged in without explanation.

To escape the gloom, Michelle had gone for a walk with her friend Sharkley, followed by the omnipresent footman. Even here Michelle did not find respite, for Sharkley had both delighted and upset Michelle by presenting her with her first letter from her brother—only three days old. Michelle remembered clearly Richard had stated that they would not be in touch except through the Duc d'Anton, so she was truly uneasy when her brother hinted vaguely about some unexpected danger. Then when Richard asked her directly for some two hundred English pounds, to be sent via Sharkley, the unease turned to alarm.

Michelle was perturbed, not because she would have to sell a drawing, for, indeed, half the drawings, despite what Richard had said in Ostend, she felt were his. She was shocked because of his request for money. Never, in times that she knew were ones of most extreme danger, had he done that. Yet now he only hinted of danger, and asked so casually. Something was, indeed, wrong with Richard, and she would speak to Jane about it the instant her nurse was in a better mood.

Even after dinner, when Michelle had looked forward to company, neither Calvern nor Sanderson nor von Reichertz was available to play even one game of piquet, but all mysteriously hustled off to Calvern's study.

It was, Michelle thought, the most tedious day she had experienced since she had arrived at Holton House.

When Lady Deirdre had summoned the girls to her room and told them the news, both Emma and Michelle had raged. Emma, who had just newly discovered the delight of her heart moving at its own sweet pace, was stung by the realization of the courtship pleasures of which Michelle had been robbed so cruelly, so unjustly.

Michelle's moonlight resolution of two weeks ago—to win Calvern's heart—was nowhere near accomplished, and here she was being forced to accept an offer of marriage within days! After a time, Michelle's rage and hurt were superseded by intense embarrassment; she blushed to think of what Calvern had discussed with von Reichertz and Sanderson after dinner.

Now it was ten o'clock: Calvern would arrive momentarily. Lady Deirdre had slipped into her dressing room, and Michelle stared out the window. The moonlight resolution of two weeks ago now seemed so far away, she thought as she glanced at the cloud-covered darkness.

"Michelle!"

Calvern was already in the room, and she turned to face him. He looked drawn, weary. Her heart sank. It was obvious that for him, there was no such thing as *la grande passion* tonight. She fought back the hot tears in her eyes and burst out, "I respect Lady Deirdre greatly, and I love Emma, but I want to go home to France, where such silly rules do not apply. Truly, it is idiocy that I should pay such a price for one night of Malfet's rudeness, Your Grace."

Michelle's chin was lifted and stubborn.

Calvern sighed. He had slipped in her estimation back to "Your Grace." He began the long, wearying climb to bring her to a state of sanity, and, he hoped, of being his fiancée.

"You are quite right, my love. In fact, I myself have used stronger words of this situation today than 'idiocy,' and you are well justified in feeling this way. It does not mean that the rules can be avoided. In France, in a similar situation, the case well might be completely lost."

For a moment she was silent, for she knew he was right. "Then am I supposed to pluck a fiancé from thin air?"

"Not thin air, but the real earth, will show you three suitors, who know the situation and are most anxious for your hand."

Three, did he say?

"Von Reichertz has asked for your hand, and I will be glad to escort you, after Napoleon's defeat, on a visit to his maiden aunt in Austria, with whom we would live for several weeks until you were married."

Michelle felt a slight shiver down her spine, but nonetheless was flattered. She smiled mischievously at Calvern. "I am surprised that even with this slight whiff of scandal, the count has not disappeared, for the chaste purity of his diplomatic reputation means so much. What did you do, Your Grace, threaten to challenge him to duel?"

She chuckled, and the duke was relieved, once again astounded at her insight. It was obvious from her easy laughter that von Reichertz did not have her heart. "And from Lord

Sanderson, I have a most sympathetic presentation. . . ." But he did not continue, for Michelle had turned to the window and was looking at the half-veiled moon.

She swallowed to control the choke in her voice, and spoke without turning back to face Calvern, for she did not want him to read how truly disappointed she would be with Sanderson. "The woman taken to wife by the lord will be well and truly cherished. He is a fine man, both strong and gentle. My father would have recognized him as a noble man."

She stopped and stood still looking out the window, afraid to gaze into the duke's perceptive face. And the third? But Calvern, too, was remaining silent. When at last he spoke, she started.

"The final suit is, of course, my own."

Michelle's heart thumped.

When she turned from the window, it was not to rush into his arms in ecstasy. She took a cautious two or three steps forward: it was Edward's love she wanted, not his duty.

"Is it in the rules of polite society, Your Grace, that a guardian must marry a ward to protect her reputation?"

Calvern became angry. "Michelle, that remark was both unkind and insulting. I am proposing because I love you, of course."

"*Love* me!" She whirled to look at him; an edge had entered her voice as well. "How am I supposed to know *that?*"

"I suppose you have forgotten Monday by the stream."

"I am not naive enough to assume that a few kisses suggest either love or marriage, Your Grace. It was probably merely gentleman's sport."

"Gentleman's sport! Michelle, that is a terrible phrase!"

"I am not English, sir, but French. In France we are more sophisticated about such things."

"And I suppose it was your French sophistication that made you faint so beguilingly when you were first kissed?"

Michelle flushed to the roots of her hair with both embarrassment and anger, but could not refute him. She continued with the argument.

"How am I to believe you love me when, for weeks after kissing me, you avoid me? When you are with me, it is to arrange the presence and suit of other men. Is that not the purpose even of this house party?"

"Michelle, these presumptions are outrageous!" Calvern's cheeks flamed. "It is not out of love, I am sure, that I stand for hours in Rault's, selecting from heaps of pearls, the three for the precise shape of a fleur-de-lys pendant. Nor is it out of love that I allow fourteen of my men to be dressed in the fashion of rebels escaped from a Turkish seraglio, and allow two of them to be driven around London in my crested carriage, presenting invitations, to prove my folly to the world? And passion for you would not cross my mind as I approach your seamstress in the lady servants' parlor to ask for silk to match your eyes, and I bring it to a dyer in my own estate village, who chuckles with mirth? Might *this* not be your long-sought *grande passion?*"

"Oh!" said Michelle simply. She turned back to the window to hide her tears of amazed relief. "If you would marry me for love, Edward, I would say yes," she said, sharp tension in her voice as she fought to control the weeping.

Calvern, who wanted nothing in this world more than Michelle's joyful acceptance of his proposal, was appalled at her tone.

"Would it be impudent of me, after your extensive inquisition, to ask *why* my lady chooses *me?*"

Oh, where was his tenderness? Michelle could bear no more; she would respond in the same tone. "If I answered that it was the dulcet gentleness of your speaking, Your Grace, would you accuse me of flattery?"

"Damn, Michelle, do you *love* me?" Calvern was almost shouting.

"I should say, sir, that is one of the other reasons."

"Pray tell, what is the first?"

"Your Grace, do you not know?" she inquired, turning toward him with a devilishly sweet smile. "You receive the Paris newspapers, and so I will be able to keep up with the fashions."

As she swept from the room, she shut the door so forcefully, the crystal pendants of the wall sconces tinkled.

A few moments later, Deirdre reentered her sitting room, her eyes sparkling with delight and mirth.

"Congratulations, 'Your Grace.' I have already heard—hearing was not avoidable, you see—that you are well and truly affianced. In fact, I would venture to say you have both met your *grande passion.* But Edward, 'rebels escaped from a Turkish seraglio'—was that not a little unkind?"

The next morning, when Michelle and the duke met in the breakfast room, and he bowed low over her hand to kiss it, the small, electric thrill of the touch made clear what they both already knew: that they were truly, lovingly, annoyingly, passionately, bound to each other for the rest of their lives. Nor did they see why the mere joyous newness of this fact meant that today they should speak to each other at breakfast.

13

AND SO IT WAS that Michelle Marie-Louise Langois, daughter of the late Pierre André St. Jean Langois, seventh Comte de Bellevue, became officially affianced to Edward Ian William Radcliffe, fourth Duke of Calvern and fifth Earl of Holton, on the twenty-first of June, 1813—five months to the day since Michelle had first encountered the duke in the library of his house on Portman Square.

It was, as they both liked to remind their grandchildren many years later, also the date of Wellington's victory against King Joseph Bonaparte at Vitoria, the battle that turned the tide of the Napoleonic wars in the Iberian Peninsula. Such a pivotal battle, they both claimed, was an appropriate symbol for the tempestuous start of their relationship. Yet even as Wellington, out of such victorious conflagrations, had remade Europe, so too Calvern and Michelle would build a new world for their family.

For seven long days after he had placed it, David Richmond, Earl of Malfet, had waited for some response to his false announcement of his engagement to Michelle.

And for that week, said his servants who were already inured to his difficult ways, the earl was more impossible than he had ever been before.

After his lackey had placed the announcements and returned with the printed copies, Malfet had retreated to his private suite in his house, placed his almost limitless supply of brandy near at hand, and closed the curtains. Leaving instructions forbidding entrance to all except his valet, Robert, and the Duke of Calvern, he retired to celebrate his certain victory by getting soddenly drunk.

A thousand times in his mind's eye he envisioned Calvern entering his chambers. The duke's veneer of aloofness, thinned by stress, would crack, and he would demand—no, beg—that Malfet take Michelle, for her reputation would survive no other course. At first he would demur, for who would want to wed the penniless daughter of a French count of the Old Regime? Calvern would be reduced to craven pleading and settle a substantial dowry upon her, which the earl would accept, only because *noblesse oblige.*

Finally he would have handed Calvern, that aloof and high-principled prig, the final defeat and humiliation: Michelle's marriage to himself, Malfet!

Then Michelle would be his—and he would remind her, day and night, that he, Malfet, was her savior, and in a multitude of agonizing ways, he would make her pay for rejecting him and causing his public embarrassment. He smiled at the thought of the exquisiteness of it. He could hardly wait, for he did not know which would offer him more pleasure: his own physical enjoyment of Michelle, or the sight of Calvern's pain watching his cherished ward suffer.

But wait Malfet did—for days.

Three and four times a day he roared for his valet to see if Calvern had arrived, or at least sent a message.

Nothing.

When, on June twenty-fourth, the correction of Malfet's announcement, and the official de Bellevue–Calvern engagement, appeared, Malfet's valet almost trembled. He waited until he heard his master snoring in a sodden stupor, then crept into the room.

The curtains had not been opened in a week. His master himself had not bathed in five days, or shaved and changed his clothes in two. The servant made the bed, set down the tray of hot food, which he knew would be congealed by the time the earl awoke, and, beside the tray, the three newspapers open to the appropriate pages, and a painstakingly written note from himself.

This was the valet's last task for Malfet.

Many of the house servants, not paid on the last quarter day in March, and fully realizing that they would not be paid on the quarter day in June, had left without notice. The valet prided himself that at least he had not violated that decorum. He had been hired for service just this week by Lord Whitsom, a friend of General Cresswell's, who, while he had wanted references from previous employers, did not even suggest asking for one from Malfet, for it would be, he said, inappropriate. The valet knew from that one remark that his master's reputation with the *ton* was damaged beyond repair.

He had hoped against reason that Malfet would be in a fit state to give him his two quarters back pay, but the earl had never been sober enough, in the last few days, for him even to ask. Well, damn him, the man thought. He just wished he could stay to see his master's face when he read those announcements. It would compensate somewhat for the abuse he had suffered these past five years. But the servant regarded his own safety as the better part of valor and forwent the salary—his last bitter taste of the Earl of Malfet. After replacing the low-burning candles in the wall sconces, he crept down the stairs and left Malfet for good.

Two days after his valet left, Malfet was awakened to a hazy focus by a young groom thudding him on the back. "Lord Edsbury to see you, sir!"

Lord Edsbury had felt uneasy about this call on Malfet. Calvern, Cresswell, and Osborne had been actively indicating in the best clubs that Malfet was no longer a desirable member, and Edsbury had been chosen by the Malfet Hunt Club to inform the earl he was no longer the master of the hunt. It was not an easy message for a lifelong acquaintance to carry, but the wisdom of Edsbury's mission was soon confirmed when he arrived at Malfet's house.

After along and thunderous knocking, a weary-eyed boy of a groom answered the door. "Excuse me appearance, sir, but me and Old John the steward is the only servants left. Old John took care of the earl since he was born, and won't leave now, and I can't leave, because I won't see me fine 'orses not fed and groomed 'cause the master's blind drunk and 'as forgot to pay us. Shall I rouse him now, sir?"

Edsbury entered Malfet's chambers. They were dank and smelled of stale smoke and food.

When he saw Malfet, he couldn't believe his eyes. The fine black hair hung in oily hanks over his eyes; he had several days growth of beard. When Edsbury demanded the earl's resignation, the man had raged that the position of master of that prestigious hunt club had always belonged to a Malfet for as long as that Malfet chose to keep it. Malfet himself was not only the club's finest rider, but its chief financial support and owner of the hound pack. How dare they make such a request!

If Edsbury had been inclined to give Malfet the benefit of the doubt before he had arrived, the earl's condition and the state of the rooms and the desertion of the household staff had destroyed all possibility of compromise. If Malfet did not resign voluntarily, the caller asserted, all the other members of the hunt would quit and start a new one. If the earl did resign, the hunt would continue, and, if and when circumstances warranted, Malfet might be invited to rejoin. Even if he did not rejoin, the existence of the club would be saved for another generation of Richmonds.

That argument struck; Malfet resigned, cursed foully, and hollered for another bottle of his seemingly endless supply of French brandy.

Malfet was not the only one affected by Michelle and Calvern's engagement. The ladies presiding over the tea tables of Mayfair were all atwitter.

"My dear, so many people have left London, and think what they have missed! I am so happy we were delayed in our departure for Hertfordshire, for think what a stir this tidbit of gossip will cause in the county," said the Countess of Willington, serving tea in her London garden.

"Well," said the Marchioness of Bridgewater, enjoying her savoy cake, "I would hardly call the engagement of the wealthiest eligible man in England 'a tidbit of gossip.'"

"It proves," said the countess, "Lady Castlereagh's point about the waltz leading to the decline of morals, for Michelle is not marrying the man she waltzed with."

"That waltz, my dear," said the marchioness, wiping her mouth daintily, "took place in public. It is the private embraces that lead to trouble."

"It is a sad day for the English aristocracy, is it not, when an English duke should choose to sully his fine family line by mixing it with *foreign* blood," sulked Lady Jane Willington, carefully selecting her third slice of white gingerbread.

"Dear Jane, I know it hurts when one is not the chosen," said the marchioness straightforwardly. "But one could hardly refer to Michelle Langois de Bellevue as foreign, for her mama was English, the daughter of the Earl of Silkington, I understand. In fact, the duke may be said to be getting the better of the bloodlines, for her papa was the *seventh* Comte de Bellevue, and he is only the *fourth* Duke of Calvern."

The marchioness sat back to enjoy watching Lady Jane fume.

The Cresswell house in Grosvenor Square, even under Lady Deirdre's cool and capable hands, was in a complete flutter. Two weddings before Christmas!

While it was, indeed, conceded Deirdre Cresswell to a friend, a little frantic to have the weddings so close together, the dates were, in fact, a testimony to the remarkable nature of the betrothed girls' friendship. Michelle had roundly announced that although Malfet, through his dastardly act, had forced her to an early decision, she was certainly *not* going to allow him to ruin the day of Emma's marriage. Emma's date and plan had long been announced: it was to be a stylish wedding, to which the cream of the *ton* would be invited, in Saint George's, Hanover Square, in December.

And that December wedding, Michelle declared, although Emma demurred, should remain the central society event.

To ensure this fact, Michelle placed her own marriage early in October. "By the time of your wedding, Emma, I shall be regarded as a thoroughly married old baggage, of no interest whatsoever, except to have dowagers speculate, every time I refuse a second helping of peas, if I am increasing or not."

Lady Deirdre, working at her needlepoint screen in the corner, chuckled. Michelle, in coming to understand the rules of society, was already manipulating it rather brilliantly, she thought.

But it was Michelle's choice for the location of her wedding that surprised everyone, and privately, delighted Calvern more than anything else she might have done. She would be married from the chapel of Holton House itself, or she would not be married at all.

To be married from a country estate chapel in the middle of the autumn Season? Was she quite sure? queried Lady Deirdre. "Some people will be reluctant to travel that far— especially since we cannot offer guest accommodation for them all at Holton House."

"Then only those who truly care about us will come," said Michelle firmly. "Anyway, I would rather have the villagers of the estate around us than many I have met in the *ton*. Mrs. Sopwith's wishes mean more to me than those of such people as the gossipy Countess of Willington. The villagers are our people; their lives depend on us. It is right that we should share our happiness with them."

Michelle turned with shining eyes to Calvern for support. "Thanks to the kindness of your father, my papa and poor outcast mama were married in that chapel. For us to be joined there—it would seem as if our parents were present to bless us."

For a moment, Calvern could not trust himself to speak, and merely nodded. Deirdre looked at the faces of both the duke and Michelle and conceded the battle.

The house fairly crackled with excitement. If Ninette's seamstresses had been busy before, they were frantic now. The general swore that the entire consignment for England of imported laces, white silks, and satins for the month of July had been taken by his one household. How could two wedding dresses—he didn't care how long the trains were— consume as much?

It wasn't just the wedding dresses—the girls giggled—it was the Other Things. The morning dresses and dressing gowns and peignoirs and nightgowns and nightcaps and chemises and . . . They trailed into embarrassed silence.

Well, said the general, wasn't that a waste of time and effort, for they were obviously working very hard to wrap up only what was going to be unwrapped.

Deirdre shot him a look that said he had gone too far.

Michelle and Calvern enjoyed their engagement immensely. Lady Castlereagh herself led off the series of small celebratory dinners given by friends; the Duc D'Anton was next. Yet several times during that particular evening, when France had been spoken of, the veiled look of pain, now so familiar to Calvern, crossed Michelle's face, and she withdrew into silence.

In the gentle darkness of the rhythmically swaying carriage on the way home, when Michelle's head in genuine tiredness rested on his shoulder, Calvern ventured a gentle probe. "Who is it in France, my love, who still troubles you?"

Michelle was tense and bolted upright within seconds. "No one troubles me at all. It is just that war itself is so very evil, and fighting it changes people so." Her voice was edged with tears.

He kissed her gently on the forehead and left many things unsaid.

When he thought about it that night, the duke concluded that Michelle loved and trusted him enough to share any secret of her own. Had she not, indeed, told him of Ulm, a most painful experience? Yet her alarm at even a gentle attempt to broach this topic was extreme. He could only surmise that this last worry was probably not hers to reveal without breaking a trust, and she would do that no more than he would. But to whom, and under what threat, did she owe such loyalty?

One thing was certain: this secret was hurting her, and if only because of that, he did not like it.

Meanwhile, in the Cresswell mansion, Michelle lay sleepless and anxious in her bed.

How uncannily astute Edward was! It felt wonderful to be so deeply understood by her own beloved—yet he was almost frightening in his accuracy. She was, indeed, troubled by someone in France, and war *did* seem to have changed him so strangely—her brother, Richard. She had written him yet another letter, once again kindly delivered by Mr. Sharkley's man, Roland, to, she understood, the hotel in Ostend, Belgium, where they had last met. In it, she had been soaring in happiness over her engagement. He had written back without one reference to her betrothal, again offered the same hints of some vague, but serious, danger—and asked for an additional four hundred pounds: double the amount sought in the last letter.

Although she kept it hidden behind her well-practiced facade of calm, Michelle was distraught.

Richard had never asked for money until recently, and certainly he would not ask for it if he did not need it. For the second time in as many months, she visited her valued friend Mr. Derby, on Jermyn Street, who had been so kind when she had brought Emma and Edward on that happy visit just months ago. The old gentleman was delighted, as always, to see Michelle. He had read of her betrothal, and wished her happiness with such fatherly affection, she almost cried. This time, when she wanted to sell three drawings, he was not surprised. "Ah, I understand, private wedding expenses, my dear." He smiled, and reimbursed her at too high a price for his own profit. It was the least he could do—his secret wedding gift—for the lovely daughter of the count who had helped out Derby himself more than once.

Then together, the old man and young beauty had bent over the wooden trays of precious manuscripts until they found precisely the ones she wanted as a wedding gift for her beloved.

Even after paying for the gifts for Edward, Michelle had

enough left over to send Richard five hundred, rather than four hundred, pounds. In the letter she begged her brother, if he was in danger, to use the extra to come to shelter with Calvern and her at Holton House, for he would be most welcome on both their parts. At least, she pleaded, could he come to her wedding? His presence, just to see him and know that he was safe, would be the crowning touch to her most glorious day.

As Sharkley read Michelle's letter to her brother, which would never be delivered, and emptied out the money in front of Roland's eager eyes, he felt ill at the roots of his very being.

Because of Michelle, Sharkley had moved up entirely into a different level of society, into the inner circles of the *ton*. No longer did he have to do the most despicable of things to eke out a living. True, the primary gentleman for whom he had exported and imported contraband goods between France and England had been indulging in heavy drink to such a degree that his business had ground almost to a halt. But Sharkley had found other sources of income, primarily gambling and lending money, to more than make up the loss on the black market trade.

But the extortion of funds from Michelle was too hurtful.

When Roland saw the pained anger in his master's eyes, as he cursed and stoutly refused ever again to trick her, Roland gave a low whistle of despair. He knew that his master was no longer foolishly mooning over Michelle, but worse still, was genuinely in love.

Had he seen what Sharkley did after the valet left the room, Roland's worst fears would have been confirmed. His master did not burn Michelle's letter in the fire, as he did all other incriminating correspondence, but folding it carefully, he opened a secret locked drawer of his desk and placed it with the pile of Michelle's other letters and her come-out invitation, all carefully wrapped in silk and tied with a ribbon.

If the treasure of Sharkley's heart was wrapped in silk and ribbons, so, in fact, was Calvern's, for silk and ribbons were what Michelle wore when she became his wife.

Their wedding day was splendid.

A bright October sun had hung high in the clear air. Thanks to Sir William's greenhouses, the chapel of Holton House was a veritable forest of French lilies and English roses, all in full bloom. The ceremony, the music, and the following celebrations were, thought Calvern, yet another example of his beloved's thoughtful, exquisite taste.

While the town guests attended the chapel service and had a large and elaborately festive wedding breakfast in the great hall, the villagers of the estate were not forgotten. At the far end of the lawn near the river was served a large picnic with seven suckling pigs, pies, apple cider, and wine while the fiddlers played old tunes. For an hour in the afternoon, their duke and his new duchess, careful to come before she had changed from her wedding finery, mingled among them, and delighted them all by leading off a country dance.

The shadows cast by the sun were growing longer as Calvern, avoiding the assisting hands of two waiting footmen, gathered his petite bride in his arms and himself lifted her into the crested coach for their trip to London for the night. They were to stay in the royal suite of the Grillon Hotel, then go on to the Cresswells' country estate in the Cotwolds for a month. His valet, her dressing maid, and four other servants had been sent on ahead to prepare the rooms and light the fires.

The door of the carriage had barely been shut before Michelle turned to Calvern, eyes shining. "Did you enjoy our wedding, my love?"

Calvern laughed, and offering her the most sweeping bow of a cavalier that the limited carriage space allowed, he seized her hand, raised it to his lips, and kissed it lightly. "My dear, you weave the most beguiling noose. Not content with just the vows, you have me well and truly married in front of the entire estate and all my friends. Now, however, will I have the run of the *ton*, pretending I am abused at home, and fancy-free?"

He looked into the veiled depth of her eyes and read the earnest question that was still there, which his flippancy, born of the exuberant joy of the day, had not satisfied: she truly wanted to know if she had pleased him. That his pleasure should be so important to her on this, her own wedding day, when the bride's own desires were traditionally preeminent, moved him profoundly.

He became suddenly serious, and turning the small, perfect hand he still held, he placed a kiss of lingering tenderness on her palm, then pressed her hand to his cheek. "Michelle, you arranged so many things, some of which I have never seen done, or would have thought of doing, yet each touch was so perfect, I would have had it no other way. How did you think of it all?"

Michelle smiled in the warmth of his appreciation. "I simply surrounded us both with those people and things we love most."

Indeed she had, and the lengths to which she went in order to achieve her aim had not only delighted, but amazed him.

At an engagement dinner, Michelle had learned from kindly old Mr. Straighton, the duke's solicitor, that during his time at Oxford, Calvern had been fond of a crusty, demanding history tutor whose insights had resulted in Calvern's own present interest in politics and foreign service. The old professor found himself not only invited to the ducal wedding, but ensconced in one of the finest guest bedrooms of Holton House —much to the pleasure of his former student. Straighton had also mentioned how the duke rejoiced in the sacred music of Tallis and Byrd he had heard in the college chapel; so it was that the clear, sweet voices of the boys of the college choir had rung like crystal through the chapel at Holton House.

If Michelle was busy seeking to give pleasure to others, those who cherished her sought, equally urgently, to please her. Michelle had discovered both Jane and the duke's venerable steward, Charles Wilson, had been at her parents' wedding, and she had hung on every word of their memories of it. Seeing how much her parents' wedding meant to their lovely bride, the two old retainers had searched every cupboard and niche in the chapel and library for the prayer book used at Michelle's parents' wedding; they found it tucked in a bookcase the old duke had kept at his bedside.

And so, dressed in silver and white, crowned by her mother's veil, which Jane had so carefully treasured, and carrying her parents' wedding prayer book, Michelle was married to her duke.

Now, as Edward again kissed her palm, a vibrant warmth overcame her, and suddenly she realized: she was, at last, alone with her husband. No Jane, no Deirdre discreetly watching. Michelle had never been so completely alone with her Edward before; she blushed a little at the mere thought of it, and smiled shyly at him.

Calvern grinned. "Not alone with me for one mile, my seductive pet, and already you are practicing your wanton wiles on me. Well, my love, let me assure you that they work now, and they always will."

Without further ado, he untied the ribbons of the small

flowered bonnet she wore, tossed the hat to the opposite seat, and did what he had been yearning to do for days. Drawing his fingers through the curling, teasing tendrils of her dark hair, he eased her head into the cradle of his arm and kissed her. Gently, gently at first, he traced the arch of her eyebrows, her cheeks, the delicate hollow of her throat, marking her features with the firm moistness of his mouth as a sculptor fingers wet clay.

The teasing lightness of Calvern's touch made Michelle's skin tingle to her very fingertips; she found her self suddenly insatiable for his deeper possession of her, and put her small hands around his face. *"Edouard."* She murmured his name in French like a secret talisman of desire; she was breathless and, with a small gasp of anticipated pleasure, drew Calvern down to the shining sweetness of her open mouth.

Because he wanted Michelle's first time with him to be a tender and perfect delight, Calvern had long treasured the thought of a slow, gentle seduction of his bride. That possibility was almost destroyed in this one wild instant by Michelle herself, by the sweet compulsion of her murmured, open-lipped invitation. He had held his passion severely in check for months; now her eager, innocent vulnerability, so close and trusting, ignited it with the hot, quick fury of wildfire.

His mouth came down upon hers, rapid, demanding; their breaths mingled, and when she felt his tongue enter, she gave a small, impassioned cry. In another instant, his lips had woven a web of fire across her brow, on the small, pink shell of her ear, in the silky hollow at the base of her throat, but always he came back, precisely, rythmically, to take possession of her mouth. The anticipation of this pattern of his kisses, his coming, entering, possessing of her, heightened Michelle's desire for him to such intensity, her fingers curled convulsively in the silk of his hair, drawing him even more closely to her. *"Encore."* Her murmur was almost a sob. *"Encore."*

Calvern had to admit, if only to himself, that by the time he undid the complex fastenings of Michelle's cloak, the five small hooks at the back of the pearl-encrusted neck of her dress, and the three complex patterns of ribbons across the bodice of his beloved's gown, his hands were shaking. "Who designed this creation, my pet?"

Michelle drew back a little, startled by Calvern's question. "Ninette, of course."

"The woman ought to be charged."

"With what crime?" she whispered.

"With attempting to preserve your innocence by thwarting your lover's desire in a maze of buttons." He grinned. "But I assure you, my love, I will not allow her malicious plot to succeed."

The heavy brocade shades of the coach, the footmen noticed with wicked winks, had been drawn almost the instant they had left Holton House; in fact, it was the hollow sound of the horses' hooves on Westminster Bridge that alerted Calvern to the fact that they were in London.

"Quickly, my pet," he said, helping Michelle to button the neck of her dress, "before all of Albermarle Street sees the new Duchess of Calvern in delightful dishabille."

If, when the duke and duchess emerged, they did not notice that Michelle's flowered bonnet lay crushed in the corner of the coach, or that the ribbons of her bodice were misthreaded in the most interesting pattern, who was going to tell them?

"Aye," said the youngest footman running to hold the horses' heads as they swung into the stable yards, "I envy the duke the joy of this sleepless night."

The coachman, who shared his opinion, nonetheless creased the calves of the lad lightly with his long whip for daring such impudence.

When the couple entered their bedchamber with its overwhelming four-poster, the duke was pleased to note the warmth of the room from the glowing fire, the tray of fresh fruit, cheese, and wine, the bouquets of violets exactly the color of Michelle's eyes around the room and on the pillows —all exactly as he had ordered. He was ready for his bride in an instant.

But if Calvern, by some insane folly, had imagined there would be a speedy release to the couple's enforced restraint, he had forgotten one thing: he was married to a Frenchwoman. Michelle instantly disappeared around her dressing screen and gave an exclamation of delight. "It's finished!"

"What's finished?"

"The special nightgown Ninette made for me, just for tonight."

Calvern drew a deep, ragged breath. "My love, I assure you, you do not have to dress to come to me."

Michelle's mischievous face, framed in dark, glossy curls, peeked around the edge of the screen, her small silver and pearl drop earrings jingling with the emphatic shake of her head. "Oh, *non, mon chérie,* what fun is an unwrapped gift?"

That argument, Calvern had the wisdom to realize, was irrefutable to any Frenchwoman, and with a sigh, he prepared to wait.

Wait he did.

From behind the screen came ten minutes of rustles as tissue surrounding silk and lace was removed, ribbons were struggled with, and a small, tense exclamation as something did not fit. He was driven almost mad with impatient desire.

"My love, do you have to do it all up?"

"Oh, yes, otherwise you will not see its delicious perfection."

Calvern was not naive enough to make the argument that the gown was not the delicious perfection he wanted to see; always the diplomat, he took another tack. "May I help?"

"Oh, no, then it would not be a surprise!"

When Michelle finally emerged, Calvern groaned inwardly. His wife, so shyly radiant, was worth the wait of a lifetime—but the gown! It was indeed a dazzling creation—for a French Royalist coronation ball. It had an intricately fastened cloak of draped lace, another of those mischievously beribboned bodices, and a swirl of petticoats tied heaven knows how. He wouldn't even put it beyond the dressmaker to have invented matching pantaloons. Curse Ninette, he thought—the woman should be hung from the highest gallows in a noose of her own ribbons.

Then, undeterred, he bent to the pleasure of the task at hand. *"Tu me passionne,"* he whispered as he slipped the first layer of silk from Michelle's shoulder and bent to kiss the even silkier skin beneath . . .

To her dying day, Michelle never revealed the secret joy of their lovemaking that she most cherished. From the first night, Calvern never shared the intimacy of her body without sharing the intimacy of her language; it was as if he paid her court, came into her world, and held it, and her, in sacred, inviolate esteem.

Michelle's naked, perfect body was nestled warm along his, and by the flickering candlelight, he glanced at the various pieces of silk and lace concoction that lay strewn across the room, flung far from the bed. "Someday, my love, you will feel easy enough to come to me nude at the start."

She instantly raised herself on her elbow, and tracing with her finger the straight bridge of his nose, the firm lines of his strong mouth, she smiled, her violet eyes glinting with mischief. "Oh, no, Your Grace, never, never will you see me nude; not even for my beloved will I come to bed without earrings."

It was not until the candles had burned low in the royal suite of the Grillon Hotel and it was almost morning that the couple remembered to exchange their wedding gifts. For Michelle, Edward had designed an exquisite necklace of pearls and sapphires from which to suspend her come-out pendant. In a small frame underneath was a special gift: Rembrandt's sketch of the head of the sleeping child they had discovered together in their first visit to Mr. Derby's. On the back of the frame was the inscription *To Michelle, my bride of the seeing heart.*

For Edward, with Mr. Derby's help, Michelle had found the impossible: a fourteenth-century copy of the Doomsday Book's description of the land around Holton House, and three other maps of the area from the fifteenth, sixteenth, and seventeenth centuries. The four pieces had been framed in mahogany, each crowned with the family crest.

Both Michelle and Calvern were delighted.

"Well," said Edward as they examined the works, "I can see what happens when a fusty history scholar marries an art dealer's daughter: the excitement of the day is the perusing of manuscripts and drawings."

She turned to embrace him: "Sir, I will tolerate your perusal, but I will not be considered less exciting than a manuscript."

"I cannot tease a manuscript," he whispered, and she discovered that even at dawn his hands, caressing so lightly, could, as quick as lightning striking tinder, start a searing brushfire that swept through every nerve in her small body.

At first Michelle was startled, almost frightened by the raging intensity of her reactions. As her lover, Calvern seemed intent on thrusting her beyond any vestige of self-control. It was like careening through the wild, spuming water of an Alpine gorge; ecstasy was close to drowning, she thought as she gasped before another even more intense rush overwhelmed her. Where was it going to stop? Yet she discovered each time she yielded to the whirlpool of the rhythmically driving, exploding sensations within her, she always came back, always discovered herself safe, looking into Edward's smiling eyes.

So, she marveled, lying warm in the morning sun in the crook of her husband's arm, this is what Lady Deirdre had meant when she had spoken to the two girls of "abandonment to delight."

The truth was, the *ton* whispered later, that Edward Calvern, the cool, witty, and dispassionate lover, had become well and truly besotted both with his lovely young wife and the state of marriage.

Certainly Calvern, even to his own surprise, had changed.

As a leading member of the *ton,* with no parental guidance after the death of his father, he had assumed the values around him. He realized that his uncle General Cresswell's marriage was as unusual as it was fortunate; Calvern did not expect to duplicate it. He knew too well the way of the world, so he took for granted sexual pleasures were to be found separately from the warmth of family, and had become master of those that could be bought.

Until Michelle.

If anyone had told him before their wedding there were pleasures of a woman's company he had never experienced, he would have laughed.

Not now.

He discovered that in their marriage bed was no hidden desire for control or gain, no sense of dispassionate sport. Edward had never, even in casual touch, hurt or alarmed Michelle; she had known only safety and comfort in his arms, so she came to him, virgin, in utter trust and openness. She knew no other patterns of desire but the ones he shared with her; their matching became perfect. She gave to him without reserve or calculation, broaching each new sensation with a sense of marveling wonder, allowing herself to be swept by passion one minute, playing coyly, coaxingly, with him the next. Yet never, in all her play and passion, did Calvern have the sensation that the tempestuous desire she so readily aroused in him was to serve any other end but their profound and mutual delight.

He was loved, for the first time, for himself.

He was no longer alone.

His marriage to Michelle quickly put the lie to another myth of the *ton.* He had been led to believe that of no wife and family could he reasonably expect support of the hours demanded by his calling in the foreign affairs of his country. Not so with Michelle. What mattered to him mattered without question to her, and she would brook no separation from any sphere of his life.

They had been holidaying quietly at the Cresswells' estate in the Cotswolds when, only two weeks after their wedding, he received word that the Foreign Office was drafting possible alliances England would form with various countries after the fall of Napoleon. He told Michelle of the message, and her reaction was immediate.

"You have always told me you wanted to influence the shape of the new Europe after Napoleon."

"Yes." He barely glanced up from the reports he was reading.

"Then are we not going back to London to allow your opinions to be included in the earliest drafts? It seems to me that is the way to be certain they receive serious consideration from the beginning. It is much harder to influence policy once it has been formed."

He looked up, surprised. "But, Michelle, we have been here only a fortnight."

She shrugged, and the mischievous dimple came in the corner of her smile. "I am willing to surrender our days to the Foreign Office, my love, but not one night."

They arrived back at Portman Square two days later.

More satisfying still to Calvern was Michelle's intense fondness for Holton House.

Early in their courtship, the duke had assumed that an elegant fashion leader who shone in the drawing rooms of politicians and diplomats would have little interest in a rural estate, but at every turn, Michelle had proved otherwise. It went far beyond her desire to hold the wedding in the chapel, or her enjoyment of the villagers. Every facet of Holton House fascinated her. Even though his wife's afternoons were dedicated to Emma's wedding preparations, and soft whisperings of secret married pleasures, every morning she was closeted with the duke's steward, learning to read the management accounts. It was Michelle who pointed out that in the last three years, the improved size of the crops forced them to have a goodly percentage of their grain milled outside. They could well afford to build their own flour mill; they could give employment to several young men of the village and probably earn a handsome profit on milling the grain for neighbors.

Calvern ordered the mill built.

One bitter day in late November, an urgent message arrived at the Foreign Office from Michelle saying that three cottages in the village had burned. Although Calvern left directly, Michelle arrived two hours earlier. The burned-out families were already sheltering in the large west wing of the house.

Michelle was tired and retired early. Alone in his study after dinner, Calvern surveyed the estate manager's report on the disaster and found a small, neat note from Michelle saying that she had already summoned the stonemason from the nearby town to discuss the duke's plan for rebuilding. He contemplated Michelle's hectic day, so directed by her compassion and interest for the estate, smiled, and rose to join her.

Warm and pink from the bath, Michelle sat in a soft robe before the fire while Jane brushed her long tresses dry. Calvern dismissed the gentlewoman with a nod and smile, and took over the brushing himself without missing a stroke.

"You love Holton." It was a statement, not a question.

"Yes."

"Why?"

"Your questions cut so close, Edward."

He glanced at her face in the mirror, never once missing a stroke of the brush. Her eyes were shining with tears, but she continued. "Our estate was seized by the revolutionary government before I was born. Papa didn't like the town house in Paris, for it had only been in the family twenty years, and Mama had died there. He rented it out when I was nine so we could afford to travel and collect art. After that, all our residences were rented. But, Edward, you have given me and our children, and theirs after them, this place to belong to. Here, what we build in stone, and more important, in love, will stay. I've never had a real home before, Edward. That was your best gift to me."

She turned from the mirror, her cheeks wet with tears, and went into his arms. He looked down into her eyes and understood what the outside world never suspected: the sparkling Michelle, at ease in so many lands, wanted home and hearth even more than the courtly, fashionable world. Holton House she wanted to become her refuge and strength and that of their family. Somehow, his dream of the future and hers, springing from such different roots, had intertwined and become one.

All he valued—his family and its honor, their mutual pleasures, the estates, his career—were as cherished in the tenderness of Michelle's safekeeping heart as they were in his own care. The profundity of the bond between them intensified his arousal almost beyond bearing. He pushed back her glistening, scented tresses and started by kissing the nape of her neck.

The *ton* was right, Calvern thought. He was besotted. The haut monde had lost its cool, dispassionate lover but gained a whole man.

14

T HE SHARP, chill February wind whacked the tall figures
of the general and Calvern as they emerged from the
War Office, lifting the collars of their greatcoats across their
faces, whipping the heavy material between their legs. The
duke's carriage drew up under the portico. The horses' nos-
trils were ringed with frost; their snorting breath hung in ice
vapor clouds.

"Bitter, this weather. Coldest in the last hundred years,
they say. First time in living memory the Thames has frozen,
and for so long. We'll not soon forget the winter of thirteen.
But one good thing—the wind that's chilling us is freezing
Boney and his men as well, and the steppes of Russia are a
damn sight colder than the streets of London." Having finished his speech in a tone of attempted jocularity, the general
risked a glance at his nephew as the two men settled into the
carriage, and realized the duke had heard not a word, so
deep was he in his own despair.

Chill? Bitter? Nothing, not the wastes of Russia itself,
could make his blood run as cold as the interview he had just
had with the secretary of war, Calvern thought. Blind! A
blind, love-besotted fool he had been, that's what; so blinded
by his love for Michelle that he foolishly ignored the signs
she was in a situation of utmost danger. Could he have
known sooner, done more to help her? The question
pounded painfully, relentlessly, through Calvern's mind, its
circling maelstrom raising a thousand intimate, tender

images of moments with his wife—images that in their turn raised other questions.

They had been married only two months when he had watched Michelle standing beside Emma at her wedding to Osgood. Michelle had been so breathtakingly lovely in crimson and white, it seemed to him that the holly and blood-red roses that decorated the church only echoed her beauty. How radiant her face had been that day as she shared her friend's happiness! Was it even in the realm of human possiblity that someone as generous, as sharing, as innocently, joyously loving as she was to Emma, to all her friends, to the villagers, and a thousand times more to himself, could be a traitor, a deceitful, deliberate traitor?

The mere idea rose like bile in his throat; it was not only an impossibility, it was an obscenity.

Yet how, how, how was he to fight it? To discover the truth? And first and foremost, protect Michelle?

As the vehicle swung into the Grosvenor Square, the general, facing opposite, cast yet another worried glance at his nephew's white, drawn face. "Do not be upset by the interview, lad. The secretary of war can be a little given to drama and intrigue at times."

"That," said Calvern grimly, "is an understatement. At one point I thought he was going to arrest Michelle for high treason, and me for complicity."

The general was surprised. "Had you not known Michelle was writing to France?"

"No. There seems to be a lot I don't know."

The general was silent. He had known his nephew from birth, and never since his father's death had he seen the supposedly aloof duke so profoundly troubled. It was obvious that Calvern himself suspected there was more in the situation than the secretary of war had implied. Yet Cresswell also knew that once the duke had had a chance to examine the myriad of details, few men would be as clear-thinking, decisive, or courageous.

"Perhaps you would care to come home for a bit of luncheon? We might mull over a few possible courses of action before you confront Michelle."

Lady Deirdre had not expected this.

Just before noon, as she was about to depart for the glove maker's to see the newly imported Italian kids, the general, stone-faced, followed by Calvern, who was ashen, swiftly entered the mansion.

"Deirdre." Calvern acknowledged his aunt with the briefest of bows, curtly deposited his greatcoat with the butler, and without so much as a by-your-leave, proceeded through to his uncle's study. The general stopped to kiss his wife on the cheek.

"Trouble at the Foreign or War Office?"

The general grunted, her husband's sign that particular information was not to be divulged. "Pretty hard on Calvern this morning."

Deirdre patted his arm. "I'll have a light luncheon sent to your study," she said, and departed to order some of her husband's favorite cold pickled tongue and hard-boiled eggs, still pondering what upset could have made Calvern so pale.

When the general came into the room, the duke was sitting in one of the deep leather chairs by the fire, his head buried in his hands. On hearing the door close, he looked up, his face drawn.

"I've been a besotted fool, haven't I?"

"Don't blame yourself, my boy. You've been married for four months, and I know men who have been married for forty years who still do not know everything about their wives."

"It is just that I am angry at my own lack of awareness of Michelle's situation. I perceived some difficulty, but did not react quickly enough to help her. She must be suffering. Less important, but it still irks, is the fact that the name of Calvern should even be remotely mentioned in the context of treasonable activity."

"I wouldn't take that too seriously. The War Office sees French spies in every wardrobe—it's the nature of their trade. Old Boney has been on the rampage so long, their naturally suspicious bent has become a permanent habit of mind. To implicate Michelle is ridiculous."

"In the War Office context, is it?"

"Look, lad, how long has the girl been in England—a year? Isn't it natural that she should correspond with people in France, her own country? Right now, there is no other way to do that but by courier. The War Office knows every courier going into France—no doubt they carry illicit information as well as legal correspondence. They thought that you, as a peer of the realm and Foreign Office advisor, should know that Michelle has been corresponding with France through a courier who is confirmed to have carried messages to known spies. Certainly the secretary offered not the least inference that Michelle's correspondence itself was anything but innocent."

"I should say not," snapped Calvern. "Not in a thousand years could one think of Michelle as a spy. It would be impossible. Never have I met a soul so trustworthy. With everything she does or thinks, she is completely open. Yet I suspect the War Office refrained from impugning her innocence only because they have not yet succeeded in intercepting her actual letters to France and examining the contents."

The general grunted his approval of his nephew's judgment, but he continued: "Yet when you ask the question, 'In the eyes of the War Office, is it?' you are implying that while *you* believe Michelle to be innocent of spying, she may appear to others to be in some—ah—compromising predicament, that her letters may, in fact, justify their suspicions."

"Precisely, Uncle. Precisely." Calvern rose to his feet and began to pace agitatedly back and forth. "There is one topic she cannot speak of, and that is something in France."

"Have you asked her directly?"

"Several times, never forcefully. She has never responded."

Calvern withdrew into himself, examining why he had never pressed the issue with Michelle. Had it been overconfidence in his ability to read his young wife's heart, combined with the desire not to disturb the shining smoothness of their newlywed joy, that prevented him from probing the gravity and pain of Michelle's situation?

The general, too, was thoughtful. "Devil of a predicament, that. Only time Deirdre refused to tell me about a dilemma was when her dim-witted cousin had pledged her to secrecy, and Deirdre wouldn't violate a pledge. Damn near cost her cousin his estate for a gambling debt, and we could have helped."

"Michelle has confided in me several situations where fear and the possibility of personal injury were most vivid; it is not fear or shyness that is preventing her from telling me. I suspect the situation springs from just such a promise as Deirdre's—a promise of loyalty," asserted Calvern.

"To whom? Who would demand such a pledge of a girl, barely beyond her come-out and newly married? No one of breeding." The edge in the general's voice betrayed his rising anger at the thought of such abuse.

"Precisely my thinking," concurred the duke. "I believe the person to be a particularly unsavory character—especially as the keeping of the pledge seems to demand a substantial sum of money."

"What?" The look of shock on Cresswell's face was profound. "Are you certain? How do you know?"

"Believe me, I shared your dismay when I discovered, barely a month ago, that, despite funds I had provided even before the wedding, Michelle has been forced to sell some of her father's drawings."

"How did you find out?"

Calvern could remember the moment only too vividly. That frosty January morning four weeks ago on Old Jermyn Street, he had felt almost as if he had been run through by a cold steel blade.

The duke had walked several steps past the store before what he had seen even registered. Discreetly placed in a corner of art dealer Derby's window were four of Michelle's Rembrandt drawings.

He stopped, returned to the window, and looked carefully.

There was no mistake.

There they were—four of Michelle's pictures he had seen the night of her coming to Portman Square and of their first kiss. In front of each there was a small, neat sign: "sold."

For a few minutes Calvern experienced a feeling he had rarely known: a burning, white-heat fury. Had he not made clear to Michelle that he understood these pictures were her patrimony, all she possessed of her father and of her life as the daughter of the Comte de Bellevue? Had he not told her, when she suggested that their sale would provide her dowry, that he would not countenance her parting with her only family treasures? She cared so much for family and tradition; how *could* she sell them?

Calvern's profound anger was followed by an even deeper sense of betrayal. Then quietly there began settling in his mind a mood that had all but vanished these last months—one of controlled, dispassionate aloofness.

He entered the shop.

When the entrance bell tinkled, Mr. Derby, whom Calvern, Michelle, and Emma had visited on that first outing together, emerged from the back of the store. As he recognized Calvern, a smile of delight creased his wrinkled face. He rushed forward and began pumping the duke's hand.

"Oh, Your Grace, how glad I am to see you, yes indeed. I have waited several months for you, yes I have. You see, I did not want to be forward, or to put you in an awkward position by writing, for, of course, you might refuse; it is so easy to refuse in writing, and much harder in person. That is why I am so glad my little ploy worked. Now you are here, and, of course, you will not deny my pleasure."

Derby had continued pumping Calvern's hand until, having finished his speech, he dropped and gave a contented sigh.

Calvern had never been more confused. "I beg your pardon? I came in to inquire about the Rembrandt drawings in the window."

"Of course you did," said Derby, beaming and offering no further explanation.

Calvern ventured again. "The drawings, are they—were they—not my wife's?"

"Of course," said Derby, beaming even more broadly and again offering no further comment.

Calvern found this conversation not only awkward, but veering toward the incomprehensible. "And they are sold."

Derby looked completely shocked. "Oh, dear me, of course not. I would not do that with Michelle's—pardon me, sir, I mean, Her Grace, your wife's—drawings."

"But they are marked sold in the window."

"That was only to guarantee that they would *not* be sold until you came."

"Until I came? You were expecting me?"

"Of course!" exclaimed Mr. Derby, with such a look of surprise, one could tell no other possibility had entered his mind.

The conversation, Calvern thought, had just slipped from the incomprehensible into the insane; he sincerely hoped old Mr. Derby was feeling all right. Gently grasping the old man's elbow, he guided him to a nearby seat and pressed him into it. "I am afraid, Mr. Derby, I do not understand at all. Could you start at the beginning and explain?"

The silver-haired old gentleman looked over his spectacles at Calvern's confused face for a full minute, then began to chuckle. "I've not been too clear, have I?"

"You have, sir, been clearer."

Derby began to laugh again. "You will have to forgive me, sir, but I have been living with this plot for such a long time, I had almost come to assume you shared in it with me. Perhaps I am getting forgetful in my old age, but it is a delicious subterfuge nonetheless, and one in which I do heartily hope you concur."

The duke nodded for him to continue.

"You see, when Michelle—excuse me, Her Grace—came in with the drawings before your wedding—with one drawing in July, and three more in August, I believe—I knew exactly why she had come. I have daughters and grand-daughters of my own, and there are always those personal little wedding expenses, aren't there?" said Derby, pleased with his own insight.

Calvern nodded again.

"Certainly I accepted the drawings, Your Grace, and paid Michelle handsomely for them. I knew instantly I was right in my thinking when, on the second visit, Michelle immediately spent a third of what I had given her in purchasing your wedding gift. You did like the page from the Doomsday manuscript? A prize piece. But never, sir, not from the first moment, did I anticipate either keeping or selling the drawings. Never! Such works are, no doubt, among Michelle's few remaining gifts from her father."

The duke concurred.

"Her dear father, the comte, helped me so much when he was in London some twenty, twenty-five years ago. He often advised me of private sales I never would have known of otherwise, and many times sent clients specifically interested in my holdings—especially in the last few years, as he became less interested in dealing in art himself. He never accepted a commission for any of his services to me—no, not one. He would only laugh and say that someday I would no longer be a struggling newcomer, and be in a position to return the favors. That day arrived when Michelle came in before the wedding.

"Then the question arose: how to return the drawings to Michelle without offending her? To offer them as a personal wedding gift would be too familiar, for even though I think of her in a grandfatherly fashion, in truth, our relationship is not a social, but a professional, one. Nor, I realized, would you, Your Grace, accept them as a gift unless you were familiar with the circumstances. Even so, if I sent them to you directly, I thought it more than likely you would offer to pay for them, and that would thwart the whole purpose. No, what I intended, I realized, could only be explained in person.

"Then I thought of it! I would put Her Grace's drawings in the window, where you would probably see them one day as you went to your club. As you probably did not know Michelle had sold them, I knew you would come to inquire—and here you are. The "sold" sign was simply to stop any other would-be purchaser from attempting to buy them before you came.

"Now, Your Grace, you will accept my gift—my assistant is already wrapping them. You will return these drawings to Michelle whenever you deem appropriate, with my compliments, and in grateful memory of her father?"

The elderly gentleman was breathless after his extensive monologue, and stopped, looking at the Duke of Calvern expectantly.

Calvern was profoundly moved by the old man's kindly—and most ingenious—gesture. "It will be my pleasure, sir, to do this for you," he said with a deep, courtly bow. "It is most insightful of you to realize the intense family sentiment behind these pictures. I will return them to my wife at an appropriate moment in the next several weeks, and I am sure she will be in to thank you herself."

That evening, in the privacy of his study, the duke opened the package. Mr. Derby had enclosed the receipt for the sums he had paid Michelle. Three hundred pounds for the first drawing, and nine hundred for the later lot of three. Michelle's wedding gifts for Calvern were superb, but the manuscripts certainly had not cost much more than a third of the total amount. That left a surplus of over seven hundred pounds! He remembered thinking that the problem must be much more severe than he supposed if it was requiring such large sums of money—an opinion with which his uncle, for whom he had briefly outlined the story, agreed.

"Seven hundred pounds! But surely for as large an amount, Michelle could have come to you, or to Deirdre, for help if she felt to use the wedding funds you supplied would not be appropriate."

"One would think so," said Calvern quietly.

"Perhaps she did not because the money represents the payment of blackmail," suggested the general.

"Blackmail!" snapped Calvern with genuine shock, his cheeks flushing with anger. "Uncle, I know my wife, and I assure you, there is no possibility that Michelle has ever had any—ah—compromising experiences."

"Sorry, lad, no offense intended. I am just asking some of the things an investigating officer might raise?"

"Extortion, on behalf of a relative or friend, is a real possibility. In which case," the duke added quietly, "parting with those much-cherished drawings was actually less painful, or less dangerous to someone, than explaining to Deirdre or me the need for such a sum."

"Did you not tell her of Derby's gift of the returned drawings, and ask for an explanation of the funds?" said the general a trifle impatiently.

"I trust Michelle, and wanted her to tell me of the funds herself, without forcing her hand by challenging her about the drawings."

Had that course of action, in fact, been right? Calvern wondered. Should he have pressed harder?

He withdrew for a moment, back to the memory of the evening following his visit to Mr. Derby's shop. As Michelle nestled with him before the fire, he told her firmly, "If you ever need money, for anything, you will tell me. There would never be any question your needs would be met."

"Of course!" She laughed. "You spoil me so dreadfully!"

Seconds later, she seemed to realize the full implication of what he had said. She raised her head, looked intently into his face, her cheeks reddening with embarrassment. Calvern deliberately showed no unusual interest or worry. She sighed and nestled again into his shoulder, seemingly unaware that the flush and question on her innocent face had revealed too much, and that her husband was profoundly hurt at being shut out once more from her evident, but secret, pain.

The general watched the difficult emotions that played across Calvern's face in response to the last question, and pressed no further on that issue.

"Do you have any idea which courier Michelle is using?" asked the general.

"Yes, I am almost certain it is John Sharkley."

"Sharkley! He was on that list I forwarded to you last June of possible Napoleonic spies working to discredit King Louis's return to France."

"Precisely. It arrived during the holiday which culminated in my engagement to Michelle. Sharkley, you may remember, was a guest at Holton House at the time—a small courtesy extended for his help in saving Michelle from Malfet."

The general nodded.

"Do you remember I said that although he spoke French, he did not have any direct access to Louis's court, and so was not the prime figure you sought?"

"Yes."

"Even so, as a precaution to protect both Michelle and the family name, as soon as I received your list, I put a footman in constant surveillance of Sharkley. While accompanying Michelle on a walk, he offered to carry mail into France for her."

"Did she use his services?" asked Cresswell.

"I was watching Sharkley; I am not in the habit of spying on my loved ones. However, after this morning's episode at the War Office, I assume she did," Calvern said softly.

The duke paced away, then turned back to face his uncle; his tone became emphatic, decisive. "Yet, Uncle, understand this: Michelle has never been secretive or defensive about her continuing contact with Sharkley. From the day she first introduced him to me in Hyde Park as the gentleman who assisted her in obtaining passage from Belgium to England, to last week, when I discovered that he was the mysterious source of suddenly plentiful French wine and brandy in our household . . ." The duke caught a glimpse of the general's startled expression and burst into laughter.

"You mean to say, Uncle, you did not notice that at Michelle's little supper for thirty for the Frost Fair outing, all those plum puddings were flambéed in so much brandy that the flames lasted for five minutes or more?"

"Preserve us! That was not *French* brandy going up in smoke? I haven't had a drop of the stuff for months. None left in my cellar."

"And I had been rationing my last two bottles like liquid gold. We both have had a chance to buy it from smugglers, and like you, it has been a matter of pride with me not to break the blockade. Here my wife, hosting her first large event, surfaces with superb brandy: she reserved the thirty-year-old cognac for drinking—the stock being burned was merely fifteen years old . . ."

At this news the general groaned.

Calvern continued, "While my friends always expect superb fare when I entertain, they have grown accustomed to the declining standards in wine as my cellar empties. Yet in the first evening we entertain as a married couple, unlimited French champagne flows."

Both men saw the humor and chuckled.

"Needless to say, after our friends departed, I questioned Michelle. She was quite open about it. Sharkley had told her he had a shipment of French brandies and wines, and that his usual buyer was indisposed and unable to purchase at the present time. He offered Michelle cases at what, even before the blockade, would have been most reasonable prices. He assured her that it was not true contraband, for it was imported via Belgium, not directly from France. Michelle believed him and purchased the lot."

Cresswell grinned. "Then, clear in your own conscience, my high-principled nephew, you are now well supplied."

"Not so quickly." Calvern laughed. "For my lovely wife outprincipled even me. After understanding how 'compromised' I was by the possession of the spirits, she was truly distressed, so the next morning she shipped the whole lot off to the military hospital for medicinal use."

The general roared with laughter. "You are a matched pair, lad, and I wish you the pleasure for her, for I suspect she will lead you a merry chase for all your life together."

As the general became quiet again, he also grew more serious. "I can, in fact, see, my boy, how vulnerable Michelle's reputation might well be in the eyes of the War Office. Even you admit that there is every likelihood that she is the victim of international extortion. She has probably written letters to France and obviously has the connections to import contraband."

Calvern nodded grimly.

"More important, look who attended your gathering for the Frost Fair. Your entertainment attracted at least a third of the senior diplomats in London!"

"Its success was completely Michelle's doing," stated Calvern proudly.

Indeed it was.

For the first time in living memory, the Thames had completely frozen over. Myriads of street vendors had set up booths on the ice, with names such as "The Hot Chestnut" or "The Eelpot." One enterprising merchant had imported the blades to be fastened to boots that the Dutch used to glide along the canals. The *ton* deemed it fashionable to have "Frost Fair" parties, simply touring the booths.

Michelle, who had been studying Russian "with friends," gave vent to her imaginative flair, and within days, a marvelous, brilliantly hand-painted troika appeared, "loaned for Their Graces' use and enjoyment," said the footmen who delivered it on a wagon. The duke was astounded.

"Exactly who have you been studying Russian *with*, Michelle?" he said as he entered her sitting room.

Michelle looked up from her needlepoint, surprised. "The Grand Duchess of Oldenberg."

"The czar's sister?"

"Yes. I met her several times with Papa. She is teaching me Russian, in exchange for some advice on art."

Calvern laughed and presented Michelle with the note that the footman had delived. It read: "Courtesy of the Grand Duchess of Oldenberg, for the pleasure of the Duke and Duchess of Calvern, so genuinely interested in things Russian, and with thanks for the several occasions on which the Duchess has advised the Embassy on the collection of art." The Russian ambassador had complemented the Duchess of Oldenburg's loan by providing two grooms, complete in cossack dress with sheepskin coats, to drive the troika "on any day of the Duchess of Calvern's choosing."

What a day the following sun-bright Saturday had been! It included their old friends from diplomatic missions, the Duc d'Anton (who was coming to regard Michelle almost as a daughter) and the Castlereaghs. Every half hour from the shelter of the Calvern tent on the shore, a small group of people would take off in the troika for a merry, wind-whipped ride past the booths and on to the open, frozen river. Michelle, particularly fetching in her red velvet cossack habit, apple-cheeked and laughing, encouraged matrons to at least try a small ride, and allowed children the treat of standing by the driver. Calvern had found the day truly delightful.

"Do you mean to imply," said Calvern, returning to his uncle's comment, "that Michelle's reputation is even more vulnerable because of the number of our friends in the diplomatic corps?"

"Just so," acknowledged the general. "Have you noticed, for instance, the precise and revealing manner in which the Duc d'Anton talks with your wife? Anyone overhearing them would learn at least a little of King Louis and the French Royalist plans for a return after the fall of Napoleon."

"That's true," admitted the duke a little sadly. He knew his Michelle treasured those times with the charming French aristocrat; in some ways, he replaced the father she so dearly mourned.

"Would it not be possible for a Napoleonic spy, working within any legation you regularly entertain, such as the Austrian or Russian, to not only give this Royalist information to our enemies, but also to make it look as if Michelle were the source?"

Calvern regarded his uncle in horror, but Cresswell did not cease his argument, for it was too vital to the family's safety. "Do you not, lad, remember the list of characteristics the War Office suggested would be most likely for an anti-

Royalist spy?: fluent in French, a means of communication with France, and close to Royalist circles."

The duke was white, his voice quiet. "That describes Michelle precisely, does it not?"

"It would certainly be easy for a Napoleonic spy to make the War Office suspicious of her—and I strongly suggest that the real spy is doing exactly that now, and quite effectively."

"Nor is that the worst of it, Uncle. Do you remember the reports of various battles, such as Vitoria, drawn from various news sources?"

"You never did give me the name of the secretary that did those for you," admonished the general. "They were exceptionally fine reports, and we could use a chap that talented; I could easily arrange his transfer from the Foreign to the War Office."

Calvern groaned softly. "Would you believe it, but should it become known beyond the two of us, even this ability could be turned against her. It is Michelle, Uncle, Michelle who wrote the reports you so much like."

The duke thought that he had never seen the general more shocked.

"It must have taken her a great deal of time to learn the format from you. Was she truly that interested?"

"That is just it. I did not have to teach her anything at all. She knows exactly what to look for, and how to present the material—including a summary of the number of men in the field, and clues to projected plans of attack provided by the maneuvers of the enemies themselves. Her father taught her all this. Michelle thinks it is the normal way to report."

"Her father must have been an active spy!"

"I tend to agree with you, Uncle, but I can swear, simply from the depth of feeling Michelle has for the king, that her father was a Royalist."

"Even so, if an active traitor to the French Royalist cause could divert suspicion from himself to Michelle, she is certainly vulnerable to accusation. In fact, although there are no grounds whatever for a charge to be laid, the War Office might think, given such a lead, that there are grounds for an investigation."

"Into what?" The duke's voice was edged with steel.

The general spoke softly. He knew what he was about to say would hurt the lad, but for the duke's, Michelle's, and, indeed, the whole family's sake, it had to be mentioned. "Treason."

Calvern had obviously been holding his breath, and now he released it in a tight, slow hiss.

The general hurried on: "There is one way to safeguard her, at least in some measure, lad, and that is to keep her away from your diplomatic friends, at least for several months, until the war situation calms down."

"You are right, yet it will not be easy. Most of our friends are in that category, and our meetings are frequent. For instance, many will be with us tonight at the Bentleys' costume ball. Even if we are not in town, Holton House is so near to London, many just come by. It almost seems that Michelle is to be punished for her very talent of bringing people together."

Both men were silent, crestfallen.

The duke turned away from his uncle and leaned on the mantel for several moments to collect himself. When he turned again to speak, his face was tense, strong, defiant—a look the general had seen on Calvern's face when, upon his father's death, the lad had vowed to defend the family heritage; he had seen the same expression on the face of the duke's brother, Tom, in the height of battle. Now, the general knew, no one—not the War Office or the regent himself —would touch Michelle or implicate her in any way without facing the white-hot, implacable wrath of Calvern.

Yet as angry as Calvern was, Cresswell knew his nephew would never allow his profound love of his wife to turn him aside from justice. The general could only pray that Michelle was as innocent as Calvern believed, for if, indeed, she had compromised the family honor, he knew both his nephew and the marriage would be irrevocably, fatally torn.

15

THERE WAS A GENTLE knock at the general's study door, and Deirdre entered. "Goodness, I had not realized cook's pickled tongue was so excellent that its enjoyment would detain you gentlemen late into the afternoon," she said smilingly, then, suddenly glancing at the tray, flushed with embarrassment as she saw that very little had been eaten. She looked quickly at the faces of her husband and nephew, and noted no relief from the tension and unhappiness that marked them both when they entered. The problem must be difficult, she thought, if these two astute and practiced men could not resolve it.

"May I remind you both," she said, her smile and cheerfulness fixed firmly in place, "that regardless of the dismal state of the world, which I have no doubt will be improved by your capable solutions, tonight is Lady Almina Bentley's Saint Valentine's costume ball." Turning to Calvern with a dainty mock curtsey, she continued, "Queen Marie Antoinette attends upon you, Your Grace, at your home in Portman Square, while I must elope with my King Richard the Lion-Hearted."

Calvern dismissed his carriage and chose to walk home through the chill damp of the darkening fog. The very briskness of his stride enabled him to think better. Yes, he decided, the wisest thing to do was to tell Michelle immediately of the danger. From the first, he had been impressed by her remarkable common sense and courage; she was sophisticated in the ways of diplomacy, would readily understand the dilemma, and would govern her behavior accordingly.

His decision made eminent sense until he stood before his wife in her dressing room.

She was standing in some long, charming lace pantaloons and a slight, short chemise while Ninette fluttered in circles around her, trying to affix three wide metal hoops on a canvas frame suspended from Michelle's slender waist. Ninette's young apprentice, meanwhile, was preparing to fit the most monstrous silver mound of a bird-cage wig on her head. Calvern could not help but laugh, and his enjoyment was echoed in Michelle's eyes.

"I assure you, sir, my beauty will be exceeded only by the elegance of my husband in his high sheep's-wool wig and satin court coat."

"Tonight am I to be your king?"

"You already are," she mouthed over the seamstress's stooped figure, and blew him a kiss.

As she stood there, so tiny in the metal hoops of her underskirt, Calvern looked at her face, and his heart tightened. Michelle had been upset these past ten days with a winter chill; her face, so alive with pleasure at seeing him, was nonetheless drawn and peaked. In truth, she actually looked tired, and there were, he could clearly discern, faint shadows under her eyes. Now was no time for a discussion of possible accusations of treason, yet for her very safety, he had to forestall her customary vivacious and wide mingling at the ball. For the first time in their married lives, he would ask her compliance without an explanation.

He would rely on her love.

"Do you know that this is the first time since our engagement that you have sat *across* from me in the carriage? I sincerely hope you are not setting a precedent." Michelle tried to make her voice sound light and gay, but a weariness colored it.

"My dear," said Calvern, also straining for lightness, "what is a gentleman to do when his beloved has barricaded herself behind four-foot-wide hoops and a wig that would be a lethal weapon if it toppled? It is Saint Valentine's Day, and perhaps tonight, to contemplate your beauty from afar, or at least from the far side of the couch, is not inappropriate."

Michelle chuckled.

"And," proceeded Calvern, "your adoring worshiper is not without his suitable offering." He withdrew a small, white velvet bag from his pocket and dangled it before her.

She reached for it; he playfully waved it higher. "Gilding the lily, or at least the fleur-de-lys." He laughed and let it tumble into her lap.

Carefully, she drew out a broad gold bracelet with the Royalist fleur-de-lys worked in a band across it in exquisite Florentine enameling. Her eyes shone. *"Merci, mon cher."*

Calvern looked suddenly earnest. "Tonight *is* special, love, for it is our first Saint Valentine's evening together. Others will swoop down upon us, but may I make this special request? I would enjoy having you close to me for the greater part of the time. Will you dance only with me?" He reached across the carriage for her hand.

Michelle was caught by the unusually serious tone in her husband's romantic words. "Is this a command, Your Majesty?"

"It is."

Her fan splayed open and hid all but her lovely eyes. "Then, my liege lord, it is my pleasure to obey."

As obedient as this Marie Antoinette intended to be to her beloved, the fates conspired as consistently against her as they had against her namesake. Lady Bentley, in her usual thoughtfulness, had seated close friends together; the Duc d'Anton's delight at discovering the Duke of Calvern and his bride at his table was obvious. Immediately the graceful older diplomat tried to claim Michelle to regale her with the latest gossip, but Calvern, with unaccustomed abruptness, snatched his wife away from him to lead her in a quadrille.

Michelle, not failing to note Calvern's glower, demurred where she could, pleaded exhaustion, and suggested often that the guests forgo the dancing to sit and converse with her husband and herself. But certain dances, particular requests, had to honored or risk rudeness. The Russian ambassador, still basking in the success of the troika, demanded a quadrille, and would not be denied. Even Count von Reichertz, who had not seen Michelle since her engagement, declared loudly that Marie Antoinette, France's wittiest and most beautiful queen, was, of course, Austrian, and he, therefore, exercised the prerogative of a countryman and demanded a waltz—a farewell waltz, as he was returning to Vienna the following week.

Even so, the duke, already tense and protective, seeing von Reichertz whisper to his wife as they danced, and d'Anton try yet again to approach her for a gossip, became furious at his helplessness in defending her, and snapped at the intruders. Few others of their friends withstood the duke's obvious ill temper toward those who who approached his wife.

Michelle watched Calvern's behavior, first with astonishment, then with growing vexation. Her husband's final rudeness to the Duc d'Anton was beyond bearing. She asked Calvern if they could leave, and he acquiesced, saying immediately was not soon enough.

Evidently the duke's behavior did not go unheeded by others. In the cloaking room, behind a screen, as a maid helped Michelle close the fastener of her cape, she overheard fragments of comments.

"Our new little duchess of French origin does, indeed, seem to have upset the applecart, for who would have guessed our aloof, controlled Calvern was even *capable* of lost composure?"

"Rumor, I admit, but it is said he is jealous of her past *amours* and now guards her like an angry bear."

"My dear! Were d'Anton and von Reichertz *both* her lovers? They seem to be the ones Calvern was angriest at."

"*Both* her lovers? Are you sure those two were all?" the matron chuckled.

Michelle swept through the farewells to Lady Bentley, cheeks flaming, with Calvern hurrying after her. Their carriage had barely drawn up to the bottom of the steps before Michelle, avoiding the duke's proferred arm, hurried down, voluminous skirts swaying, and stepped up into the vehicle with only the footman's assistance. She spread her skirts, her fan, her reticule, across the entire width of the seat so that her husband could not possibly sit beside her and stared fixedly, silently, out of the coach window.

Odd, thought Calvern, slouched in the corner opposite with seemingly imperturbable elegance (a pose he had succeeded in assuming only in the carriage), but Michelle seemed to have lost a little weight over the last several weeks. It was worrying, but it did heighten the delicate curve of her flushed cheeks and slender arch of her neck, making her even more beautiful. The coach lamps affixed outside the carriage cast through a warm, yellow glow within; and by their light, near her fleur-de-lys pendant he could see the pulse beating at the base of her throat, the small flutter he always kissed.

Quite simply, he had never loved her or hungered for her more, yet feared so greatly for her safety, or felt more unable to ensure it. The maelstrom of emotions churning relentlessly through him froze suddenly as he realized that although Michelle's face was impassive, her cheeks were glistening with tears.

He had never before in their marriage been the cause of her tears, and he despised himself for it.

Wordlessly they left the carriage, wordlessly they ascended the stairs of Portman Square, both clearly aware that to whisper even a syllable would start a rage that no servant, no other being, should be allowed to witness. By common, unspoken consent they entered the small private sitting room adjoining their bedchamber; it was neutral territory and appropriate for battle.

As Calvern closed and locked the door against intruding servants, Michelle swirled her cape from her shoulders. "What do you think I am—an object to be purchased at the price of a few trinkets?" She drew Calvern's heavy Valentine's bangle from her wrist and fired it at him. He dodged, and it struck the door.

"Do you think that because I'm now your wife you can boorishly monopolize my company, be rude to any of our friends who dares to speak to me?" Her sapphire ear bobs flew across the room and rolled under his writing desk.

"By look, or word, or action, have I ever implied that I was interested in another? What justification have you ever had for such insanely possessive jealousy?" She slipped a large ornamental ring from her finger and dropped it onto his inkwell tray with a clatter.

"For let me make this clear: I cannot be purchased or possessed. I came to you freely because I was loved and respected; I love you, but I will not spend my life being handled as chattel by a sullen boor." She reached for the clasp of her pendant and struggled with it; it would not give.

In two strides, Calvern was behind her, opened it, and dropped the ornament into her hand. "My dear," he said, his voice soothing, "I could not bear to see the rhythm of your magnificent tirade broken."

Furious, she whirled to face him, and was stunned by the expression in his eyes: there was not the arrogant, dispassionate amusement she had anticipated; there was something very close to sorrow, to gentle expectancy.

For long seconds she gazed at him.

"Then your behavior tonight was not possessive jealousy."

"I freely admit to enjoying your company so intensely that at times I find myself annoyed by the intrusion of others, but I hope my social graces are fine enough not to allow such annoyance to show. I have, however, never, not for one minute, ever doubted your loyalty or faithfulness."

"But tonight you were so rude. You snarled at von Reichertz, practically barked at the Russian ambassador, and what distressed me most of all, genuinely affronted the dear old Duc d'Anton, who had mentioned he had something important to tell me. Why, you have never been as rude since the Earl of Malfet first asked you if he could call on me."

"Perhaps I have the same reason now, as I did then— your safety."

At this Michelle's eyes grew wide. Again she searched Calvern's face: it was marked by no anger, no fear, only the same clear sorrow. His statement was in earnest.

"Whatever danger could there be for me in my husband's company among friends at a private gathering?"

Calvern sighed and strode away from her to the hearth. "Although it is invisible, danger as real and more insidious than that on any battlefield." He came toward her, placed his hand under her chin, and tilted her face up to his; his voice was gentle. "The time has come, my love, to tell me what troubles you about someone in France."

At this, Michelle's eyes instantly filled with tears. For the first time in her married life, she turned from him because she could not speak freely.

"I can't. I'm pledged to a silence that, once broken, might cost the life of another." She faced him, fighting back the tears. "Oh, Edward, isn't it enough that you know all about me, everything that I can possibly think of to tell you, about Papa, about traveling, about all that happened during these terrible, terrible wars? There is not a thing on my own behalf that I have been reluctant to reveal. Surely, surely this must be enough to justify your trust. But I cannot betray the life of another."

"I knew it! I knew that such vital strictures on truth would not be your choice."

Suddenly she realized the impossibility, the horror of the situation: to solve the dilemma of her husband, she would have to betray the life of her brother! The enormity of it overwhelmed her; tension snapped through her body like a whip. She staggered back, crumpling, covering her face.

Her lover reached her, embraced her before the first sob broke. He held her, caressing her back for minutes on end. "Do you know the time I learned I loved you, and would love you for all my life?" he whispered.

She shook her head as it lay on his breast, not daring to look up.

"When you trusted me enough to share what happened to you at Ulm. I knew then that you were completely honest and without fear. I knew there was nothing that I needed to know about you that you would not tell me. I trust you absolutely; I always will. But this thing that you cannot tell me may hurt you more than you would believe, and without information to protect you, I cannot help."

She pulled away from him and gave him a long, searching look. "Hurt me? How?"

"It is all quite simple, too simple really. Some Napoleonic spy is sending detailed information on all of King Louis's plans for his return to France for his proposed constitutional monarchy. Every major step Louis is attempting for his restoration is anticipated and then negated or confused by Napoleon's counterattacks.

"The War Office knows that this spy has three characteristics: he must be fluent in French, be intimate with details of Louis's court in Buckinghamshire, and have regular means of communication with France.

"This morning, the secretary of war called me to his office; my uncle had been previously informed, and he came with me. For half an hour they outlined their information, then concluded by saying quite simply that while they were not "officially suspicious" of you, they did know that you were communicating regularly with France, by means of a courier who regularly contacts known spies. They did not state the courier's name, but I deduced it is John Sharkley."

While Calvern had been speaking, the horror on Michelle's face grew. She understood very clearly what was implied. "The War Office thinks there is a possibility, if not a likelihood, that I am that spy."

The duke could only nod. "And I am so glad that I haven't added inadvertently to your danger. You know the reports that you do for me, the analysis of the foreign newspapers? They're superbly done, better than those written by any of my secretaries at the Foreign Office. There isn't a man among them who can touch the caliber of your work. The minister has assumed that it is a secretary I have hired privately, and he has been asking constantly for his name so the Foreign Office can offer him a position. Thank heavens I've never stated that it is your research! The only one who knows your identity is my uncle, whom I told this afternoon.

You see, your father trained you beautifully in exactly the format for spy reports."

The instant surprise and horror on Michelle's face brought a flood of relief to Calvern; it was obvious that she had had absolutely no previous conception of that fact. She was speechless.

Calvern clapsed both her hands. "So, my love, I could not explain all this to you in the half hour before we went out to a ball. I only hoped that by keeping all contacts with you to a minimum, I could forestall the real spy, who is possibly among our 'friends' and uses you to get information about King Louis. I also attempted, most awkwardly I admit, to reduce your time with the the the Duc d'Anton, which would ease War Office suspicions about you a little. The only way to limit those contacts was by being rude."

"Oh, Edward." Michelle blushed furiously. "I overheard in the ladies' cloaking room two gossips saying you were guarding me like a bear, probably because of all my previous *amours*. They think I am a woman of questionable virtue."

Much to her amazement, Calvern laughed. "Why, that is wonderful. It means no one suspects what I was really doing, which is all the better for your safety; and time and our behavior toward each other in the future will lay that untruth to rest. But now I must think of a way to safeguard you without admitting too noticeably that we are withdrawing from contact. I had thought of our going to Holton House for a few weeks, but that would be proof, in the War Office's eyes, that I thought you might be guilty and had therefore spirited you away. We would never want such a slur on the name of Radcliffe."

Michelle raised her chin indignantly. "If it is an insult to the name of Radcliffe to be a Napoleonic spy, it is ten times more dishonorable for the Royalist name of de Bellevue."

The duke glanced at her oddly, as if she said something that he had never before considered. "That could conceivably be a fitting revenge, couldn't it?"

"What do you mean?" his wife asked in puzzlement.

Perhaps it was the tiredness or the strain in her voice, but Calvern looked sharply at Michelle. If she had appeared a little drawn before the start of the evening, she was now white with exhaustion. The shadows under her eyes had deepened to dark marks, and her hand, as it brushed back her hair, had the faintest tremor. In seconds, he had swooped her up into his arms, the hooped shirt of her costume bouncing in the air.

"We should not call your maid, not at this hour of the night. I'll try to release you from that bird cage of hoops Ninette so proudly bound you into, and then to bed."

He laid Michelle down on their bed; she was asleep almost before he had undressed her.

Her sleep that night was disturbed and restive. At one moment, she was hiding, heart in mouth, in that thornbush in Ulm; at another, she was standing with Richard in the inn at Ostend, pleading not to be sent to England. In one dreadful scene, the look of Malfet as he had struck her across the face swirled past; she awakened with a cry. She turned toward Edward, but he was not in the bed; he came running across the room, only partly undressed. She sat up, half-awake.

"Edward, you have not come to bed."

"Sh, sh, my love. I could not sleep, so I have been sitting in the chair, thinking." He held her and smoothed back her hair. "Lean against me; I'll be here." In seconds she had fallen back against his shoulder and slept, this time more peacefully.

In the darkness, Calvern had come to realize what he must do. Michelle would not violate her pledge any more than he would under similar circumstances. What she could not tell him, he would have to find out by other means. He knew that the Duc d'Anton had known Michelle's father; he would start his investigation there. Unfortunately, he knew the diplomat had started the journey back to King Louis in Buckinghamshire immediately after the ball; Calvern would go there as soon as possible. But meanwhile, with Michelle resting safe in his arms, he could sleep.

The next morning, when she awoke, the first thing Michelle saw beside her bed was one pink rose, and her bracelet, ear bobs, ring, and pendant neatly placed on the small white velvet bag. There was a note beside them: "the armaments of love," and a small sketch of a male figure dodging a flying object. She laughed and felt the warmth of Calvern's love for her.

Somehow, that warmth made what Michelle had decided to do even more right. She asked her maid to have Jane come to her immediately.

Jane was not happy, not happy at all.

The old governess and loyal companion sat with ramrod stiffness in her chair, her hands smartly folded—Michelle recognized it as her most disapproving posture. "Just be-

cause someone at the War Office has made vague mention of
the fact that you are French and therefore possibly a spy—
for that is all the grounds they can have—is no reason to go
trotting off across the channel to find Richard at any time,
and certainly not now, in the middle of Napoleon's retreat."

"Oh, Jane." Michelle's voice was one of both pleading
and impatience. "It is much more serious than you recognize. Edward was questioned yesterday by the secretary of
war—and they implied that they knew all about my writing
to Richard. They did not tell Edward that I have been using
Sharkley to deliver the letters; Edward deduced that himself."

At the news that the War Office had gone so far as to
apprise the duke of the situation, Jane did, indeed, look
troubled.

Sensing that Jane might be won to her cause, Michelle
continued rapidly: "And then, I am seriously perturbed
about the welfare of Richard himself. Do you know that he
gave no comment on my engagement and never even mentioned the invitation to our wedding, despite my pleadings
with him to come?"

Jane was, indeed, surprised. "Did he thank you specifically for the money you sent?"

"I have not heard from him since I sent the five hundred
pounds." Michelle was close to tears, and now Jane fully
shared her anxiety.

"Well, girl, do you have his letters here? May I see them?
For something is indeed not right."

Michelle pulled a small, neat bundle from her handkerchief drawer, and the two women sat together, opening and
reading the letters. Jane held the envelopes to the light. "It is
certainly Richard's seal."

Michelle nodded. "I checked that most carefully."

The governess adjusted her quizzing glass. "And it appears to be Richard's handwriting. But there is something
most strange. We were most poor right after the Revolution,
when Richard learned to write. As a young lad, he did his
lessons on slate with chalk, and your papa allowed him to use
paper only on the most special occasions, so he learned to be
most economical with it. I have never seen him write with
such wide and generous spacing in my life"

The two women fell silent for a moment, contemplating
the dilemma.

"I am certain, under such strange circumstances, your
pledge to Richard might be set aside. Why not tell Edward

fully of the situation, including these odd letters? In fact, Edward would probably try to find Richard for you himself."

"So he would, but," Michelle countered, "would Richard reveal himself to a man he had never seen before, claiming he was my husband? Even if Edward should carry personal items from me, Richard, I know, would still not take such a chance. Such caution is why he has lived this long."

"Then you are convinced you must find Richard yourself."

"Yes."

"Well," said Jane, rising to her feet and sighing, "there is one last thing to be considered. I suppose you have not yet told Edward of your delicate condition?"

"N-no," stuttered Michelle. "Two or three weeks simply does not seem long enough to be sure, and Edward believes only that I have a winter chill from the Frost Fair."

"Any consideration of your condition would not be enough to stop you from going to Europe." The old nurse knew Michelle's nature, so it was not so much a question as a statement.

Michelle nodded. "On the contrary, is it not now more important than ever that the Radcliffe and de Bellevue family names stand above reproach? And the only way that can be done now is to bring Richard to England and let him explain to Edward, the War Office, and even to the prime minister himself what is going on."

Jane was convinced, but she was still not happy. Michelle took her hand and smiled. "'Would you feel any less guilt if I told you that I am going to find Richard with or without you, so you have, in fact, not consented to the decision and are simply accompanying me for my well-being and safety?"

Jane nodded, grateful for Michelle's understanding. "Only on condition you will tell His Grace."

"Of course I will—otherwise Edward will worry. I will write him a note telling him what I am doing and why, and assuring him that I am safe, have sufficient funds, and will communicate with him at the earliest moment. I will not say where or how we are going, for he would follow and stop us, without a doubt. Now, to our plans."

Jane was as satisfied as she could expect to be in such circumstances and mentally noted to herself that if she could not betray her mistress by telling the duke, at least she could be forgiven for telling her own dear Charles Wilson, the duke's butler, a few more details than Michelle would reveal in her letter. And so putting her conscience to rest, she set about helping Michelle to prepare.

The two were most efficient, for they had not traveled about war-torn Europe for years without learning to pack quickly, travel lightly, and plan wisely. Within an hour, they were ready.

Dressed for a normal morning's outing, they each carried a small case—imported silk, they told the maids, for a friend in Regent Street. They had deliberately chosen Regent Street, which architect Nash was developing for the prince, for it was notorious for traffic and a jumble of construction, and near to their first destination. Because it was obvious the duke's heavy coach would likely get caught in the construction timbers and mud, the thoughtful Duchess of Calvern offered to walk the last two hundred feet and dismissed the carriage. The coachman, appreciative of so considerate a mistress, drove off.

As soon as the coach was out of sight, Michelle and Jane entered a hired hackney and sped off to the address Ninette had been able to scribble down for them from memory—Mr. Sharkley's, master of her attentive and amusing Roland, who now accompanied the jolly seamstress on almost every shopping trip.

Despite the fact that his extortions had been both tidily conducted and lucrative, Sharkley had always known that for his deliberate deception of the matchless Michelle, there would be reserved for him a special hell, and he recognized that he was confronting that torture now.

Here she was, even more perfect than he had remembered (the delicacy of her face seemed enhanced—was she a trifle thinner?), sitting on the new satin settee in his drawing room, nodding daintily as she took a slice of new pound cake and a cup of tea from Roland, who was serving with the elegance of a butler to the king. Even that old gray-haired Cerberus, her companion, seemed to be nodding in appreciation as Michelle praised him, Sharkley, until he thought he would writhe in his very seat from the agony of his deception.

"However can I thank you, sir," said Michelle, honest appreciation shining from her eyes, which seemed more incredibly violet than even he had remembered, "for your kindness in undertaking to deliver for me those letters which mean so much to me? Why, you would not even accept a twopence to cover your expenses, yet I know how difficult and dangerous the task has been."

The sincerity of her voice was so unnerving that even Roland's hand shook as he poured tea for Jane.

"Mr. Sharkley, you have rescued me twice already, at Ostend and from the perfidious Earl of Malfet. Alas, I am afraid I must come again, needing your help and trusting in your most kind and forthright nature."

This is it, thought Sharkley. This is hell.

"A most dangerous situation has suddenly arisen, and I find that I must go to my brother, Monsieur de Varennes, immediately. Your delivery of the letters to him has been so efficient, I know that you will be able to help me find him quickly."

Michelle's worried frown intensifed the trusting pleading of her look, and Sharkley recognized that it was no small matter that had driven the vulnerable beauty before him to seek his help. He would have preferred to be assaulted by a hundred screaming demons with hot pokers, or to face Malfet himself roaring, violently drunk, before he would utter one word to deceive the gentle Michelle in her need.

He was rendered speechless.

"Me master is most 'umble about 'is accomplishments in finding people, Your Grace, and I am afeared that your praise has embarrassed him not a little." Roland shot his master a glance: Black Jack was still frozen, immobile. "It is a full six months since we have seen the gentleman in question, since afore Your Grace's wedding." Here Roland made a little bow and, momentarily turning his back to the guests, glowered warningly at his master. "'Owever, the last time we saw Monsieur de Varennes, it was in the same inn in Ostend where we first encountered Your Grace."

Sharkley managed the faintest of nods.

"And I am sure 'ow me master would recommend to start the search there, by inquiring of the innkeeper. Now, even a stable boy would remember 'orseflesh as fine as the gray one ridden by Monsieur de Varennes when we last clapped eyes on 'im."

Sharkley managed another nod.

"Is . . . is that all?" faltered Michelle, paling with disappointment.

"Come, my dear," said Jane, immediately grasping the futility of the situation, and rising. "I am sure the gentlemen have given us all their information, which will be quite enough if we use our heads and tongues wisely. We do thank

you for your hospitality and kindness." Jane marched firmly
to the door, with Michelle, dazed, two steps behind.

Sharkley followed dumbly to the threshold, grateful that
Roland had so gracefully handed them their cloaks and
escorted them to their carriage, but he never expected Roland's comment as the servant returned.

"Well, no crested coach for the new duchess but an 'ired
'ackney, told to wait! 'Ho would 'ave believed it of little Miss
Innocence, barely four months married to 'er duke, and already off to see 'er lover in France!"

For the first time in all their months together, Sharkley
struck Roland. He seized the servant by the lapels and threw
him into the settee so forcefully that it skidded on the carpet.

"Not only am I certain that is *not* her intent, my man, but
I want to know exactly what you have been telling our beloved Earl of Malfet when you have made your weekly
brandy deliveries these last few times, for I suspect you have
been betraying the duchess to her worst enemy. You know as
well as I the messages we carry for him to France are probably for spies, and even now, if my guess is right, the earl is
arranging to have Michelle suspected of *his* own treachery.
What have you been saying to Malfet?"

Here the enraged Sharkley picked the shocked servant up
by the lapels, then drew the trembling Roland's face to
within inches of his own. "If you hesitate to confess, I'll turn
you over to the War Office myself."

"So Ostend, is it, my girl? 'Where we start, we end,' as
the proverb goes," said Jane as they settled into the hackney.
"Down to the docks?"

Michelle shook her head. "Edward is much too clever for
that, I fear. As soon as we are missing, he will approach
every passenger agent in London, and probably all the coach
houses on the road to Dover. I do not know my new country
too well yet, Jane. Is there another port?"

"No, you are quite right. Canterbury to Dover would not
be at all the thing. Let me think—Maidstone and Ashford to
Folkestone, that is it! Folkestone is a fishing village a scarce
few miles from Dover, but it does have small vessels going to
Ostend. We shall try that, but only on one condition, my
girl."

"What?" Michelle already felt weary.

"That we hire not one of those bouncing chaises, but a
well-sprung private coach. Gone are the days when we must
tolerate the vagaries and inconveniences of shoddily kept

conveyances, and now, especially with your condition, I will not hear of it. If you refuse, I will go straight back to the duke."

"Such blackmail," Michelle laughed, and, indeed, although she never would have confessed it, she was most grateful for whatever meager comforts could be provided.

Even in London, with substantial funds, it took them until afternoon to find a well-sprung vehicle and a coachman willing to make the journey in a straight run. A tall, redheaded, lanky lad finally agreed.

"Mind, it will take a good twenty-four hours for the ninety miles, for if it rains any harder, the roads turn to mud tracks going into a small village like Folkestone."

The rain, fortunately, did not arrive until almost midnight.

They reached Sevenoaks in time for a late evening supper, which was indifferent. In spite of the small travel pillow Jane had brought for her charge, and the warmth of her favorite lavender cloak, which she hugged around her only wishing it were Calvern's arms, Michelle found sleep impossible. If dinner at Sevenoaks was indifferent, a late breakfast at a small inn beyond Ashford was worse.

Once, as they approached Folkestone, they heard the thundering hoofbeats of a horseman behind them, and the young duchess caught herself wishing it were Calvern.

It was exactly twenty-two hours later and midafternoon as they reached Folkestone. The young coachman had driven well and was amply rewarded for his efforts.

A small gray-stone inn stood high on the cliffs overlooking the harbor. The landlord could not only provide a small private sitting room with a roaring fire in the hearth for their use, but would book them on the first packet available for Ostend as well. As Jane made the final arrangements, Michelle slipped the hood of the cape over her head and stepped out into the gentle mist for a walk on the leas, the gardens on the cliff tops.

How would it be when she came back to England, if, indeed, she came back at all? (She had seen enough of war to know that disasters were possible, and that civilians could be victims.) How had Richard changed? Why had he become so callous, so mercenary? Would he consent to come back to England with her, and if he did, how would Edward receive him? For her beloved duke, would the de Bellevues always be tainted as spies, even though they were Royalists? That thought was too painful to be borne.

Suddenly she was so exhausted that her very bones seemed leaden. These questions were too big; tonight they seemed insoluble. For the first time since leaving London, her cheeks were wet with tears.

For minutes she cradled her reticule to her, with its small collection of treasures from the people she cherished above all else—the pendant, necklace, and valentine bracelet Edward had given her; her parents' prayer book; the latest letter from Emma on her wedding trip to Devon—as if by doing so, she could draw healing warmth from their love of her.

She glanced down.

Below, she could see the masts of ten or twelve small vessels bobbing in the harbor. From the height of the cliff, they looked like children's toys, and somehow that was comforting. Through it all—the discomfort, the damp, the loneliness, and the uncertainty of the outcome—she knew one thing: she was right to undertake this voyage. The question of her own and her family's integrity had to be settled, and that well before the birth of their child.

She would pursue her course to the end.

She glanced down at her damp feet. Suddenly she realized that she was standing in a patch of wild spring crocuses, blooming this early, this bravely. Yellow and violet! The colors reminded her of her first splendid drive in Hyde Park. It seemed so long ago, though it was only ten months. And the crocuses might well be in bloom at Holton House, the only home that she had ever known, and was fighting for now. She stooped, picked several, and held them close as she returned to the inn.

She was not superstitious, but just this once, she allowed herself to believe the flowers were a sign and promise that she would return to England, and to her beloved, vindicated.

16

WHEN THE FRONT knocker rang out resoundingly, Sharkley answered it himself, for he was servantless.

"Good afternoon, Your Grace; I've been expecting you."

"You have?" Calvern was astonished; indeed, it was the
only positive remark that he had heard all this terrible day.
Before Calvern had had a chance to leave for the Duc
d'Anton's in Buckinghamshire, the general had arrived, saying that just last night a statement had been sworn naming
Michelle as a spy. The duke sent the shortest of notes to
d'Anton, pleading for help on behalf of his wife, then he and
the general rushed to the War Office. This interview with
Sharkley was Calvern's first stop after what had been, without question, the worst day of his life.

"Would you please come into the parlor? Care to be
seated? May I offer you a little brandy, a morsel of fruitcake
iced with marzipan?"

Sharkley sincerely hoped Calvern would say yes, for less
than half an hour ago, he had given his landlady a full pound
for the dainties, to be refunded in full if a *real* duke showed
up in a crested carriage. Calvern, in fact, had ridden over,
and Sharkley just hoped that a groom holding a horse with a
crested saddle blanket would be as acceptable to the old ter-
magant.

The Duke stationed himself by the mantel. "Nothing to
eat; perhaps just a little brandy." Calvern knew it was contraband, but today it did not matter.

"I apologize for serving you myself, but my man, Roland,

departed today under circumstances that will become clear."

"Sir, I am not here to investigate the status of your servants, but to inquire about my wife's correspondence, through you, with France." The duke felt sorry; he had not meant to sound rude, but today had tried him almost beyond his limits. Fortunately, Sharkley did not appear to be in the least perturbed. "You see, there is some serious question about the nature of the correspondence, and I should like to ascertain from you to whom the letters were addressed."

Sharkley was learning to understand Calvern a little better, and now knew that he was so formal, so aloof, only when a true crisis loomed. He felt almost sorry for the man. Yet—yes he would, he would play his high card in this first hand and impress the duke with his knowledge.

"Is it true then that Michelle—excuse me, Her Grace—is threatened with accusations of being a spy?"

Calvern was surprised. "It is."

"Is it also true that those accusations have been formalized by a complaint to the War Office—a complaint signed by a peer of this realm?"

The duke was completely astonished. He himself had obtained the information that it was the Earl of Malfet who had sworn the affidavit naming Michelle as a spy only an hour ago, after the general and he had elicited the support of every friend they had in the War Office up to the prime minister. He nodded at Sharkley. "It is."

"Then, Your Grace, it is my pleasure to offer some considerable assistance to you."

"The name of the person with whom she corresponded would be a splendid help."

The interview was going much better than Black Jack would ever have dared to hope; he permitted himself a small, graceful bow. "Sir, it is my pleasure to offer you something much more substantial even than that."

Calvern took a small sip of brandy. He had that distinctly odd feeling—as he had had with the old art dealer—that he did not know at all what was going on. He inclined his head. "Please continue."

"I have here, sir"—with a flourish Sharkley produced a packet of letters, neatly tied with ribbon, on a silver tray—"Her Grace's complete correspondence with France."

Calvern felt himself grow almost weak with relief. He seized the letters instantly—they guaranteed the recognition of Michelle's innocence. "Copies?" Even though they would be of significant help, Calvern felt his fury rising. No one had a right to copy his wife's letters, whatever the circumstances.

"No, Your Grace, not copies—the originals."

Calvern gasped.

"For whatever the War Office says, Your Grace, or the Earl of Malfet in his sworn statement, or even Michelle herself, no word she has written has ever left London."

"How do the originals come to be in your possession?" Calvern demanded testily.

Part of the truth was as good as the whole, Sharkley had always said, and he wanted to be acknowledged as once again saving Michelle; the departed Roland could well afford to bear the blame. "It appears that my man, Roland, was extorting money from the duchess by sending her letters that she believed were from a certain Monsieur de Varennes, but were, in fact, forged."

"How can that be? Were they not sealed?"

Sharkley pulled a small occasional chair to the duke's side, seated himself, and leaned forward, speaking in a confidential whisper, although no one else was in the flat. "It seems that Roland stole the gentleman's seal in an encounter in Ostend, as well as a sample of his handwriting. He used a forger to write notes and offered them to Her Grace as legitimate correspondence from Monsieur de Varennes."

"Why did Roland keep her responses? Surely they are incriminating?"

Sharkley shrugged; the question had touched a tender point with him. "I believe Roland's extortion extended to many people, Your Grace, but Michelle's letters were the only ones he kept. An unusual fondness for her, perhaps? I found them among his personal belongings after his departure."

Calvern felt ill at the thought of some disreputable criminal reading Michelle's thoughts and laughing and discussing possible responses at some shilling-house forger's. Nonetheless, he was grateful. "This is, indeed, a major assistance. It is the proof that my wife sent nothing to France, and so will save her reputation. We are most indebted to you."

Sharkley almost winced at the sentence; it reminded him of the phrase the duke had used at Michelle's come-out.

"But, if I may ask, sir, how did you know the peer signing the complaint was the Earl of Malfet?" The information, I believe, exists only in the War Office."

Sharkley remembered another maxim of thieves, taught him by the departed Roland: "Confess what is already known."

"As you may know, sir, due to pressing financial circumstances, I have become . . . ah, an importer of contraband. The person for whom I worked, I am profoundly ashamed to say, was the Earl of Malfet." (Black Jack thought for a moment of expounding upon his shame and contrition, but noting that Calvern's face was drawn and impatient, he hurried along.) "It appears that Roland, in making his weekly deliveries, was paid by Malfet to give him information he had gleaned from the duchess's seamstress—Ninette, is it? So of course, the earl knew the details of Her Grace's activities, of the gossip from the French court in Buckinghamshire, and used that, and Roland's talking of a 'de Varennes correspondence,' to implicate her as a spy. Roland confessed to me before he departed—with rather undue haste."

"So Malfet hates her that much, does he?" the duke mused, almost to himself.

"I beg to differ, sir," said Sharkley, himself surprised by both his sudden insight into the earl and his own sympathy with him. "Perhaps he loves her, in his own perverse way, so much that he would rather see her dead than belong to another."

The thought was astounding, thought Calvern, yet it was all so simple, so obvious. But then, from what he knew of foreign affairs, the resolutions of catastrophes and evil are most often simple. He glanced down at the letters, secure in his waistcoat, relaxed a little, and took another sip of what he now had the leisure to recognize was excellent brandy.

Black Jack, too, was thinking. For one wild moment, he thought he might tell the duke that Malfet himself was the spy they sought, but then he thought better of it. He would only confess enough to save Michelle; the War Office would soon find the real spy for themselves. In fact, if he said anymore, it was conceivable that he, Sharkley, could be arrested as a traitor's accomplice for having carried the messages. It was bad enough to have admitted being in the black market.

The duke raised his glass to Sharkley. "Thank you for the letters. For a third time you have saved Michelle. No one will hear from me of your 'importing' activities. Indeed, we shall look forward to using your services after Boney is put to rest and the blockade is lifted, which, from what we hear, should be soon."

Black Jack nodded in appreciation. One could always trust a true gentleman to understand.

At just that moment there was a large, clear thump of the knocker. Calvern heard Sharkley open the door, then, to his amazement, he discerned the precise, modulated speech of his butler, Charles Wilson. Never in the last twenty years had this senior retainer left the house to deliver a message. There were footmen, grooms, stable boys, for that. This must be urgent: Michelle! Even before Wilson had requested permission to see the duke, Calvern was behind Sharkley at the door.

"A most important message, Your Grace. I've brought the carriage for your convenience."

Calvern had made his thanks and departing bows in a minute and was off in the carriage.

Sharkley was so delighted he almost whooped. Not only had the interview gone superbly, but the landlady had witnessed the arrival at her house of both a crested carriage *and* a steed. Those two items should be good for *another* fruitcake with marzipan.

"So, Charles?" inquired the duke before they were both barely seated in the carriage.

"It is the duchess, Your Grace, and Jane Malton with her. They have left for Europe."

"Good God!"

"It appears, sir, to be a mission to find a certain Monsieur de Varennes, a personage that the duchess seems to feel can retrieve her reputation, sir, though I doubt it was ever lost. The information is in this letter to you from your wife, sir."

Calvern looked at the envelope—it was still sealed—then glanced at his trusted servant. "How do you know...?"

"Jane Malton, sir. She and I are friends of some considerable longstanding. Since the duchess forbade Jane to tell you, Jane has told me, and I am to tell you, they are voyaging to Ostend, not by Dover but through Folkestone."

"A channel crossing in mid-February? Devilishly treacherous, and ships leaving Folkestone are smaller. Why did they choose Folkestone?"

"Her Grace thought it would be a route you would not likely take to follow her; Jane thought it would be a slower route and give you a better opportunity to catch up. She also insisted the duchess hire a heavy traveling coach rather than a regular one, to slow things down even further. Jane will try in every way to delay the channel crossing until you arrive."

"I do hope her attempt is successful," the duke said vehemently.

"I share your wish, sir, for you see, there is a slight difficulty with the duchess."

Even thought he could not see it in the unlit gloom of the carriage, Calvern could feel the elderly gentleman's embarassment. "Please, do not hesitate."

"Jane is most terribly worried about the crossing, sir, because your wife is with child, and not at all well."

Calvern was stonily, utterly silent.

Wilson knew the young duke well enough to realize that he was behaving like a true Calvern: all feelings, no matter how profound, were being locked away in order to think clearly about what had to be done, immediately, successfully.

"Will you please have the groom bring the horse behind us, ride to the Cresswells', and request that the general join me for the ride to Folkestone?"

"After I spoke with Jane, Your Grace, I presumed to anticipate your instructions and had the general informed of all except the . . . ah, intimate details. He is awaiting you at Portman Square with his best mount, sir. He estimated that on horseback, with two grooms and three horse changes, you ought to be able to make the ninety-mile journey in sixteen hours, and so have every reasonable chance of catching the duchess before she embarks."

Before he leaped from the carriage as it drew up before his stables, Calvern put his hand on Wilson's shoulder. "I am blessed in my family and my retainers, my good man."

And we are blessed in him, the old butler thought.

Through the fog the four men heard Big Ben sound nine as they thundered across Westminster bridge. Three hours out of London the fog turned to a driving downpour; the road became barely visible. The general was mounted on Warrior, a large, dark horse with exceptional speed and staying power, a fine match for Calvern's favored gray, Smoke. Yet they rode the twenty miles to Sevenoaks in five hours— slow time.

While the Duke's groom began the rubdown of Smoke and Warrior (he would stay the rest of the night in Sevenoaks and return with the horses to London on the morrow), the general's second man was selecting and saddling the horses for the run to Maidstone. Calvern took advantage of the quarter-hour respite to slip into the now almost deserted tavern of the hostelry and, in the private inglenook behind the hearth, to read Michelle's letters, addressed to the same de Varennes whom Wilson had said she was seeking in Europe. Who was this de Varennes that he should inspire such tender concern? At first he had hoped he might be the brother she had mentioned, but there was not one mention of any family name or relationship, not one reference to the past.

Her first epistle had been written after several days of the holiday at Holton House. Although Michelle was clearly anxious about the possible circumstances that he inspired this unexpected contact, her happiness at being in touch with de Varennes shone throughout the letter. Further, the unguarded description of her suitors assured Calvern that de Varennes was not her lover. For von Reichertz she had little patience; Robert Sanderson she found a considerate, upright man whose company she quite enjoyed. But concerning himself, Calvern, she was most confused: she confessed that "even though this duke is most precisely English," he could at moments, "make her heart sing with something that might become *ma grande passion*"; yet at other moments, Michelle vowed, Calvern seemed prepared to "throw her to others." He ached at the pain her misreading of his attempt at disinterested fairness to other suitors had cost her.

In the next note, dated three weeks later and enclosing some two hundred pounds, she was perturbed by de Varenness's request for funds, concerned for his well-being, and most gentle. Of her engagement to Calvern, she did not explain the circumstances, but called it a "precipitous joy"—a phrase the duke secretly cherished for the length of his life.

But it was the third letter that upset him. In it she alternately glowed with happiness over their engagement and was distraught with worry over de Varennes's need for four hundred pounds. She begged the gentleman to come to their wedding and to discuss his situation with the duke, her fiancé, "for he is a man who knows the nature of both justice and mercy, as you do."

While Calvern rejoiced in his beloved's confidence in him, he was infuriated by the price, not only in money but in anxiety and pain that Roland's lucrative game of extortion had extracted. If he could but lay his hands on the blackguard!

Two hours before dawn, when the night was blackest and the road muddiest, Cresswell's horse threw a shoe. The remaining groom surrendered his horse to the general and walked the shoeless animal to Maidstone, some twelve miles forward, while his master and the duke galloped ahead. The two men began to gain the time lost and arrived in Maidstone by eight. Although the breakfast was foul, the horses were fine, and Calvern was enheartened to hear his wife was only some six hours further on. With luck, two riders on horseback could easily catch up to a coach.

It was luck that, from here on in, they did not have. Five miles short of Ashford, Calvern's horse went lame; they did not reach that town until five in the afternoon, and there, had to wait an hour for suitable steeds. Rolling fog from the sea was so dense, and the track so muddy, that they were slowed even more. It was nine in the evening before they arrived at gray-stone inn at Folkestone.

"A delicate little thing the lady is, sir, with dark hair and very large eyes, wearing a lavender cape?"

"Precisely."

The hosteler stepped back and surveyed Calvern and the general. He had not run an inn on the smugglers' coast for forty years without having seen young ladies fleeing hostile husbands or treacherous lovers—although rarely were the women as lovely or well dressed. He could not decide whether the striking blond man, or the gray-haired one of distinctly military bearing, was pursuing the girl. Whichever it was, neither man looked cruel, and he would take a chance.

"Aye, set sail on the evening packet for Ostend at high tide not more than an hour ago, they did. The maid 'ad booked them on one tomorrow morning, but my lady, she would leave tonight. And it looks like it's the devil they'll pay, for there's a sudden channel storm rolling in."

The general glanced out the window. Where before it had simply been raining, now it was a wind-driven deluge, and in the distance he could see forks of lightning fast approaching.

"I'd like to hire a yacht—now!" said Calvern, his voice edged with hard authority.

The hotel keeper eyed him warily. So he was her husband.

"I'd advise waiting till morning, or at least till the storm blows by, guv, for that's a mean sea."

"Perhaps the gentleman is right," ventured the general, but before he had even completed the sentence, Calvern had sent a gold piece spinning on edge across the counter. The innkeeper snapped it up instantly.

"It's yours if you name the man who would, for twenty-five more guineas, set sail within the half hour," said the duke.

So the little lady was worth that much, was she? Well, good luck to her, and who was he to gainsay her fate? thought the host. "Billy Martin and his brother are the only ones gold-blind enough to take your offer on such a night, and it's no yacht they have, but a mere fishing vessel, and a small one at that. My lad here will take you down to their cottage."

However well-worn the path to the shore, at night in a storm such as this it was a fool's climb, even for two strong men and a nimble boy, but they made it to the Martins' cottage. Even then Billy himself had to stand at the door, looking at the storm and thinking, before he accepted the gold.

"Aye, I'll do it, but twenty-five guineas are not near enough for myself and my brother. Forty, or we don't go."

"Thirty-five."

"We're away."

Calvern, the general, and the two brothers all had to push waist-deep into the driving surf with the dingy in order to jump in and row to a small, bobbing vessel. Boarding was a feat, for as the dingy pitched down, the *Maryanne* rolled and yawled up and away, so the distance between the dingy and the vessel heightened to some ten feet without a ladder, at four or five feet apart. Martin's brother slipped into the surf, but caught a thrown rope and clambered up.

"The devil take it!" said the general, cursing as he attempted to stand on the narrow, heaving deck and keep his balance by holding the swing rope rails. "This ship, if it can be called that, must be Admiral Nelson's revenge on the army."

"I say, guv, I've never thought o' her in quite that way afore," said Billy, a newfound respect for the old girl in his voice.

The duke said nothing as he concentrated on ducking the swinging boom, noting only that this was the first fishing vessel he had known that didn't smell of fish.

Shortly before dawn they were becalmed just two miles from the Belgian shore. A red gash in the clearing sky declared daylight. Calvern was scanning the dock with a spyglass—Michelle's vessel had clearly made shore—while the general lay, recuperating, wrapped round with a piece of burlap that had been thrown over bolts of worsted cloth sheltered in the bow. The general suddenly recognized the nature of his makeshift bed and gave yet another oath.

"Isn't this worsted cloth the Oxford Blue of the Royal Regiment of Horse?"

"Maybe it was, sir, maybe it was this week past." Martin laughed. "But next week it will be the bonny blue of Boney's own Imperial Guard."

"The devil," the general said, and sank back while Calvern smilingly noted that being at sea had certainly shrunk the vocabulary of the landlubber soldier.

They made port some three hours later.

The *Maryanne* had scarce tied up before Calvern leaped from the deck and began running. He had been scanning the wharf and shore ceaselessly since sun up, and for the last fifteen minutes, he could swear he had seen through the spyglass a diminutive figure in lavender walking through crowds in front of a block of shops facing the harbor. She was small, and he frequently lost sight of her as the crowds surged in front of him, but every several minutes he would catch a glimpse of an unmistakable cloak, ever nearer. Finally, he was not fifty yards behind her, and he froze on the spot.

Michelle was looking in the widow of an antiquarian bookshop, but she was not alone.

With her was a man, dark-haired and even slightly taller than Calvern himself. They were standing close together, so close, in fact, that the man had nestled Michelle by his side and had so surrounded her with his greatcoat against the early morning chill that only the lavender hood of her cloak showed above his sleeve. Something in the window had attracted her, and as she pointed it out to him, a look of such open and tender delight animated her face that Calvern felt as if he had been hacked from behind by a broadsword.

He was across the street in five strides.

"Michelle!" He bellowed her name like a cannon shot. "Sir, unhand that lady—*now!*"

The stranger turned so quickly, his greatcoat swirled in a swath; he had already pushed Michelle behind him for safety.

"Who *dares* address my sister in such a tone?"

And Calvern looked straight into a pair of eyes as violet as Michelle's own.

Yes, the general concurred with the effervescent Michelle, today was the most exceptional day of a lifetime. Certainly, he agreed, that she should arrive in Ostend the same day as her brother, who was coming to her assistance on the instructions he had received five days ago from the Duc d'Anton, was remarkable. Of course, it was most wonderful that Edward and Richard, though they had never met until two hours previously, would think so similarly about the inevitability of Napoleon's defeat, the importance of the upcoming congress, and the certainty of Louis the Eighteenth's eventual coronation as king of all France.

The general would have agreed to anything, to fire on his own brigade, if only the horizon in the window beyond him would stay steady, and the inn table at which he sat would never, ever heave.

No, not even in this, Michelle's happiest hour, would the general agree to partake of a little luncheon.

"Michelle."

The coal fire glowed red in the grate, its intense warmth filling the dark-paneled bedchamber of the inn at Ostend. Michelle nestled deeper into the feather bed and pulled up the heaping quilts. A hot bath, this warmth, her beloved's loving—it was enough to drive the horror and chill of the journey from London to Ostend from her mind as well as her body.

"Michelle!" The first time Edward had said her name, it had still been husky with desire; now it had an edge that commanded her attention. She opened her eyes and smiled.

He stooped to her, tracing her profile with the tip of his finger. "None of your beguiling wiles, my lady, while I am discussing something so eminently serious."

She giggled.

"No, my pet. Serious."

Michelle looked into the duke's eyes. They were intense, earnest. She sobered instantly. "I'm listening."

"I want you to make a vow to me—one as sacred as any you made to Richard or at our wedding. The vow is this: you will never, as long as you live, agree to keep anyone's confidence that cannot be shared with me. If you must hold a trust, it is a trust to be held by us both. Those who would ask such a thing would know neither of us would break a bond of confidentiality."

Tears glistened in Michelle's eyes. "Richard's safety, his life . . ."

Edward brushed a tendril of hair from her cheek; his smile was tender. "You were not wrong to keep Richard's promise, for when you gave him your word, you had not even met me. One of the thousand reasons I love you is that we both share that same sense of honor. But never, ever again must a commitment come between us. Promise me."

Michelle nodded solemnly. "I do."

"You know, my darling, there you would have been, traipsing across Europe in the wake of Napoleon's retreating army—"

"You were only six hours behind me."

"And would I have succeeded in finding you if you hadn't discovered Richard here on the wharf at Ostend? You'd have been halfway to Paris, war or no." Calvern raised both his wife's hands to his lips, kissing them between each phrase. "I don't think I've ever been as afraid in my life, afraid for you, for our child. If the Duc d'Anton hadn't called Richard to England days before I even suspected you were in danger, what would have happened?"

Michelle's eyes suddenly narrowed. "Edward, you . . . you don't think my dear duc could actually be King Louis's spy master, do you?"

Calvern was surprised and pleased with the innocence of her question. "Where you are concerned, my love, I imagine he thinks he acts in the place of your beloved father—especially since your official guardian had the presumption to become your husband."

But before he had finished even these words, Michelle, weary, warm, her hands still clasped safely in her lover's, had fallen softly asleep.

For four days it rained, and the channel was boisterous; on no account could the general be induced even to leave the inn for a walk by the sea wall.

On the fifth day, Michelle, waiting for the duke to confirm with the passenger agent their bookings for the channel crossing in the largest ship available (the general would countenance no other), had strolled past several stores to the lace shop when a hand touched her lightly on the shoulder and she turned to stare directly into Roland's bleary-eyed and bewhiskered face.

"Aye, so it is me past master's one and only true love, is it?" he said with an obsequious bow. He had obviously been drinking, for he almost lost his balance and pitched forward. "And now, how much is it worth to the little lady to ensure that her duke, her very fine duke, never learns that she came to him as his ward by a *forged* will, mmm?"

Roland waggled his finger menacingly in Michelle's face; as he did so, a fist sailed over Michelle's left shoulder and landed squarely on Roland's jaw. The lackey staggered backward and quickly received another blow in the midriff from a dark figure on the right that was so severe he doubled over into a refuse heap in the alley beside him.

"I think, Calvern, that that remark, even coming from the mouth of a liar and criminal, does bear explaining," said de

Varennes to the duke as both men pulled their gloves back on. They walked back to their private parlor at the inn, and as Michelle served pastries and tea, Richard began to explain.

"For months following my father's death, I tried to support Michelle, Jane, and Ninette by my art dealings, as well as to report to King Louis on Napoleon's doings in that incredible year of 1812. Of course, Louis needed more and more information, and I would never accept pay from my impoverished sovereign in exile. Things became impossible. Although I have never encountered three more able, imaginative, or frugal women than Michelle, Jane, and Ninette, the worry of having to earn an income for them, while my sovereign claimed almost all my time, was severe.

"Several years ago, my father had placed his will with a notary in Paris, who holds the original in safekeeping to this day. The notary's letter reached me, as executor of the estate, some months after my father's death. In it, he gave the terms of the will, one of which was that in case he should die, Michelle was to go to her godfather, the Duke of Calvern. My father knew the duke would be a wise and gentle guardian, and as the count had expressed the wish several times to me personally, and Michelle's safety in France was becoming questionable, I realized I had no other course but to send her to her godfather—or as it turns out, to you.

"Because I knew that it would be dangerous for either Michelle or me to return to Paris and pick up the original will, and because I knew its terms precisely, I did, in fact, force Michelle to present you with a 'forged' will, signed and sealed, not by my father, but by me. The document may have violated the letter of the law, but, I assure you, not the spirit.

"In my profession I cannot guarantee I will be alive the next day; I preferred to leave Michelle protected by legality rather than charity. Would you, Calvern, have let her go to a strange man—however generous he was reputed to be—with only the verbal claim of being a goddaughter?"

The men smiled at Michelle in such a way that she blushed; Calvern shook his head firmly.

Calvern rose and shook de Varennes's hand. "Please believe me, brother, I would have done the same thing."

That night, without explanation, and with short farewells as was his custom, de Varennes left. The next day dawned bright and clear, and while the channel could not be said to be as smooth as glass, even the general conceded it was calm, and the Calvern party sailed for London.

In London, on Tuesday, the fifth of April, 1814, every church bell in the city pealed for fifteen minutes, for the news had arrived that the allied sovereigns had entered Paris.

On Wednesday, the twentieth of April, King Louis the Eighteenth of France journeyed from Buckinghamshire to London, where he was greeted by thousands in Hyde Park. In a splendid public cavalcade of some six royal carriages, preceded by a hundred gentlemen wearing costumes festooned in gold lace braid, on horseback, flanked by trumpeters, and followed by the King's Life Guards in their resplendent uniforms, King Louis was greeted in a public ceremony before Grillon's Hotel, Albemarle Street, to the music of the hundred men of the Duke of Kent's band.

That night, a state reception in the large and lavish halls of the Prince Regent's Carlton House sparkled with more of British and French nobility than had been seen together for a generation. But only a short time before the doors opened for the reception, a duke of England and his French-born duchess were invited to the prince's private apartments to pay their respects to the English regent and the French monarch. Michelle, resplendent in a white and silver gown, wearing the fleur-de-lys pendant on her pearl and sapphire wedding necklace, curtseyed to kiss the hand of her beloved king.

Later in Paris, King Louis issued on the noble lists the name of one Richard Phillippe de Varennes to succeed to the title of his natural father, and thenceforth be known as the eighth Comte de Bellevue.

At a May tea, as she ate her third *pâtisserie,* Lady Jane Willington could not but allow how much a pleasure it was to be an intimate of those who were known and received by the royalties of two countries.

Early in June, in the warm gardens of Royal Pavilion, Brighton, Prinny laughed with delight at Michelle's stories of the invasion of the new Royalist Paris by British travelers. And in September, upon the birth of the Duke and Duchess of Calvern's son and heir, the regent wrote to say that he was instructing the College of Heralds to affix to the Calvern crest a fleur-de-lys.

Only, wrote Michelle in her letter of thanks, with a twinkle in her eyes, if His Royal Highness charged the Heralds to be sure not to place it too near the paws of the lion rampant.

And when a new upstairs maid was assigned to the ducal apartments, she commented to Her Grace's companion, Jane, upon how curious it was that, as the duchess was usually so fastidious and orderly in the keeping of her clothes and jewels, she would occasionally lose an ear bob under a writing desk, a bracelet by a hearth, or a ring in a letter tray.

And Jane agreed yes, how curious, and said not another word.

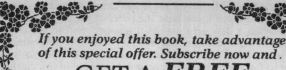